HYPHENATED RELATIONS

DANIEL MAUNZ

To Kristi,
For the love of
families in whatever
shape they take.

Black Rose Writing | Texas

The author grants the final approval for this literary material.

First printing

This is a work of fiction. Names, characters, businesses, places, events, and incidents are either the products of the author's imagination or used in a fictitious manner. Any resemblance to actual persons, living or dead, or actual events is purely coincidental.

Cover art: Stephanie Ciccotta
Copyediting: Adrienne Marie Barrios
Author Photo: Irene Bello

ISBN: 978-1-68513-189-0
PUBLISHED BY BLACK ROSE WRITING
www.blackrosewriting.com

Printed in the United States of America
Suggested Retail Price (SRP) $21.95

Hyphenated Relations is printed in Garamond Pro

*As a planet-friendly publisher, Black Rose Writing does its best to eliminate unnecessary waste to reduce paper usage and energy costs, while never compromising the reading experience. As a result, the final word count vs. page count may not meet common expectations.

For my wonderful in-laws Walter and Patricia,
who inspired this particular story.
Congratulations on your 50th anniversary!

ACKNOWLEDGMENTS

Long before I ever set out to write a novel, I often heard writers lament that as hard as it is to write a first book, the second is even more difficult. I did not fully appreciate the truth behind such whines until I started work on this story. It was not always easy, but I was ultimately able to see this novel through to the end with the help of many others to whom I am indebted.

My first, and loudest, expression of gratitude goes, as always, to my beautiful wife, Lynne. Her work on this book behind the scenes is plentiful, whether it be offering feedback on story ideas, serving as my first test subject for the finished product, patiently proofreading, or just pushing me (in her gentle way) to keep writing. There are few joys in my life as profound as hearing Lynne giggling to herself in another room as she reads something I gave her to review. Even if no one else ever read this book, that laughter, in and of itself, made it all worthwhile.

I'm also thankful to, and for, our five-year-old son Patrick. The stories I write are generally more positive and hopeful than what I consider to be my inherent nature, and that is largely a result of me trying to view the world these past years through his joyful and wondrous eyes.

Thanks are also owed, once again, to my mother, Barbara Lush, for instilling in me early on a love of books and planting the seeds for my need to put the stories in my head to paper. She remains a valuable source of feedback in reviewing early drafts of this novel, and I'm very appreciative for what a fierce advocate she is for all my books.

I am grateful for my in-laws, Walter and Patricia Anderson, for their constant encouragement and for sharing their thoughts after reading this story while it was a work in progress. I also owe thanks to their other daughter, Tracey Kappenberg, for her interest in reviewing this story early on and for her passionate feedback, which was a great motivator when I really needed one.

I'm generally not one to sit around discussing the process of writing with others, but a notable exception to that is Ed Dougherty, who is regularly my sounding board for story ideas or just to discuss writing in general. I've fallen into the habit of texting Ed, or sending him voice memos, multiple times a day with random thoughts about writing and crafting stories, and I'm always very appreciative of his feedback and knowledge. (I'm not normally so earnest with Ed, but since he only pretends to read my books, he'll never see this anyway.)

My first book did not require much in the way of research (with some notable exceptions), but this story required me to dip my toe into some medical topics that are well outside my area of expertise, and I am very grateful to Dr. John Reagan and the nursing power couple of Nick and Kaitlin Montella, who each worked with me in crafting certain plot points and patiently answered all of my silly medical questions.

I was once again very fortunate to have Adrienne Marie Barrios apply her copyediting expertise to this novel. As with my first novel, Adrienne worked on this manuscript with love and care, and her impressive knowledge helped fix many errors that were not even remotely close to being on my radar. She is always incredibly patient and responsive in addressing my various grammar questions (which, fittingly enough, largely centered around hyphen usage this go-around), and I can't thank her enough for her work in helping to make this novel as polished as possible.

I also consider myself very lucky for convincing Stephanie Ciccotta to design another beautiful cover for this book (as she did with my first novel). It is such a joy to give Stephanie some basic thoughts for a cover and then watch her run with her own interpretation and ideas, which ultimately yields artwork far greater than I could have ever imagined or hoped for.

Thank you again to Reagan Rothe and everyone at Black Rose Writing for their work in making stories that deserve to be heard available to be read and for their tireless efforts in ensuring that these stories do not stay under the radar for long.

I once again must thank my cats, Admiral and Captain, who were often my only company on nights when I was up late writing. Even on those occasions where they felt like taking a more active role by stomping across the keyboard as I was typing, I was always glad to have them with me.

I also thank everyone who took the time to read my first novel, Questions of Perspective, and particularly those who went through the effort of trying to introduce it to others, whether it be through posting reviews, discussing it on blogs, or starting up conversations about it on Bookstagram. It's not always easy to summon the energy to keep writing, and knowing there are passionate readers out there willing to take a chance on new authors was all the motivation I needed at times.

And, of course, if you are reading this, thank you as well. I put everything I have into this story, and it's an honor to have you check it out.

I hope you enjoy it.

HYPHENATED RELATIONS

CHAPTER ONE

Monday, August 19, 2019

Sam Daly arrived home from work to find her father-in-law, Harold, sitting in her living room, studying her underwear.

She had left a pile of clean clothes, fresh from the dryer, on her couch before she left for the office that morning. That pile was a remnant of an ambitious plan to run a load of laundry, swap it to the dryer and then fold it, all before running out to catch the train to Manhattan. Somewhat predictably, Sam only made it about two-thirds of the way through that agenda before darting out, leaving a small hill of clothing behind.

A hill that her father-in-law, whom she hadn't seen in over two years, inexplicably discovered and, even more bizarrely, chose to explore.

Harold was approaching seventy, and his hearing had been an issue since Sam first met him a few years earlier, so he didn't look up when she entered the house, which gave her some time to study the scene. She knew indignation and outrage would eventually come, but all she felt in the wake of that initial shock was a morbid curiosity about Harold's intentions toward her undergarments.

Please don't do anything creepy, she prayed. After a moment, she amended that thought. *Well, creepier*.

It was a small comfort to see that her father-in-law's investigation did not appear to be sexual in nature. Rather, his odd ritual consisted of holding up an item of clothing and studying it like a patron at an art gallery admiring an abstract painting, only to throw it—with an unmistakable air of disappointment—toward the far end of the couch. After three rounds of inspection, Sam found her voice.

"Dude," she said loudly, and Harold froze. "Even for you, this is weird."

Harold turned slowly toward her, armed with his most charming smile. The kind of shit-eating grin that often earned him a free dessert from the older waitresses at his local diner. Sam had seen it often and enjoyed a solid immunity to its wile. She was a trifle offended, though, that Harold believed it had even a chance of working on her.

"Sam!" he said, rising to his feet, arms spread for a hug. Sam crossed her arms and stared at his right hand, which was holding a bra. Harold frowned in confusion before following her gaze.

"Oh. Right!" With a laugh, he threw what he had been holding onto the couch and moved toward her. Sam, maintaining her crossed-arms position, reflexively took a step back, which caused Harold to stop in his tracks.

"Don't tell me you're angry!" he said, sounding hurt. "I mean—I can see how this might look bad. But there's a perfectly good explanation, I promise you." Sam shook her head.

"I've gotta tell you: I don't think there's a combination of words in the English language that could constitute a 'good explanation' for this. What are you doing here, Harold?"

Harold hesitated, gathering his thoughts. It had been several years since Sam last saw him, and, in that moment of pause, she was struck by the extent to which his features mirrored those of her husband. The same slender nose. The same old-fashioned haircut, parted neatly on the left side. The same thin lips. Only the eyes were discernibly different. While Harold's bright blue eyes tended to switch between impatient indignation and seductive charm, the eyes of his son could not help but mirror what was transpiring in his heart at any given moment. *Guileless*, Sam thought. *Mike's eyes were guileless*. Sam noted, not for the first time, that Harold was otherwise a very good approximation of what Mike would have looked like in thirty years.

Harold sat back down on the couch, patting the seat beside him.

"Please, sit down. We have a lot to talk about. And yes, I'll explain this." He gestured at the pile of clothes to his left.

Sam eyed the open spot next to Harold before moving to a separate chair near where Harold was sitting. If Harold registered the rebuff, he did not acknowledge it.

"Go ahead," Sam said, taking a seat. "I'm all ears as to why you broke into my house to play with my underwear." Harold winced.

"I wasn't 'playing' with your—with your things. And I didn't 'break in' either." Harold punctuated each of his points with finger quotes. "Mike gave me a key a few years ago, to hold in case of an emergency."

"This is an emergency?" Sam asked, raising an eyebrow.

"Well, no. I suppose not. But I did have to talk to you!"

"And a phone call wouldn't have sufficed?"

"I tried!" Harold threw his hands up. "I called your number, and I kept getting someone speaking Italian. Or maybe it was Portuguese. Something that sounds kind of like Spanish, in any event. I don't think it was Spanish, though."

Sam flushed, feeling a smack of guilt. She had changed her number shortly after Mike's death, and she hadn't bothered to give Harold the new one.

You caught him playing with your underwear! she reminded herself. *Do* not *start feeling sorry for him!*

"Ok, fine. You couldn't reach me by phone. How about an email?" Sam waited for a response, and Harold blinked in confusion.

"Oh, I didn't realize you had an email. I just got one of those myself." He cleared his throat, eager to get back on point. "Look: I wanted to talk to you in person, so I made the drive up here from Long Island, figuring I'd catch you when you got home from work. I may have misjudged your commute by an hour or so, and I took the liberty of letting myself in to wait for you. And if that was crossing a boundary, I humbly apologize."

Harold lowered his head, looking contrite. Sam was not prepared to forgive him so easily, but she was curious about what had brought him up to her home in Westchester.

"You shouldn't have done that. It's creepy—and invasive—even without you rifling through my laundry. I mean, what was *that* about?"

"Like I said, I can explain that."

"Then get to it."

Harold paused again, unsure of where he should start. Then three words poured out of him in a torrent: "I'm in love!"

He seemed to be waiting for Sam to leap out of her seat and embrace him in a celebratory hug. Sam wordlessly declined the implied invitation to partake in such a tender moment. Instead, she sighed and waited for Harold to continue. When Harold realized that he had not yet managed to thaw the ice between them, he went on.

"Her name is Marcie. We met about four months ago." He stopped to study Sam's impassive face, which had not moved. "Now, don't give me that look. Just because we became widows on the same day, and you apparently threw yourself into a life of chastity, doesn't mean that I have to do the same."

Sam maintained her blank facade. *We didn't just lose our spouses on the same day*, she noted. *It was probably the same second.* A Mother's Day dinner ended prematurely by a drunk driver doing fifty on the wrong side of the road.

"Widower," she said.

"What?"

"Widower. You're not a widow. You're a widower."

"Widow what?" he asked, confused. Sam's patience started to slip.

"You know, you really do need a hearing aid. You'll be amazed at what you're missing," she said in a louder voice. Harold raised his hands in protest.

"Oh, no! I'm not getting one of those. They make you look old."

Sam didn't bother to hide her eye roll. She stood up and walked toward the kitchen.

"Yeah," she muttered as she walked away. "Nothing screams youth like yelling *what?* every two seconds."

"What?"

"Never mind," she said, mostly to herself, before raising her voice again. "You want a beer?"

"Wha—yeah, sure. Why not?"

Sam grabbed two bottles of Brooklyn Lager and popped the caps with a magnetic opener on her fridge. She brought the beers back to the living room and handed one to Harold. He took it and started to take a sip before realizing that Sam was holding hers out, angled toward him. Removing the bottle from his mouth, he awkwardly clinked it against hers.

"Congrats," she said. "You've fallen in love. How beautiful."

They each fell silent to take a long pull. Sam sat down again and chewed on the lip of the bottle, trying to make sense of Harold's reemergence in her life. As if remembering an appointment elsewhere, Harold abruptly stood up and walked to the back door.

Impulsive as ever, Sam thought, not that she had any reason to think he would have changed in that regard. She followed him into the backyard, annoyed at having to stand up again so soon after finally getting settled.

Outside, the sun was well into its descent, but there was still enough light to see the state of the small yard. The lawn had been mowed a few days earlier by the landscapers who came once a week, but, otherwise, it was obvious that the yard hadn't been shown any love for some time. A patch of empty dirt was all that remained of a garden along one of the fences. A small shed sat in the back corner of the yard, in desperate need of a paint job. In the middle of the lawn, next to its lone tree, a life-sized statue of a raccoon peering out of a hole in a ceramic log had fallen onto its side. Harold wordlessly took in the backyard before speaking.

"What happened to your garden? You used to get great tomatoes out of it."

"That was really more Mike's project."

"Well, he's dead now," Harold said with his standard bluntness.

"Oh, yeah. I think I remember hearing something about that." Harold frowned, and Sam instantly felt ashamed. *He lost a wife and a son*, she reminded herself. *His entire family. Take it easy on him.*

"Don't get all sarcastic on me," Harold said. "I'm just saying that I used to love your yard. It's a shame that it's—well, 'trashy' is probably too harsh of a word, but . . ."

Harold trailed off and walked over to the fallen statue. After carefully placing his beer on the ground, he swiveled to pick up the raccoon and correct its orientation. After some thought, he packed some dirt around it to prevent the ornament from being knocked over again.

"There!" he announced from his knees. Holding out a hand, palm up, he added, "That will be fifty dollars!"

"Add it to my tab," Sam replied. She glanced at the sun, which offered at least another hour of daylight. She couldn't remember the last time she had a beer in her backyard. *Might as well take advantage of a decent summer evening*, she thought.

"The question remains," she said, walking toward Harold, who had resumed standing and was dusting off his hands. "What does your falling in love have to do with my laundry?"

"Right. That." Harold stooped to pick up his beer. "I had mentioned Marcie—oh, is she wonderful! You will never meet a kinder woman if you spent three hundred years walking this earth. And she is funny and smart. I can also add"—Harold winked and lowered his voice, conspiratorially—"that she's a bit of a demon in the sack, if you know what I mean." Sam choked on the beer she'd been sipping. Harold's eyes danced; he was tickled by her shocked reaction.

"Do you really think I want to hear about your love life?" she yelled. "No! I don't!" But that only served to further amuse Harold.

Something about the entire conversation struck Sam as odd, and, after a moment, she was able to place it: This was probably the first time she'd had a chance to speak with Harold alone. She was used to having Mike at her side, ready to jump in and be the bad guy when his father's lack of a filter got out of hand. It didn't feel that uncomfortable to play the heavy herself, though. She once walked on eggshells around Mike's parents, desperate to impress her in-laws. But those bonds had been severed for some time, and Sam no longer truly saw Harold as her father-in-law. She wasn't sure what he was to her, at that point, other than a sixty-eight-year-old man who had invaded her home to ramble about his newfound sex life.

"Alright! Alright! It was just a little joke. You know, you *used* to laugh at my bad jokes."

"I'm not above politely laughing at a joke, but my politeness goes out the window when a person breaks into my home and—"

"Ahhhhhh!" Harold interrupted, embarrassed. "Again with that? Well, I'm getting there. Anyway, Marcie and I have fallen in love. She's wonderful, but I said that already. And she has four kids, who are just the best. They all love me, I tell you. Marcie even has a daughter—Sadie—who is just about your age. I can easily see you becoming best friends with her." Sam let out a skeptical grunt, but Harold did not seem to notice.

"The other three are boys," he continued. "Great kids. Well, adults. Kids to me, though. One of them is gay, but I forget which. He's kind of under the radar about it, whoever it is. The interesting thing about Marcie's kids is that they each have a different father. Marcie had married four times, but those husbands kept dying on her." Harold laughed, but Sam was confused.

"You're dating a woman who has buried four different husbands?"

Harold, still smiling, nodded.

"Is she—" Sam stopped. "Are you involved with a black widow?"

"You mean did she kill these guys?" Harold laughed again. "No. No, absolutely not. Like I said: She's probably the nicest person on the planet. Just a series of bad luck. Ended up being good luck for me, though!" Sam was dubious. Harold tended to see the best in people, which didn't always make him the most reliable judge of character.

"So, what's she doing with you?" Sam asked, and Harold chuckled.

"God only knows!" he said. "I mean, I told her I was rich, so maybe that has something to do with it." He laughed, but Sam just looked at him.

"Why did you tell her you were rich?"

"Oh, it was just a joke. We kid around a lot. *She* appreciates my sense of humor." Harold gave Sam a meaningful look.

Sam had no idea where this all was going. She was not all that confident that Harold knew, either. A glance at her phone revealed it was 6:45. *I'll give him another five minutes, and then he's getting the door*, she thought.

"This all sounds very lovely for you," Sam said, trying to muster up some semblance of enthusiasm. Harold beamed in response. "But I have to start dinner soon, so—"

"Right. Right. The thing is—we have decided to get married!"

"Oh."

"Oh?"

"I mean, congratulations. Again," Sam said, stammering a bit. "Congratulations again. I was just surprised. You said you met her four months ago?" Harold nodded.

"Yes, but when you know, you know, right? We don't see any point in waiting. We haven't even worked out any of the details yet; we just know we want to keep the wedding small. Family and close friends only. And we wanted to get everyone together—give the two families a chance to meet each other—so we're having a barbeque this weekend at Marcie's home. And I came here to invite you! We're going to announce the wedding there, so please don't tell anyone else beforehand." Harold seemed to be serious. Sam frowned.

"You're inviting . . . me?" She couldn't imagine why. Now it was Harold's turn to frown.

"Yes, of course. Why wouldn't I?"

"Well, we haven't really spoken much in the past two years, for one."

"So what? We have a chance to change all of that now. I mean, we're family!"

Sam opened her mouth to speak and paused, taking the time to choose her words carefully. Her anger over the underwear incident—which remained unexplained—was not maintaining as much as she would have liked, and she felt a wave of sympathy for Harold. Still, she wasn't particularly inclined to be dragged along into some new family dynamic that she never signed up for.

"Look, I'm honored to be invited, but—this really isn't my thing." Harold started to speak, but Sam talked right over him. "I married your son. '*Til death do us part*, I believe we said at the ceremony. Well, that has happened. Death has parted us. I'm glad you found a woman and a new family who apparently love you, but I personally need to just move on at this point." Harold took half a step toward her, his face a mix of anger and hurt.

"That's just ridiculous. You're my daughter-in-law! Of course you need to be involved in this wedding! I told Marcie all about you—she's dying to meet you." Harold paused before repeating, "You're family!"

"Maybe I *was* family, once, but things are different now," Sam said as kindly as she could. "Don't you see that?"

"You know what I think this is really about? You resent me for moving on, when you're not willing to do that. But you're—what?—thirty-six years old? You're still attractive—you can find someone else, if you really wanted to."

"Gee, thanks. It's nice to know that I don't have to be resigned to becoming a spinster."

"You know what I mean!" Harold finished his beer and placed it on the ground in front of him. "Man, you can twist anything I say into something offensive, can't you? But I didn't come here to argue. Here." Harold reached into his pocket and fished out a rumpled piece of paper before shoving it at Sam, who took it instinctively. "Those are the directions to Marcie's house, with all of the other information you'll need. I'll see you Saturday." Harold stood up and walked toward the side gate, not looking back. Sam realized that he was leaving without even bothering to say goodbye. She trailed after him.

"Wait! You never explained what you were doing with my laundry!"

Harold stopped in his departure and turned back to face her.

"Wow. You don't let up, do you?" Harold initially seemed annoyed and embarrassed, but he quickly reset himself with a chuckle and a grin. "That was nothing. I was sitting here waiting for you to get home, and I was thinking to myself, *Hey! I should get Marcie a gift on the way back later!* Now, she's a bit of a hippie dippy, so her style isn't always . . . great. So I notice this pile of laundry, and I think to myself, *Sam is a cool girl! Let's see what she's wearing!* You know—just to get an idea or two as to what to get for Marcie. I was rifling through your stuff, and I thought, *Maybe I can get Marcie some sexy underwear—spice things up!* Now, I'm not quite up to speed on women's undergarments, so I was looking for a bit of a hint by checking out what you are wearing these days."

Sam stared at him, slack-jawed, but Harold misread her look.

"See!" he said. "I told you it was nothing. And to be quite honest: I'm not so sure you don't have room for improvement under there." Harold gestured vaguely at Sam's outfit. "I think what you're wearing would have been out of style when *I* was a kid. I heard someone on tv once refer to 'Grandma Panties'—is that what they were talking about?" Sam felt her cheeks flush.

"Dude," she said. But she was rendered speechless. "Dude," she said, again. Harold shrugged.

"Anyway, that's just my two cents. Goodnight. See you this weekend." Harold got halfway across the yard, and Sam finally found her voice again.

"I told you, I'm not coming to the party."

"I know you'll do the right thing," Harold said over his shoulder without looking at her. He opened the gate and marched toward the sidewalk without breaking his stride. Sam ran to the gate that he'd left open behind him.

"I *will* do the right thing," she called to him. "But that doesn't involve me going to your engagement party!" Harold stopped on the sidewalk to look back at her.

"See you Saturday!" he called out with a grin, before speed-walking down the street to his car, robbing Sam of her chance to get the last word in.

CHAPTER TWO

Tuesday, August 20, 2019

Miguel arrived at Outback Steakhouse half an hour before the scheduled time. He had anticipated hitting traffic as he traveled from his home in Queens to the restaurant, which sat in the middle of Long Island, but the roads were uncharacteristically clear, and he ended up making great time. Not that arriving early was necessarily a bad thing. Miguel figured he could nurse a beer while he waited for his siblings to arrive, but upon entering the establishment, he was surprised to find his older brother, Jeremy, already sitting at the mostly empty bar.

Technically, Jeremy was Miguel's *half*-brother, but Miguel never really thought of him that way. Jeremy, ten years older than Miguel, was a constant presence in the house where they grew up. Their relationship was, for all intents and purposes, that of brothers, and that was good enough for Miguel.

Miguel noticed that Jeremy didn't have a drink and surmised that he had only just arrived himself. Jeremy, focused on getting the bartender's attention, didn't notice Miguel as he slid onto the stool next to him.

"Hey, Jeremy!" Miguel said. Jeremy threw a quick glance at him before resuming his stare down of the bartender.

"Oh. It's you," Jeremy said. He let out a deep exhale as he tried to will the bartender into looking in his direction. "Shitty service here, am I right?"

The bartender, a preppy-looking guy in his late twenties, was flirting with the other bartender, a woman with short black hair and what looked to be a Spider-Man tattoo running up her right arm. The two bartenders bantered with one another, and Jeremy finally lost his patience. He snapped his fingers twice in rapid succession in the direction of the male bartender.

"Can I get a drink over here, chief?" Jeremy asked. The bartender, annoyed, gave a subtle nod to Jeremy, prompting him for his order.

"Jack and Coke." After a pause, Jeremy turned to Miguel. "You want something?"

"Beer is fine. Sam Adams?"

The bartender cracked open a bottle for Miguel and then got to work on Jeremy's drink. Miguel noticed that he filled the glass almost entirely with soda before adding a splash of Jack Daniels. Miguel wondered if it was an intentional slight. Jeremy, satisfied with successfully ordering a round, didn't seem to notice. In fact, when the drink was finally delivered, Jeremy took a delicate sip before sighing with relish.

"Ah," Jeremy said. "They make 'em good here." He turned to Miguel, shoving his glass in his face. "Try it!" Miguel took a diplomatic sip. As he suspected, it tasted just like a Coke, with perhaps a subtle hint of alcohol.

"Mmmmm," Miguel said without conviction as he handed the glass back to Jeremy. "Tasty." Jeremy grunted his agreement.

Without warning, Jeremy snapped his fingers in Miguel's face. Miguel couldn't help but flinch.

"Hey! You know what? You and I should totally plan a trip to go on Spring Break. Gotta do it before we get too old, right? Tons of college chicks—it'll be awesome."

Too old? Miguel thought. *I'm pushing thirty, and you're pushing forty.* But there was another issue with Jeremy's proposal.

"Well, I'm gay. Remember?" Miguel asked. Jeremy's face scrunched in confusion, and Miguel felt obligated to add, "I came out at Thanksgiving a couple of years ago?"

"Oh, yeah. That thing." Jeremy laughed. "It's funny—I always forget about that. You seem so—well, I don't want to say *normal*, but . . ."

Normal? The insult didn't slip by Miguel, but he wasn't tempted to challenge it. He knew if he called out Jeremy on every inappropriate thing he said, that would define their relationship. All of their interactions would be Miguel correcting Jeremy, with Jeremy never growing any wiser. Recognizing the folly of wasting energy trying to fix the unfixable, Miguel was resigned to the fact that Jeremy simply was what he was.

This was not the first time since Miguel had come out to his family that Jeremy had seemingly forgotten about that emotional event. Emotional for Miguel, at least. Miguel had once theorized that Jeremy was just playing dumb, in some roundabout way of mocking him. A friend who was aware of Jeremy's forgetfulness had proposed an alternate possibility: that Jeremy was subconsciously rejecting Miguel as a gay man because, deep down, he was uncomfortable with seeing Miguel in that light. It took a few years, but Miguel finally settled on what he believed to be the reality of the situation: Jeremy was simply too self-involved to remember. Still, Jeremy was his brother, and Miguel couldn't help but forgive him—even when no forgiveness was asked.

Jeremy, struck by a thought, once again snapped his fingers a few inches from Miguel's face.

"Hey! If you're gay, I've got the perfect show for you to watch! *Vikings*—have you heard of it? You would love it. The main character, Ragnar—well, he's something, alright! You should check it out."

Miguel smiled at Jeremy's enthusiasm. *This is Jeremy trying to be helpful.* It was an odd gesture, but Miguel found it somewhat reassuring. *His heart is in the right place.*

"Yeah, I'll have to check that out." Before Jeremy could offer any further awkward suggestions, Miguel asked, "So, any idea what this meeting is all about?" Jeremy grunted.

"No point in going over it until everyone else is here."

He has no idea. Sadie, their adopted sister—or adopted half-sister, depending on how you looked at it—had called for the meeting earlier that day with a vague text to her three half-brothers: *We all have to talk tonight. In person.* Sadie was a few months younger than Jeremy, who felt slighted whenever she usurped what he considered to be his leadership role as the eldest of the siblings. So, in an effort to maintain some illusion of control, Jeremy quickly responded to the text by declaring the time and venue for their meeting: *Outback. 7:00.* Sadie did not respond. Miguel assumed that she, like him, had decided that you had to pick your battles when it came to Jeremy.

"She's late," Jeremy said. Miguel glanced at his phone.

"It's only 6:55. She still has a few minutes." He looked at Jeremy, who grunted again.

"Yeah, maybe. But still." Jeremy finished his Jack and Coke and smacked his lips in appreciation. "Sadie is out of her mind if she thinks Colin is coming, though."

Colin was their other half-brother. Three years younger than Jeremy and seven years older than Miguel, Colin had evolved over time to become the recluse of the family. Ten years ago, he made it to almost every family affair. Five years ago, his attendance was downgraded to just the major holidays. Last year, to Miguel's knowledge, the only time the rest of the family saw Colin was on Christmas, which was unsurprising: Colin had always liked getting presents.

Miguel was about to agree with Jeremy's observation about Colin but stopped when he realized that Jeremy was distracted by something near the entrance. As Jeremy's face evolved from a look of surprise to an unconscious visage of lust, Miguel deduced, somewhat sadly, that it wasn't *something* as much as *someone* that had arrived.

Specifically, their sister, Sadie.

Jeremy rarely spoke of his lifelong fascination with Sadie, but it was clear as day every time their paths crossed. A sizing up of her outfit that lasted a bit too long. A casual touch that extended a second or two longer than was appropriate under the circumstances. Jeremy's eyes searching the room whenever Sadie fell outside his line of sight. Everyone in the family, including Sadie, seemed to notice these subtle clues that collectively amounted to a flashing billboard, but it was not discussed.

Although Miguel viewed Sadie solely as a sister, regardless of the absence of any blood ties, he could objectively appreciate Sadie's appeal. She was tall—nearly six feet in heels—and her slender frame, coupled with her natural grace, suggested a background in ballet. It was obvious that Sadie exercised rigorously, but it was difficult for Miguel to imagine her doing so since he had never seen her sweat. Not once. Nor did she ever seem to have a single hair out of place, regardless of the weather. Sadie reminded Miguel a bit of a Pixar character come to life, in that the absence of any readily apparent physical flaws made her seem almost unreal.

Aside from Jeremy, just about every man and woman noticed Sadie, one by one, as her entrance into the restaurant predictably commanded their attention. Sadie was accustomed to drawing the attention of a room, and she paid no mind to the stares. Her focus, to the contrary, was on the skulking presence at her side—their other half-brother, Colin.

Colin clearly didn't want to be there. Granted, he was *dressed* to go out: a light blue Ted Baker button-down shirt tucked neatly into a pair of Prada khakis. But Miguel knew that was Colin's regular outfit for a day spent at home, in his basement, playing video games . . . which is how Colin spent most of his time. Colin went out of his way to avoid leaving his house and, particularly, to avoid unusual venues filled with unfamiliar people. It typically took a substantial force to drag him out of his safe place.

A force like Sadie.

Indeed, Miguel noted that although they were not touching, Sadie and Colin together conveyed a sense of her physically dragging him along, against his will, by an earlobe. Miguel's assumption that Colin's presence at the restaurant was a product of duress was largely confirmed by his sulky expression.

Sadie scanned the restaurant and located Jeremy and Miguel. Miguel was relieved to see that Jeremy had finally managed to wipe the lust off his face. Still, Jeremy was overeager as he flailed his arms to get Sadie's attention.

"Over here! Over here!" he called. Sadie, pausing only to check that Colin had not escaped, made her way toward them. Miguel could see from her pursed lips, as she studied the restaurant, that she did not approve of the meeting spot. But she didn't give any voice to her dissatisfaction—the four of them were there, and a change of venue was not worth the effort. Sadie was not one to waste words.

Jeremy, of course, misunderstood Sadie's act of surveying the restaurant. "Yup, great place here!" he said. "You have these idiots going to these fancy-schmancy steakhouses in Manhattan, paying over fifty dollars for a steak, when you get something just as good here for twenty. Sides included!"

"Do we have a table?" Sadie asked, ignoring him. Jeremy happily produced an electronic device from his back pocket.

"I checked us in. Just waiting for—" He stopped short when the device sputtered to life, vibrating and flashing lights. "Oh! Perfect timing!"

Jeremy darted to the greeter at the front of the restaurant, waving his flashing contraption. Miguel watched as Jeremy was led to a table on the far side of the restaurant. Sadie sighed.

"A booth," Sadie said. "Lovely."

She led Miguel and Colin to the table where Jeremy was already sitting. She directed Miguel to take the seat next to Jeremy and gave Colin a small shove into the booth on the other side. Only once they were settled did Sadie sit herself. Jeremy glared at Sadie, annoyed that she had positioned herself diagonally from him.

"We need some apps over here," Jeremy muttered. He spotted a waiter walking by and snapped his fingers at him. "Hey! Chief! We're going to need two Bloomin' Onions over here to start." The waiter blinked.

"Ummm, I'm sorry, but someone else has this table. I'm sure they'll be over here—"

"Just put in the order," Jeremy said, interrupting. The waiter, thrown off, sputtered before giving a curt nod and walking back to the kitchen. Through all of this, Sadie remained still. But Miguel knew her well enough to register the flicker of annoyance in her eyes.

"If that is settled?" Sadie spoke in a soft tone, and everyone turned their attention to her. Even Jeremy.

"You may be wondering why I asked you all here tonight," she continued. Jeremy opened his mouth as if he was about to protest, but he didn't speak. "Something has come to my attention that concerns all of us, which I believe warrants some discussion." Sadie paused to make sure everyone was paying attention before continuing. "Mother is, once again, getting remarried."

Both Jeremy's and Colin's eyebrows lowered as they digested this information. *How wonderful!* Miguel thought, but he knew better than to voice that opinion. Not with this crowd.

"To the old man?" Jeremy was the first to speak. Sadie rolled her eyes at the inanity of the question and gave a quick nod.

"When?" Colin asked. "And how do you know this?"

"I don't know when," Sadie said. "And I know because Mother told me last night." Jeremy did a sharp double take.

"She told *you*? You? And not us?" he said. Miguel reached out to try to calm Jeremy down, but Jeremy shook off his grasp. "That's bullshit! I'm the oldest—why wouldn't she tell me? I mean, you're not even—"

Jeremy shut up when Sadie turned her gaze toward him for the first time since they sat down. She didn't speak; she simply stared at Jeremy impassively until he was no longer able to hold eye contact. After a long beat, Jeremy turned away, maintaining his annoyed face in a last-ditch effort to hold onto some dignity. Sadie's poker face was legendary, and any casual observer wouldn't notice anything amiss, but Miguel knew she was livid.

"I do not know why she told me," Sadie said, turning her attention back to the rest of the table. "But it is not important, and it does not warrant any speculation on our part. What matters is that she apparently intends to remarry—and what that will do to us."

Colin nodded, deep in thought. A moment later, Jeremy also bobbed his head in agreement. Miguel's mind was racing, but his failure to react was noticed. Three pairs of eyes swiveled to him.

"I assume I need not explain to you—to any of you—why this notion of a wedding is not in our best interests, do I?" Sadie asked, staring hard at Miguel. Miguel gave an involuntary nod.

"No," Miguel said, and everyone relaxed a bit. "But"—Miguel tried to ignore the reemergence of Sadie's hard stare—"I mean, if it makes her happy, is it that big of a deal? Harold seems nice enough." Jeremy rolled his eyes.

"Oh, God. Here we go," he muttered. Colin simply shook his head in disbelief. Sadie studied Miguel, calculating. Miguel wasn't comfortable being scrutinized in that fashion, and he tried not to squirm. Thankfully, Sadie didn't take long to complete her analysis, and her eyes softened.

"Miguel," she said, reaching out to place a hand over his. Miguel noticed Jeremy's eyes narrow at that nominal physical contact. "I am honest enough to recognize that you have the biggest heart here, so it does not surprise me one bit to hear you say that. But the four of us—we are a family. Not a conventional family, sure, but we are always there for each other when push comes to shove. You know this."

Miguel nodded. He liked to think that was true.

"I hope you can appreciate what this marriage would do to me. What it would do to Colin and Jeremy. Because if we are going to stop it, it will take all of us. Including you. *Especially* you. And sentimentality aside, it is not in your own interests for this wedding to take place. Do you understand this?"

Sadie continued to stare at him, green eyes wide. *How many times has she enchanted a man into doing her bidding with that look?* He was immune to the spell himself, but he saw the truth of what she was saying. Miguel was often the force binding his siblings together, and if he was not with them on this . . .

It was easy to imagine their family splintering without him.

"You're right," Miguel said. "I was just saying that Harold isn't a bad guy, and Mom deserves happiness. But big picture . . ." He didn't finish his thought, but Sadie seemed satisfied with what he had said.

"There will be a party this weekend at Mother's house," Sadie said, turning back to the rest of the table. "They intend to announce the engagement then. It is very important that we are all prepared for this, and that we make it clear, albeit in a subtle way, that we do not approve of this marriage."

"That's it?" Colin asked.

"For now," Sadie said. "I am making other arrangements to ensure that there will be no wedding."

"What other arrangements?" Jeremy asked in a harsh tone. He clammed up once another waiter arrived, dropping off two plates loaded with deep-fried onions. Before the waiter could speak, Jeremy waved him away with an annoyed flick of his wrist. Sadie waited until the waiter was out of earshot before answering.

"That is no concern of yours. I am taking care of it. Just do your part."

"Easy enough!" Colin said. "To be honest, I'm not even sure if I'll go to this party."

"You had better be there," Sadie answered. "Or will you need a chaperone again?"

Colin's cheeks flushed, and he looked away. Silence descended upon the table. Miguel could see their waiter in the distance trying to gauge whether it was safe to approach.

"The old man," Jeremy said, breaking the lull. "He has a daughter."

"A daughter-in-law," Miguel corrected. "He talks about her a lot."

"Whatever. She's single now, right? Her husband died. Maybe we should bring her to our side?"

"How on earth do you plan to do that?" Colin asked, taking out his phone. He proceeded to tap and swipe at it, looking for something.

"I don't know. I can seduce her. Charm her," Jeremy replied before stuffing his face with fried onion.

"You wouldn't have two ex-wives if you still had the ability to seduce anyone!" Colin said with a laugh. Jeremy couldn't respond with his mouth full, so he simply flipped Colin off. Once he finished laughing, Colin held out his phone for the table to see. It displayed a picture of a couple that had been posted to Facebook.

"That's her," Colin said. "She's named Sam—pretty awful name, if you ask me. For a guy, but particularly for a girl."

Miguel leaned forward to see the picture. It was a couple standing in front of a river together. The woman was short—she only came up to the man's armpit—and she beamed happily with the man's arm draped around her shoulders. Miguel assumed that was her deceased husband—Harold's son. Sam's round face was partially obscured by her long dark hair, whipping in her face from the wind, but her smile, which was plain to see, was genuine.

"Oh, she's pretty!" Miguel said. Jeremy leaned in to take a better look and grunted in agreement.

"Yeah, I'd fuck her." Jeremy made it sound as if it was a grand concession on his part. Miguel sighed but otherwise managed not to wince outright at the remark. Sadie, by contrast, made no effort to hide her annoyance.

"No," she said, pushing Colin's phone down to the table so no one could see it. "There is no reason to involve Harold's dead son's wife. None." But Jeremy wasn't giving up.

"I'm just saying we can work Mom on our end, and if we get this girl on our side, she can do the same with Harold—help convince him that this wedding isn't a good idea. I know if I talked to her—"

"You will do no such thing," Sadie said, cutting him off. "You will not talk to her. You will not approach her. You will not get her involved. Do you understand?"

Jeremy's eyes brimmed with rage, but Sadie didn't seem to care. Colin and Miguel instinctively exchanged a look with one another—shared relief at being on the periphery of this confrontation. In the end, this battle, like most disputes between Jeremy and Sadie, ended before it could start, with Jeremy looking away in an unspoken defeat.

But that wasn't enough for Sadie.

"I need you to say it," she said. "Tell me you will not do anything with this daughter-in-law. I need to hear it."

Jeremy took a deep breath.

"Fine," he said, spitting out the word. "I'll stay away from the girl. Happy now?"

CHAPTER THREE

Thursday, August 22, 2019

Jeremy, restless, paced back and forth in front of a deli in downtown Manhattan. He felt very exposed, but he didn't want to miss her when she left for the day. It took a fair amount of effort to find out where Sam worked, but a few creative Google searches revealed that her office was on the ninth floor of a downtown skyscraper looking out toward Brooklyn across the East River.

Jeremy had considered conducting his stakeout in the lobby of the building, but he wasn't entirely clear on when Sam would finish work. Loitering in front of security for a prolonged period of time would only invite trouble. A quick bit of surveillance confirmed that the building had two main areas of egress, both of which were visible from Jeremy's vantage point in front of the deli. So that was where he waited, and would wait, regardless of how long it took. He was in no rush. Throughout the school year, in his work as a middle school gym teacher, Jeremy always found himself counting down the days until summer break, but when it finally arrived, he was inevitably amazed at how soon he was bored with it all. This surveillance was the most exciting thing he'd done in a month.

Sadie really thought she could order me not to make contact with Sam? Jeremy chuckled to himself. Part of him wondered whether, had Sadie not challenged him so, he would have gone through the effort of taking the train into the city to spend hours waiting to find his future stepfather's daughter-in-law.

"Enough is enough," Jeremy muttered to himself as he paced back and forth on the wide sidewalk. Sadie had been a thorn in his side since she entered his life at the age of thirteen, after his mother had married Sadie's father, Victor. The stuck-up girls at school generally avoided Jeremy, so it seemed a godsend when a new girl—hotter *by far* than anyone in his class—had moved into his house, taking a bedroom just down the hall from his own. But Sadie made it plain from the outset that Jeremy's presence was a mere annoyance in her life that would be waved aside on those occasions it couldn't be ignored outright.

Except, of course, when Sadie needed something from him. Then she wasn't at all shy about barking out her commands and orders.

"Fuck her," Jeremy growled. A young couple walking down the street, pointing at the various structures of lower Manhattan, overheard him and wordlessly altered their path to give him a wide berth. Jeremy noticed and gave them a hard stare as they arced around him.

"And fuck those tourists," he added, watching them walk away. A moment later, he felt a tinge of guilt. It was, after all, a tourist who had managed to steer Jeremy in the right direction earlier in the day, when he inadvertently took the 2 train uptown, leading him to disembark, disoriented, in Harlem. The misstep delayed his arrival by nearly an hour, but he still managed to retrace his steps and get to Sam's building before 4:00. It was unlikely that he missed her, even with that hiccup, but the mere possibility of that happening was enough to make Jeremy anxious. Aside from the fact that such an outcome would make the day a complete waste, Sadie would continue to think that Jeremy had once again bowed to her will without a hint of resistance. And so, Jeremy resolved to continue his vigil, shuffling back and forth, head swiveling between the two exits from the building, looking for her.

Because Jeremy knew that once he located Sam, the rest would be easy.

• • • • •

Sam sat in her small cubicle, staring at the giant clock on the far wall as it crept toward 5:00. Around her, co-workers made idle small talk with each other, but, somewhat curiously, no one seemed to be packing up to leave. *Whatever*, Sam thought. *I'm out of here*. She glanced at her phone—

sometimes the clock on the wall was off by a minute or two, depending on the state of its batteries. *4:54. Close enough to leave for the day?*

Yes. For sure.

With a few quick clicks of her mouse, she powered down her computer while simultaneously opening the lower desk drawer with her foot. Before her computer screen even had a chance to go black, Sam had snatched her backpack out of the drawer and bounced out of her chair.

As she turned to step away from her desk, she saw her manager, Nick, a meek man in his mid-forties, approaching with a document in hand at his side. Even from a distance, she could see that it was covered with red edits. With a sad exhale, Sam slumped back into her chair, dropping her backpack to the floor, to await Nick's arrival.

"Hey, Sam," Nick said. "Just returning this to you." Nick placed the document on her desk. Sam glanced at it and saw it was a disclaimer letter she had drafted for Nick's review earlier that day. Sam assumed, from the number of revisions on the first page alone, that Nick had recently acquired a new red pen that he was having fun with.

"The edits look worse than they are," Nick added, reading her thoughts. "I mostly just had to cross out about sixty adverbs and adjectives. This is a letter disclaiming insurance coverage. You should save those juicy adverbs for your book reviews." Nick grinned as he said it, but Sam felt her face flush with embarrassment.

"You read my book reviews?" she asked, prompting Nick also to blush.

"No, no," Nick said, stammering a bit. "I mean, I stumbled across one a week or two ago. I wasn't googling you or anything like that. It was good! It got me to order the book."

Sam barely heard him. She was frantically trying to recount everything she had ever put on her Bookstagram account and struggling to remember if there was anything unsuitable for work. She generally kept it a PG affair, but . . .

"Nice job otherwise on the letter," Nick said, desperate to change the subject. "Your writing is finally catching up to your negotiating skills. Just make those edits and get it out. I don't need to see it again." He paused, noticing Sam's backpack at her feet, and frowned. "You weren't leaving, were you?"

"Ummmmm . . ." Nick's tone suggested that yes would be the wrong answer, but Sam couldn't figure out why that would be the case. "Maybe?"

Nick looked pained. "We have drinks after work for Arthur's retirement, remember?"

"Oh. Right." Arthur was the grizzled veteran on their floor—a fierce warrior who had devoted the better part of his life to adjusting insurance claims. Sam knew him well enough to smile politely at him in the elevator, but that was the extent of their relationship. It wasn't so much that she had *forgotten* about his retirement party as she had immediately diagnosed the announcement of the get-together as irrelevant for her purposes.

"I didn't think that was mandatory," Sam said, adopting a casual tone, which prompted Nick to raise a skeptical eyebrow.

Sam knew that Nick was a pretty good boss, all things considered. He had handled Sam with kid gloves ever since Mike died, excusing her from any social gatherings that she didn't feel up to attending. Which, as it turned out, was basically all of them. Sam had no desire to fraternize in the immediate aftermath of Mike's death and, as she settled into the life of a recluse, any interest she may have once had in mingling never resurfaced.

She knew that her social immunity had a shelf life, and there would come a time when she would be expected to reenter the civilized world. She didn't know when that time would come—all she knew was that when it did, it would not be of her own volition.

"Look," Nick said. "I appreciate everything you've gone through. And I can't imagine how difficult it must still be for you. But we're a team here, and it's important for us all to be able to get together at times and bond outside of work."

"So, you're saying this is—"

"Yes," Nick said with mild irritation. "You should consider it mandatory. Have a drink or two and sneak out—I don't care. But you should at least show your face." Nick looked apprehensive, like he was bracing for Sam to put up a fight. But instead, Sam slumped slightly in her seat and shrugged.

"Ok. Fine." She paused, looking around. No one seemed to be preparing to leave. "What time is this thing starting?"

"Well, some of the people here work from 10:00 to 6:00, so we will all head over together after they finish up for the day." He noted Sam's aggrieved expression and chided, "It said as much in the announcement email."

The email she had ignored. *Of course.*

"Well, looks like I have another hour to kill!" Sam said, forcing a grin. Nick gave a small grateful smile in return and headed back toward his office. Moments later, Sam's computer was fully rebooted. With nothing better to do, Sam got to work on revising her heavily edited disclaimer letter.

But it turned out Nick was right. The revisions were easy and straightforward—just a matter of mindlessly deleting unnecessary, albeit colorful, adverbs and adjectives. It didn't take much effort at all for Sam to drain the life out of that letter.

• • • • •

Jeremy was getting tired. Physically tired—pacing around a New York City sidewalk in the sun for two hours was exhausting—but mentally, as well. The past hour or so had generated a continuous stream of people leaving the building across the street, and Jeremy was doing his best to eyeball all of them as they filtered out to ensure that Sam didn't sneak by him. He had found a couple of pictures of Sam online, so he *thought* he would be able to recognize her when she emerged. Still, there were a few misfires. On one occasion, Jeremy ran up to a woman shouting "Sam! Sam!" Only when he was right in the woman's terrified face did he realize he had accosted the wrong person, and he sheepishly returned to his strategic vantage point.

Fewer and fewer people were leaving the office building as it got closer to 6:00. *What if she slipped by me?* Jeremy wondered. *Maybe she dyed her hair blonde or something and I missed her*. It would be a shame. Aside from the wasted afternoon, Jeremy had spent a great deal of time online learning as much as he could about Sam: her favorite movies, her favorite books, her favorite music—he even learned that her favorite color was green!

Perhaps I'll get a chance to use that information down the road, he thought. Granted, he wasn't sure he could muster up the energy to come back into the city tomorrow, and the barbeque was the day after that. But maybe he'd find an opportunity *at* the party to work his magic. It wouldn't be as satisfying as showing up to the gathering with Sam as a newly acquired ally—*that* would certainly make Sadie's jaw drop—but it was probably the best he could do.

Jeremy prepared to leave, looking up and down the street for a subway entrance. *It'll be humiliating if I have to get directions from another fucking tourist*, he thought. But as he was getting his bearings, a throng of people, perhaps a dozen, emerged from the building across the street. And there, in the middle of them all, looking extremely bored, was Sam.

She looks just like her photos. But there was something off he could not immediately place. Then it occurred to him: her smile. In all of the photos he found of Sam online, she wore a giant effortless smile—the kind that would inevitably lead to the formation of crow's feet around the eyes. But as Jeremy studied her from across the street, he noted that her face looked blank and disinterested.

"A little grumpy today, I see," Jeremy muttered to himself. He wasn't concerned. It was just a factor to consider when he approached her.

Jeremy followed the group at a distance, waiting for Sam to emerge from the pack. But she never did. Instead, the cluster of people moved together through the streets like a flock of birds dancing in unison across the sky. Jeremy began to question how long this would continue. *Do they all share the same apartment?* he wondered. But everything made sense once the mob arrived at a small Irish pub a few blocks from their office.

Ah, a happy hour. Jeremy stopped to collect his thoughts and decided this was a positive development. *Just give her some time to get a drink or two in, and then I'll talk to her inside.* It would be much easier than if he had approached her on the street. He could even make it look like a random encounter—the last thing he wanted to do was come off as creepy.

Jeremy took out his phone and set a timer for twenty minutes. That should give Sam enough time to relax and have a drink. Sure, it involved more waiting on the sidewalk for Jeremy, but he didn't mind.

He was in the driver's seat now.

• • • • •

Sam stood at a far end of the bar, nursing a beer. Her unit had taken up the back half of the pub, and Sam had spent the last twenty minutes navigating the room, making sure she was seen by everyone important. She was satisfied that a sufficient number of eyes had registered her presence, and she was calculating how much longer she had to stay.

As she was checking her phone for the Metro-North schedule to find a convenient train to take home after her unexpected late day, she felt a presence sidle up to her. Glancing up, Sam noted her co-worker Mitch hovering at her side.

"Fun party, right?" Mitch said in his monotone voice. Sam grinned in artificial agreement and tried to steal a glance at her phone, which had finally loaded the train schedule.

"So, I don't know if you've heard about the restructuring," Mitch continued, and Sam felt her face blanch. Even though they worked for a company that employed thousands, Mitch had seemingly managed to memorize the entire organizational chart. It was, to Sam's knowledge, his greatest passion in life.

"Apparently," Mitch said, before embracing a dramatic pause. He pushed that moment of silence to its limit before continuing. "In November, Drew's unit will begin reporting to Tina. They had been reporting to Rebecca. Now, as I understand it, Chad's group will continue to report to Rebecca, but that seems to be the anomaly. It's crazy—just last year, Rebecca had four direct reports. And now she's down to one? Really makes you wonder what's going on over there."

"Sure does," Sam said. She took a long sip of her drink.

"I can't help but wonder if Tina can handle the added workload. I think she now has *seven* direct reports? That can't be a long-term solution. In fact—"

"Oh, I'm sorry," Sam interrupted. She was slightly breathless from the effort of chugging her beer as quickly as possible. "I'm all empty. I'm going to go grab another drink." Sam glanced at the glass in Mitch's hand, which was nearly full, before venturing to add, "Do you need anything?" Mitch looked down at his beverage.

"Thank you, but I'm fine for now."

Sam, with an over-enthusiastic grin, gave him a thumbs up and waded back into the crowd, emerging shortly thereafter at the bar. Looking back through the mass of bodies she had just navigated, she could make out Mitch repositioning himself next to another colleague left vulnerable by the recklessness of being a wallflower.

It occurred to Sam that if she could see Mitch, then he would be able to see her. It would look odd—or, more accurately, rude—if she were to just leave after announcing an intent to get a second beer. Checking her phone once again, Sam confirmed that she had at least another half hour to kill before leaving to catch the next train home. *Oh well.* She moved to the bar and waited for the bartender to come around so she could throw another drink on the corporate tab.

As she waited, Sam heard music coming on from the front of the bar. There had been no background music up to that point, so the sudden onset of a song was a bit jarring. *I guess someone found the jukebox.* It was difficult to identify the song at first with all the conversations around her, but the beat of the tune gradually lodged in her head. Sam couldn't help but smile when the song finally registered.

"The Warrior" by Scandal. It was Sam's favorite song growing up—one to which she periodically returned when she needed to feel uplifted or empowered. She hadn't heard the song in several years, though. Her adversity during that time had reached levels that transcended the healing abilities of *"The Warrior."*

As she waited for the bartender's attention, Sam found herself bopping along to the music. The song was barely audible; really just the bass and drums coming through the din of the crowd. But it was enough to spur the soundtrack in Sam's mind, and despite herself, she allowed her body to sway in rhythm while she waited at the bar.

Sam was jolted out of her reverie toward the end of the song when a gravelly voice spoke directly into her ear: "You're welcome."

Sam looked over her shoulder and saw a tall, lanky man, roughly her age, looking down at her. He wore a collared shirt with short sleeves, which revealed a few scattered tattoos on his forearms and biceps. His head was angled sharply downward to account for the significant height difference between them, and he wore a confident grin that suggested he knew her from somewhere.

"Excuse me?" Sam said, thrown off.

"I couldn't help but notice you enjoying the song. I happen to be the one who put it on the jukebox a few minutes ago. So, as I said, you're welcome."

"Oh. Right. Thanks then. Excuse me." Sam shouldered past the strange man but stopped when he called out after her.

"You're Sam Daly, aren't you?"

Sam looked at the man again, studying him more closely.

"I am. Do I know you?" He didn't look at all familiar to her. The man threw back his head and laughed.

"No, no. At least, not yet. But my name is Jeremy. And I understand that we may share something in common."

Is that supposed to make sense to me? Sam continued to stare at Jeremy with a perplexed expression.

"You see," he continued, "I've learned that my mother will be marrying Harold Lindgren. It's a terribly kept secret, although they haven't yet formally announced it. Harold is your father-in-law, right?"

Sam's mind was racing. *I need a moment to think.* Seeing the bartender approach, she stepped past Jeremy to order her drink. In a mirror behind the bar, Sam managed to make out Jeremy's smile slipping—he didn't appreciate being ignored. Sam looked back at him over her shoulder and held up her index finger—*one sec*—and turned back to wait for her beer before Jeremy could respond. When her pint glass was finally delivered, Sam took a long sip, collecting her thoughts. Only once she felt fully reset did she turn back to Jeremy. She took a few steps away from the bar, where it wasn't as crowded, and gestured for Jeremy to follow.

"I'm sorry!" she exclaimed. "I've been trying to get that bartender's attention forever. You know how that goes." Sam made a big deal of noticing that Jeremy wasn't holding a drink of his own. "Oh, you need a drink, too!

I would have gotten you one, but we have a company tab going. I'd probably get in trouble if they saw me buying drinks for random people here. You understand, right?" Jeremy grunted sourly.

"Anyway—" he started.

"Right!" Sam cut in. "You were saying that your mother is marrying Harold. That's exciting!" Sam took a thoughtful sip, then widened her eyes, as if she just had a thought. "By the way, how did you know who I am?" Jeremy's smile reasserted itself. *He was anticipating the question*, Sam noted.

"Well, Harold talks about you all the time. One night—fairly recently—when we were all hanging out, he showed us your picture. I guess the image must have stayed in my head, because imagine my surprise when I just happened to spot you here! I had to come over and say hello, of course."

"Of course." Sam looked around. "Are you here with friends? Do you work in the city?" Jeremy beamed at the question. *That didn't catch him off guard either*, Sam thought.

"No," he said, all confidence. "I work on Long Island. And I'm a teacher, so not technically working right now, but we'll start up again soon. I was actually here to meet a woman I met online. She was supposed to be here a half hour ago, but it looks like she stood me up! I figured I'd just grab a beer before I head back home. And then I saw you." Jeremy seemed proud of his answer—like a second-grade student successfully reciting his two lines at a school Thanksgiving pageant.

"Fancy that." Sam was struggling to diagnose whether Jeremy was being deceitful or whether he was just socially awkward. *Possibly both.* "Sorry to hear you were stood up. What was her name?"

"Her name?" Jeremy's cockiness evaporated instantly, and Sam knew she found a hole in his prep work. He glanced down at his arms before answering. "Uh, it's . . . April. Why do you ask?"

"April, huh?" Sam took another look at Jeremy's tattoos and noticed a ninja turtle on his right forearm. *Someone's got April O'Neil on the brain*, she thought. "Is she a redhead?"

"What?" Jeremy blinked in confusion. He seemed to have just enough self-awareness to realize a joke had flown over his head.

"Never mind. So, about this wedding—"

"Yes!" Jeremy interrupted. "The wedding. Right. Well, my siblings and I, we have some concerns, you see. It's not that your father-in-law isn't a great guy, it's just—"

"Look," Sam said, cutting him off. "I'll be honest with you. I haven't had a great deal of contact with Harold since—well, we haven't spoken a lot in the past few years. And I'm happy for him. But I don't see why this marriage has anything to do with me."

"Well, that's the thing," Jeremy pressed. "They're having this barbeque on Saturday to announce it, even though, like I said, it's not much of a secret at this point, but I was thinking—"

"I'm not going to that party."

Jeremy's head jerked.

"You're . . . not going?" He looked confused. "But aren't you, like, Harold's only family?"

"I'm his ex-daughter-in-law. Or former daughter-in-law. I don't know what the correct term is. But it's a stretch of the concept of 'family,' in any event. I like Harold and wish him the best, but I'm trying just to move on with my life at this point."

Jeremy digested this in silence. As Sam watched Jeremy's gears turn, a hint of a smile touched his lips, and Sam realized something that struck her as truly bizarre.

Jeremy was pleased that she was not planning on attending the barbeque.

"Well, ok then!" he said. "That largely moots what I had planned to say! Anyway, it was a pleasure to meet you, and best of luck to you." Jeremy turned to make his exit, leaving Sam confused by the abrupt end to their encounter. But after a few steps, Jeremy turned back to face her.

"Say, would you mind if I told people that I convinced you not to go to the party? I mean, I doubt anyone will check with you, but just in case—would that be cool?"

Sam stared hard at him.

"You can say whatever you want," she answered carefully. Jeremy seemed satisfied with that response.

"Great!" He offered her a closed fist, and Sam, with great reluctance, knocked her own against it. "Well, check you later!" Jeremy strode out of the bar, leaving Sam to puzzle at why he looked so pleased with himself.

CHAPTER FOUR

Saturday, August 24, 2019

Sam lay on her couch, absorbing a line of afternoon sun. She had spent the past few hours trying to make a dent in a new novel—a fantasy book nearing nine hundred pages—but she was finding it difficult to focus.

I love fantasy when I'm in the right mood. But when I'm not . . . my word, is this tedious. Just about every sentence had one or two made-up words that necessitated referencing a glossary at the end of the book, and she was weary of flipping back and forth to try to make sense of any of it.

She briefly considered putting off the book and going out somewhere to take a fun picture of it—something to use when she got around to reviewing the novel online. But she decided against it. Sam was very careful in how she photographed books—she liked to let the story decide where and how the book should ultimately be shot. But the prologue in which she was mired had not provided any hint of an appropriate place to conduct a photoshoot. *It's a fantasy—probably any picture of the book in a forest would work*, Sam thought. But she knew it was an uninspired choice that she would not act upon.

Truth be told, it was hardly the novel's fault that Sam couldn't focus. No matter how hard she tried to concentrate on anything else, her mind kept jumping back to the strangeness of the past week, starting with Harold's unexpected reentry into her life and ending with Harold's future son-in-law seemingly stalking her at a work happy hour.

"But aren't you, like, Harold's only family?"

Jeremy had asked that rhetorical question not as a matter of judgment, but as a surprised reaction. Still, the question gnawed at her and triggered unexpected pangs of guilt. It was tempting to answer it in the negative, as she had to Jeremy: *"No, I am not his family. Not anymore."* Of course, Sam knew if that was true, then the unavoidable result was that Harold was alone.

A fiancée who had already seen four prior husbands die. Four future stepchildren that had "concerns" about the wedding, one of whom was a stalking creep. As sure as she was that something was off about Harold's new family, Sam was equally certain that Harold, with his tendency to only see the best in people, would be blind to it, without backup from a cynical set of eyes to steer him right. And Sam could not shake off Jeremy's accurate pronouncement: aside from her, there was no one else to do it.

Sam groaned and tried, once again, to distract herself with her book. But after rereading the same sentence five times and stubbornly refusing to go to the glossary to translate it into something other than gibberish, she gave up. With a loud sigh, Sam half-threw the book onto her coffee table, scattering a collection of unsorted mail from the past week. Sam sat up and collected the various envelopes, stacking them into a neat pile. As she did so, a single piece of paper fell out and fluttered to the floor.

It was the directions to Harold's engagement party, which he had left at the end of his visit earlier that week. Sam cocked her head to make out the details on the paper and noted that the party was starting in less than half an hour. Unmoving, Sam stared hard at the piece of paper on the floor. She wished she had the will to throw it out and erase it from her memory, but she knew that road would lead to crushing guilt. Shoving her head into the sand was not a realistic option, so Sam made the only decision that was left to her.

"Damn it," she muttered.

Just because it was the only decision, it didn't mean she had to like it.

• • • • •

Miguel stood alone in a corner of his mother's backyard. The party was supposed to start at 3:00, and Miguel, in his naïveté, arrived at that time only to be greeted by an empty yard. Various seating options were scattered throughout the freshly mowed space, and a table holding a variety of covered-up snacks had been placed near the fence.

There was no sign of anyone outside. Not Miguel's mother. Not Harold. None of his siblings. Not even any of the strange New Age crew his mother tended to hang around. Deciding to make the best of the situation, Miguel found a cooler filled with beer and ice and grabbed a bottle to sip as he killed time.

Earlier that week, he had debated whether to bring Kevin, a high school physics teacher he'd been seeing for about two months. It was a long enough period of time to introduce Kevin to his family, if Miguel was so inclined, but still short enough to wait a bit longer. Miguel decided against it, not wanting to make this day about him.

Miguel was honest enough to admit that his decision was also driven, at least in part, by his discomfort with how his siblings—particularly Jeremy—would react to meeting Kevin. The best Miguel could hope for was a bored indifference, but Miguel could also imagine things going much worse than that. It was also unclear to Miguel how Sadie and his brothers intended to react to the wedding announcement itself, given their stated opposition to the marriage. Sadie tended to hand out her marching orders as late as possible, so Miguel could not rule out the possibility that there would be some dramatic and uncomfortable scene later that afternoon. All of those uncertainties made it easy for Miguel to decide to fly solo for the day.

A couple soon arrived: a pair of aging hippies Miguel assumed were friends of his mother. He gave them a wave, and they smiled and began walking in his direction. Moments later, another pair of older hippies arrived, and the original pair diverted their path to talk to them instead. Miguel felt mildly relieved. His mother's friends, as nice as they were, tended to freak him out a bit.

Miguel was finishing his beer and on the verge of getting another when Jeremy arrived. Jeremy stopped upon entering the yard and looked at Miguel and the separate quartet of hippies.

"Wow, some party," he proclaimed in a loud voice. The cluster of hippies ignored him. Noting Miguel's empty beer, Jeremy mimed a drinking gesture from across the yard and adopted a puzzled expression. Miguel pointed at the cooler, and Jeremy gave him a tight thumbs up in response. Jeremy was at his side a minute later with two beers, one of which he handed to Miguel. Jeremy took a long pull but sputtered after taking in what Miguel was wearing.

"That shirt," he said, wiping his lips with a sleeve. Miguel looked down at his plain blue shirt.

"What about it?"

"It's pretty gay, man." Jeremy laughed. Miguel frowned.

"It could not be a more boring blue shirt. And besides, your shirt is purple." *As if colors can be gay*, Miguel thought. Jeremy looked down, as if he had forgotten what he was wearing.

"Nah, it's maroon," Jeremy said. "So, is this it? Party-wise? Where's Mom and the old man?" Miguel shrugged.

"Beats me. I would've thought it had been canceled if these four hadn't shown up." Miguel tilted his head toward the hippies, and Jeremy grunted.

A few minutes later, Sadie and Colin came into the yard, once again arriving together. Colin, as always, looked sharp in a red dress shirt and black chinos, and Sadie looked almost demure in a yellow sleeveless sundress with an intricate flower pattern, her long hair falling gently over one shoulder. Colin detected Jeremy's amusement upon joining them.

"For the record," Colin said in a clipped tone, "I arrived on my own. Sadie just happened to be parking when I got here."

"Of course," Jeremy said, sarcasm dripping from each word. Sadie ignored the exchange between the two half-brothers and quickly assessed the scene.

"Where is everyone? Is Mother here?" she asked.

"This is it so far," Miguel said. "Just us and them." He nodded toward the other group, talking excitedly amongst themselves. Colin laughed.

"If we had a basketball hoop, we could challenge them to four-on-four," he said. Sadie rolled her eyes and began checking her phone.

As they stood together in the back corner of the yard, attendees began to trickle in, and the party slowly came to life. It was painfully obvious that most attendees were associates of their mother, while a smaller subset—dressed more conservatively and appearing a bit frightened of the larger, more eccentric group—were friends of Harold. Harold himself soon arrived and immediately took to welcoming all of the guests. His progress was slow—he seemed to get drawn into a long, boisterous conversation with every group he approached—and Miguel figured it would be some time before he made his way over to them. There was still no sign of their mother.

"Mom is as popular as ever," Colin noted, scanning the crowd. "Small showing for Harold, though. Looks like it's mostly people from his old job." Harold was retired, but Miguel recalled that he had spent the past few decades working for a cable company.

"Yeah," Jeremy said, jumping in. "Hardly anyone here to support Harold. It actually would have been more than this, had it not been for me." He paused, waiting for someone to ask a follow up question. Sadie's eyes narrowed, but she didn't say anything. Colin merely frowned in confusion. Jeremy was beginning to look annoyed at the lack of response, so Miguel figured he would just give him what he wanted.

"What do you mean?" Miguel asked. Jeremy, looking relieved, chuckled.

"Let's just say I had occasion to make acquaintance with Harold's daughter-in-law. Cute girl. We hit it off right away. I managed to convince her to steer clear of this party. Don't get me wrong: it was challenging—I didn't want to tip her off as to *why* we didn't want her here—but I pulled it off in the end." Jeremy stretched, extending his arms toward the sky, looking very pleased with himself. "Yeah, I thought about bringing her to our side. But then it occurred to me: *What if we just take her off the game board completely? Keep the old man isolated and alone, while we work Mom on our end?* Seemed like a no-brainer, so that's the way I went with it." Jeremy paused, as if waiting for thanks or congratulations, but he was met with blank stares. Miguel stole a glance at Sadie to see what she thought of this development, but she only looked thoughtful. But as Sadie processed this turn of events, Miguel noticed a slight crease in her forehead that revealed that she was, in her usual subtle manner, distracted by something. Her eyes refocused—not on Jeremy, but, rather, on something behind him in the distance.

"You unbelievable idiot." Sadie's pronouncement was barely audible—not much more than an exhale. She seemed more amazed by Jeremy than annoyed. Colin followed her look and barked out a laugh.

"Looks like you weren't quite as charming as you thought!" Colin said to Jeremy. Jeremy, startled, looked over his shoulder. It took a moment to register, but when it did, Jeremy's face darkened with pure rage.

"Oh, fuck her!" he snarled.

• • • •

Sam entered the unfamiliar backyard filled with an odd collection of men and women in their late sixties. Most were laughing and singing with no care for their surroundings, although a smaller group huddled together to one side as if intimidated by the unorthodox majority. Sam did not see Harold or Jeremy—the only two people she would be able to recognize. Given her height, it was difficult to see the rear of the yard over the wall of people closest to her. Sam figured it was possible Harold and Jeremy were lurking somewhere in the crowd.

Before leaving her home earlier that afternoon, Sam struggled to decide what to wear. Harold hadn't given her a great deal of information about how formal the event would be. He had described it as a barbeque, so she made an educated guess of casual dress, which she manifested by throwing on a green blouse with jeans. Sam was concerned about missing the get-together entirely—she was already late—so she only allowed herself a few minutes to apply a nominal amount of makeup and throw her hair in a ponytail before driving down to Long Island.

Upon arriving, Sam realized that her worries were misplaced, as there was no discernible dress code amongst the guests. Some men were in shorts and t-shirts, and others looked business casual in khakis and polos. The women all seemed to wear long flowing dresses of various colors and patterns that wouldn't seem out of place in vintage shops. It was an eclectic group, and Sam sensed that most of them were not Harold's crowd. *And that means they're with the increasingly mysterious Marcie*, Sam thought.

As she started her cautious entrance into the bowels of the gathering, a voice from behind spoke directly into her ear.

"I knew you'd do the right thing and come."

She turned to see Harold, looking like he was dressed for a round of golf, with a self-satisfied smirk on his face. Sam surmised that he'd circled around behind her without her realizing it. Although Sam generally had no issues with her height, she recognized it as an inconvenience when it came to matters of reconnaissance.

"Look," Sam said, "I wasn't going to come, but I changed my mind about an hour ago. There's some weird stuff going on that I want to talk to you about. Jeremy—"

"Oh, Jeremy?" Harold interrupted. He looked about the backyard and pointed. "He's over there, with the rest of Marcie's kids."

As a trio of partygoers shifted, Sam could finally see the area of the yard where Harold was pointing. Jeremy, in a bright purple shirt, was glaring at her from across the yard with naked malevolence. Next to Jeremy stood two men and a tall, beautiful woman, each dressed in a different primary color. They looked on impassively at Sam, although the one in the blue shirt seemed to give her a subtle shy wave of the hand, which hovered around his waist.

"They look like an evil version of the Wiggles," Sam said, uncomfortable under their collective scrutiny.

"The what? And no—they're not evil! You should go talk to them. Here, I'll introduce you." Harold took her elbow and started to march toward the rear of the yard, but Sam shook her arm free.

"No! I really need to speak with you first!" Sam looked again at Marcie's children. Jeremy still looked like he was barely suppressing his rage. The woman's head was tilted slightly to the side, eyes narrowed, as she watched Sam interact with Harold. *She's studying me*, Sam realized. *That's the expression of someone in the midst of a chess game.*

"We can talk later," Harold insisted. "I—" He was interrupted by another couple, who had just arrived at the party and beelined to him to say hello. "Joan! Brad! I'm so glad you were able to make it!" He guided the new arrivals to the drink cooler, turning back once to throw a reassuring smile at Sam.

Well, now what? Sam did not fully understand what she was trying to accomplish. *Just get the general vibe, maybe try to figure out what the kids are up to.* Harold ultimately had to live his own life, but Sam continued to feel something was amiss. *Just come up with something, more tangible than a vague feeling of unease, that you can take to Harold*, she thought. *It's up to him at that point what he does with it.* Sam figured that if she could accomplish that, at least, her conscience would be clean, regardless of whether Harold acted upon whatever information she delivered to him.

I guess I have to go introduce myself to Marcie's kids, Sam thought, not relishing the notion. She turned toward them and was instantly blinded by a wall of purple. Taking a step back, Sam looked up and realized that Jeremy had crept up on her the moment Harold left her side.

"You told me you weren't coming today!" he snapped. "You're a liar!"

"I changed my mind," Sam responded. She felt her temper rising. "Why do I owe you any explanations for whether I was going to come or not?"

"You said you weren't!" Jeremy pressed. "It's just a little thing called 'integrity'—ever hear of it?"

"Why does it matter to you?" Sam said. Jeremy took a quick glance over his shoulder toward his siblings, and Sam remembered one of the many strange things that Jeremy had said to her two nights earlier: *Would you mind if I told people that I convinced you not to go to the party?* Sam guessed that Jeremy's rage stemmed from his embarrassment over being caught in a lie about her more than her actual presence.

Jeremy's two brothers approached. *Half-brothers*, Sam reminded herself. She made a mental note to draw up a family tree later to try to decipher this family. Sam looked for the sister, or half-sister, and spotted her making small talk a few yards away with an older man, although she didn't seem to be paying much attention to what he was saying. A subtle tilt of her ear suggested that the sister had merely positioned herself to listen to Sam's interaction with the three brothers without having to engage herself. The youngest of the brothers smiled and extended a hand.

"Hi, I'm Miguel. You must be Harold's daughter-in-law. Sam, right?"

Sam dutifully shook his hand and glanced at the other brother, who gave no inclination that he would introduce himself.

"That's Colin," Miguel added, and Sam nodded at the blonde-haired older brother. "And it seems like you know Jeremy."

"Yeah, we met," Sam said in a neutral tone.

"We heard from Jeremy that you weren't coming," Colin said. Jeremy's face reddened once again.

"She told me she wasn't coming," Jeremy said in a whiny tone. "Is it my fault I believed her?"

"Like I said, I changed my mind," Sam said. Colin, although playing it cooler than Jeremy, seemed less than thrilled by her arrival, and Sam had a moment of inspiration. "To be honest, I had no intention of coming, but then Jeremy pointed out to me that Harold really had no other family to support him, and I thought he should at least have someone from his side of the family here. I assume you know what this gathering is all about, right? Jeremy told me."

Sam was uncomfortable identifying herself as part of Harold's family—she was still unsure how she felt about that. But Sam knew the arguable white lie was worth it upon seeing Colin and Miguel turn toward Jeremy in disbelief, with Jeremy too flustered to do anything but stammer in his defense. Out of the corner of her eye, Sam noticed Sadie watching from a distance, but the beams she stared at Jeremy confirmed that she was well within earshot.

"I didn't—" Jeremy sputtered. "She already knew about—" He paused to collect himself. "Look. We are getting sidetracked. The point is—"

"The *point* is that I go where I please, and I don't owe you any explanation for where I might end up." Sam took half a step closer to Jeremy to emphasize her point, and he reflexively backed up.

"I'm not afraid of you," he blurted out. Miguel, embarrassed, covered his face with a hand. Colin also looked bewildered. "I mean, I know Tae Kwon Do," Jeremy added, feebly.

"Ah, sweet Jesus," Miguel muttered, walking away with his hands raised, as if he was surrendering. Colin also seemed mortified and looked around for something to save him from the awkwardness. Jeremy's head swiveled between them, sensing something was amiss but seemingly unable to pinpoint it.

"You know Tae Kwon Do," Sam said softly. "And how, pray tell, is that relevant to anything going on right now?"

Jeremy's mouth moved wordlessly, but Sam continued.

"Do you really see you and I having a physical fight here? A martial arts match?" She took another step closer to Jeremy. He towered over her by about a foot, so Sam had to crane her neck to look at him, but she wanted to highlight the size difference between them. She knew it would make him feel even more absurd.

"No," Jeremy said in a sullen tone. "I don't want to fight you. I was just saying—"

"Yeah, I heard what you were just saying. Maybe don't say things like that in the future, eh?" With that, Sam walked toward the cooler. She could feel Sadie's eyes following her from across the yard, but she didn't care. *Hope she enjoyed the show*, Sam thought while she cracked open a beer. As she took a sip, Sam tried to collect her thoughts. *Now what?* She looked around for Harold, but he remained out of sight, as did his bride-to-be.

Sam detected motion to her right and noticed Miguel sheepishly approaching.

"Hi," he said, awkward as anything. "Ummmmm . . . I'm sorry about that?"

"It's not your fault," Sam said. She held her sweaty bottle against her forehead to cool off. Miguel continued to stand there uncomfortably.

"Miguel, huh?" Sam said. "My husband's name was Mike. He was Harold's son."

"Yeah, I know," Miguel said. He grabbed a beer of his own. "Jeremy used to call me Mike. Still does sometimes, but he's getting better." It was clear from his tone that he did not care for the deviation from his given name.

"You don't like 'Mike'?" Sam asked.

"Nah, it's not that. It's just—" Miguel paused, collecting his thoughts. "My dad, who moved to New York from Puerto Rico when he was a teen, died when I was a toddler. An aneurysm just suddenly took him out. I don't remember him at all. But I know his culture was a big part of who he was and that he would have passed it along to me if he was around. But he wasn't. And I feel a bit guilty that I lost that part of me. Hell, my Spanish doesn't go much further than telling someone where the library is. So I try to hold onto my name as firmly as I can, out of respect for my dad. I know it's a feeble gesture, but—"

"No, I get it," Sam said. "That makes complete sense to me." She extended her bottle toward Miguel. "To your dad."

"To Dad." He clinked his bottle against Sam's with a small grin.

"And anyway," Sam said. "Dónde está la biblioteca?" Miguel blinked and looked around with a confused frown.

"I actually don't know!" he admitted with a laugh and a shrug. "No sé."

Sam found herself loosening up around Miguel. After Jeremy's horrendous first impression, she felt mildly better about the family that was absorbing Harold.

"I'm sorry about before, too," Sam said, but Miguel quickly waved away her apology.

"No, no. You were fine. Jeremy can be a bit . . ." Miguel paused, looking for the right word. "Much. He can be a bit much."

"I'm pretty sure he stalked me from work this week," Sam noted, prompting Miguel to sigh.

"Yeah, it's possible," he said, sounding resigned. "But he's harmless, I promise you."

"Harmless? It's pretty scary knowing a stranger was following me around on the streets of lower Manhattan!"

"Yes, yes! Of course!" Miguel shuffled and looked around to make sure no one was listening to them. "I just meant . . . he's my brother. I can't always defend what he does, but he's my brother. If that makes sense." Miguel was suddenly distracted by something over Sam's shoulder. "It appears I am being summoned," he said with a deep exhale. "Anyway, it was really nice to meet you. And for what it's worth, my family isn't that bad, even if first impressions aren't always our strong suit."

Sam watched Miguel walk away toward his three half-siblings, huddled together. The woman—Sadie—seemed to sense Sam's look and took a moment to stare back at her, impassive and calculating, before turning back to talk with her brothers.

"Nice to see you still have some life in you!" Harold had once again managed to sneak up on her, causing Sam to jump.

"What?" Sam asked, disoriented.

"I saw you go at Jeremy before. Really put him in his place. It was sweet to watch, actually. Brothers and sisters tend to fight, and pretty soon, they will practically be your stepsiblings."

"No!" Sam said. She looked back at the four half-siblings, who were still gathered together. It looked to Sam like three of them were trying to convince Miguel of something. "That's not—" She took a deep breath. She did not want to go into this again. "Where is your fiancée, anyway? I haven't seen her."

"Shhhhh!" Harold looked around to see if anyone was listening. "Most people here don't know about the wedding yet. We're going to surprise them in a bit. Anyway, Marcie is—"

Out of nowhere, Sam was knocked to the side by a small force of nature flying into her. Before she could turn to see what had hit her, Sam felt her arms pinned to her sides, nearly causing her to drop her beer. From her trapped position, Sam managed to turn her head just enough to realize that she was being held by the wiry arms of a small woman.

"I'm sorry!" the woman said into the side of Sam's head, not loosening the bearhug at all. "I just came out here and saw you talking to Harold, and after hearing so much about you, I could not help but introduce myself with a big hug. I am Marcie. And you must be Sam!"

Marcie finally relinquished the embrace but continued to grip Sam's arms with surprisingly strong hands. As Marcie pulled away, Sam could finally see her: a slender woman with long gray hair in her late sixties, standing a few inches taller than Sam, wearing a smile that radiated joy.

"Yes, I'm—" Sam started, but she was soon interrupted by another crushing hug.

"I'm sorry!" Marcie said in a cooing tone, speaking to the back of Sam's head. "But I just couldn't help myself to another hug! I hope you don't mind."

Even if Sam minded, there was nothing she could do to stop it. The embrace drove all of the air out of her lungs, depriving her of any opportunity to object. Her arms were once again pinned to her sides, so all Sam could do was helplessly wait for the second hug to end. After some time, Sam managed to slightly redirect her head to make eye contact with Harold, who was holding in a laugh at her expense. Eventually, the second hug ceased, and Sam regained control of her body.

"I am so sorry I am late," Marcie said, her brown eyes wide.

"Yeah, what were you doing in there?" Harold asked, sounding a bit grumpy.

"You will not believe it!" Marcie's eyes darted between Sam and Harold, making sure they were both paying attention. "I was doing some laundry downstairs before the party started, and I came across this little hopping bug. Like a grasshopper, but darker in color. It was just jumping happily around the basement. So, I found a plastic container and a piece of paper and caught the little fellow to let him out a window on the side of the house. And then I went back to the laundry, and wouldn't you know it? There was another one jumping around by the washing machine! So, long story short, I spent the last two hours or so catching all of those bugs in the basement and letting them out the window. I think I finally managed to free them all!"

"Jesus, Marcie, *that's* what you've been doing? We've had all these guests waiting out here for you." Marcie didn't look remotely perturbed by Harold's grouchiness. Instead, she patted him fondly on the cheek.

"Oh Harold," she said. "I'm sure you did a wonderful job entertaining our guests without me." Harold grunted, but he didn't press the issue.

"And so, Sam," Marcie said, turning back to her. "I have heard so much about you, I feel like I already know you! I wish we could just spend some time here getting to know each other—really know each other—but this isn't the ideal place for that sort of thing." Marcie gestured around the yard at the other guests to emphasize her point before adding, "Tell me, are you free next weekend?"

Sam didn't have to check her calendar to know that she was. She was tempted, out of habit, to make up an excuse—a simple lie about a prior engagement—but she reminded herself that her whole purpose in coming to the party in the first place was to figure out the weirdness behind Harold's engagement. Marcie was nothing like she had anticipated, although Marcie's demeanor only raised additional questions in Sam's mind. Since she had resolved to investigate this strange family on Harold's behalf, it only made sense to get to know Marcie better. *May as well go all in*, she thought.

"Yes," Sam said. "I believe I'm generally free next weekend." Marcie, delighted, clasped her hands together.

"Oh, how lovely!" she exclaimed. "On Saturday, Harold and I are attending a fire ceremony not too far from here. We would love for you to go with us!"

"Wait," Sam said. "A fire ceremony? Does that involve walking . . . on fire?" But Marcie laughed at Sam's apprehension.

"Of course not! It will be wonderful! Don't worry about anything—all you have to do is show up. Come here next Saturday around six o'clock, and we can all drive over together. It's a shame—I also invited Sadie, but she has plans that night and can't make it."

Sam looked around and noticed that Sadie had again positioned herself within earshot of the conversation, about ten feet away. She gave the appearance of being engaged in conversation with a man who looked like one of Harold's friends from work, but it was plain to Sam that her attention was focused on her conversation with Marcie.

"That is a shame," Sam said, without conviction. Marcie started to reply when Harold took her gently by the arm.

"It's time, Marcie," he said, pointing at his watch. Marcie glanced at the time before nodding.

"I am looking forward to next week, Sam," Marcie said as she was led away by Harold. "I think it will be an amazing experience for us both." Harold steered her to the back patio before Sam could respond.

Once Harold and Marcie were positioned by the back door, slightly elevated above everyone else, Harold called out for quiet.

"Excuse me! Excuse me!" He waited impatiently for the din to die down. "Thank you all for coming today. Marcie and I are so happy to be here on this beautiful afternoon with our friends and family, and we are so glad you all could make it." Harold looked fondly at Marcie and placed an arm around her shoulders. Marcie responded by beaming and leaning into him affectionately, accepting the hug with enthusiasm. "We did want to share a bit of positive news with you all, although I'm not sure how newsworthy it will be to a lot of you. I was never good at keeping a secret." The small crowd laughed politely, and Harold paused dramatically to soak it in before continuing. "But in any event, we wanted you all to know that in the very near future, Marcie and I will be getting married!"

It seemed to be a tighter secret than Harold thought because the crowd let out an audible gasp, followed by a loud cheer. Marcie lit up at the reaction. She looked over the crowd, waving now and then to a specific friend, and she even threw Sam an earnest thumbs up when they made eye contact.

As Marcie continued to survey the guests, Sam noticed her smile dissolve until her face was lined with concern and confusion. For the first time since Sam had met her, Marcie wasn't bouncing with positivity.

Sam followed Marcie's gaze. Standing on the side of the backyard against the fence stood her four children. Not one of them was clapping. In fact, they looked as if they had just received catastrophic news. Marcie looked down at them, puzzled by their non-reaction, and the three boys stared back at her. Disapproval was written all over Jeremy and Colin's faces as they wordlessly walked out of the backyard together. Miguel trailed them, and as he exited, he briefly looked at Sam. His face was unreadable.

From the patio, Marcie turned to Sadie, her eyes pleading for an explanation for her three sons' abrupt departure. But that silent question didn't reach Sadie, whose attention was centered elsewhere—specifically, a laser-focused look at Sam, who was uncomfortable under the sudden scrutiny. Sadie wore a hint of a smile that conveyed its own wordless message, which Sam found quite easy to decipher:

Your move.

CHAPTER FIVE

Tuesday, August 27, 2019

Miguel lounged on his couch reading an *Entertainment Weekly* while Kevin worked on dinner in the kitchen. A new meal—*tofu stir fry*, as Kevin described it—and Miguel could already register its intense smell. Not bad, per se. Just intense.

"Is there anything I can do to help?" Miguel called out from his prone position. He thought Kevin might appreciate the lip service.

"You can set the table," Kevin answered back, and Miguel sighed to himself. *He called my bluff*, Miguel thought. He stood, reluctantly.

"And I don't mean the coffee table," Kevin added. "We're not eating at the couch. You have a dining room table. I think it's about time you learned how to use it."

"Aren't *we* getting fancy?" Miguel muttered, shuffling to the circular glass table. It was covered with clutter—unread mail, some documents he brought home from work, and even some toiletries he had picked up at the store earlier in the week. Lacking the energy to sort it all out, he scooped the contents of the table into his arms and simply dumped it on the floor of his bedroom.

I can't remember the last time I ate at the table, Miguel thought. *I should probably give it a good wipe down.*

Miguel made his way into his tight galley kitchen where Kevin was busy chopping broccoli and snatched a roll of paper towels and a spray bottle of cleaner. As he maneuvered past Kevin back out of the kitchen, a loud buzzer sounded. Miguel and Kevin exchanged a confused look and waited. Moments later, the door buzzed again. Miguel made his way to the kitchen window where he had an unobstructed view of the entrance to his building. Jeremy was on the ground level, peering up at him.

"Open the door!" Jeremy called out. "What's the matter with you?"

Miguel froze. Kevin stared straight ahead—he didn't say anything, but waves of annoyance radiated from him. *Damn it Jeremy*, Miguel thought. Jeremy was largely raised on sitcoms from the 1990s and thought nothing of just popping in without any sort of warning.

"I didn't know he was coming over," Miguel mumbled as he exited the kitchen. He pressed a button next to the door and heard a door slam open two stories below them, followed by heavy footsteps stomping up the stairs.

"It's my brother," Miguel said. "Jeremy."

"Well, I assumed it wasn't the brother that's afraid to leave his house," Kevin replied.

"No, Colin's never been here. I'm not sure what Jeremy's up to. I'll just see what he wants and gently show him the door. What's the ETA on dinner?"

"Twenty-five minutes or so?"

"Got it. No problem."

The door flew open, and Jeremy strode into Miguel's apartment. Without any preamble, Jeremy lifted his nose into the air and sniffed.

"Smells good in here," he said. "What is that? Fish?"

"Uh, no," Miguel said. "I think it is sriracha."

"Oh, right," Jeremy said. *He's never heard of sriracha*, Miguel thought.

"It's great to see you, man," Miguel said. "But we're just about to eat dinner, so—"

"*We?*" Jeremy asked. He glanced in the kitchen and noticed Kevin standing at the counter. "Hey, didn't see you there." Jeremy extended a hand to Kevin, who awkwardly shook it with his left hand due to the oven mitt on his right. "Are you guys watching a ballgame or something? Seems like a pretty fancy meal for the Mets."

"No, we're just having dinner. This is Kevin. He's—" Miguel paused. Their relationship was in that awkward stage where it was not entirely clear if it was a relationship at all. But even Jeremy was able to pick up on the vibe.

"Oh. Oh! Gotcha." Jeremy winked at Miguel. "I just wanted to talk to you quick. About this past weekend, and that stuff with Mom."

Miguel didn't want to get into any of that in front of Kevin. He still felt dirty from his own role in ruining their mother's big announcement. The last thing he wanted was for Kevin to get wind of that story. Miguel took Jeremy by the elbow and gently guided him toward the door.

"Why don't we take a walk?" Miguel suggested. "Let Kevin finish dinner without us annoying him?" He glanced back at Kevin, who nodded gratefully. "I think I have twenty-five minutes or so before dinner is ready."

"Twenty-three minutes," Kevin corrected.

Miguel led Jeremy back down two flights of stairs and outside onto the streets of Bayside, a town on the periphery of Queens that managed to feel more suburban than a part of New York City. Miguel instinctively started walking toward Bell Boulevard—a commercial street in Bayside—and Jeremy fell in beside him.

"Sorry to interrupt your date," Jeremy said. Miguel thought he detected a sarcastic inflection on *date* but wrote it off to paranoia. "Are we walking anywhere in particular?"

"Let's go into town," Miguel said. "Pick up some dessert." Kevin would probably be less annoyed if he reaped some tangible benefit from the interruption. Jeremy grunted, noncommittal. They walked a bit in silence before Jeremy spoke.

"We didn't get a chance to talk after we left that party this weekend. What do you think?"

"What do I think?" Miguel said. "I feel pretty bad about it, to be honest with you. Mom called me afterward, wondering why we all stormed out like that. She didn't sound angry, just concerned about my well-being, which only made it worse."

"Yeah," Jeremy said. It wasn't clear whether he had registered anything that Miguel said. "I think Sadie may have screwed us with that move."

"What do you mean?"

"The three sons leave, looking unsupportive and awful. Sadie stays behind as the caring daughter. I believe she set us up."

"Oh, I don't think so. Sadie knew about the engagement beforehand. I mean, we all did, but Mom *knew* Sadie knew. It wouldn't have made sense for her to leave with us."

"Yeah, maybe. But still. I just don't see the point of us doing that. The wedding is still on, as far as I know."

"Sadie said it was important to plant seeds in Mom's head. Give her a reason to question whether we are all on board with this new marriage. I don't think it was meant to accomplish much more than that."

"I think it accomplished plenty for Sadie," Jeremy said. "But I don't think you or I have anything to show for it."

They reached Northern Boulevard and waited for the light to change. Jeremy looked around and spotted a CVS on the corner.

"Look, why don't we just go in there and get some cookies, if you need dessert?"

"I'm not bringing back a box of Entenmann's, Jeremy," Miguel said. Jeremy snorted.

"Well, excuse me, Prince Miguel!"

The light changed and they crossed the street. The northern side of the boulevard, where the heart of Bayside was situated, was more populated than the area around Miguel's apartment, and Jeremy had to walk close to Miguel to accommodate the pedestrian traffic.

"I'm just saying that maybe we shouldn't blindly go along with what Sadie says," Jeremy continued. "What was that business about her taking steps of her own, without telling us what that's about? That made no sense, right?"

Miguel shrugged, although he knew why Sadie would hold her cards close to the chest on that one. *She doesn't trust us.* It was hard to argue against the point, given that Jeremy's blunder had already resulted in Harold's daughter-in-law entering the fray, even though she seemed predisposed to stay out of it altogether. But, of course, that wasn't something Miguel could point out to Jeremy.

"I don't know," Miguel finally said. "It's hard for me to get too invested in this whole thing. I want to help you guys out if I can, but I'm starting to feel guilty about what we're doing to Mom. And Harold, who seems like a pretty good guy himself."

"You want to help us out," Jeremy said in a mocking tone. "Some help you are. I saw you all buddy-buddy with that Sam. Cavorting with the enemy."

"She's not the enemy," Miguel said, rolling his eyes. "She seems perfectly nice."

"I thought so, too," Jeremy said, "but she's an established liar. Told me she wasn't coming, and then she just shows up. Nearly made me look like a fool."

"Yes," Miguel said. "Nearly." Jeremy's head jerked, and he looked hard at Miguel to see if he was being mocked. Miguel felt a touch of shame. *Jeremy has it rough*, he thought. *I shouldn't pile on.* Granted, most who met Jeremy found him to be unworthy of sympathy, but that only made it easier for Miguel to summon pity for him. Although Miguel was a bit grumpy over Jeremy intruding upon his evening, he didn't intend to antagonize him over it.

"We're here!" Miguel announced as they approached the bakery, happy to change the subject. Inside, the establishment was packed. Fortunately, the business was adequately staffed to handle that volume, and the line moved quickly.

"I'm going to get a cherry pie," Miguel told Jeremy as they waited. "Do you want anything? My treat." Jeremy waved him off.

"No, it's fine. I'll just try some of that pie later."

"Later?" Miguel blinked. "Do you . . . Do you plan on staying for dinner?" Jeremy frowned, then forced a laugh.

"No, no, of course not. I'd hate to interrupt your *date*." This time the emphasis on *date* was unmistakable. "I'll just take a chocolate chip cookie for the drive home."

As it turned out, Jeremy couldn't wait for the ride home to dive into his cookie, which he devoured on the walk back to Miguel's apartment. Jeremy had neglected to take a napkin, and his hands were covered in chocolate by the time he finished. It looked at one point like Jeremy would wipe his hands clean on his jeans, but he seemed to decide it would be more dignified to systematically lick the chocolate off his fingers instead.

"You know, you won't have to worry about this stuff with Mom much longer," Jeremy said after polishing off a ring finger with his lips. "This will all be wrapped up soon."

"Yeah?" Miguel asked. "How do you figure?"

"Colin told me earlier today that he's going to blow up the whole engagement this weekend. Little bastard was quite confident about it. But I have to admit that I've never seen Mom deny Colin anything, so he may be right."

"Hmmmm." *Jeremy may have a point*, Miguel thought. Although their mother doted on each of them, she always went above and beyond when it came to Colin. It probably came down to Colin being the most shameless about exploiting their mother's generosity. Miguel recalled the various meals their mother had prepared for them in their youth that didn't meet Colin's approval. Colin was never shy about voicing his objections, and their mother, in turn, never hesitated to prepare a new dinner from scratch that was more to Colin's liking. Jeremy, and even Sadie on occasion, would tease Colin about his childish antics, but Colin never showed even a hint of embarrassment, so long as he ultimately got what he wanted.

Does that extend to Colin wanting Mom to put an end to her engagement? He couldn't remember Colin ever making such a significant ask of their mother, but it was likewise impossible for Miguel to imagine their mother denying Colin *anything*.

They arrived back at Miguel's apartment building. Looking up two floors, Miguel could make out Kevin in the brightly lit kitchen, staring down at them from the window.

"Well, thanks for coming out. I'm sorry we didn't have more time to talk," Miguel said to Jeremy, hoping he would take the hint.

"Yeah, no problem. Shame you had to give me the bum's rush." Miguel started to protest, but Jeremy waved him off. "Anyway," Jeremy said, "thanks for the cookie. Have fun tonight." Jeremy's wink was too salacious for Miguel's liking, but Miguel didn't think it was worth acknowledging.

"Oh," Jeremy added. Miguel glanced back up at the window where Kevin was still looking down at them. "Assuming Colin accomplishes what he says he's going to accomplish, we should start thinking of how to best position ourselves. Like I said, I trust Sadie about as far as I can throw her. I have no doubt she's already scheming against us, so we need to get on the offensive. We can talk later about it."

Miguel wanted to argue, but that would only further prolong the conversation, and he could feel the weight of Kevin's eyes looking down at him from above, so Miguel offered what he considered to be a noncommittal nod, and Jeremy, satisfied, strode to his car.

Miguel waited to watch Jeremy drive off as he tried to quell the sick feeling in his gut. It was bad enough being caught in the conflict between his mother and his siblings, but Miguel was disheartened at the realization that whatever alliance existed amongst his siblings was, in all likelihood, temporary in nature. It wasn't hard to imagine a scenario in the future where each member of his family tried to pull Miguel to their side to the disadvantage of the others. Miguel didn't know how much longer he would have the luxury of sitting on the fence, but he knew deep down that he'd be forced to stake out a position at some point.

One way or another.

• • • • •

Sadie pulled into the nearly empty lot of the office park. Even the handful of cars in the vicinity seemed on the verge of departing, as evidenced by the clusters of office workers walking at varying speeds away from the buildings. Sadie was surprised by the complex, which was nicer than she had envisioned. *What was I imagining a private investigator's office to look like?* Sadie thought. She had been preparing herself to face a hard-drinking, chain-smoking, bitter ex-policeman, lounging about in a filthy office littered with cartons of half-eaten Chinese food. She allowed herself a brief moment of irritation at being caught off guard due to her buying into tired tropes, but she did not permit that internal scolding to linger.

There was nothing to be gained by that.

She was a few minutes early for her six o'clock appointment, so Sadie took some time to collect her thoughts before entering. She did not know much about the investigator she was meeting, other than his name—Raymond Lawrence—and his stellar reputation. And that he was retired police—that cliché was true in this case, at least. He had no social media presence, which Sadie thought was a plus in his favor. Sadie was largely dealing with a blank slate, but she was not put off by her ignorance. In fact, she felt somewhat invigorated.

As much as Sadie tried to avoid entering any transaction with less than complete information at hand, she enjoyed the sport of improvisation—assessing the landscape and the parties involved, then reacting on the fly. Granted, some degree of improv was required in any situation, but Sadie had prepared for this meeting by leaving herself as flexible as possible.

She wore a dark gray, one-shouldered sheath dress that was revealing enough to draw Raymond's interest, if needed, but still allowed her to maintain an air of professionalism that would ensure she was taken seriously. Her black, open-toed heels brought her height to six feet even, which she hoped would be roughly eye level with the investigator when they were both standing. Not wanting to be encumbered by a bulky bag, Sadie opted instead for a small leather clutch.

Dressing herself was the easy part. Deciding what intangible items to bring was more difficult. *Does the truth stay in the car?* Sadie wondered. She was an adept liar when the situation warranted, but if this investigator was as good as his reviews suggested, any deviations from provable facts may present an unnecessary risk. *I should not need to embellish at all for this meeting*, Sadie decided.

And if that changed—well, she could always improvise.

At 5:57, Sadie exited her car and walked toward the building. She knew the office was on the first floor, so she would not have to account for any elevator-related delays. Indeed, it did not take her long at all to locate the door to his suite, which was adorned with a simple sign: Lawrence Investigations. After checking her phone for the time—5:59—Sadie relaxed the muscles in her face to hint at a pleasant smile and entered.

It was a small office, with a vacant receptionist's desk up front. From her vantage point near the door, Sadie could make out a man, perhaps ten years older than her, typing away at a computer at the desk toward the back of the room. His dirty blonde hair was beginning a transition to gray, and Sadie thought she could make out something of a bald spot, although it was largely hidden by his short military-esque haircut. The man glanced up at Sadie's arrival before resuming his work on the computer.

"You must be Sadie," he called out. "I'll be right with you."

Sadie glanced at a chair by the door and noted a stain in the fabric, so she decided to remain standing. She did not have to wait long before the man stopped typing and bounded over to her, hand extended.

"Nice to meet you," he said as he shook her hand. "I'm Raymond Lawrence. Feel free to call me Ray." *Nothing inappropriate about that handshake*, Sadie thought. *Appropriate duration without lingering.* If Ray found her attractive, he was not showing it.

"Nice to meet you as well," Sadie said. "And yes—I'm Sadie. Thank you for seeing me on such short notice." Her smile was polite and purposely short of suggestive. Ray gestured to the back of the office.

"Please, come on in. Let's talk—see if I can help you out."

He extended an arm, and Sadie walked ahead of him, taking note of his wedding ring. She found a chair at the far side of the room, which was thankfully cleaner than the one up front, and sat. Ray maneuvered to a seat on the other side of his desk. A collection of photographs was displayed on the wall behind him. The pictures were mostly nature shots that Sadie assumed Ray took himself; there was nothing particularly professional about them. There were no pictures of Ray's wife or children, if he had any. Sadie wrote that off to caution on Ray's part about putting too much of himself out there for his clients to see.

Sadie noticed one picture of Ray, looking thirty or so years younger, wearing football gear, sans helmet, as he posed holding a football up as if he was about to pass it. His blond hair, longer in the photo, was strewn across his forehead. Sadie could not see the name of the school on the blue and gold uniform—all she could make out was a giant 4 on the jersey. Glancing around the office, she noticed that the number four was a common theme in the decor. A wall clock shaped like a four. A desk lamp also in the shape of that particular digit. *There's a vanity there*, Sadie thought.

I can use that.

As Sadie crossed her legs, she noticed Ray's eyes flicker toward the movement and then snap back to meet her eyes. It was an involuntary reflex. *He wants to look at me, but he's resisting the urge*, Sadie thought. Open flirtation would not get her far—that would only cause him to get defensive. But a pretty young woman in need of assistance? That would appeal to him, while allowing him to maintain his honor.

And Sadie knew what role she would have to play.

"We spoke briefly on the phone," Ray said, grabbing a pen and a fresh legal pad out of his desk drawer. "But why don't you walk me through what your issue is, from the beginning?"

Sadie pursed her lips, creating the appearance of being deep in thought. A few quick blinks seasoned the look with a hint of nervousness. A deep breath to calm herself, and then she began.

"Well, I had mentioned to you that my mother, Marcie Porter—and that is not her maiden name, by the way—recently met a man named Harold Lindgren. You see, my mother has gotten married four times in the past, but those husbands each died a few years into the marriage." On Ray's look, Sadie added, "Nothing nefarious, I assure you! Two heart attacks, one stroke. My own father died of cancer almost two years after he married my mother. I should also mention that she is not my biological mother—she died during childbirth—but I was adopted by Marcie right around the time she married my father." Sadie decided a small laugh would be appropriate and let one out. "She said that she had no idea how to be a stepmother, but since she knew how to be a mother, that was what she would be for me. Are you following?"

Ray, who had been taking notes, nodded and gestured for Sadie to continue.

"I have three brothers, or half-brothers I suppose. There was a fair amount of change for my brothers growing up, with our mother constantly remarrying, but I came in toward the end, so I had a mostly stable upbringing after my father passed. But my brothers all turned out ok, even though they were brought up in a home that was constantly changing." Sadie had no qualms about that white lie. It was, after all, a matter of opinion—no one would be able to call her out for it. "Mother did the best she could. Actually, that's not fair. She did amazing. Her 'best' was amazing. She is an unbelievably kind woman. It is her greatest strength. But it can also be her greatest weakness, at times." Sadie looked up and took a long inhale. She eyed a box of tissues on the desk to suggest that tears *may* be in the forecast, but she thought it was still too early to go there.

"Like I said, my brothers and I are all adults now, and our mother seemed to have retired from the dating life after my father, Victor, passed away nearly twenty-five years ago. But recently, out of nowhere, this new man—Harold—is in her life. They dated for a few months, and he seemed nice enough. If he made my mother happy, that was good enough for me." Possibly another white lie, but again, Sadie was not concerned—the statement was impossible to disprove.

"But I've just learned that Harold and my mother are planning on getting married, even though they only met about five months ago. They haven't announced a date yet, other than telling us all that the wedding will be very soon. And frankly, this started to ring some alarm bells."

"How so?" Ray asked, leaning back in his chair. He had stopped taking notes once Sadie's account of the background facts had ended.

"We don't know much about this guy," Sadie said. "I'd like to think that he has our mother's best interests at heart, but . . ." She trailed off. *Better to let him finish the thought himself.*

"Are there financial considerations?" Ray prompted, and Sadie nodded.

"Yes, that is certainly part of it. My mother became quite wealthy after her various husbands passed, for a variety of reasons, even though she is not a financially minded person herself. And maybe I am just being paranoid and overly concerned about my mother. But with this engagement coming out of nowhere, and this rush to get married—well, something just didn't smell right to me, if you know what I mean?"

"Alright, fair enough," Ray said. "I think I can help you out." Sadie let out a relieved breath.

"Oh, thank goodness."

"I can take a look at this guy, and check out whether anything in his history suggests any sort of ill intent. I mean, I'm not a mind reader, but I can certainly conduct a background check, see if it turns up any red flags that give you concern. Just how in depth of a vetting process are you looking for?"

"Please, be as thorough as you need to be. I don't care about how much it costs, if it can give me some peace of mind with regard to my mother's well-being in retirement." Sadie paused, feigning indecision, before reaching into her bag to pull out a folded-up piece of paper. "I wrote down all of the information I have regarding Harold, and my mother, if that's of any help to you." Ray took the paper and unfolded it before looking it over.

"Yes, this is a good place to start. Alright, I'll put together an estimate and email it to you later tonight. If that works for you, I'll get started on this tomorrow."

"I'm sure the estimate will be fine, but thank you." Sadie stood up. Ray joined her and extended a hand, which she took. She held onto the hand as she added, "And seriously: thank you so much. I feel bad, in a way, like I'm spying on my mother, but—"

"You're just doing your due diligence. You're a good daughter." Ray didn't try to shake off her hand. Sadie molded her face to convey a smile in relief before releasing her grip.

"Thank you. That is very reassuring to hear." Sadie turned to leave and paused, as if she had just remembered something. When she turned back, Ray cocked his head in an inquisitive look.

"There is something I forgot to mention," Sadie said. "Harold has a daughter-in-law. Sam Daly. I guess she chose to keep her own last name when she married? Anyway, her husband, who was Harold's son, died in the same car crash that killed Harold's wife a few years ago. As I understand it, this daughter-in-law has been out of the picture since then. She apparently wanted nothing to do with Harold. But as soon as Harold and my mother announced their engagement, she popped back into his life. And, it seems, my family's life. It just struck me as a bit—"

"Odd?" Ray finished for her. Sadie nodded, appreciative.

"Yes! Odd! That is the exact word I was looking for."

"So do you want me to take a look into her as well?" Ray asked. "It will obviously cost more, but—"

"Yes, please. Like you said earlier, I want to make sure I conduct this due diligence on my mother's behalf properly. She can be overly trusting, you see." Sadie made a point of keeping the concern in her voice. Ray nodded.

"I understand. If you email me whatever you have on the daughter-in-law, I'll see if there's anything going on with her as well."

"Yes, I will do that." Sadie actually had another sheet of paper with everything she knew about Sam in her bag, but the way the conversation had played out, it did not make sense to hand it over now. "And I really can't thank you enough."

"My pleasure," Ray said as he walked her to the door.

Sadie allowed herself to feel good as she strolled back to her car. She had accomplished what she had set out to do, and her brothers—particularly Jeremy—were not even positioned to screw it up. There was still work to be done, of course, but it was a solid first step. *And I didn't even have to lie that much to get the ball rolling*, Sadie thought. *I managed to keep my risks at a minimum while completing my objective.* To be sure, the next steps would be more difficult, but Sadie found herself looking forward to the challenge.

She could not remember the last time she felt so exhilarated.

CHAPTER SIX

Saturday, August 31, 2019

Sam spent the week questioning the various actions she had taken that threatened the walls of the cocoon she had built around herself over the past two years. Whether it was the initial decision to get involved in Harold's engagement or her making an apparent enemy out of Jeremy (and possibly even some of those other siblings), she found her own behavior at odds with the *modus operandi* she'd established since Mike's death. And her willingness to accept Marcie's invite to a fire ceremony, whatever that was, was out of character. Whether that was a positive or negative development for Sam remained to be seen.

Sam's trepidations about the fire ceremony extended beyond stepping out of her comfort zone. She had briefly tried to research the ritual online, but the descriptions she found were so vague and abstract they were essentially useless. In the end, she decided to just go in blind and trust Marcie when she said that all Sam had to do was show up. The ceremony itself would probably be a few hours of weirdness, but it was a chance to dig deeper into Marcie and her family to try to get a better read on the situation. Even though Sam had to concede from her brief meeting with Marcie that it was possible she *was*, in fact, the nicest person in the world, as Harold had described, she wanted to investigate further.

Sam was also honest enough to admit that it was nice to have weekend plans for a change, even if they were only with her father-in-law's odd fiancée.

What was clear to Sam was that her work was not finished. Confiding in Harold had gotten her nowhere: He thought it was funny that Jeremy had stalked her at work. "See, you still got it!" he told her with a laugh. Sam realized she would have to come up with something rock solid to knock the rose-tinted glasses off of Harold's face, which of course meant a lot more sleuthing.

Fortunately, free time was something she had in spades.

When the following Saturday rolled around, Sam departed in the late afternoon for Marcie's house on Long Island. Although she left herself plenty of time to get there, traffic on and around the Throgs Neck Bridge made it so that she only arrived at Marcie's house shortly after 6:00. *She said to come* around *6:00*, Sam told herself. *I should be fine.*

At the front door, Sam could make out the muffled sounds of a television inside, operating at high volume. She raised a hand to press the bell but stopped once she realized it was broken, dangling helplessly from the side of the door. Sam shrugged and proceeded to pound the door with a closed fist three times in tight succession: *boom, boom, boom.* Seconds later, Marcie appeared at the door in a long blue dress, looking thrilled to see Sam.

"You came!" Marcie said as she opened the door. When Sam entered, she found herself ensnared once again in a fierce embrace. "Oh, don't think you can sneak by me without a hug, Sam!" Marcie said in a slightly chiding tone.

"Sorry," Sam muttered, her face pressed into Marcie's shoulder. Once she was released, Sam took a few steps further into the house, where the television was blaring a Yankees game. Sam peered through a doorway and found Harold sprawled out on a couch, watching the action.

"Hi Sam!" he yelled, raising a hand in greeting without getting up or lowering the volume. Marcie laughed and waved him off.

"Don't mind him," she said to Sam. "Come, let's talk in here while he's finishing his game." Marcie gestured to a small sitting room on the opposite side of the house.

"Oh," Sam said, glancing back at the front door. "Aren't we going to that fire ceremony thing?"

"We are!" Marcie answered. "But that doesn't start until eight, and it's only about a half hour away, so we will have plenty of time to get to know each other beforehand. Can I get you some tea?"

"Ummmm, sure. Thank you." Marcie darted into the kitchen, and Sam dutifully took a seat in the sitting area. On the far side of the house, Sam could hear Harold cursing loudly at something that transpired in the ballgame. Sam felt a bit discombobulated—she had been mentally preparing for the fire ceremony but was coming to the realization that it would be a later night than she envisioned. Still, having more time to figure out what was going on with Marcie and her children wasn't necessarily a terrible thing in Sam's mind.

Marcie entered the room carrying two small mismatched plates, each holding a steaming cup of tea. She placed one on a small table at Sam's side before situating herself into an adjacent chair.

"Thank you," Sam said. Marcie merely smiled in response, not breaking eye contact for an uncomfortably long time. Desperate to puncture that awkward moment, Sam picked up her cup and took a sip, only to instantly gag. Marcie's eyes went wide with concern.

"Is something wrong? Perhaps I used too much garlic? Or maybe I went heavy on the ginger—I can never quite remember how much to use. But it's supposed to be very healthy."

"No, nothing's wrong. I was just expecting something more like Earl Gray." Sam placed the strange tea back at her side. "It tastes . . . well, it certainly tasted very healthy."

Marcie smiled in relief and took a sip of her own drink before also choking.

"Oh my!" Marcie exclaimed once she stopped coughing. "I definitely have to use less turmeric next time! I think that's where I went wrong. But yes, it does taste *healthy*." Marcie laughed. "Thank you for being so polite."

Marcie's mouth moved silently as she tried to work the foul taste out of it. All the while, her eyes danced about as she giggled internally at her own antics.

"So, Sam," Marcie finally said. "Tell me about yourself."

"Me?" Sam asked lamely. "What do you want to know?"

"Oh, anything. Everything!" Marcie laughed. "How about your name: Sam. Is that short for Samantha?"

"No, it's just Sam." Marcie continued to smile at her, and Sam felt obligated to continue. "My dad's favorite show when I was born was Cheers, so he wanted to name me after his favorite character. At least, I always assumed it was his favorite character. Maybe he just didn't like the names Diane or Carla." Marcie didn't respond, and Sam felt compelled to add more. "Or Rebecca. Or Lilith. Although I think those characters showed up later in the show's run."

Is she just going to smile at me until I name every character on Cheers?

Sam stopped speaking and braced herself for more awkward silence. She hoped Marcie would accept her explanation—she didn't know how much more she could expound on the origin of her name.

"My goodness," Marcie said once it was clear that Sam had nothing further to add. "And how wonderful that your father wanted to associate you with his favorite show. That really demonstrates tremendous love, don't you think?"

"Yeah, I guess."

"Tell me: where is your father now?"

"He died when I was in college. He had been sick for a while, so it wasn't all that unexpected when it finally happened." Sam said it all quite matter-of-factly. Marcie gasped.

"I am so sorry. And your mother?"

"She died some time ago as well." Sam shrugged, trying to convey that it was not something she wanted to delve into.

"Do you have any brothers or sisters?" Marcie asked, sounding legitimately concerned.

"No, I was an only child. Honestly, though, it never bothered me." Sam noticed that Marcie looked dubious.

"And then you lost your husband a few years ago. You're all alone." Marcie's eyes looked as if they were on the verge of shedding tears.

"No, it's—I'm doing ok, really."

Marcie frowned, deep in thought. But then, out of nowhere, her face resumed its default smile, brighter than ever.

"Well, how wonderful that the universe has arranged things so that you are now positioned to join our family!"

"Ummm, yeah." Sam, uncomfortable, forced herself to take another sip of the awful tea. On the other side of the house, Harold was cheering alone to something happening in the baseball game.

"He's a wonderful person, you know," said Marcie, apparently in response to Harold's exuberance.

"Sure," Sam said. "He's a good guy." *I don't know if I'd go with "wonderful" myself,* Sam thought, *but to each their own.* Her lack of conviction must have come through because Marcie pressed the point.

"He is! He's kind, generous, and very funny. And he thinks the world of you. He always sounds so proud whenever he talks about you," Marcie said. Sam put her tea back on the table and leaned in toward her.

"See," Sam said, "that doesn't make a whole lot of sense to me. Why would he feel pride about me? I'm not his daughter. Aside from visiting him a few times a year with Mike after we got married, I didn't have all that much to do with him. I don't see why he would feel *proud* about me in any way." Sam leaned back in her seat as Marcie thought that over.

"I think," Marcie said, speaking slowly, "that he holds you in high regard. He always tells me that he respects your strength and toughness. If I had to guess, his pride stems from his raising a son who was worthy of your love."

Sam stared and felt a familiar tightness in her throat. *Oh shit, I cannot start crying.* Memories of Mike threatened to rise, but with a few deep breaths to calm herself, she managed to stuff them back down into the recesses of her memory. If Marcie picked up on the fact that Sam was on the brink of tears, she gave no sign. She merely sipped at her tea and giggled at its putrid taste.

"He told me about the incident with your underwear, by the way," Marcie said, and Sam felt her cheeks blush. "I don't know that I necessarily need new undergarments myself, but it's sweet that he was thinking of me."

"Yeah, that was a weird way for him to reenter my life."

"He's certainly not perfect. None of us are." Marcie paused, as if reflecting on her own faults. "But if the worst thing you can say about a person is they don't always appreciate or respect certain boundaries, I don't view that as a dealbreaker. In fact, I've come to appreciate Harold's lack of filter. I know that the worst he has to offer is coming out of that mouth of his, so I don't have to wonder about any darkness hiding away in there. It's strangely comforting. And, to be honest, a lot of the unfiltered stuff he says just cracks me up!"

She means it, Sam realized. Any theories she had about Marcie marrying Harold for some malevolent purpose were evaporating. *This is a woman in love.* That was becoming clear to Sam, even if the pairing itself remained a bit of a mystery.

"He means well," Sam said. It was the most she could offer just then. *How well do I even know Harold now? Until a few weeks ago, I hadn't seen him in years.*

"You probably know this," Sam added, "but after Mike and his mother died in that accident, Harold and I didn't have a lot of contact with each other. We had the two funerals to get through together, and from there, we just kind of went our separate ways. I probably—" Sam cut herself off, not wanting to say too much. Marcie leaned forward in her chair and reached to pat Sam on her knee in consoling fashion.

"I probably should have been a better daughter-in-law to him," Sam said. "He lost his son and his wife in the same night. He needed someone, but I couldn't do it. I hoped, now and then, that he had someone there for him. But I—" Marcie leapt out of her chair and wrapped her arms around Sam's head, making shushing sounds.

"You stop right there," said Marcie. "You were grieving. You had to take care of yourself. You were in no position to take care of others. Don't you blame yourself for any of that. I can tell you, Harold certainly doesn't. He is just happy to have you here with us now. As am I."

Marcie didn't end the hug. After an unbearably long time, Sam awkwardly reached up to tap Marcie on the shoulder—an unspoken request to be released. Marcie understood and sat back in her seat.

"Right around the time Harold and I met, he told me what happened to Carol and Mike on that Mother's Day," Marcie said. "He still struggles with it, but he was really in a dark place when I first started seeing him. I'm sure he's told you, but I've had my own similar losses."

"You had four prior marriages, right?" Sam asked. Marcie nodded—her smile was tinged with sadness.

"Yes. Four wonderful men, all taken too early. I thought I was equipped to help Harold process his loss, and I suppose I succeeded to some degree, as he is in a much healthier space now. And, in full candor, part of the reason I was so eager to meet you was that I was a few years younger than you are now when my first husband—Barry—passed away. Our time together was cut way too short. Jeremy wasn't even two years old at the time. I know the struggle and pain you must have gone through with your own loss. Continue to go through. I wanted to help you if I could in any way."

Sam looked away. *What a crappy detective I am. I'm trying to figure out this woman and her family, and this entire conversation has been about me.*

"Thank you. I appreciate that." Sam tried to smile, but she wasn't quite sure it got there. "I'm doing ok. At least, I'm getting by. It's not easy, of course. I just—" Sam paused. "Look, as much as I appreciate your concern, it's just not something I'm particularly comfortable getting into."

"Of course," Marcie said, nodding. "I don't mean to pry. Just know that I am here if you ever need a set of ears."

Before Sam could reply, Harold wandered into the room, looking expectant. Sam noticed that the television had been turned off at some point without her realizing it.

"Yankees won," Harold announced. Marcie's face lit up as she clapped her hands, but Sam could tell she wasn't particularly invested in the outcome of the game. "Are you all ready to go?"

That question triggered a small degree of chaos, with Marcie explaining that she needed a few minutes to get ready herself, and that it was too early to leave in any event. Harold seemed impatient and announced that he'd be waiting in the car for everyone. As he walked out of the house and Marcie darted upstairs to get ready, Sam was left to wonder what she should be doing herself. Feeling uncomfortable on the main level of the house alone, she wandered outside and took a seat in the back of Harold's SUV.

"You guys have a good talk?" Harold asked, looking at Sam in the rearview mirror.

"Yes, actually. She seems like a very nice person."

"Yeah, I told you—she's great. Not sure what she's doing with me."

"I was wondering that myself," Sam said drily, and Harold laughed.

"If I had one complaint about her," he said, "it would be that it takes her a half hour to get ready, no matter what we are doing. But she never realizes it. If we have to be out the door at 7:00, start getting ready at 6:30, you know? The math isn't hard."

"I'm sure she'll be ready soon," Sam said, arching her head to look at the upstairs windows of the house. All of the lights were on—Marcie's preparations seemed to be ongoing.

Forty minutes later Marcie emerged, looking much as she did when Sam had seen her earlier. It was not clear what Marcie had accomplished while Sam and Harold waited for her, and Harold grumbled about having to sit in the car for so long.

"No one told you that you had to wait in the car," Marcie gently reminded him. Harold grunted but couldn't argue the point.

It was getting dark by the time they finally got on the road. Marcie did her best to serve as Harold's navigator, but her instructions usually came about a split second before any given turn that should have been made. Harold's frustrated sighs grew louder and louder, but Marcie ignored them all. It occurred to Sam that she was witnessing the personification of impatience meeting a limitless well of tolerance. She found it interesting to watch.

Shortly before eight o'clock, they arrived at a small unremarkable cape house further out on Long Island. Only the collection of vehicles parked in front of and around the home distinguished it from the other homes on the street.

"We are here!" Marcie announced. She exited the vehicle and Sam did the same. It took her a beat to realize that Harold wasn't leaving the car.

"What about him?" Sam gestured toward Harold.

"Oh, he prefers to wait in the car. He will just listen to the radio, I imagine. Very nice of him to drive us, though."

Through the window, Sam could see Harold looking at her and chuckling to himself. *Is he laughing at me?* she wondered as Marcie led her toward the house.

They walked down a path adjacent to the sidewalk that took them through a gate and into a small backyard, which was immaculately landscaped with small trees and an artificial pond in the back corner. Sam took note of a fire pit in the center of the yard with a small pile of logs beside it, and she assumed that was where the fire ceremony would take place. But Marcie ignored the fire pit and instead led her to a basement door that she entered without knocking.

A dozen people milled about inside, making small talk with each other. The grouping consisted almost entirely of women, with the exception of a bearded man in his fifties and a young, intense-looking man hovering at his side.

"That is Arlo. He will be conducting the ceremony," Marcie whispered, gesturing subtly toward the bearded man. "He comes through about once a year. I think the man with him is his . . . apprentice? He was here last year and travels with Arlo as far as I understand. I'm not certain of the exact nature of the relationship between them."

Marcie took Sam around and introduced her to the various women, who were all roughly the same age as Marcie. As Sam was making small talk about the weather with one of them, Arlo cleared his throat. Everyone immediately quieted and sat on the floor in a circle, and Sam followed their lead. Marcie took a seat to her left and adopted a meditative pose. Sam was a few spots away from Arlo, which gave her some comfort that she'd be able to act as an observer before being asked to do anything herself.

"Good evening to you all," Arlo announced, smiling warmly around the circle. "It is wonderful to see so many familiar faces again. For anyone new, or anyone who needs a refresher, we are here together to partake in a fire ceremony. Or, as some may call it, a burning ritual. To me, the nomenclature largely depends on your intentions, because fire has the ability to create—and it has the power to destroy. The threshold question you should be asking yourself is whether your goal is to invoke—whether there are feelings and circumstances that you seek to welcome from the universe, or whether there is something internal that no longer serves you that you wish to discard. There are truly no wrong answers. The most important thing is that we are all grounded and focused before announcing our intentions. So let us start with a basic meditation."

With that, Arlo led the circle through breathing exercises. Sam sporadically stole a glance at Marcie, to her left, and copied her poses. *This isn't bad*, Sam thought. *I can handle this.* As the meditation continued, Sam even found herself relaxing to some degree.

Sam felt lighter when the meditation ended with a gentle instruction from Arlo for everyone to open their eyes. When she did, she noticed that a small piece of paper and a pencil had been placed in front of each person.

"Now," Arlo said, "we are going to go around the circle and have everyone state their intentions for the universe. Once you do, write it down, and hold onto that piece of paper. We will need that for the end of the ceremony. And remember: There are no wrong answers. Let's start here."

Arlo gestured to the intense man sitting at his left. The man stood up, and Arlo's slight disapproving frown suggested to Sam that this was an exercise where everyone was expected to remain seated.

"I long," the man intoned, before pausing dramatically. "I long to become more passionate . . . about my passions."

The man sat down, looking pleased with himself. Arlo chewed his lip.

"That was—well, I don't want to say 'wrong,' but . . ." Arlo thought it over. "Perhaps you can state a more direct intention for the universe?"

The man nodded and closed his eyes, deep in thought. He opened his eyes again and started to stand up but was stopped with a hand from Arlo.

"You can remain seated," Arlo said, not unkindly. The man bowed his head in acquiescence and gathered himself.

"I am a crystal," the man announced.

Everyone froze, waiting for more, but that was apparently the extent of the man's intention. He started to write it down, but Arlo stopped him once again.

"No, that's not—" Arlo looked frustrated. "You're just saying words, you're not—Why don't we come back to you."

The man clasped his hands together and bowed his head respectfully before resuming his meditative position.

"How about you?" Arlo gestured to the next person in the circle, who was the woman sitting to Sam's right.

"Hello!" she said brightly. "My name is Mary, and I would like the universe to help my daughter lose weight. You see, she's really a pretty girl but—"

"No!" Arlo said, nearly losing his patience. "That isn't what we are going for here. This should be about you. So, for example, if you are struggling with accepting your daughter's weight, you can—" The woman stared at him blankly, and Arlo sighed. "We can come back to you as well." Arlo shifted his attention to Sam. "Alright, you're up. If you would, please state your intention."

Damn it, Sam thought. *Those two didn't really give me much of a template to work from.* She threw a bitter look at the man and woman sitting to her right. The man continued to stare straight ahead at . . . something, and the woman still seemed to be processing being skipped.

"I—" Sam paused. *What can I possibly say?* "Look, this is my first one of these . . . things. Maybe you can skip me for now?"

Sam's smile was hopeful. And a tinge desperate. Arlo studied her calmly before shaking his head. Standing up, he walked to a corner of the room, started digging through a duffle bag, and pulled out an assortment of percussion instruments: small drums, a shaker, and even a cowbell. One by one he handed out the instruments to those in the circle. Sam received a tambourine, and Marcie seemed delighted by the small bongo drum that was given to her.

"This is what we're going to do," Arlo said as he continued to pass out instruments. "I think we can all use a reset at this point, so we are going to play these instruments, as a group, and let our heads clear. And then we will get back to stating our intentions."

Arlo sat back down, holding two drumsticks. As everyone watched, he started hitting them together in a slow but steady rhythm. The group, catching on, started to follow along in staggered fashion. Soon, the entire group was operating at the same speed, chuckling to each other at their impromptu, albeit minimalistic, song.

Sam dutifully shook her tambourine in time. *How long is this going to continue?* After a few minutes, Sam started looking around, watching for a sign that it would wrap up soon. A few minutes later, Sam started to entertain the possibility that the percussion exercise would continue all night long. All the while, she continued to shake her tambourine to the rhythm.

No one else seemed concerned about the possibility that the song would never end. They all blissfully hammered out a beat with their eyes closed. Not wanting to stick out any more than she assumed she already was, Sam also shut her eyes. The loss of visual stimuli resulted in the beat being her sole sensory input, and she soon began to detect subtle discrepancies in the rhythm that made it more than just a steady banging. At one point, the group seemed to start putting a greater emphasis on every third note: *bang, bang, BANG, bang, bang, BANG.* Later, the rhythm gradually sped up, without anyone explicitly directing the change in tempo. Sam felt her individuality fade away as she continued to operate her tambourine, and she didn't fight being part of the group's collective energy.

The rhythm continued. Sam was no longer worrying about the ceremony, or the possibility of the beat continuing into the morning. Her mind had become consumed by the improvised song performed as a single entity. Sam entered a true meditative state, unencumbered by worry, no longer confined by the walls she had constructed for herself over the course of the past several years.

Sam didn't sense when Arlo knelt a few feet in front of her, and his whisper didn't register as something external but rather as a question that arose from the very depths of her soul.

"What is your intention, Sam? What is it you wish to release?"

The drumming continued. Sam didn't allow herself to reflect on the question posed to her—she continued to swim in the serenity that the rhythm provided. She breathed in deeply and released it, her breaths unconsciously dancing to the beat of the song. Sam barely noticed when a word escaped her lips, riding the crest of an exhale:

"Fear."

The beat continued around her, and Sam fell out of her meditative state as the import of her proclamation hit her. *Fear? Fear of what?* Glancing to her left, Sam noticed that Marcie had also stopped drumming and was looking at her with a puzzled expression.

Gradually, the rhythm slowed and faded, until it was just the intense-looking man banging a bongo alone with his eyes closed. Arlo laid a hand on his shoulder and the man took the hint and stopped, bringing silence back to the room.

"Thank you," Arlo said to Sam. "Please write that down."

Sam blinked, forgetting that she had a pencil and paper. She snatched them up and hastily wrote "fear" before quickly folding up the paper so she would not have to look at the word. Marcie smiled at her in encouragement before announcing her own intention.

"I would like the universe to help me with my ability to forgive," Marcie said, before writing "forgiveness" on her own piece of paper. Sam, looking down, frowned in confusion. From the little she knew of Marcie, it seemed like patience and forgiveness were the least of her problems. *It's funny how differently we see ourselves from how the outside world views us*, Sam thought.

Once Sam and Marcie had set the tone for what was expected of the group, it didn't take long for the rest of the circle to state their intentions. It ended with the intense man professing a desire to become more aerodynamic, and he beamed when Arlo gave him a high five in response to what was apparently an adequate answer.

"Now that we have all stated our intentions and memorialized them in writing, we will cast those papers into the fire to propel them into the universe."

I should have known we weren't done, Sam thought. *Can't have a fire ceremony without the fire.*

The group slowly rose, and Sam noticed a few people stretching, trying to pump some life into extremities that had fallen asleep during their time seated on the floor. They made their way to the backyard, which was illuminated by the burning wood in the center of the fire pit. Everyone milled about uncomfortably, unsure of what to do. Finally, at Arlo's prompting, the intense man stepped close to the fire, holding his piece of paper up before him like it was a sacred scroll. The man closed his eyes, gathering his energy, before shouting into the night.

"I . . . am . . . aerodynamic!"

With a flourish, he threw his piece of paper toward the burning wood, but an upwind from the flames caught the paper and blew it off course, causing it to swoop and stutter to the ground five feet away. The man cursed under his breath, bent for the paper, and crumpled it into a ball before casting it into the fire.

Those that followed were less dramatic. One by one, they approached the fire pit, meekly announced their intention, and carefully dropped their papers into the flames. Sam had been hanging back, but she soon realized that she was the only one remaining with a piece of paper.

"I relinquish fear." Sam mumbled as she dropped her own paper into the pit, although she didn't quite understand what that meant to her. She didn't feel particularly less fearful as she watched her paper wilt and burn away. Sam was ripped out of her reverie by Arlo and the rest of the group breaking out into a small applause. Sam was momentarily taken aback, thinking the clapping was for her specifically, until she realized that was the end of the ceremony.

Sam hung back as Marcie went around to her friends to give them hugs and wish them a good night. As Marcie circled around the yard, Sam stared into the fire pit, which had not yet been extinguished.

Why on earth did I blurt out "fear"?

Sam felt a tap on her shoulder. She turned, and Marcie gestured with her head toward the gate. Sam waved goodbye to those in the backyard and walked with Marcie back to the street.

"I feel much lighter!" Marcie said as they walked, and Sam could tell that she meant it. Marcie seemed to be bouncing down the sidewalk.

"That was interesting," Sam said, remaining truthful but diplomatic.

"Oh, it is!" Marcie gushed. "There is tremendous power in simply stating your intentions to the universe. Give it time, and I think you will be amazed at how you are changed." Marcie paused, growing thoughtful. "This may not be my business, and of course you do not have to tell me if you don't want to, but you relinquished fear earlier."

"Yeah, I don't know why I—"

"What is the nature of this fear you want to let go?" Marcie asked, ignoring Sam.

"I don't know. I don't feel afraid." Sam shrugged. Marcie stopped walking and stared quizzically at Sam, as if trying to solve a puzzle. Sam was uncomfortable under her gaze and glanced down the street. She could just make out Harold's parked car, and he looked to be sleeping in the driver's seat. But when Sam looked back to Marcie, she was still studying Sam with that same calculating expression.

"Ah!" Marcie suddenly exclaimed. "I think I see it now. You fear death." Sam couldn't help but laugh.

"Trust me, I have plenty of issues. But a fear of dying is not one of them, I promise you," Sam said as she resumed walking. But Marcie remained rooted to the spot, and Sam stopped to look back at her. Marcie, unmoving, looked directly into Sam's eyes before speaking.

"I didn't say it was your own death that scares you."

CHAPTER SEVEN

Saturday, August 31, 2019

It wasn't easy to wake up Harold, snoring in the partially reclined driver's seat, but soon they were driving back to Marcie's house as Marcie regaled Harold with tales of the fire ceremony.

"You should have seen Sam!" Marcie said, proud as anything. "She was the one that kicked off the entire thing! She was the first to state her intention, and everyone followed her lead."

"Wow," Harold said, making eye contact with Sam through the rearview mirror and winking. "Sounds like I missed a great time."

It was nearly ten o'clock when they got to Marcie's home. Sam was about to head to her own car when she was stopped by Marcie.

"It's late, and you have a long drive," Marcie said to her. "Please, let me make you a quick cup of tea at the very least, to give you a bit of pep for the ride. I promise it will be better than the one from earlier."

"Sure." Sam's sleep was erratic, at best, and she was in no hurry to go to bed. It had been a while since she was out of her house after dark, and she was enjoying herself more than anticipated. She wasn't sure what she had accomplished by way of reconnaissance, other than confirming that whatever issues there were with her children, Marcie appeared to be authentic and kind to the point of approaching sainthood.

Inside, Harold beelined for the television, and Marcie went to the kitchen to make the tea. Sam followed Harold and took a seat beside him on the couch, watching as he rapidly flipped through the channels. Even though he didn't settle on any particular show, Harold paused at one point to turn the volume up.

A few minutes later, Marcie entered, looking distraught. Harold caught her look and muted the television.

"Colin left me a message," Marcie said. "He wants to talk to me right away."

"It's after 10:00!" Harold said. "Did he say what it's about?"

"No, he just said he wanted to talk to me as soon as possible, in person. Can you take me over there? I just know I won't be able to sleep tonight until I figure out what this is all about."

Harold looked pained—he clearly wasn't relishing the thought of going back out into the night.

"I'm happy to drive you," Sam said, jumping in. Harold looked at her, his expression radiating gratitude. "I'm feeling pretty wired after that ceremony, to be honest. Harold can stay here and relax."

"I'm fine with that plan," Harold said, picking up the remote. Marcie teasingly swatted at his knee.

"Sure, I'll bet you are! And thank you, Sam—that is very gracious of you to offer. Let me just give Colin a quick call to tell him that I'm coming over."

Marcie exited again, and Harold, with a flourish, unmuted the tv. As he continued cycling through the channels, he glanced at Sam and mouthed: *I owe you one.* Sam noiselessly responded: *Obvi.*

"Alright, I'm ready!" Marcie called from the front door. As Sam stood to leave, Harold extended a fist toward her, which, after a moment, she pounded with a fist of her own before leaving.

Sam was a bit embarrassed by the messy state of her car, but Marcie didn't seem to notice as she climbed into the passenger seat.

"Colin only lives about ten minutes away," Marcie said. "And I really can't thank you enough for this."

Marcie directed Sam as she drove, taking her north. Several minutes later, after meandering through a suburban neighborhood in an affluent area of Nassau County, she pointed at a driveway where Sam could park, adjacent to a well-kept colonial.

"Nice house," Sam remarked.

"Oh, yes," Marcie said. "Colin always insists upon the nicest things."

Sam grunted to give the illusion of a response and exited the car. Marcie walked briskly up the steps and opened the door without knocking.

"Colin told me he's working in the basement, and I should just let myself in," she explained. As they entered the house, they were greeted by a barking puppy—what looked to Sam to be a tiny black Labrador.

"This is new!" Marcie cried, bending over to let the puppy lick her face. "And what is your name? What is your name?" As she cooed, the puppy rolled over to expose her belly for a good rub, and Marcie was happy to oblige.

Sam glanced around the house while Marcie played with the dog. The home was, in Sam's opinion, simply immaculate, with staging that suggested that it had been laid out by a professional interior decorator. The modern furniture looked to be from Pottery Barn, and the walls were painted in an intricate colored pattern of oranges and greens. Sam could see the kitchen at the rear of the house, which was completely white with the exception of a dark quartz countertop.

Marcie continued to pet the Labrador as Sam took it all in.

"I can just cuddle with you all day!" Marcie told the puppy. "But I need to find your daddy! Come, let's go find your da-da!"

Marcie scooped up the dog in her arms and led Sam to an open door leading to a basement. She descended the steps cautiously, careful not to fall or drop the puppy. Sam followed behind and was somewhat amazed to see that the basement was just as decadent as the ground floor. A long sectional faced a massive television mounted to the wall, and the wall behind the couch was decorated with rows upon rows of Star Wars action figures, still in their original packaging. Colin lounged on the couch with a controller in his hands, staring intently at the tv. He waited a good minute before pausing his game to look up at Marcie.

"I'm sorry to interrupt your work!" Marcie said. Sam started to laugh but stifled it when she saw that Marcie was being sincere. Colin noticed Sam's confusion and glowered.

"It's fine," Colin said. He peered behind Marcie at Sam and grimaced. "What is *she* doing here?"

"Sam was kind enough to drive me over to see you! Isn't that nice?" Marcie didn't seem to notice that Colin's frown remained. He didn't seem pleased to see Sam at all.

"You're . . . working?" Sam asked, looking pointedly at the controller in Colin's hands.

"It's research," Colin said. When he didn't offer more, Marcie piped in. "Oh, yes! Colin hosts a very popular show. It is called a podcast, am I getting that right? He discusses a different video game each episode. I listened to a couple, and I really enjoyed them, although some parts went a bit over my head. But I know a lot of people love his show!"

"Cool," Sam said. "What's the name of the podcast?"

"*B.A. Start*," Colin said. "It's a reference to—"

"Yeah, I get the reference," Sam said. She had played enough Nintendo in her youth to remember the code to get thirty extra lives in certain games put out by Konami. The name of the show was just the tail end of the code itself, although Sam figured that the code, in full, would be too unwieldy for a podcast name. Marcie smiled, but it was clear that she needed a translator to follow the conversation.

"Anyway, who is this pretty little girl?" Marcie asked as she lowered her head to receive more puppy-kisses.

"Ah, that's Samus," Colin said. "I got her this past week. She looks cute, but she's a pretty terrible dog. Keeps pissing and crapping inside the house. It's getting tiresome."

"Colin!" Marcie laughed. "She's a little puppy! You have to be patient and train her." Colin shook his head.

"I tried, but she doesn't listen. I think something's wrong with her. I drove all the way out to Pennsylvania last week to get her. And now I have to do that drive again to take her back. It's a real pain in my ass."

Marcie gasped.

"No! You can't take her back. I will take care of her. I will train her, and maybe when she learns to go to the bathroom outside, you will want her back?" Colin shrugged a *maybe*.

"If that's what you want to do. But I'm telling you: She doesn't want to be trained."

Marcie ignored Colin's skepticism and instead clasped her hands together, looking thrilled. She didn't seem at all put off by the imposition. "How wonderful! I'm so excited to get to know little Samus better. And don't worry—I promise to take great care of her!"

Colin didn't look worried. If anything, he seemed lightened at the prospect of being relieved of his burden.

"Is that why you wanted to see me, Colin?" Marcie asked, putting the puppy down to allow her to sniff around the basement. "The troubles with the puppy?"

"No. There was something else I was hoping to discuss with you. Privately." Colin's eyes flickered to Sam, and Marcie caught the hint.

"Sam, would you mind going upstairs for a bit? You can bring Samus and play with her. Thank you so much!"

"Sure, no problem," Sam said. She tried to grab Samus, but the puppy eluded her grasp and ran to the other side of the basement. Sam could feel Colin's eyes on her as she staggered about the basement, trying to corner the elusive dog. Finally, once Samus was effectively trapped, she rolled over in submission. Sam chuckled, gave her belly a quick rub, and carried the dog upstairs, leaving Marcie and Colin behind.

Sam took a seat on the couch in the living room. She was curious about how extravagant the other rooms of the house looked, but she didn't feel comfortable exploring the place on her own. Samus lay at her feet but quickly became restless and started scratching at the furniture. *I'll probably get blamed for this*, Sam thought before getting down on the floor to distract the puppy. Samus, eager for a playmate, bounded to her side and quickly darted away, as if wanting to play tag. As tired as she was, Sam crawled after her, scratching Samus's ears whenever she managed to catch her.

• • • • •

Twenty minutes later, Marcie emerged from the basement. Her eyes were red-lined—it looked as if she was holding back tears.

"We can go now," Marcie said to Sam in a soft voice. Sam blinked, disoriented. She had never seen Marcie in such a state.

"Are you ok?" Sam asked, and Marcie, tight-lipped, nodded. Sam looked toward the basement door, wondering what had happened in her absence. It was clear that Marcie just wanted to leave. "What about her?" Sam finally asked, looking down at Samus.

"I will have to get things ready for her at home," Marcie said without looking up. "I will come back tomorrow to get her. She can stay here one more night."

Sam shrugged and gave Samus one last scratch behind the ears before leaving the house with Marcie.

As she drove Marcie home, Sam stole an occasional glance to her right. Marcie remained deep in thought and still seemed as if she might start crying at any moment.

"Are you sure you're ok?" Sam asked at one point, breaking the silence, and Marcie nodded.

"Yes, I'm fine." She did not elaborate. She clearly was not fine, but Sam didn't know how to respond. *How can I get her to talk to me?* she wondered. She suddenly recalled an exchange earlier in the night when she had resisted Marcie's efforts to discuss the grief Sam experienced after Mike died and realized they had stumbled into something of a role reversal.

And Sam knew what she had to do.

Sam pulled off at the next exit onto a turnpike. If Marcie registered the detour, she didn't comment on it. It didn't take long until Sam found what she was looking for: a diner on the side of the road. Sam pulled into the lot and parked.

"Do you mind if we grab a quick cup of coffee? Or tea?" Sam said. "I have a long drive back to Westchester ahead of me, so I could use the caffeine."

"Of course." Marcie sounded more polite than enthusiastic about the stop.

Sam and Marcie took a booth inside the diner. The restaurant was relatively empty for a Saturday night. There were a few people finishing up a late dinner, but it was still too early for the drunken college kids looking for cheese fries to storm in from the bars. A waitress came by to take their orders, and then Sam and Marcie were alone.

"You asked me earlier about what it was like after Mike died," Sam said. Marcie, lost in her own thoughts, blinked and looked at Sam with renewed attention. Marcie nodded at her to continue.

"The immediate aftermath was a blur, but there were moments I recall that are so vivid. It took some time before I began to feel like myself again, even a little bit. But even then, I wasn't truly myself. I felt broken."

Marcie bobbed her head in acknowledgment but didn't speak.

"It was maybe a month or so after the accident before I even tried to do anything for myself. I guess I had some form of survivor's guilt? Anything I did that was remotely pleasurable just felt *wrong* to me. Even having a slice of pizza. So, I ate to keep myself alive, but I wouldn't allow myself to do anything more than that. I know this sounds silly."

"No, not at all," Marcie said. It was obvious that she had her own thoughts brewing, but she was patiently waiting for Sam to finish before sharing them.

"The first thing I allowed myself, not tied to mourning, was just reading a book. I couldn't watch tv back then—Mike and I used to binge-watch shows together, so even that was too difficult for me to do alone. But Mike was never a reader. That was an activity that was largely untainted by any memories of him. With some exceptions." Sam paused, on the verge of remembering details, before forcing herself to continue. "Still, reading was something I thought I could handle. So I read a novel. And in doing so, there were times when the accident wasn't at the forefront of my brain. It was some relief, even if it was never long-lived. Do you want to guess what I did when I finished that book?"

"You read another," Marcie answered.

"I read another. And then another. But I soon realized that I couldn't stay a hermit, reading book after book. Sure, friends would swing by to check in on me, but I needed a reason to get out of the house that was just for me—to do something enjoyable. It took me some time to find it."

"What was it?" Marcie asked. The waitress arrived with their orders: coffee for Sam and green tea for Marcie. Sam waited for the waitress to depart before continuing.

"I was online looking for book recommendations, and I came across Bookstagram. Have you heard of that? It's basically people reviewing and discussing books on Instagram."

"Instagram?" Marcie asked. "Is that some sort of website?"

"Yeah. Well, kind of," Sam said. "People will put up a picture of a book they want to talk about with a caption, and people can respond in the comments. A lot of people get very creative with their photos, too. I was itching for a taste of human contact, even if it was merely discussing a book with strangers online, and I was desperate for a real excuse to leave my house, so I created an account and ventured out into the world to take a photo of the book I was reading. It was a novel about stock traders, so one Saturday I took a train into Manhattan and took a nice picture of the book next to the Wall Street sign. It was really just a reason to go outside and take a little day trip, but I ended up grabbing some lunch downtown and had a decent day. Then I put the picture on Instagram, wrote up my thoughts about the book, and felt slightly more human than I had in some time. I did it again the following week, only I drove out to a casino in Connecticut to take a picture for a book I was reading about a card counting scheme."

"That sounds lovely!" Marcie said, sounding energized for the first time since they had arrived at Colin's house earlier. "I would love to read your write-ups. Where can I find them?"

"You can find me on Instagram—my account is called samisreadingbooks." After a moment of reflection, Sam added, somewhat defensively, "I came up with the name of that account at a particularly uncreative time in my life."

"And people read what you put on there?" Marcie asked.

"Yes. At least, I think so. I have a few thousand followers at this point."

"A few thousand?" Marcie gasped, placing a hand over her chest. "My goodness! I had no idea I was talking to a celebrity!"

"No, it's . . . it's not like that." Sam didn't think it was worth the effort of trying to explain it to Marcie. *Maybe I can just show her later.*

"It is funny," Marcie said, sounding thoughtful. "There is power in just writing down your thoughts. Or typing them, as the case may be. That is why writing our intentions was such an important part of that fire ceremony. I imagine it must be quite therapeutic for you to have that outlet and be able to express yourself through your reviews. My goodness, after Barry—my first husband—passed away, I had so many thoughts bouncing around in my head that it became practically impossible to think at all. I got in the habit of trying to calm that mental chaos by memorializing my musings in a journal, which was incredibly helpful." Marcie sighed. "I thought it was a temporary project at first, but, unfortunately, I never seem to avoid adversity for too long. The journal is quite filled at this point. I shudder to think what I would be like today if all of that noise was still trapped inside my skull."

"I think I know what you mean," Sam said, although she didn't quite have the same experience with Bookstagram, where she actively tried to avoid writing anything remotely personal. *It's therapeutic as a creative outlet*, Sam thought, but she wondered whether she would be better served by being more forthcoming about herself in her writing.

"How much time do you spend on these book reviews?" Marcie asked.

"It's hard to quantify," Sam admitted. "When I'm not at work, I'm generally reading or out in the world taking a picture of what I'm reading. Or writing about what I just read. So, a good amount of time, to be sure."

"That certainly seems like a fun habit," Marcie said. "But is it fulfilling in and of itself?"

"It gets me through the day." Sam shrugged. "Most days, at least." Marcie sipped at her tea, looking pensive.

"You had said earlier you were broken. That jumped out at me because that's exactly how I felt after Barry passed away. Broken. It was hard for me to conceive of moving on. I had Jeremy to raise, so that forced me to continue to some extent, but it definitely felt like I was just doing the best I could with demolished parts. But you know what?"

Marcie paused, pointing a spoon directly at Sam.

"I realized that it's easy to feel broken when you go through something tragic that hurts you. You come out of that experience changed, and you just assume that the change within you is a manifestation of the breaking you suffered. But it took me a long time to appreciate, and to celebrate, that I had *evolved* because of the time I had together with Barry. He was a wonderfully generous man. We got married when we were in our twenties, and we were as poor as anything. Barry worked two jobs just to keep us afloat, and not once did he complain about it. After he died, trying to raise Jeremy through that grief was the hardest thing I've ever gone though. I tried to hide the breaking I felt inside to be a better mother. The thing is, though, that once I dug through the pain, I could finally see that my time with Barry had only made me stronger. Made me better. I realized that my transformation was more than just the anguish I felt at his passing. Considering myself 'broken' would dishonor the impact he had on me through the totality of our relationship."

Sam stirred at her coffee absently.

"That seems like a really positive way of looking at the loss of a loved one. I don't think I can pull that off, though."

"Well, are you a different person now than you were before you met Mike?" Marcie asked.

"Yeah. Sure. Of course."

"How?"

"How?" Sam blinked. "I'm not sure if that's something I can put into words."

Marcie frowned, deep in thought, and then, with a laugh, clasped her hands together in delight. A few others in the diner noted the commotion and looked over in their direction.

"What a wonderful answer!" Marcie said. Sam squinted, wondering if Marcie was mocking her.

"What do you mean?"

"Well, let's see. How many words are there in the English language?"

"I don't know. Two hundred thousand or so?" Sam vaguely recalled seeing that number somewhere, possibly on a Snapple cap.

"Ok, let's go with that," Marcie said, growing excited. "Now, think of all the people on the planet. All of their intricacies. Do you think any combination of words can adequately describe *anyone* beyond broad strokes? Of course not! I think, from now on, when asked to describe myself, I will also answer, 'That is not something I can really put into words.'"

Sam stared at Marcie before letting out a hearty laugh. She was surprised at not being repulsed by Marcie's positivity. In fact, it may have been rubbing off on her—Sam's inherent cynicism seemed to have thawed over the course of the evening.

"It must get exhausting being so positive all the time," Sam said with a small grin. Marcie blinked.

"Exhausting? No, never! It only gets exhausting when I allow negativity to seep in." Marcie grew serious. "And thank you for sharing your experience with me. I know it's not always easy to talk about such things. I am honored that you are comfortable enough to discuss that with me."

Sam nodded. Marcie took a deep breath, and Sam could see her make a decision.

"Colin asked me to call off the wedding," Marcie finally said.

"What?"

"And I agreed."

"What!"

Marcie looked forlorn.

"Colin told me that it was very hard for him growing up to have two new stepfathers after Russ—Colin's father—passed away. He said he's really struggling with the idea of having yet another new stepfather. It seems to be causing him a lot of stress. And I promised myself years ago that I would always put my children's interests above my own, and that is an oath I have never wavered from."

Sam stared, slack-jawed.

"How old is Colin?" Sam asked.

"He's thirty-five. Why?"

"I can't speak to how having a new stepfather can potentially impact a child," Sam said, "but I am fairly certain Colin is past the age where you can really impact his development that much." Marcie shook her head.

"Oh, Colin has always been a very sensitive boy. Why, I remember once, when he was young, we were celebrating Christmas. All the children were taking turns opening their gifts around the tree, and I noticed that Colin seemed sadder and sadder each time he opened a new one. Finally, when there were no more presents to open, he looked up at me, on the verge of tears. That look broke my heart, I tell you. I will never forget what Colin said to me: 'Mom! All of these presents are terrible!' I tried to apologize, but Colin ran to the front door, and I heard him drive off in his car. I didn't know what—"

"Wait," Sam interjected. "I'm sorry to interrupt. Just how old is Colin in this story?"

"Oh, I think he must've been in high school," Marcie said. "Perhaps college."

Sam felt a need to vomit.

"Ok. Please continue."

"Anyway, a few hours later, he finally returned. I had hoped that the drive would have cooled him down, but he still seemed quite agitated. It wasn't until he went into the living room and saw all the new presents I had wrapped for him that he finally looked happy again. You see, Colin's birthday is in January, so I fortunately had a number of gifts stashed away for him that I was able to quickly wrap while he was gone. Thank goodness he liked that crop better! We were all ultimately able to have a wonderful Christmas after all." Marcie stopped, and Sam realized that was the end of the story.

"I'm not sure I'm picking up on your point," Sam said in a measured tone.

"My point is simply that Colin has always been more sensitive than other children his age. If he was that upset over getting presents he did not like, I can't imagine how bothered he must've been every time a new man entered his life as a father figure. It had not occurred to me until he told me earlier, but I was acting very selfishly by even thinking of doing that to him again."

"Oh," Sam said. She took a long sip of her coffee to hide her expression, but Marcie picked up on her disapproval.

"What are you thinking?" Marcie asked. She sounded genuinely curious.

"Well, how much honesty are you looking for?"

"All of it," Marcie said. "Always."

"Ok." Sam gathered her thoughts. "I obviously don't know Colin—or any of your children—that well, but from what I've seen, and what you've just described, it sounds to me like Colin's issues relate more to being spoiled than being hypersensitive."

Marcie winced, but she did not seem angered by what Sam said. *I may have struck a nerve*, Sam thought. *Well, she asked for the complete truth.*

"Like I said, I'm not qualified to offer an opinion on how having a new stepparent, or multiple stepparents, can impact a child," Sam said. "But I think there is a time in everyone's life where you're responsible for your own happiness, and you can't blame what others are doing for your mental state. I don't know what that point is, exactly, but—you said he is thirty-five years old?"

"Yes. He will be thirty-six next January," Marcie confirmed. Sam let out a small laugh.

"Yeah, he is past that point, whatever it is."

Marcie mulled this over.

"What makes you think he is spoiled?" she asked.

"Aside from throwing a temper tantrum over Christmas presents when he was old enough to drive a car? Well, he seemed very comfortable passing off his dog to you when the responsibility seemed too large, which only took about a week. He's trying to dictate what you should do with your life when you're both adults, focusing solely on how it may marginally impact him without any consideration for your own happiness. I mean, even his house—what does he do for a living?"

"As I mentioned earlier, he has his podcast."

Sam stared at Marcie in disbelief.

"That's it? His house must cost a fortune, not to mention how it's decorated. How can he afford that only by playing video games and doing a podcast?"

Marcie looked away, uncomfortable.

"I don't like to discuss money, but Colin's father was very knowledgeable about stocks and that sort of business and left a fair amount of money for Colin after he passed. I think it was in some sort of trust, if I'm getting that right. Colin used that money to buy his house and decorate it and get some other things. I also help him out financially when he needs it. But like I said, I don't like to think about money."

Money, Sam thought. *Of course.*

"I assume you're well off yourself," Sam said gently, and Marcie blinked in surprise.

"What makes you say that?"

"Well, generally speaking, only rich people have the luxury of not thinking about money."

Marcie's cheeks flushed as she looked away.

"You are right, of course," Marcie finally said, turning back to Sam. "Colin's father—and my other husbands—were all wonderful as far as ensuring that the children and I would be financially protected. I only meant that what fulfills me generally does not have a dollar sign on it. Two weeks ago, Harold found a heart-shaped stone on the beach that he gave me, and that gift is more valuable to me than any piece of jewelry I ever received."

"I don't doubt it." Sam felt bad. Marcie seemed even further saddened by her diagnosis regarding Colin being spoiled. "Like I said, I don't know you or your family that well, and I have no doubt—zero doubt—that you showered all of your children with love when they were young and continue to do so to this day. And I get that when you love someone, your instincts may be to put their interests above your own. I'm just not sure you're doing Colin any favors by catering to his every whim. He should've learned by now that he's not an island and the world doesn't revolve around him, but if he hasn't, I think he'll be a stronger person in the long run once he figures that out. So, if you want to marry Harold, I think you should do it." Marcie was quiet, but Sam could see the gears moving behind her eyes.

"I will think on what you've said," Marcie finally said. "I will meditate and pray on it. You've given me a fair amount to reflect upon."

Sam nodded. *It's probably the best I'm going to get from her right now.*

"You are right about one thing," Marcie said. "My chief strategy as a mother was to make sure that none of my children were ever wanting for love. And I can say, with confidence, that I succeeded in that regard. But sometimes I wonder if that was enough. As my children have gotten older, I can feel them drifting away from me at times. Not Miguel—he is very proud of being a mama's boy, as he puts it. But Jeremy, Colin, and Sadie—I can detect hints of losing them, now and then, and I am not always sure what to do about it. Or if there's anything to even be done about it. It may just be the nature of watching your children grow up. But, for example, I had invited Sadie to come to the fire ceremony, and she had no interest whatsoever. I'm so thankful you were able to come with me, but it would have been wonderful to spend time with my daughter as well."

Sam thought back to the weirdness of the ceremony. *I'm not sure that would've been Sadie's scene*, she suspected, even with her nominal knowledge of Sadie.

"Maybe it's just that things like the fire ceremony aren't aligned with Sadie's passions," Sam said. "I assume she has different interests than you. You may simply have to meet her on her own terms." Marcie slowly nodded.

"Yes. That is very wise. I should not expect her to share my interests. Although you were kind enough to do so tonight."

"Well, that was largely driven by my lack of a social life," she said with a laugh.

"Be that as it may," Marcie said, "it occurs to me that I should extend the same courtesy to you. You opened your heart by sharing one of my passions with me. I would welcome the opportunity to return that favor. Is there a hobby of yours we can do together? Perhaps something relating to your book reviewing project?"

Sam hesitated.

"Unfortunately, reading and reviewing books are difficult to turn into a group activity."

"You also said you photograph the books that you review," Marcie pressed. "Perhaps I can assist with that?"

"There's not much to it," Sam said. "I just drive to a locale, take a picture, grab a coffee, and wander around." Marcie let out a squeal and clapped her hands together.

"That sounds like so much fun! Where are you going for your next book?"

She's not letting up, Sam realized. *And she genuinely wants to come with me.*

"A good chunk of the novel I'm currently reading takes place in Woodstock," Sam said. "I was thinking of going up there to get a picture of the book near a town sign, or something like that." *Oh no*, Sam thought as Marcie's eyes widened at the reference to Woodstock. *I should've seen that coming.*

"How lovely! Next weekend? Oh, this will be so much fun! I actually grew up not too far from there. I am so excited—thank you so much for inviting me!"

"But I—" Sam decided to let it go. "My pleasure. It will be fun."

The waitress came by to drop off their bill, which Marcie insisted on paying, and then they left the diner together to resume their drive home. Marcie was mute for the remainder of the ride, lost in her own thoughts.

When they arrived back at Marcie's home, the tv was still blaring loudly, broadcasting a new baseball game. Harold had fallen asleep on the couch, but he stirred when Marcie and Sam entered the room.

"Everything ok with Colin?" Harold said groggily over the noise of the tv.

"Everything is fine," Marcie replied, struggling to project her voice over the television. "Enjoy your game. I'm going upstairs to pray."

Marcie walked over to kiss Harold on the forehead, and then she came back to Sam to grab her in a rocking hug.

"Goodnight, Sam," Marcie said. "Thank you for everything. I'm so excited to spend some more time with you next week."

With that, Marcie went upstairs, leaving Sam and Harold alone together in the living room. Sam, not wanting to scream over the television, gave Harold a wave before turning to leave.

"Oh," Harold said. He fumbled for the remote to mute the television, and Sam turned back to him and waited. "I wanted to thank you for all you're doing with Marcie. She's into some outlandish stuff, and it means a lot to her—and me—that you're willing to do this weirdness with her." He laughed. "Also takes a lot of pressure off of me to participate in her witchcraft!"

"It's not witchcraft," Sam said. *At least, I don't think it is.* "And it's totally fine. She's a lovely person. You're lucky to have found her."

"I know you and I haven't had a chance to talk much since this whole engagement thing started," Harold said, "but Marcie was really excited to get to know you, and I thought it was important that you two spend some time together. So please don't think I've been ignoring you."

Sam nodded in understanding and turned to leave.

"By the way," Sam said from the front door. "I'm flattered that you actually muted the tv to talk to me just now." Harold chuckled.

"Well, it's a commercial anyway, so—"

Sam, with a grin, rolled her eyes and left.

As she drove back to Westchester, Sam reflected on the productive day. After learning that Marcie was wealthy and being exposed to Colin's spoiled nature, Sam figured she was very close to pinpointing the reason behind her children's objection to the wedding. She still wanted time to reflect on the situation and how to proceed, but she sensed that she had all the information she needed to guide Harold and Marcie, to the extent they could be persuaded of anything.

There was not a lot to be gained, from an investigative standpoint, from spending another weekend with Marcie. Still, Sam noted that she was not at all tempted to cancel the planned trip to Woodstock. It didn't take her long to self-diagnose in this regard: After having spent years where the goal each day was to simply get through it, it was refreshing to finally have something to look forward to.

CHAPTER EIGHT

Sunday, September 1, 2019

Colin was having a solid weekend, with a number of boxes checked off on his to-do list. He managed to finish "Axe of Madalia," an old-school RPG for the original PlayStation, and recorded a new podcast episode about the game that he planned to put up on Monday. It was a solid episode, too. Colin even thought it was one of the better ones he had recorded. Despite all of that work, he still found time to unburden himself of his untrainable puppy and, on top of that, end his mother's engagement, which was something even Sadie had not yet been able to accomplish.

He was feeling quite proud of himself that Sunday when he invited his siblings to come over in the evening to tell them the news. He wanted to see their faces in person when he revealed that he had single-handedly accomplished their collective goal. It was fitting in a way—most of the money at issue had come from Colin's biological father.

Colin had an incomplete view of his father, Russ, who passed away when he was only three years old. His mother was always happy to discuss Russ with him—she thought it was very important for the children to understand their respective fathers. And so, Colin developed a view of his father as being affable, with a very easy laugh and a natural ability to get by without ever seeming to work that hard. But his mother's aversion to discussing financial matters left Colin with a spotty image of how his father accumulated his wealth. Colin understood that his father had a knack for investing wisely, although that appeared to be more a product of luck than business acumen. Things always had a tendency to work out for Colin as well, and he often wondered if luck was hereditary.

Of course, dying before the age of forty strongly suggested that there were limits to Russ's good fortune.

Colin understood that Russ was well off when he met and married his mother in the early 1980s, but that his wealth grew exponentially during the course of their marriage, which lasted four years. Investments he made that seemed sound from the outset proceeded to explode, pushing his net wealth from high six figures to eight figures. To his credit, Russ had arranged for a sizable trust in Colin's name to be established upon his death, which had funded Colin through the entirety of his adult life, but the majority of Russ's estate passed to his mother. She remarried twice after that, and on both occasions, she made a point of making sure her wealth was shared with her new husband—his mother truly bought in to the notion that marriage is a partnership. Colin had no doubt that she would have done the same upon marrying Harold.

That is, until Colin managed to steer his mother clear of that contemplated marriage.

He continued to hold out a hope that he would end up seeing the lion's share of the funds, although he imagined that his half-siblings would argue that he was already rewarded by way of the trust that his father set up for him before he passed away. That argument was, of course, bullshit. Jeremy, Sadie, and Miguel should consider themselves lucky to see even a piece of his father's legacy. It was downright degrading that Colin even had to plead his case for why he should end up with more than a quarter of that money. *Maybe their tunes will change once they realize that I was the hero with regard to this entire affair?*

Colin was still basking in pride at what he had accomplished when his mother arrived to pick up Samus on Sunday afternoon. It wasn't a long visit—his mother explained that she had spent the morning gathering everything needed to care for an untrained puppy, so all that was left for her to do was collect the dog itself. But before she left, his mother handed him an envelope and asked him to read and reflect upon it when he was in a state of peace. The envelope was thick—it seemed like at least ten pages of paper were stuffed in there—and Colin immediately disregarded it. *Probably just some prayer she figured would inspire me*, he thought dismissively.

Later that evening, about a half hour before his siblings were scheduled to arrive, he came across the envelope, which he had flung onto his kitchen counter, and he looked at it with fresh eyes. It occurred to him that there may be a check in there, amongst all the other papers. His mother had been known to slip him money when she thought he could use it, or even if he just seemed to need a pick-me-up.

He opened the envelope, removed the sheets of paper, and shook them out, waiting for a check, or cash, to flutter to the ground. Nothing. Mildly curious, he glanced at the handwritten letter from his mom. He skimmed the pages quickly, so only certain portions of the letter registered.

I am dedicated to living a life of being in my heart space . . .

After quiet meditation, which is the lifeline to my soul and a connection to the Creator of our Universe . . .

Honoring the direction given by the Guide Within . . .

Colin frowned as he tried to decipher his mother's spiritual ramblings. Eventually he reached a section of the letter that was quite easy to understand and immediately caused his heart to sink into his stomach:

I have determined that it is my purpose to proceed with marrying Harold, despite our conversation last night.

"Shit."

He heard a car pull up in front of his house. He peeked out his front window and spotted Jeremy's Mustang parked on the street. Miguel exited from the passenger seat—they'd carpooled.

"Damn. Damn it, damn it, damn it."

From his vantage point behind the curtains, Colin saw another car pull up. *Sadie*, he realized with horror. Even though the temperature in his house was quite cool, he felt himself begin to sweat. He turned the lights off in his living room so he couldn't be seen from the street as he continued to watch through the window. Sadie, Jeremy, and Miguel spoke briefly to one another on the sidewalk and then made their way as a group to his front door. Moments later, his doorbell rang, and Colin froze.

Should I text them and tell them to go home? he wondered. They had each driven at least half an hour to get to his house. It was unlikely they would leave without a valid reason.

As he mulled his options, he was jolted by three quick bangs on his front door.

"Hey weirdo!" Jeremy's voice, muffled through the door. "Hit pause on whatever you're playing and let us in."

This is humiliating, Colin thought. It reminded him of when Jeremy had bragged about convincing Sam to stay away from the engagement party, only to have her show up almost immediately after. Colin had delighted in Jeremy's embarrassment at that incident, but he was finding it much less pleasant to be the humiliated party.

Sam. That was it. He realized how to spin this fiasco.

Colin turned the lights back on and opened the front door.

"Sorry to keep you all waiting," he said, forcing a smirk. "I was just tied up in the bathroom." Jeremy frowned and stepped into the house, with Sadie and Miguel following. Miguel looked around, and Colin couldn't recall if this was the first time he had seen his home.

"Nice place, Colin!" Miguel said, confirming that this was, in fact, his first visit. He paused when he spotted a pair of bowls on the kitchen floor. "Do you have a dog?"

"Yes," Colin said. "Well, no. Not anymore. The dog was terrible, so I gave her to Mom."

"That sounds about right," Jeremy said. He barked a mirthless laugh. "Maybe you should think about getting a vasectomy? Mom is probably too old to raise a child at this point, so it'll be hard for you to foist a baby onto her when you lose interest in it." Jeremy looked around, waiting for laughs that never came.

"Do you have news about Mother?" Sadie asked, getting right to the point. She eyeballed Colin's furniture before sitting on the couch. "That is why you wanted to meet with us all, no?"

Miguel took a seat next to Sadie, and Jeremy seized a large recliner for himself, leaving Colin without a place to sit.

My own house, and I'm stuck standing?

Colin went back to his kitchen and grabbed a chair. He placed it gently in the living room, taking care not to scratch the floor, before sitting.

"Well, yes," Colin said. "About that. I spoke with Mom this weekend about the wedding. Told her how I felt and convinced her to call it off."

Jeremy and Miguel exchanged a look. Colin thought he saw Jeremy mouth *told you* to Miguel. Sadie, seeming to sense that he was not at the end of his story, waited for Colin to continue.

"The weird part is, Mom showed up today with this long rambling letter. I only skimmed it, but the gist is that she's going through with the wedding after all. Which is a complete one-eighty from what she told me last night." Colin stood and went back into the kitchen to fetch the note. When he came back, Jeremy snatched it out of his hands and began reading to himself. "The thing is," Colin said as he watched Jeremy read, "I had asked Mom to come over for us to speak in person. But then she showed up with that Sam. I pulled them apart to talk to Mom privately, but Sam had *quite* the attitude when she was here. I'm certain she was the one who changed Mom's mind."

Sadie remained still as she processed this development. Jeremy, half-listening, continued to read the letter from their mother.

"She gets pretty personal in here, bro," Jeremy said without looking up from the letter. He started to read a portion out loud. "*I fear I have, through a desire to leave you as unburdened as possible, led you to a point where you are not adequately equipped to care for yourself, and I apologize for my failures in that regard.*" Colin's mouth tightened.

"Like I said, I only had a chance to skim the letter."

"She's calling you lazy and spoiled."

"Yeah, I got that."

"Do you want to hear the part where she says you're not really contributing to society? I mean, it's vague, but I think that's what she's getting at."

Colin squirmed. It was never good to be in a position where Jeremy felt comfortable mocking you.

"It's that damn daughter-in-law," Colin said. "She's meddling in our business." Jeremy nodded.

"Yeah, I told you she sucks."

"Well, we wouldn't be dealing with her at all if you hadn't screwed things up," Colin said, eager for an opportunity to seize the offensive. Jeremy flushed.

"Hey, at least I was trying to help us all out. That's a lot more than I can say for this guy," Jeremy said, jerking a thumb at Miguel. Miguel raised his hands, defensive, but Jeremy didn't let him get a word in before continuing. "Hell, Sadie acts like she's directing this whole thing, but I haven't seen her do anything yet, either."

"I'm doing plenty," Sadie said in a muted tone. She rubbed her chin, deep in thought. "It's becoming more apparent than ever that the daughter-in-law is a disruption. We have to get rid of her."

"Do you mean *kill* her?" Jeremy blurted out. Miguel's face blanched, and Colin looked to Sadie, waiting for her to clarify. She scoffed at Jeremy, derision written across her face.

"No. Of course not. Do you actually think you're smart enough to kill someone *and* get away with it?" Jeremy winced, as if physically struck by the insult. Standing up, he walked toward Sadie, glowering. Unfazed, Sadie also stood and stared, unflinching, into his eyes. "I meant that someone will have to disentangle Harold's daughter-in-law from our family's affairs. And by 'someone,' I mean me. *You* don't have to do anything, although you have somehow managed to screw that up once already. Which is, frankly, a level of stupidity I did not think was humanly possible. You need to come to terms with the fact that you are a buffoon. I promise you: the world will make a lot more sense to you once you do."

Something in Jeremy snapped. Colin saw it—a dilating of his eyes revealing that he was no longer in control of his actions. Filled with rage, Jeremy raised his hand across his face, poised to backhand Sadie. Colin heard Miguel gasp, but he was otherwise too shocked to move or act. Colin was also too surprised to intervene—he was powerless to do anything other than watch the unexpected drama.

Sadie was unmoved by the threat of violence. She stared hard at Jeremy, as if daring him to hit her. After a beat, Colin could see sanity slowly return to Jeremy's eyes, and he lowered his hand. He continued to glare at Sadie with unbridled hatred while he collected himself. Sadie's lips curved upward in a small smile as she watched Jeremy back down, but her eyes continued to stare daggers.

"Lowering your hand just now was the smartest thing you've ever done," Sadie said in a measured tone. She took her time collecting her purse from the couch before making her way to the front door. She opened it, as if to leave, before stopping to look over her shoulder at Jeremy. "But raising it to me in the first place was probably the dumbest," she added. Jeremy didn't respond. He looked down at the floor, fists clenched at his sides.

"I will take care of the daughter-in-law," Sadie said from the doorway. "You three can continue to do nothing. Please try not to screw that up." With that, Sadie departed, closing the door behind her.

No one moved until they heard Sadie's car start up and drive away. Even then, the trio of half-brothers was too shocked to speak. Jeremy returned to his seat in a daze and sat down with a thud. Colin glanced at Miguel, who looked horrified, although he didn't speak.

"I don't know why she seemed annoyed at me when she left," Colin finally said. "I don't see what *I* did to get under her skin."

Jeremy gave him a look but didn't say anything.

"That wasn't cool, Jeremy," Miguel said, finally finding his voice. He looked uncomfortable challenging his older brother. "You shouldn't have done that."

"Done what? I didn't do anything," Jeremy muttered.

"I hate this," Miguel said. He stood up and began pacing about, as if he was contemplating leaving himself. "I hate that we are conspiring against our own mother. I hate that we're turning against each other. It's not worth this. Nothing is worth this."

"Turning against each other?" Colin asked. He forced a chuckle. "I've seen you guys more since Mom got engaged than I have in the last three years. This has brought us together, believe it or not. It's not like we had this tight Brady Bunch unit to begin with."

"But that's the point!" Miguel pressed. "There's no reason we can't all be in each other's lives even without a conspiracy. Just think about how great it would be if we were all hanging out without this needless stress!"

"Easy for you to say," Colin said. "This is mostly *my* father's money we are talking about here. You're lucky you may get a piece of it at all. But you'll forgive me if I think these occasional hiccups are worth it to secure my father's legacy."

"Legacy?" Miguel shook his head. "Do you hear yourself?"

"She goaded me into it," Jeremy muttered. "Like she always does." It was unclear whether he had been listening to Colin and Miguel at all. Jeremy abruptly shook his head, as if it was an Etch-a-Sketch that he could clear away. "Well, this was a giant waste of time. Let's go, Miguel." He stormed out of the house before Colin or Miguel could respond, and, shortly thereafter, they heard Jeremy's engine roar to life.

"I guess I'm leaving as well," Miguel said drily. "Look, I don't want to fight with you. It's just—"

"Yeah," Colin said. "I get it. It's hard now, but it'll be worth it in the end. I promise."

Miguel shrugged, unconvinced. With a half-hearted wave, he also departed, leaving Colin alone in his house. He listened for Jeremy to pull away before looking around at his empty house, wondering what he should do with the remainder of his night. *May as well get some work in*, he thought.

With a sigh, Colin descended into his basement and powered up his Nintendo 64.

CHAPTER NINE

Saturday, September 7, 2019

Sam spent the morning puttering about her house. She was feeling a bit of cabin fever and was eager to get on with her day, but she had to wait for Marcie to get started. The two of them were supposed to meet at Sam's house at 11:00, and Marcie claimed she would shoot Sam a text when she was on her way. Sam glanced at her clock, which read 10:45, and hoped that Marcie had left without bothering to text her. *It's an hour drive*, Sam thought. *She can't possibly be* that *late.*

A moment later, Sam's phone vibrated. "Leaving now! So sorry for being late!" the text read. It was followed by a small army of heart and angel emojis, which Sam imagined must have taken Marcie some time to input.

Oh well. Sam plopped onto her couch. At least now she had a rough estimate for when Marcie would arrive.

Sam reckoned she finally had a handle on what was going on between Marcie and her children, although she remained unclear about how to proceed. Throughout the week, she'd pondered the issue, which appeared to be money. *I should've guessed that from the outset*, Sam thought. Although by no means rich herself, money wasn't something that Sam often worried about. Mike had taken out a substantial life insurance policy that paid out several times his annual salary in the event of his untimely demise. It was enough to allow Sam to pay off their mortgage, with some funds set aside. Her salary, as meager as it was in comparison to Mike's, was sufficient to cover the property tax and utilities, which allowed her to remain living in an area of Westchester that would otherwise have been unaffordable to her.

Even in death, he's looking out for me, Sam noted at one point, but she didn't allow the thought to take root—she knew it would lead to reopening wounds that still hadn't fully healed. She forced her attention back to the problem of Harold and Marcie.

Marcie is rich, but she seems genuinely indifferent about it, she thought. *The kids seem like they are generally well off, but that's not necessarily a deterrent to wanting more.*

Sam managed to decipher part of the problem at work earlier that week. She was in the midst of processing the financial ramifications of Harold marrying Marcie when Nick dropped a marked-up letter on her desk.

"Nice work," he said. "I only had to delete about twenty adverbs this time. Make those edits and get it out." He turned to leave, but Sam had a thought and spoke up.

"Hey, Nick," she said. "You're a lawyer, right?"

Nick frowned, confused.

"Well, yes. I mean, I graduated law school, and I am admitted to practice in New York, as well as in federal court in the Southern and Eastern Districts of New York, although my status is presently inactive since I am not currently practicing law. Why do you ask?" Sam rolled her eyes. *No need to check his diploma—that was as lawyerly a response as they get.*

"Can I ask you something quick?" she asked. Nick nodded.

"I'll help if I can. Of course, since I'm not practicing, you should not consider this legal advice, and you should independently obtain counsel to the extent—"

"Yes," Sam said, cutting him off. "I understand the fine print. My question is: What happens to a person's money if they get married? Does that automatically become both of their property?" Those questions had never come up in the course of Sam's own marriage.

Nick rubbed his chin, deep in thought.

"Now, granted, my specialty isn't matrimonial law, and—" He stopped himself at Sam's impatient look. "From what I understand from law school, whatever a person brings into a marriage is considered separate property, although once they are married, anything the couple acquires is presumed to be marital property. I guess there can be disputes about whether certain property is separate or jointly owned, so it may make sense in some cases to avoid a fight down the road with a prenuptial agreement, or even a postnuptial agreement. Now what happens to that property if they get divorced, or if one of them dies . . . that's a more complicated question. Why do you ask?"

Sam ignored the question and thought hard. *If Harold and Marcie marry, her wealth wouldn't automatically transfer to Harold. But if Marcie's kids are still afraid of that possibility, maybe they can be placated with a prenup. Is that the answer? Would a prenup satisfy Marcie's brood and get them to stop meddling?* Granted, Sam was not certain whether Marcie and Harold would agree to such an arrangement, but it was a possibility worth exploring.

"Can a prenup just state that each spouse keeps what they bring into the marriage?" she asked.

"I don't see why not. I think it can be tailored to almost any arrangement that the couple agrees to. You will sometimes see them invalidated for various reasons, but it's a fairly common practice nowadays. Are you thinking of getting remarried?"

Sam frowned again, as she continued to work through the problem of Marcie's family. Nick misunderstood her look and started to look a bit panicked.

"That's none of my business, of course! I am sorry I asked; I was just trying to get some context to help you."

Sam waved off his concerns.

"No, no. It's fine." She paused. "Thank you. I think this was helpful."

Nick wandered away at that point, left to puzzle how he had managed to be of assistance. But Sam was starting to get an inkling of what she had to do—a path to a resolution that would leave all interested parties satisfied.

If they all went along with it.

Sam continued to think through the problem that Saturday as she waited for Marcie to drive from Long Island to her home. But soon after receiving Marcie's text announcing her departure, Sam's phone buzzed again and, after checking to see who was calling, Sam answered.

"What's up, Harold?" Sam asked into her phone.

"Sam?" Harold's voice, sounding like he was on speaker. "Wow! I'm glad to know that you didn't give me a fake number!"

"You must've caught me in a moment of weakness," Sam said. "What's going on? Marcie left, right?"

"Yes. She just left. She's a very good driver. Hates driving at night though, which is why I have to be her chauffeur now and then. So you better make sure she leaves well before sundown! I don't want to have to drive up to Westchester to rescue her later."

"Will do." Harold didn't immediately respond, and Sam checked her phone to see if they'd been disconnected.

"Look," Harold finally said, "It's hard to talk to you sometimes with Marcie around. But I wanted to thank you for what you did. Marcie told me that Colin was being weird about the wedding, and that you straightened her out. I appreciate it immensely. This whole wedding thing means a lot to her. Me too, of course. But she's particularly excited about it."

"Sure, no problem."

"I don't know what's up with Colin. He and I get along so well, and now he's getting anxious about a wedding? Ah, well, it doesn't matter. Marcie loves her kids, but she's always erred on the side of spoiling them. I'm glad you talked some sense into her."

"Yeah, about that . . ." Sam hesitated. She hadn't quite figured out what she wanted to tell Harold, but this was as good a time as any. "I know Colin said that he didn't want a new father figure in his life, but, well, I think it may be about something else. Marcie told me about the money."

"She did?"

"I mean, not in any great detail. Just enough to know that there's a lot of it there. And I think the reason Colin and, as far as I can see, the others, are against this wedding is because they are afraid they will lose out on the money somehow."

"Oh, that's ridiculous!" Harold said, indignant. "Are you suggesting that I'm marrying her for money?"

"No!" Sam collected herself. "I just think that it's possible that Marcie's kids don't want to see the two of you married because they're afraid that Marcie's wealth will end up with you."

There was a long pause. Sam checked her phone once again to make sure the connection wasn't lost.

"Marcie's kids are all very secure financially," Harold finally said in a low voice. "It's hard for me to imagine that they would put greed above their mother's happiness. But it's all moot, in any case."

"Moot? What do you mean?"

"This is really none of your business, but"—Harold paused—"Marcie and I have a prenuptial agreement in place, to ensure that all of our individual assets stay ours, even after we are married."

"A prenup? Why do you—Do the kids know about it?"

"I don't know what Marcie told them in that regard. I'd be surprised if she had mentioned it to them, though. The arrangement is something she wanted to do, so we got it taken care of shortly after we got engaged. Ok?"

"Yeah, ok. Got it." Sam was surprised to hear that Marcie had pushed for a prenup. *Maybe she's not so indifferent to her finances after all*, she thought.

"Good." Harold let out a long exhale. "Anyway, can you do me a favor and not mention any of this to Marcie? She'd be heartbroken if she thought you even suspected her children were trying to manipulate her for money. And she's always uncomfortable discussing that kind of stuff anyway."

"Yeah," Sam said. "I won't say anything to her."

"Great. Thank you. Well, you two have a fun day, alright? What are you up to, anyway?"

"We're going to drive up to Woodstock together and take a picture of a book I just finished reading," Sam said. Harold was quiet as he digested that.

"Sounds like a hoot," he finally said. Harold was laughing as he ended the call.

"Well, she kind of invited herself," Sam muttered defensively as she put her phone back on the coffee table.

• • • • •

Marcie arrived a little over half an hour later. Sam met her out front, and Marcie let loose a litany of apologies.

"I'm so sorry, I have no excuse, I simply lost track of time."

"It's fine," Sam assured her. "We're taking a picture of a book, not seeing a Broadway show. Woodstock will wait for us."

Marcie looked grateful as Sam led her to her own car, which she'd cleaned out in anticipation of the minor road trip.

"This is so exciting!" Marcie squealed as she buckled her seatbelt.

Is it? Sam wondered. It was something to do, at least. She drove off and started the hour-plus journey to the northwest.

They rode largely in silence, with Marcie taking in all the surrounding trees, still lush and green despite the threat of autumn on the horizon.

"I forgot how beautiful it can get up here," she whispered at one point, nearly to herself.

"You grew up in this area, right?" Sam asked. Marcie nodded.

"Yes. About twenty minutes from Woodstock. Perhaps we can swing by after, if there's time? I'd love to see my old neighborhood."

"Of course," Sam said. "I have nothing but time."

"It's funny." Marcie slouched down slightly to get a better view of the wooded mountains to the left. "I grew up here, but it took a fair amount of traveling as an adult before I could really appreciate that this is one of the most beautiful spots on earth. I suppose familiarity does tend to breed contempt, not that I ever held real contempt for this area. Still, seeing a good amount of the world certainly helped me to look at the Hudson Valley with a renewed perspective."

"It is beautiful here," Sam agreed. She stole a glance to her left, trying to see the scenery through Marcie's eyes. Marcie resumed looking out her own window, occasionally remarking on a landmark that she remembered from her childhood or a new feature of the landscape that caught her eye.

"I've been thinking a lot about what you said last week," Sam finally said during a lull. "About me being afraid of death?"

"Hmmmm?" Marcie continued to look at the forest lining the road in wonder.

"I didn't know what you meant at first. But then I remembered something that happened at work about six months after Mike died. Someone circulated an email about this puppy who needed a new owner. I think a woman got the dog, and their kid was allergic to it—anyway, it doesn't matter. The email included a picture of this adorable black-and-white puppy. It may have been part dalmatian. And I thought to myself: *I could use another soul around the house right now. Maybe I should step up and get him.*"

Sam glanced in her periphery. Marcie had stopped looking out the window and was listening intently to what Sam was saying.

"I was on the verge of responding to that email to say I was interested, but I didn't. Instead, I did an online search for the life expectancy of a mixed-breed dog. It was something like thirteen years. I did the math, and I imagined the pain I would undoubtedly have to go through around the time I turned fifty myself. In a best-case scenario, that is; it could have been sooner. And I decided against it." Sam paused. "Someone else ended up taking the dog, so he's ok, at least."

"Oh, Sam. You were still grieving. Trying to make sense of it all."

"Sure. I guess." Sam noticed movement up ahead—two deer milling about by the side of the road—and slowed the car until the deer were safely behind them.

"But even now," Sam added, "I look back at my time with Mike, and I can't help but wonder if it was worth it. Four years of happiness measured against whatever I am now. And presumably will be going forward. Whatever that is." At Marcie's look, Sam added, "Even if I fall short of being entirely broken."

Marcie turned to face Sam, who was thankful she had the excuse of watching the road to avoid that eye contact.

"Of course it was worth it, Sam," she said, her voice heavy with understanding. "You wouldn't be hurting so badly now if it wasn't."

As Sam was about to respond, she noticed a sign for Woodstock. She made a quick right onto a less populated road.

"I called it a fear of death," Marcie continued. "But maybe it's more accurate to call it a fear of life. When you embrace life, you're opening yourself up to everything. Joy. Pain. Love. Sorrow. You have to take the good with the bad, unfortunately. But I promise you: the good will ultimately outweigh the bad."

"Right," Sam said without conviction. Marcie's look suggested that she knew she was being placated, but she didn't press the issue. "Just a few more miles," Sam said, and Marcie squealed with excitement.

Minutes later, they turned onto Mill Hill Road, which would lead them into the town of Woodstock. Marcie stared, amazed, as they made their way down the narrow road lined with small quirky stores and restaurants.

"It's so much more built up than the last time I was here," Marcie marveled. Sam pulled onto a side street and found a place to park.

"I have no real agenda," Sam told Marcie. "I can take my dopey photo anywhere. So, if there's anything in particular you want to check out . . ."

"Oh, I'm happy just to be here and feel the energy. And don't you dare call your photo dopey! I think it is a wonderful hobby you've stumbled upon!"

Leaving the car, the two of them walked into the heart of the village. Almost immediately, Marcie spotted a tea store and stopped to gaze through the window. Sam noticed a young woman inside, looking puzzled at the sight of Marcie fogging up the glass with her breath.

"We can go inside if you want," Sam asked, feeling mildly embarrassed.

"I'm just window shopping. I'm sure they don't mind."

A minute or two later, Marcie pried herself away from the window and they resumed their walk. But they only made it another half of a block before Marcie stopped again, this time to stare at a restaurant. A sign on the door identified it as The Peach Grove.

"I used to eat here all the time!" she exclaimed. She looked up at a tall oak tree above them. "I used to always ask for a seat by that window." She pointed to a window on the second floor of the establishment. "You have the most amazing view of the tree from there." Marcie looked around and spotted a t-shirt in the window that was displayed for sale. "Maybe I should buy a shirt in remembrance of my time here?"

Sam took a closer look at the pink shirt, which read "The Peach Grove," with an unidentifiable emblem. The back of the shirt said "Juicy. Succulent. Raw."

"I think that shirt may have a sexual connotation," Sam said in a cautious tone. Marcie leaned in for a closer look and laughed.

"Oh, my! Yes, I see it now. I suppose I would look somewhat silly in that!"

They continued down the street. A fork in the road marked the heart of the town, which was bustling. A significant amount of the foot traffic was clearly tourists, but a sizable portion of the crowd represented real Woodstock. Or, at least, people going through the effort of emulating what they considered to be "real" Woodstock: An older man with a gray ponytail played a mandolin, with a woman in a vintage dress singing in a shrill tone at his side. Another woman simply danced in front of them, paying no attention to the traffic she was disrupting on the sidewalk. A young man, with a gray cat lazily lounging on his shoulder, gently stepped around the dancer and made his way to a restaurant a few buildings down the road. Across the street, a half-dozen protesters held up signs painted with peace symbols and hearts as they chanted against unspecified military action.

"How wonderful that they are so passionate about their cause!" Marcie said, pausing to take in the commotion. Sam shrugged.

"I don't know how many minds they are going to change, protesting here. Seems like they're preaching to the choir to me. But anyway, this is as 'Woodstock' as I think I'm going to get. Would you mind helping me with this picture?"

Marcie was, in fact, delighted to assist. After Sam showed Marcie how to operate the camera on her phone, she dug out the book she was going to review from her backpack and held it aloft, trying to catch as much of the Woodstock chaos behind her as she could. Marcie took her time in finding the perfect angle, to the point where Sam started to feel a bit moronic at holding up her book in a Statue of Liberty pose in the midst of a crowd. But Woodstock had set the bar for weirdness too high, and no one paid her any mind.

Marcie finally took the picture and handed the phone back to Sam.

"I hope it's ok," Marcie said, sounding nervous.

"I'm sure it's fine," Sam said. But after she pulled up the picture, she handed the phone back to Marcie.

"Would you mind taking another?"

"Why? Is something wrong?" Marcie looked chagrined.

"No, it's a good picture. You just got my face in it."

"Of course! It's a beautiful face!"

"Well, thanks. But I tend to keep my face out of these book shots. Sorry, I should have mentioned that before."

"I think your face would only enhance the shot, and I have no doubt your audience would love to see it." But Marcie, with some reluctance, took the phone and snapped another picture, this time focused on the novel.

"Better?" Marcie asked, handing the phone back. Sam looked at the picture—the book was in focus, perfectly centered, flanked by the colorful energy of Woodstock in the background.

"Well, you got a little bit too much of my wrist in this one," Sam said, eyes twinkling. Marcie, with a playful gasp, placed her hand over her heart and adopted a shocked face.

"I'm just kidding." Sam laughed at Marcie's exaggerated relief. "It's perfect. Thank you."

They walked around the town a bit more, but there wasn't much ground to cover. Marcie seemed more interested in feeling the energy on the street than exploring any of the quirky shops, so after wandering for about half an hour, they were back at the car.

"That was lovely!" Marcie said. "I mentioned earlier, if you still have some time, would it be possible to swing by where I grew up?"

"Sure thing."

As they drove, Marcie gave Sam point-by-point directions to get to the Kingston-Rhinecliff Bridge, which was a mile-and-a-half bridge that took them east over the Hudson River into Dutchess County. From there, it was just a few minutes to the town of Red Hook. Marcie navigated Sam through some back roads and then finally directed her to park on a residential street. Marcie hopped out of the car and spun around, taking it all in.

"This area has been built up so much," she marveled. "There was hardly anything here when I grew up."

Sam looked around. The area seemed anything but "built up." Large houses, sitting at varying elevations, were scattered along the street, with small wooded areas serving as effective boundaries between the properties. Marcie pointed at one house on a hill, sitting in front of a forested area.

"That was my house, until I moved out to live with Barry some forty years ago," Marcie said. "That's what brought me to Long Island, where I've been since."

"Are you ever tempted to move back here?" Sam asked. Marcie shook her head.

"No. Not really. All of my children are down there. Still, it is wonderful to be here again, if only for a short visit. Anyway, my old home isn't what I want to show you. Come."

Marcie took off down the street. There were no sidewalks, but the road was wide enough to allow them to walk comfortably side by side without fear of passing cars. Marcie led Sam to a small stone bridge, perhaps fifteen feet wide, spanning a stream. With a pleased exhale, Marcie walked to the midpoint of the bridge and rested her arms on the thick stone walls. Sam, following her lead, adopted the same position next to her. Below, a shallow creek bubbled around several protruding rocks. Trees on both sides of the rivulet leaned toward each other, creating the illusion of a leafy tunnel that absorbed the waterway as it meandered to the northwest.

"Ah, this is the view I remember. There are more houses here, to be sure, but this creek—and this bridge—hasn't changed. I used to always come here to clear my mind when it got too cluttered. Meditation before I even knew what that was. Isn't it peaceful?"

It is, Sam thought. The gentle waters generated pleasant white nose that made it effortless to clear her mind. The old stone bridge, coupled with the view of the stream winding its way deeper into the forest, reminded Sam of a song from her childhood that seemed outdated even in her youth. *Over the river and through the woods, to grandmother's house we go . . .*

"Don't get me wrong, I love Long Island," Marcie said. "Long Island has its own beauty. The beaches. The marshes. The hills of the north shore sitting over the Sound. But I can feel that beauty fade over time, with all the development taking place there. It's a shame we have to drive so far to find relatively untouched creeks and forests."

"Did you come to this bridge a lot as a kid?" Sam asked. Marcie nodded.

"Oh yes. I made a point of coming here every day, if only for a few minutes. I would stare at this creek and imagine it running to the Hudson

River, which, in turn, connects to the Atlantic. And from there, you're connected to the rest of the globe. Standing here always made me appreciate my connection to this planet and all of the creatures upon it. In fact, a lifelong wish of mine, for after I die, is to have my ashes deposited right here, so that they can be taken downstream and spread out across the world." Marcie paused, before adding thoughtfully, "I really do need to let Harold know about that at some point."

Sam found it hard to imagine Harold carrying out those wishes. The long commute, in and of itself, would be a major deterrent for him. *He would probably just drop the ashes off at the closest beach and consider it good enough.*

"Unless he goes before you," Sam noted, and Marcie laughed.

"Oh, he told me that when he dies, he wants to be stuffed and mounted in my den so I'll never forget him. Always the kidder!"

They resumed watching the water. The view never got boring to Sam—the sun darting through the trees of the forest, coupled with the bubbling water, maintained an unpredictable pattern of light dancing across the surface of the creek that continued to stimulate Sam no matter how long she stared. Marcie, too, seemed like she could happily remain there all afternoon.

Their moment of tranquility was interrupted by a random ringing. Marcie blinked in confusion before digging in her bag to pull out a cellphone. She glanced at it and murmured to Sam, "It's Miguel."

The normal one, Sam thought. She started to move away to give Marcie some privacy, but Marcie waved for her to come back.

"Hello, Miguel, is everything alright? Just calling to say hi? Well, I am up in Red Hook with Sam, so . . . Oh, how far away are you? Just a second." Marcie covered the phone with her hand and turned to Sam. "Miguel and his friend are apparently on their way to Rhinebeck, which is about ten minutes from here. I had no idea they were coming up this way. Would we be able to swing by and say hi real quick?"

Sam gave her a tight thumbs up. She was in no rush to get home.

"Yes, we will see you there in a few minutes," Marcie said into her phone. "I am so looking forward to it!" Hanging up, Marcie beamed at Sam. "Thank you so much, Sam. I am so sorry to have hijacked your day, but I am having a wonderful time. And as I mentioned to you, I fear my children are getting further and further away from me as they get older, so when one of them reaches out to me—"

"Really, it's fine," Sam said. "I'm having fun." And she meant it.

Rhinebeck was, as advertised, only a short drive away. Sam found a municipal lot in the village and parked.

"Are we supposed to meet them anywhere in particular?" Sam asked. Marcie was about to respond, but her face lit up at seeing something over Sam's shoulder.

"Miguel!" she cried, striding past Sam. Sam turned and spotted Miguel, looking much the same as he had at the barbeque a few weeks earlier, walking toward his mom with his arms outstretched. Marcie caught him in a fierce embrace and didn't let go. Sam wanted to laugh at Miguel's trapped expression—she imagined it was much the same as hers when she found herself caught in one of Marcie's inescapable hugs.

Miguel finally managed to pry Marcie off.

"Good to see you, Mom," he said. He spotted Sam and waved. "You too, Sam. Sorry to intrude on your day. We had no idea you were coming up here today." The reference to "we" reminded Sam that Miguel was not alone. She looked around, which Miguel noticed.

"Oh. Right." He waved at another man, slender and blonde, who was lurking a few cars away in the parking lot, and the man shuffled toward them. "This is Kevin. He's—" Miguel trailed off, and Kevin, crossing his arms, looked thoughtful at Miguel's hesitation. But Marcie saved Miguel as she lunged forward to hug an unprepared Kevin.

"Kevin!" she said from her embrace. "It is wonderful to meet you! I want to know everything about you." She ended the hug but held onto Kevin's arm tightly. "Come. Let us walk a bit and get to know each other."

Marcie dragged Kevin out of the lot toward the sidewalk as Kevin looked back with pleading eyes. Miguel, in return, gave him a small helpless shrug.

"I guess we should follow them?" Sam asked.

"I suppose so," Miguel replied.

• • • • •

Miguel fell in comfortably beside Sam as his mother marched down the street with Kevin. He could see her chatting without pausing for breath, but he couldn't make out what she was saying over the noise on the street. *Kevin is a cool customer*, he thought. *He can handle Mom.*

"It's nice to see you again," Sam said. "You and Kevin are a cute couple. If that's what you are?"

"I guess we are? I don't know. We're kind of in that relationship gray zone. I like him, though. Are you and Mom having fun?"

"For sure," she said. "Her enthusiasm for life is a bit infectious."

"It can be. Although some are immune. I always enjoy seeing her, though. She has turned around plenty of my crappy moods. Or at least made them slightly less crappy."

Miguel thought of his siblings, who would often roll their eyes at their mother's colorful antics. Their cynicism was at its worst when they were together in a group, which suggested to him that any annoyance they felt toward their mother was more performative than anything.

"While we have a minute alone, I'd like to tell you something," Miguel said. Sam seemed to sense that the conversation was turning serious and gave him her full attention.

"I don't fully understand how, but you've apparently managed to get under my sister Sadie's skin," Miguel said.

Sam let out a small laugh.

"That's ridiculous! I've literally never even spoken to her," she said. Up ahead, Marcie and a helpless Kevin turned a corner, so Sam and Miguel accelerated their pace to keep up.

"I'm not saying it makes sense. But it's true, nonetheless." He assessed that Sam wasn't overly concerned.

"Well, I'll be sure to file this away in my *Tough Shit, Sadie* drawer," she said. Miguel remained serious.

"You don't understand. Sadie has a way of breaking people who get in her way. I can't even describe it. She will just analyze them like a puzzle, find the weak spots, and poke away until she gets what she wants. I've seen her do it since I was a little kid. Hell, she's done it to me when it suits her."

"She sounds like a lovely person, Miguel," Sam said.

"She can be," Miguel insisted. It sounded weak in his own ears. Of course, *anyone* could be a lovely person, if it suited them. "I mean, she's not perfect, but she's the only sister I have. If I paid too much attention to my siblings' faults, I wouldn't have any family at all." Sam arched an eyebrow, and Miguel was left with the impression that she thought he might be better off without his siblings.

"What are their faults?" was all she asked, and Miguel gave the question some thought.

"They can be self-absorbed," he finally said.

"How so?" Sam asked. "Not that I disagree with you."

"Here's an example," Miguel said. "A few years ago, I decided to come out to my family at Thanksgiving. I suspected some of them already knew. I'm sure Sadie did, at least. But it wasn't anything we ever discussed amongst ourselves." Up ahead, Marcie and Kevin had stopped to look through the glass window of a vintage toy shop. Miguel and Sam stopped a few yards behind so they could continue to speak privately. "I spent the week leading up to that Thanksgiving psyching myself up to do it. That particular holiday was just the five of us: me, Mom, Jeremy, Colin, and Sadie. No spouses or girlfriends around for that one. Mom, of course, insisted on saying grace before the meal, and before we could all dive in, I told everyone I had an announcement to make. And I told my family I was gay. Can you guess how they reacted?"

Sam shook her head.

"Indifference. Maybe a scattered 'cool' or 'congrats,' but that was it. They otherwise just jumped into the meal."

"Surely not your mom!" Sam said in disbelief.

"Well, no," Miguel conceded. "Not her. She jumped up and ran over to give me a giant hug, with tears streaming down her face. But, in all honesty, she probably would have done the same if I had announced I was taking up racquetball." Sam barked a laugh and then looked a bit guilty about it.

Miguel chuckled to let her know she hadn't offended him before growing serious again.

"But no: I have no issue with my Mom's reaction. I was disappointed in my siblings, though. All week, I mentally played out how it might go. Massive acceptance? Open mockery? Would they start arguing amongst each other, taking different sides? I ran through all of those scenarios, and I thought I was ready to deal with anything they threw at me. But I was entirely unprepared for what ultimately happened: complete apathy. It was almost worse than if they had reacted negatively."

Miguel collected himself and shrugged. He had not told that story to anyone, not even Kevin. He was surprised that it still had the power to hurt him. Sam placed a hand on Miguel's shoulder in sympathy before continuing to walk. When she spoke again, Miguel could detect the anger in Sam's voice.

"That all brings me back to the question of why you seem to be carrying so much water for your siblings," Sam said. "Do they actually deserve it?" Miguel didn't hesitate in nodding.

"I see the good in them," Miguel said. "It's hard at times, but it's there. And like I said, they're my family. I didn't get to choose them, but I'm not going to take them for granted. Even if they don't always return the favor."

While Miguel and Sam spoke, Marcie and Kevin had managed to get out fairly far ahead of them. Through a small crowd on the sidewalk, Miguel could make out his mother and Kevin turning around to walk back toward them, having reached the end of town.

"But I digress," Miguel said quickly, trying to wrap things up while he could still speak with Sam alone. "All I'm saying is you should be careful of Sadie. Try to figure out whatever it is you did to piss her off and stop it."

"God," Sam said, laughing. "You talk as if she's going to have me killed!"

Miguel thought it over.

"No," he said. "I think the odds of her murdering you are pretty low."

"Pretty low?"

"She's . . . tough. She enjoys the sport of conflict. And getting her own way."

"Some people say I can be tough, too," Sam said. Miguel appraised her, thoughtful.

"I don't doubt it," he conceded. "But Sadie is also something I don't think you are."

"What's that?" Sam asked quickly. Marcie and Kevin were on the verge of returning to them, so Miguel mouthed his response to avoid being overheard:

Ruthless.

• • • •

They spent more time walking around the village as a quartet, stopping for coffees (and one tea) that they carried around in to-go cups. After another round of walking up and down the same main street again, Marcie finally stopped, and the others followed her lead.

"Well, it was lovely to see you, Miguel. I certainly don't want to intrude on your day any more than we already have. And it was a pleasure to meet you, Kevin!" Marcie turned toward Miguel. "Did you know that he plays the guitar? I asked if he would play for me one day, and he said he would!" Sam thought Kevin looked a bit grumpy at the thought of performing for Marcie.

"Thanks, Mom," Miguel said. "And yes. Kevin is very talented. For what it's worth, I play the guitar, too."

"And amazingly so! What a talented couple the two of you make!"

They worked through all the permutations of goodbye hugs before Miguel and Kevin wandered off to find a place to have dinner. Sam and Marcie went back to the parking lot and found Sam's car.

"What an amazing day that was!" Marcie said, closing her eyes as she settled into the passenger's seat.

"It was fun," Sam agreed as she started up the engine. She glanced at Marcie, who looked exhausted. "Are you going to be ok to drive home? We still have a few hours of sunlight, but you look pretty beat."

"Oh, I'll be fine dear, if you don't mind me resting my eyes for a spell."

Sam pulled out of the lot and started the hour-plus drive home. Marcie sat with her eyes closed, wearing a small smile on her face. Sam wondered if she was sleeping and having a pleasant dream.

"Do you have any thoughts on the wedding?" Marcie asked out of nowhere. Sam jumped in her seat and looked at Marcie, whose eyes remained closed.

"What do you mean?"

"I just mean the details and logistics of the wedding. Frankly, I'm not interested in all the planning that goes into a big ceremony. I would just like to get together and celebrate with my family."

"Hmmmmm." Sam thought about it. "Have you considered a destination wedding?" Marcie's eyes opened.

"A destination wedding? What do you mean?"

"You know, just visit somewhere you've always wanted to go, invite a handful of people, have a quick ceremony, and just enjoy yourself. Is there anywhere on the globe you're itching to get to?"

Marcie closed her eyes again, deep in thought.

"Did you know that more than half of the people who live in Iceland believe in elves? I read that somewhere and never forgot it. Every now and then, I will read a story about some road or tunnel they had planned to build in Iceland, only to have those plans altered because they interfered with the local elf and fairy community. It's wonderful how respectful they are of others, don't you think? I always imagined Iceland as one of the last places on earth where nature is allowed and encouraged to truly thrive." Marcie fell silent.

"So, are you saying you'd like to get married in Iceland?" Sam asked. Marcie opened her eyes and blinked.

"Oh, yes. It would be quite an experience, don't you think? A lot of our friends probably wouldn't be able to make it, although I would be perfectly content to have a small wedding with just you and the rest of the family. I'll have to discuss it with Harold, of course, but I just know he'll be open to it. I'd love to do it soon, though. There's nothing to be gained by delaying this. Do you think we can manage to have an Icelandic wedding within the next month or so?"

"I don't see why not, if you keep it small enough," Sam said. Marcie clapped her hands together and let out a little squeal.

"I'm so excited! To think that all of our family could be together in Iceland to celebrate our wedding in a matter of weeks. I—I have no words!"

"That sounds like a wonderful plan, Marcie."

"So you would come?" Marcie asked. She froze, bracing for rejection.

"Of course. I would be honored." Sam realized that she meant it, too. Marcie squealed again, and then grew still, as if remembering something.

"Oh, but before the wedding, there is one other thing I wanted to ask of you. I feel a bit uncomfortable making this request, after all that you have done for me, but . . ."

CHAPTER TEN

Tuesday, September 24, 2019

"A bachelorette party?" Sadie asked in disbelief.

"Oh, no! Certainly not a bachelorette party," her mother responded.

They were sitting together at a small table on the sidewalk outside a café near Sadie's home. For the past few weeks, Marcie had been reaching out to Sadie to inquire about spending some time together. Sadie received another such call the prior day, but, for the first time in her adult life, she had not been pressured by Marcie to come to an angel reading, or a meditation, or any of Marcie's other passions that were of no interest to Sadie. Instead, Marcie made it clear that she wanted to do something in Sadie's world. Sadie was thrown off by the ask—she had no intention of taking her sixty-six-year-old mother to a Pilates class—but she found it difficult to reject such an open-ended request to spend time together. In the end, Sadie suggested that they just meet for coffee and chat.

"I certainly do not consider myself to be a bachelorette," Marcie added as she sipped her green tea. "But I would enjoy an opportunity for some of us girls to get together before the big day. A weekend getaway is all. My friend Doris already said she is interested in coming, and I spoke with Sam a few days ago, and she said she would come. Now, granted, it is a weekend of quiet meditation, which may not be your thing, but it really would mean the world to me if—"

"Sam is going?" Sadie interrupted.

"Yes. It is very kind of her. I don't know how interested she actually is in this, but I appreciate her keeping an open mind to humor me. But that being said, I know you don't always care for my 'hippy dippy' stuff, so please don't feel obligated . . ."

Sadie thought hard as her mother continued to speak. She knew she would have to deal with Sam face-to-face sooner than later, but she felt unprepared to do so just yet. Still, she had a meeting with Raymond Lawrence later that morning to go over the results of his investigation, which could change her perspective.

"I don't know," Sadie said once her mother had finished speaking. "I will have to check my calendar and get back to you." Sadie thought that left her sufficient flexibility to go or not go, depending on what she learned from her private investigator. Marcie seemed mildly disappointed by Sadie's failure to commit, but she tried to hide it with a smile.

"Well, thank you," Marcie said. "I know you are very busy, and it is late notice, so I will certainly understand if it is just not doable for you."

A few minutes later, Marcie finished her drink and Sadie took the last sip of her iced coffee, and they said their goodbyes. Sadie watched her mother return to her car and drive off, and only after she was out of sight did Sadie head to her own vehicle. She glanced at the clock and calculated that if she went straight to Ray's office, she should arrive twenty-five minutes early for their ten o'clock meeting. Long Island traffic being what it was, though, Sadie ended up making it to the parking lot a mere two minutes before the scheduled start time. She had hoped for more time to collect herself and get into the mindset of the character she had created at her initial meeting, but she felt less pressure to deliver an artful performance now that the work was completed and paid for. After she exited the car, Sadie walked into the building with as much speed as she could afford without looking undignified.

Inside, the office was once again empty except for Ray Lawrence himself, sitting at his desk at the back of the room. Ray looked up from his computer and quickly waved Sadie over before turning back to his work. Sadie was mildly annoyed at the lack of a personal greeting, but she followed his cue and took a seat in front of his desk. After a moment, Ray clicked his mouse with a flourish and a printer behind him came to life. Ray handed the printouts to Sadie, who noted with a glance they were two documents titled "Investigative Report." One appeared to be for Harold, the other for Sam.

"Hello Ms. Porter," Ray said to Sadie. "It is great to see you again. Thank you for coming in." Sadie nodded, impatient to get to the heart of the matter.

"I completed my assignment, which is summarized there." Ray nodded toward the papers in Sadie's hands. "I thought it might be helpful to have a conversation about what I found and answer any questions you may have. But first, please let me know if there have been any developments on your end."

Sadie adopted a slight frown.

"Nothing of note, although I am glad that you have wrapped your work so quickly, as the wedding is now scheduled to take place in about a week and a half. In Iceland, of all places. So, time is now truly of the essence."

Ray nodded in understanding.

"Well, to be clear, I am not a mind reader, and I can't tell you what is going on in the head of Harold Lindgren or Sam Daly. But I will share with you what I've learned. My investigation consisted of reviewing publicly available databases, some interviews I conducted as part of a standard background check, and even some information I obtained in going through their trash."

Sadie gasped. "Is that legal? Or ethical?" She truly did not give a shit either way, but it seemed like an appropriate thing to ask.

"Once your garbage is off your property for pickup, it is fair game legally. As far as ethically?" Ray shrugged. "That's more of a question for a philosopher, I suppose. Digging through trash like a raccoon isn't my favorite part of the job, I'll tell you that much. But it's amazing what you can learn about someone by going through their debris."

"Fair enough," Sadie said. Ray cleared his throat and looked at his computer monitor.

"Alright. Let's start with Harold Lindgren. Sixty-eight years old, recently retired. His wife—Carol—was killed in a car crash, along with their son Michael, in the evening of May 14, 2017. Happy Mother's Day." Ray paused, skimming his monitor. "But you know all this, I'm sure. The long and short of it is there is not much that I would deem to be noteworthy with regard to Lindgren. No criminal convictions, no large debts I can see. His former co-workers all swore up and down that he is a great guy. He golfs a lot—every Monday and Wednesday, as far as I can tell. There is only one thing I found that may or may not be significant."

Sadie leaned forward. She had not truly been expecting Lawrence to come up with any significant dirt on Harold, so she was curious what he found that he considered noteworthy.

"The title of your mother's home was transferred to Lindgren last week." Ray leaned back in his chair and exhaled. "I honestly cannot tell you what that means. I can think of a few reasons they might want to transfer that property before their wedding, but I admit that would be pure speculation on my part."

Sadie, a prominent real estate agent on Long Island's affluent north shore, had her own thoughts as well. She knew from her own experience that home ownership was a point of pride for many men, particularly those from Harold's generation. She also knew that Harold intended to sell his own home and move in with her mother after the wedding. *The thought of living in a home that his wife owned undoubtedly irked him to no end*, Sadie thought. *He probably couldn't even handle being a mere co-owner. I'm sure Mother agreed to transfer the title just to appease him.* In the end, it did not greatly concern her. Her mother's house was modest, and although it had worth simply because of Long Island's lucrative real estate market, the value of the home was still a drop in the bucket compared to the entirety of her mother's estate.

"I don't know what that means either," Sadie said aloud, playing dumb. "I will have to reflect upon that. Did you spot anything of concern with regard to Sam?"

Ray shook his head. "No smoking guns, if that's what you mean. As I just mentioned, her husband died about two-and-a-half years ago. From the information I've gathered, it seems she has been largely reclusive since then. Like you mentioned in our first meeting, any contact she had with Harold Lindgren for most of those years was nominal, at most, so if they have renewed a relationship in the past few weeks, I agree that would be somewhat suspicious. There is something else."

"Oh?" Sadie tried to hide her irritation at Ray's dramatic pause.

"I was able to get my hands on some of Sam Daly's bank records, which she tossed in the garbage without shredding," Ray said. "It seems like she is well off financially, even if she falls short of what I personally consider to be wealthy. The mortgage on her home was also paid off completely in the past two years. I believe that she is probably making a five-figure salary as a claims adjuster. Low six-figures, tops. Not enough, in and of itself, to account for her current financial state."

Sadie cocked her head, inquisitive. "Where do you think those funds came from?" she asked.

"Two likely sources," Ray said. He had clearly given the matter some thought. "First, her husband was a partner at a very prestigious accounting firm. It stands to reason that he would have had a sizable life insurance policy, of which Sam Daly would almost certainly be the primary beneficiary. That would have easily given her adequate funds to pay off a $500,000 mortgage." Sadie nodded slowly. *It makes sense*, she thought.

"What else?" she asked.

"She also brought a lawsuit against the estate of the guy who killed her husband and Lindgren's wife. The estate was sued because the drunk driver died himself in the accident. Looks like it settled within a few months, but the terms of that settlement appear to be confidential. I assume an insurance company somewhere paid out a pretty penny to make that litigation go away."

Interesting, Sadie thought. She needed time to process this information, but she already could imagine how it could be useful.

"Did Harold also bring a wrongful death action?" she asked.

"No," Ray said. "He didn't. I suppose he could have, although I suspect it would not have been nearly as valuable as the suit commenced by Sam Daly, given her husband's young age and future earnings potential."

"Thank you," Sadie said. "This has all been very enlightening. I'll have to reflect on what you said, and obviously discuss the matter with my siblings." Sadie had no intention of doing the latter, but it seemed like a reasonable thing to say.

"Of course. And a more detailed account of my investigation is in the papers I gave you."

"I can't thank you enough," Sadie said. "I've felt very helpless these past few weeks. It's been a tremendous comfort having a professional conduct some due diligence and help protect my Mom."

"It's been my pleasure, Ms. Porter."

Sadie shook his hand and exited the office. As she walked back to her car, she took stock of the ammunition she had gathered. She had already conducted her own impromptu psych evaluation of Sam Daly a few weeks earlier at the wedding announcement when she surveilled Sam's interactions with her brothers from a comfortable distance. Above all else, Sam struck Sadie as being tough and proud, either of which could be a strength or a weakness, depending on the circumstances. Sadie knew she could ensure they would become Sam's kryptonite.

As for the additional information she had obtained from Ray Lawrence, Sadie suspected that it would be more than sufficient for her purposes. Granted, Sadie wanted to take her time in deciding how to best utilize those newly acquired bullets. *I can work out the details*, Sadie thought. But what she had obtained gave her the confidence to make a decision on the spot.

In the car, Sadie took out her phone and called her mother, who answered on the first ring.

"Good news, Mom!" Sadie said brightly into the phone. "I checked my calendar, and I'm perfectly clear to go away this weekend. I can't wait to spend some time with you and to finally get to know this Sam that I've heard so much about!"

CHAPTER ELEVEN

Friday, September 27, 2019

"Why do you get a bachelorette party while I'm stuck babysitting the dog?" Harold was trying to make a joke, but Sam could hear something of an authentic whine behind the question. As could Marcie, apparently.

"It's not a bachelorette party, silly," Marcie said. "It's a weekend of quiet meditation. The opposite of a party, really. But feel free to go out with the boys, if you want. Go see an exotic dancer for a true bachelor party experience, if you like. I don't mind." Harold thought it over. Sam could tell he was intrigued by the idea, but he hesitated, sensing a trap.

"No," he finally said. "I'll just watch the dog. What kind of name is Samus, anyway?" He turned to Sam and asked, "Was this dog named after you?"

"It's from an old video game," Sam explained. "Metroid, for early Nintendo. There was a big twist at the end of the game when the main character, named Samus, removed a helmet to reveal that you were playing as a woman the entire time. It was more shocking in the 1980s, I suppose." But Harold had already lost interest and was absently flipping through the sports section of a newspaper laid out on the kitchen table.

"I think Samus is a beautiful name," Marcie said as she darted around the room. "As is Sam," she added, patting Sam gently on the cheek before disappearing through another doorway. Samus, who had been laying on the kitchen floor, woke up, as if detecting the compliment, and took to following Marcie about the house.

"Who else is coming?" Sam asked, hoping that Marcie was still close enough to hear the question.

"Let's see," Marcie called out from the other side of the house. "Aside from me and you, my dear friend Doris, who you met at the fire ceremony, is coming with our mutual friend Hazel. The three of us will room together. Sadie is driving up by herself later today; she said she will be a bit late. I hope you don't mind, but I've arranged for the two of you to share a room."

"Great," Sam muttered. *At least Miguel reassured me that Sadie was* probably *not going to have me murdered*, she thought. Marcie strode back into the kitchen, Samus on her heels.

"And thank you so much for driving me up there. I know it is out of the way for you. Sadie already said she'd be able to take me back on Sunday, so you'll be able to go straight home."

"It's no problem at all."

"No problem for you!" Harold piped in. "I'm the one stuck here alone with the untrained dog!"

Samus, sensing Harold's glare, rolled over on the floor, exposing her belly. Harold laughed and bent over to rub her stomach, groaning with the effort of lowering himself to the ground.

"I'm just kidding, sweetie," he said to Samus. He looked up and noticed Marcie, waiting expectantly.

"Don't tell me you're ready?" he asked, incredulous. At her nod, he rolled his eyes in disbelief and turned to Sam. "She's on time when you're driving. When it's me, I'm stuck waiting around for at least forty-five minutes."

Marcie laughed. "It's a silent retreat, silly. The whole point is to pack light." She gave him a kiss before leading Sam out to the driveway, where she turned to wave at Harold standing forlorn by the front door.

"Oh, he'll be fine," she whispered to Sam. "Don't worry about him."

"I wasn't." Sam gave Harold a thumbs up and grinned at his discomfort before settling into the driver's seat of the car. Marcie blew Harold a kiss as she took a seat on the passenger side.

It was about a three-hour drive into western Massachusetts. As they got further and further away from New York City, civilization began to evaporate, replaced by nature that was largely untouched. Marcie was quite talkative in the car, regaling Sam with various stories involving her four prior husbands.

"I had planned on only marrying once," Marcie was saying. "If I had known I would have four husbands—soon to be five—over the course of my life, I would have kept my own last name from the get-go, like you did when you got married. It was very confusing, adopting a different last name every few years. Why, if you were to shake me awake in the middle of the night and ask me my last name, I think I would get it wrong half the time! I had just gotten used to being Marcie Porter, but in another few days I will have to learn to be Marcie Lindgren."

"I told Mike I wanted to keep my name when we married," Sam said. "All I said was that I was used to it, and I liked it. He didn't take it personally. As I recall, he shrugged it off and said something about 'a rose by any other name . . .'" Catching herself, Sam shoved the memory that threatened to surface back into the deep and tried to refocus on driving.

"I can certainly understand where the two of you were coming from," Marcie said. "I think it was my path in life to wear a variety of names. Each version of 'Marcie' feels like a different person to me. I was born Marcie Durand, and she was a sweet, albeit naive girl. Then I married Barry and became Marcie Fischer, who learned from Barry not to sweat the small stuff in life and to keep things in perspective. That was the first time I felt like I had earned anything approximating wisdom. Four years later, I transformed again to Marcie Davies. She learned from Russ that avoiding stress, and just being one with the universe, is a worthy goal in and of itself. That was who I was for seven years, until I became Marcie Burgos when I married Miguel's father, Ramon. That's the period in my life where I learned to appreciate beauty, whether in nature, art, or music. And then, a few years later, I married Sadie's father, Victor, and Marcie Porter entered the world. And that is who you see today!"

"Wow," Sam said, wondering how much of that timeline she would be able to retain. "What will Marcie Lindgren look like?"

"I don't know!" Marcie said, smiling devilishly. "I haven't met her yet!"

"Fair enough," Sam said. She gave a sidelong look at Marcie. "I think I learned more about you in the past five minutes than I have in the rest of the time we spent together."

"Oh, I don't believe that," Marcie said dismissively. "Every minute we spend together we are learning about each other—even if we aren't reciting names from the past. I just happen to be in a chatty mood right now."

"Why is that?"

"Simply getting it out of my system, I suppose," Marcie answered. "We are supposed to be quietly meditating this weekend, so this may be my last chance to stretch my vocal cords for a few days."

"Does everyone actually remain silent all weekend?" Sam asked. The thought of sharing a room with Sadie under a veil of awkward silence was unsettling, but probably better than having to make small talk for two days.

"Some people take it more seriously than others," Marcie admitted. "Certainly, if you're with the group, there is an expectation of silence. But if you're in your room or walking the grounds, no one is going to shush you for talking quietly."

It was mid-afternoon when Sam finally reached an unpaved road that took them into a forest. Fifteen minutes later, the road led to a clearing with a small parking area surrounded by clusters of cabins. There did not seem to be much activity, but several women were in the process of carrying bags from their cars to their assigned rooms.

Sam parked, unsure of what to do. Marcie, sensing her unease, gestured for her to exit the car and follow. Sam allowed herself to be led to a cabin on the periphery of the settlement. After consulting a sheet posted on the door, Marcie guided Sam inside to an unmarked room, where a woman was sitting on the lower level of a bunk bed.

Sadie.

"I was able to finish up work early," Sadie explained by way of greeting. Marcie winced and gently placed a solitary finger to her lips, gesturing for quiet. Sadie looked at Sam and rolled her eyes in an exaggerated fashion before smiling broadly. Sam frowned, confused at the display of camaraderie.

Marcie wordlessly embraced Sadie, who returned the hug warmly. Not wanting to intrude upon that mother-daughter moment, Sam studied the room. Aside from the bunk beds, the only furniture was a basic four-drawer chest, an uncomfortable-looking wooden chair, and a matching desk. Sadie had already taken to unpacking her bags, with her clothes laid out on the lower bed.

I guess that leaves me on top, Sam thought. She wondered whether it would be possible for her to manage to climb to the upper bed without looking ridiculous.

Sadie hadn't attempted to escape the hug, and after an inordinately long time, Marcie relinquished it. Stepping back, she beamed at Sadie—a look Sam interpreted as *I'm so glad you're here*. Sadie smiled in return, and Marcie exited with her hands pressed together, bowing slightly. A wordless *namaste*.

Once Marcie had departed to find her own room, Sadie glided across the floor to close the door behind her before letting out a relieved sigh.

"God, this looks to be a long, tedious weekend," Sadie said to herself. As if suddenly remembering Sam was also in the room, she added, "Oh, sorry. Are you ok with me talking when it's just the two of us in here? I don't know if I can handle a weekend of complete silence myself, but I don't want to ruin anything for you, if that's what you were going for."

"I'm not quite sure what to expect this weekend," Sam said carefully. She felt a bit thrown off, both by Sadie's unexpected early arrival and her outward friendliness. Sadie seemed to detect Sam's wariness.

"Right, I should have probably introduced myself," Sadie said. "I'm Sadie, Marcie's daughter. Which you probably picked up on by now. I keep forgetting that you and I haven't actually properly met yet. I've heard so much about you, I feel like I know you. I'm sorry we did not get a chance to speak at the barbeque a few weeks ago."

Didn't get a chance to speak? Sam thought. *She was actively avoiding me then, for whatever reason. Am I being gaslit?* But Sam didn't see any advantage to calling out Sadie on her revised account.

"I'm Sam. It's nice to meet you." Sam spoke softly. The walls seemed thin, and she was nervous about being overheard by their neighbors.

"I'm looking forward to getting to know you this weekend," Sadie said. "I hope you don't mind that I took the bottom bed. I tend to toss a bit in my sleep, and I've always had a fear of falling out of bed in the middle of the night."

"No, it's fine. I mean, so long as you don't mind giving me a boost at the end of the night." The mattress for the top bunk was a few inches above Sam's head, and she was still wondering about how to climb up. Sadie, who stood about a foot taller than her, looked like she could have hopped onto that mattress with only a small jump. Sadie threw back her head and laughed. Sam looked for a sign that Sadie's merriment was inauthentic, but she couldn't spot one.

"I promise, we'll find a way to get you up there when you're ready." Sadie paused and grew serious. "Look, I hope we have a lot of fun together over this weird weekend, but I just wanted to tell you at the outset that I'm so sorry about what happened to your husband. Everything I've heard about him from Harold made it clear that he was a wonderful person, and you have my deepest sympathies for your loss."

"Thank you." Sam again searched Sadie's face for a hint of insincerity but came up short. "That was a long time ago. I'm trying to get past it."

"I can't imagine." Sadie shook her head sadly. "And Harold! He lost his wife and his son in the same night. His entire family! What he must have gone through!"

"It was rough," Sam said, uncomfortable with this line of conversation.

"Well, as hard as it was, I'm sure Harold is thankful that you were there with him to share his grief and help him try to get through that calamity."

Sam froze, struggling to maintain a blank facade. *Was that a passive aggressive attack?* she wondered. *Or was it just an innocent observation?* Sam wondered whether Sadie could somehow know that she had largely stayed away from Harold after that night when both of their spouses died. *Maybe Marcie told her? Or Harold himself?*

Sam took a deep breath to calm her thoughts. *If that was an attack, I'm only giving her what she wants by overanalyzing it.*

"I'm just happy to see Harold so happy now with your mother," Sam finally said. "He seems very excited to be a part of your family."

Sadie, with a small smile, nodded in return and resumed unpacking her clothes. Sam, following Sadie's lead, took to emptying her own bag into a drawer in the single chest in the room. A few minutes later, after their bags were unpacked, Sadie spoke again.

"Do you want to get out of here and explore a bit? I saw something about a group meditation at a fire pit, but I wouldn't mind wandering around and seeing what other options we have here."

"Sure." Sam was looking forward to getting outside, where she would once again presumably be protected by the silence mandate.

They left the room together and took a quick peek into Marcie's room, which was unoccupied. They found Marcie outside, flanked by two of her friends as they sat around a fire in a meditative position with their eyes closed.

"That looks like a blast," Sadie muttered, barely loud enough for Sam to hear. She took a seat near Marcie, and Sam followed. Marcie, sensing their arrival, opened her eyes and smiled a greeting at them before resuming her meditative state. Sadie, with a sigh, closed her eyes, leaving Sam alone with her thoughts.

She tried to avoid thinking of what Sadie had said earlier. She knew dwelling on it would only be giving in to Sadie's manipulation, if that's what it was. But Sam soon found that actively trying to avoid thinking of Sadie's comments made it all but impossible to do so.

Do people assume I would have been there for Harold after his family died? Sam's world in the aftermath of the accident was one of self-directed survival—simply withstanding an onslaught of grief long enough to make it to the next day. Harold's was probably the same, although he almost certainly put on a braver face than Sam was usually able to muster, as was his nature. Sam, in the months after Mike died, found herself constantly surrounded by those looking to make her life even moderately less painful. Acquaintances were upgraded to the role of friends. Friends, in turn, transformed into constant presences in her life. Those relationships dissolved and weakened over time, of course. Some well-wishers had children and no longer had the luxury of looking after Sam. Others seemed to think that there was an expiration date on grief and considered any obligation they had to Sam to be terminated upon arriving at that arbitrary point in time. Sam didn't begrudge them in this regard. She was grateful for being afforded the luxury, even on that temporary basis, of never sitting alone too long with her grief. With her regrets.

But Harold? Who was there for him? Maybe an old friend or two from his job had taken him out for a beer at some point. But did he have any family to help him through that unimaginable loss? Sam knew deep down that the only thing approximating a family Harold had after that fateful Mother's Day was her, and she cursed herself for spending that time focused entirely on herself.

Mike would have been ashamed of me for not helping his father when he needed me. The thought nearly brought her to tears, and she closed her eyes tightly to keep those water ducts from opening.

Sam was jolted out of her self-admonishments by a light elbow at her side. Everyone in the vicinity continued to meditate, eyes closed, except for Sadie, who looked bored and restless. With a toss of her head, Sadie wordlessly gestured toward a dirt path meandering into the woods. She rose and quietly walked away, gesturing for Sam to follow, which she did with some reluctance. Before reaching the line of trees, Sam looked back with longing at Marcie, still deep in a meditative trance. She was wary of going off alone with Sadie, but she couldn't think of a graceful way to avoid it.

"Can I make a confession?" Sadie asked once they were far enough away not to be overheard by the group at the fire. At Sam's nod, she continued. "I felt a bit threatened by you after I heard that Harold and my mother were getting married. Growing up with my brothers, I took a sort of fierce pride at being the only girl. I felt special. When I learned that Harold was joining the family, and you with him, I didn't know quite what to make of it. I'll admit it was a touch unsettling. But even though we just met a short while ago, I'm starting to see the upside of it. Colin is so self-involved, and Jeremy is just a mess. It's not always easy to talk to them."

Sam, sensing a trap, didn't voice her agreement. Not that she necessarily disagreed.

"Miguel seems nice enough," Sam said, diplomatically.

"Miguel has a good heart," Sadie conceded. "He's a bit younger, though, so he's not someone I always think to confide in. I suppose I should make a point of reminding myself that he's a fully grown man now. All I'm saying is that it's nice to have a woman my own age to vent to, when the need arises."

What the hell do I say to that? Sam wondered.

"I'm glad to hear you say that," Sam said. She remained dubious of whether that was true. "To be honest, I didn't feel particularly welcomed by your brothers, except for Miguel. I'm sure you heard about Jeremy following me from work to convince me not to go to that engagement party a few weeks back?"

Sadie grimaced and shook her head, forlorn.

"He really can be a bit of an ass," Sadie said. "But in his defense, there was some concern amongst us, at least at first, that Harold was simply trying to marry our mother for financial gain. I see now, of course, that he genuinely loves her. But we were not sure of his intentions, or yours, at the outset. So that is where Jeremy was coming from, even if he can be a tactless buffoon."

"It's interesting to hear you say that," Sam said. "Because I had questions, at one point, about whether you were all looking to keep the marriage from happening for monetary reasons as well." Sadie blinked in surprise, and then threw back her head and laughed. At Sam's confused look, she stopped to explain herself.

"So much miscommunication, all around! We really should have all gone through more of an effort to know each other at the get-go, don't you think? A lot of this mistrust could have been avoided. But that largely falls on me, I admit." Sadie stopped to study Sam's face. *To see if I am buying this*, Sam thought.

"I don't know if this eases your concerns at all," Sadie finally said, "but for what it's worth, I'm pretty well off financially. I'm one of the top realtors on the north shore of Long Island, and I can often make, through a single sale, more than any of my brothers see over the course of the entire year. Is Mom sitting on a great deal of money? Sure. But it's really not anything I personally *need*. And it's certainly not anything that would warrant impeding my mother's happiness, from my perspective. She raised me as one of her own, and I only wish the best for her." Sadie paused, as if deep in thought. "Now, can I say with certainty that none of my brothers wouldn't act selfishly? I like to think not, but you never know with Jeremy or Colin. But to the extent you were worried about me at all, I hope I can put your mind at ease this weekend."

Sam slowed to a stop in the middle of the forest, and Sadie did the same. It was brisk, and the late afternoon sun, largely obscured by a tapestry of green and orange leaves, seemed like it was on the verge of plummeting beneath the horizon.

"Maybe we should head back?" Sam ventured. Sadie nodded, and they turned around to make their way back to the camp.

"You sound as if you no longer distrust me," Sam said. "Why is that?"

Sadie gave the question some thought.

"A large part of it is just hearing about you from my mother," she said. "She likes you and trusts you, so that carries a lot of weight with me. But Harold also mentioned to me fairly recently that you're quite well off yourself, financially speaking. He said something about you taking out a large life insurance policy on your husband, and then settling a big lawsuit relating to his car accident? In any event, he gave me the impression that you're now set for life. It's strange—he seemed almost annoyed that you profited off of his son's death, but I tried to explain to him that you were just trying to protect yourself. A life insurance policy is just a way of mitigating risk; there's nothing sinister about it. And why shouldn't you sue to get some money if a person is reckless enough to kill your husband? I can see how the thought of someone's son's death being reduced to a dollar amount is off-putting, but—are you ok?" Sadie had noticed Sam's face, frozen in shock.

Just what is she up to? Sam wondered. *Did Harold actually tell her about Mike's life insurance or the lawsuit? Is she purposely twisting the facts?*

"That's . . . that's not accurate. Mike took out a life insurance policy himself, through his job, to protect me, just in case. I was barely aware of it. And the lawsuit was something I was told I should do for the insurance. I certainly was not *profiting* off his death!"

Sadie held up her hands in apology.

"I'm sorry, I'm sorry. I didn't mean to offend. He told me this a few weeks ago; it is possible I have some of the details mixed up. My point was simply that I know you are living comfortably, and it's unlikely that you would be participating in any big scam to go after my mother's money. That's all I was trying to say."

Living comfortably? Sam felt enraged. *If she only knew the torture I've been through over the past two years.* Torture that had only recently and mercifully downgraded, for the most part, to a general sense of malaise, with occasional spikes of anguish piercing through the numbness at the most unexpected times. Sam held her tongue though. She didn't see any advantage in revealing more to Sadie, who she continued to distrust, than was absolutely necessary.

"Mike was wonderful and looked out for me," was all Sam said. "And I loved him and tried to return the favor as much as I could. I certainly did not 'profit' from his death. I assure you—I'm very much in the red."

"Of course, of course," Sadie said quickly, in an apparent attempt to mollify Sam. "I did not mean to suggest otherwise. Please forgive me."

Sam gave a short nod, merely to allow them to move on from the topic, and continued to walk. When they finally emerged from the forest, the small group that had been clustered around the fire was milling about. Sam and Sadie tracked down Marcie, who beamed at them and made a spooning gesture toward her mouth. *Dinnertime.* Sam was famished, but she was skeptical of what might be available to eat at this strange retreat.

The meal was a pleasant surprise. Trays of vegetarian fare were spread out on tables in a large room, and Sam filled her plate with a salad and some type of marinated tofu. She sat with Sadie, Marcie, and Marcie's two friends and ate in silence. Sam found it pleasant to focus solely on the act of eating, without the pressure of making small talk, and she started to appreciate at least some of the benefits of a silent retreat.

It's not like talking to Sadie was such a joy.

After dinner, the group went back to the fire for further meditations as the sun continued to set. Sam feared that Sadie would again drag her off to initiate another uncomfortable conversation, but she didn't. Sadie seemed perfectly content to sit alone near the fire, her mother at her side, with her own thoughts, leaving Sam to do the same.

Unfortunately, Sam didn't consider her thoughts to be welcome company just then. Despite her best efforts, she couldn't avoid dwelling on the seeds of doubt and guilt that Sadie had planted all afternoon. Sam experimented with meditation years earlier and had managed, at times, to reach the desired goal of focusing on nothing but her breath. She desperately tried to summon that ability, but it eluded her.

What the hell do I have to feel guilty about? My husband was killed two years into our marriage, I grieved for a long time—and continue to grieve, even if my mourning has evolved—and I live a comfortable life because Mike made plans for me in the event of his passing. There is nothing there that warrants an apology.

Sam remembered dark and lonely days in the immediate aftermath of the accident, where each day seemed to stretch on forever, only to eventually reach a night where sleep was unattainable. *What was Harold doing during those times?* she wondered. *Undoubtedly mourning, in a manner different from my own grief, but in pain nonetheless. Perhaps worse than my own, if that were even possible. He did lose a wife* and *a son*.

Harold had an undeniable ability to put on his best face, even when confronted with indescribable adversity. *He was probably hiding a lot of what he was feeling. Who knows, even now, what he is hiding?* Sam had assumed, from the time Harold unceremoniously broke into her house to announce his new marriage, that he wanted Sam back in his life. *Is it possible he's masking resentment toward me? For not being there when he needed someone? For collecting money off of his son's death?*

With a start, Sam realized she would much rather be subjected to Sadie's passive aggressiveness than repeatedly pummeled by her own dark thoughts. But Sadie showed no signs of moving. Her meditative pose looked natural and relaxed and nearly mirrored that of her mother.

Not knowing what else to do, Sam continued to sit by the fire, eyes closed (with an occasional peek to see what everyone else was doing). She couldn't bring herself to anything resembling tranquility, but her blank façade didn't hint at the cacophony of self-imposed torture operating beneath the surface.

No one moved from the fire even after the sun completed its descent. The cluster of women sat together, with only the crackling of the fire serving as a soundtrack for the evening. Despite being surrounded by people, Sam could not recall the last time she felt so alone.

An hour or so after sunset, groups started to peel away from the fire toward their assigned bedrooms. It was still early—probably not much later than 7:30—but there was little incentive to stay up late in the absence of conversation. Sam assumed that many of the women wished to head back to their rooms simply to share some muffled gossip, without infringing upon the sanctity of the silent retreat.

Sadie managed to make eye contact with Sam and gestured back toward the sleeping area with a subtle tilt of her head and an inquisitive raise of an eyebrow. Sam nodded, and they rose together. Marcie took note and rose as well to accompany them back to their room.

Once they were inside, Marcie carefully closed the door behind them and spoke in a hushed whisper.

"Please don't tell anyone I spoke out loud," she pleaded. "But I wanted to thank you both for coming here this weekend. I know this is probably outside of your normal comfort zones, but I really appreciate the two of you being here. You are each incredibly special to me, and I can't imagine going through with this wedding without you both."

Marcie put a finger up to her lips before Sadie or Sam could respond and exited. Sam and Sadie exchanged a look and began changing into their pajamas. Sam, despite herself, stole a glance at Sadie while she was in the midst of dressing and marveled at her figure. *Does she do yoga for five hours a day?* She felt short and squatty in Sadie's presence.

"I guess I'll turn in?" Sam said after they had both changed. Sadie shrugged her agreement.

"I don't think I've gone to bed before eight o'clock since I was three years old, but I'm not sure what else we should be doing." She glanced at her phone. "Of course, there's still no service here."

Despite her prior concerns, Sam managed to climb into the top bunk fairly easily and lay on her back, staring at the ceiling. Once Sam was settled, Sadie switched off the lights, casting the room in darkness, save the moonlight piercing their window, which provided some minor illumination. Sam did not feel particularly tired and resigned herself to a few hours of looking blankly at the barely visible plaster above. Below, Sam heard the sounds of Sadie crawling into her own bunk. Sam wondered whether Sadie had the ability to fall asleep at will.

The room was quiet for a few minutes, and Sam began to suspect that Sadie managed to nod off. She was on the verge of leaning out of her bed to steal a peek when Sadie spoke.

"My mother cares for you a lot, you know."

"She seems to care about everyone she interacts with," Sam said in response, speaking directly into the ceiling above.

"True. But I can tell you're special to her. Just look at how she spoke with us earlier. She had us on equal footing, even though I'm her daughter."

"Please," Sam said. "She clearly adores you. What could she have said? 'I'm so glad you're both here, but more so Sadie?'" Sam forced a small laugh, but Sadie didn't join. A silence reasserted itself. Sam couldn't relax, knowing there was more to come.

"Shortly after my father died, my mother arranged to adopt me," Sadie said. "I think she was concerned about my mental state, and maybe Jeremy's and Colin's as well, because she decided around that time that we had to get a dog. She consulted all of us, although Miguel was just a toddler at the time. I wanted to get a Boston Terrier, and Jeremy and Colin wanted a Golden Retriever, as I recall. But in the end, she ignored all of our requests."

"How so?" Sam asked, not knowing where this was heading.

"She took us all to a no-kill shelter. She was adamant about getting a dog from there. I don't remember if the notion of a 'rescue dog' was around back then, but that's what she had in mind. As she took us around that shelter, Jeremy, Colin, and I would occasionally point out a puppy that caught our eye. But again, she mostly ignored us."

Sadie, who had been speaking in a hushed voice, paused dramatically. Sam waited, somewhat impatiently, for her to continue and get to the point.

"Eventually she came across a small puppy with three legs. I don't recall why the dog had to have its other leg removed, but it seemed happy enough. That was the dog my mother was dead set on getting, so we did. My brothers and I were disappointed, of course, and whined incessantly about our mother's pick. Over time, we all grew to love the dog, and named him Baxter. I think Jeremy picked the name. Baxter was surprisingly mobile and was a huge part of our childhood. Even after all of us kids moved out, with the exception of Miguel, Mom continued to shower that dog with as much love as if it was one of her children. Baxter lived to be over fifteen years old. He was really lucky to end up in the care of someone like my mother, where he could live a life in which he was constantly bombarded with love."

"Your mom seems like an amazing person," Sam said.

"That's just who she is," Sadie replied in the dark. She didn't sound boastful of her mother—she was simply stating a fact.

"Case in point," Sadie added. Sam heard Sadie get out of bed and saw her turn on her cellphone's flashlight. Sadie found her bag, extracted what looked to be a note and returned to bed, keeping the light from her phone on.

"Mother is big on handwritten notes," Sadie explained. "She never took to email, so I will get a long note in the mail from her now and then. This is one I received yesterday."

Sam heard the sound of paper being unfolded, and then Sadie began to read:

Dear Sadie,

I cannot tell you how excited I am that you will be coming to the silent retreat this weekend. You are very much your own person, and our interests do not always align, so I think it is wonderful that you are willing to connect with me in my world. Of course, I hope we have the opportunity to further connect in other areas that are more in tune with your own passions. Or maybe we can just make a point of going out for coffee and tea together every now and then? I am so glad for the time we spent together earlier this week.

I'm also thrilled that Sam will be able to join us. I know you haven't had a chance to get to know her yet, but she is a lovely person, and I am sure you will find it very easy to befriend her. I certainly have over the course of these past few weeks.

As I'm sure you've heard, Sam lost her husband—Harold's son—a little over two years ago. She's been very isolated since then, and I really feel like the absence of a family has been hurting her all this time. It is a very sad situation, and I'm so thankful that Sam is opening up to allow us all to help her. I hope she thinks of me as a friend, as I do her, but I suspect that she would welcome your friendship as well. I've gone through similar losses, and I know how important friends and family are during those periods of feeling broken.

XOXOXO,

Mom

Sadie stopped reading and slowly refolded the note. She then meticulously turned off her phone's light, plunging the room back to darkness.

"That's just who my mother is," Sadie said. "She is the kind of person who will seek out the damaged—those who are in more desperate need of her love—and ensure they get it. Baxter was lucky to be found by my mother." Sadie paused. "So are you."

Sam was stunned into silence. She heard Sadie shuffle about below her, putting the note and her phone away, before resettling in her bed. After a few minutes, Sadie seemed to realize that she was not going to get a response from Sam.

"Goodnight, Sam," Sadie said softly. Sam could hear her below, rolling onto her side to try to find sleep. Sam continued to stare into the dark above her.

I threw myself into this situation to help Harold, she thought. *And once I got to know Marcie, I wanted to help her as well.* Sam viewed her role as being the protector of that elder couple—a shield to hold off Marcie's scheming children. But now she found herself questioning that perspective.

I thought I was the hero of this story. But do others see me as the damsel in distress? Sam always refused to view herself as a victim, even in the aftermath of Mike's death, and it troubled her greatly that others, such as Marcie, saw her as a fragile egg in need of gentle handling. She didn't want to be the object of anyone's pity.

Perhaps Sadie is lying about that note? Sam decided against it. It sounded like Marcie's voice to her, and besides, it would be too easy for Sadie to be caught perpetrating such a fraud. After spending the day with her, Sam was beginning to understand Sadie's tactics. *A quick strike, couched in language that affords her plausible deniability, followed by silence to allow the weeds to take root.*

And it was working.

Sam knew she was being manipulated, but she was surprised to find she didn't really care. The thought of being a charity case to Harold and Marcie was too much for her. She was comfortable throwing herself into the family drama in an effort to help others, but she could not stomach the thought of Harold and Marcie thinking her a broken mess that needed fixing. Sam also questioned how much Harold actually resented her, and she began to speculate whether he had reached out to her in the first place because Marcie forced him to do so out of pity.

Sam decided then and there to remove herself from the situation entirely.

She carefully climbed down from her top bunk. Deep breathing from the lower bunk suggested that Sadie did not have any trouble falling to sleep after all. In the dark, Sam stealthily changed and collected her belongings. Marcie and Sadie would undoubtedly note Sam's absence in the morning, and there would be questions at some point, but those were all problems for another day. Sam felt suffocated, and her need to escape trumped any other long-term concerns that threatened to show up on her plate down the road.

Leaving the dorms, Sam scurried under the starry night to her car. The loudness of the engine startled her in the stillness of the forest, but she quickly recovered. As quietly as she could manage, Sam navigated out of the parking area and began her long drive home.

CHAPTER TWELVE

Sunday, September 29, 2019

After arriving home late Friday night, Sam spent an anxious weekend wondering when she would face her reckoning for her abrupt and unannounced departure from the retreat. Early Saturday morning, Sam received a worried text from Marcie inquiring about her whereabouts. Sam felt bad—she knew Marcie must have driven some distance to find cellphone service to send that message. Sam responded with a few vague sentences about departing because she felt ill, which she hoped would prevent Marcie from leaving outright to check in on her. It seemed to have worked, as her excuse managed to buy her a few days of peace.

At least from the outside world.

Sam remained frazzled, in a state of unrest. Unable to focus on any of the books she had been reading, Sam tried to keep herself busy by gardening and landscaping her yard, which helped to keep her from sinking too deeply into her own thoughts. By the end of Saturday, Sam was so exhausted from yard work that she passed out in her bed immediately after showering.

Sam woke up that Sunday morning, thankful for a night of sleep untroubled by insomnia, and resolved once again to drive herself to the point of exhaustion through manual labor. After a quick bite to eat in the morning, Sam set out to clean up her property to the best of her ability. So focused was she on her work that she did not notice Harold's arrival mid-afternoon.

Sam was weeding near the fence when Harold entered her backyard. He coughed loudly to get Sam's attention before surveying her progress, and his face registered his appreciation for what Sam's hard work had accomplished. Sam knew she had successfully transformed her property over the course of the past day and a half, driven by a need to distract herself from guilt and doubt. The flower bed was pristine—the only plants remaining were those that were meant to be there. Sam had even given the small shed in her backyard a fresh coat of white paint. There was no evidence that the tree in her backyard was in the process of shedding its leaves, as Sam had diligently raked the freshly mowed yard.

"Looking good, kiddo," Harold said in his standard loud voice. He frowned as a thought occurred to him. "I thought you were feeling sick. Isn't that why you left Marcie's thing?"

"I'm feeling better now," Sam muttered. Harold shook his head—he clearly couldn't hear what she had said—but he seemed to decide it wasn't worth pressing.

"I tried to call you earlier," he said. "So did Marcie. But when we couldn't reach you, we got nervous and drove up to check on you."

"*We?*" Sam asked. "Is Marcie here, too?"

Harold nodded and gestured with his head toward the street.

"She's out front with Samus. She thinks you may be mad at her, for some reason. I said I'd come back and check since I'm too lovable for you to ever be angry with me." He grinned, waiting for a playful rejoinder from Sam. But Sam did not take the bait.

"I'm not—" Sam started. *Am I mad at Marcie?* She was not entirely sure what she felt. She was no longer comfortable with the odd role she had assigned herself as the protector of Harold and Marcie's engagement, but she couldn't pinpoint any transgression on Marcie's part that would warrant hostility toward her.

"I'm not mad," Sam finished. "She can come on back."

Harold went to the gate and waved. Moments later, Marcie walked into the backyard, holding a canister in one hand and a leash affixed to Samus in the other. Samus sniffed the grass enthusiastically, but she didn't try to pull away from Marcie.

"Hello, Sam," Marcie said, looking somewhat shy. "I was just looking at your floral life in the front. What is that gorgeous orange flower by your front door?"

Sam thought it over. "I think that's just a weed I haven't gotten to yet," she said.

Marcie laughed. "Well, it's beautiful regardless. To be honest, I've never quite understood the distinction between a weed and a non-weed." She held up the canister she was holding. "I'm so sorry to hear that you felt ill during the retreat. We missed you terribly. I brought some tea to help you feel better. And don't worry—I went easy on the turmeric this time."

Sam took the tea, but as she did, Samus managed to slip out of her collar and run deeper into the backyard, only to immediately defecate next to the tree.

"Samus!" Harold scolded. "You should have done that at home!" Marcie placed a calming hand on his shoulder.

"Now, Harold, when you have to go, you have to go." Marcie turned to Sam. "If you would be so kind as to get me a plastic bag, I will be happy to clean that up."

"It's fine," Sam said with a shrug. "I'll take care of it later."

They wordlessly stood together as Samus patrolled the small yard. When the three of them were together a few weeks earlier, Sam felt like she was a part of something bigger than herself. Even if it did not reach the level of "family," there was a sense of camaraderie that suggested a commonality of interest. But now, Sam very much felt a third wheel—a crasher at a party to which she was not welcome. It didn't matter that Harold and Marcie had come to her. She didn't feel like part of their team.

She felt like charity.

"I'm sorry I left so abruptly," Sam finally said to Marcie, just to puncture the awkwardness. "It was . . . interesting. I appreciate being invited."

"Of course!" Marcie replied. "No need to apologize at all. I'm sorry you got sick. I'm just thankful you are feeling better."

Sam felt a tinge of guilt at her lie and did not respond.

"We were all a bit confused yesterday morning when we realized you had left," Marcie continued. "Sadie felt terrible. She thought she might've inadvertently said something that offended you and caused you to leave."

Sam managed to avoid grimacing. *What would happen if I was completely honest and recited everything Sadie said to me?* she wondered. Sadie's passive-aggressive attacks had been cloaked in a veil of plausible deniability. Complaining about them would only make Sam look thin-skinned and paranoid, particularly to Marcie and Harold, who tended to view Marcie's children with rose-tinted glasses. *There's nothing to be gained by getting into that*, Sam concluded.

"Well, it's good you've recovered," Harold said. "We have the ceremony next weekend, thanks to you. I can't believe we put together a wedding in Iceland in just a few days. Hell, I can't believe you convinced Marcie to get married in Iceland!"

"No," Sam said. "I didn't—"

"It will be lovely, Harold," Marcie said, taking a hold of his arm affectionately. "A small wedding, with just our families, in the middle of nature, surrounded by the elves and the fairies. I cannot wait!"

"It will be a small one alright, although I can't blame my friends for not wanting to fly up to the north pole for a wedding. It's fine though." Harold didn't truly seem that bothered by having an intimate wedding. Sam knew he just liked to find things to complain about sometimes.

"The hardest part," Harold continued, "was finding someone to watch the dog on short notice. We're leaving in a few days to get things squared away, but none of our friends were free this week. Finally, one of Marcie's hippie friends—"

"Oh, Ellen isn't a hippie," Marcie cut in, but Harold didn't seem to hear her.

"—said they were willing to watch Samus, but only if she could do it at Marcie's house. She lives in a crappy area of upstate New York, so I think she's just treating herself to a free vacation on Long Island. But she's doing us the favor, I suppose, so I can't judge her too harshly." Harold shook his head, as if fighting the urge to complain more. He took a deep inhale to calm himself and exhaled slowly before visibly relaxing. *Marcie taught him that one*, Sam concluded.

"So anyway," he resumed, "I think the airport was supposed to email you your flight information. You'll be on the Thursday night flight with the rest of the gang. We even sprung for you to get your own hotel room, although Marcie wanted you to share with Jeremy—"

Marcie, with a frown, elbowed Harold. "I did not!"

"I'm kidding, I'm kidding! Like I said, you'll have your own room, the wedding will be Saturday, and then—"

"I've decided not to go," Sam said meekly. Harold didn't immediately hear her and continued to talk but was quieted with a gentle touch from a wide-eyed Marcie.

"What?" Harold said, annoyed at the interruption. He calmed when he noticed Marcie's distraught face. "What did I miss?"

"You're . . . not coming?" Marcie asked. Harold looked around, bewildered, but Marcie's eyes were fixed on Sam. She sounded pained, and Sam found it hard to meet her gaze.

"I'm sorry," Sam said, looking down. "I appreciate the invite. I've just been going through some stuff, and I don't think I'm in the right mental state to go." A long silence followed, but Sam couldn't bring herself to explain further.

"Well, that's ridiculous!" Harold finally exclaimed. "You seem fine to me. What is this really about? Do you have a problem with me remarrying so quickly?"

"No! Not at all! I think you're both very lucky you found each other. And I really wish you the best. I just . . . I don't see any reason for me to be a part of it."

"A part of it?" Harold continued to look perplexed. "All you have to do is come on a free trip and stand around during a ceremony. I don't understand why you—"

Marcie, who had been wordlessly processing this entire exchange, finally spoke.

"It's ok, Harold."

Harold's attention swiveled to her.

"What do you mean it's ok? It's—"

"An invitation is not an obligation," Marcie said. Sam thought she was trying to maintain a brave face that hid the hurt she was feeling. "If Sam does not wish to come, we have to respect that."

Harold froze, unable to hide his anger.

"Fine," he finally spat out. "Do whatever you want. I'm not going to argue."

"I'm sorry," Sam told him, and he shrugged.

"I called the airline," Sam added. "They said they would refund the ticket and—"

"It's fine," Harold responded coldly. "Don't worry about it. Come on Marcie, let's walk Samus before heading home."

Marcie, with a nod, knelt down. Samus bounded to her side and allowed Marcie to put the collar back around her neck.

"Goodbye, Sam," Marcie said. After a brief hesitation, she gave Sam a short hug. "I'm sure we will see you after the wedding. I hope you feel better."

"Right." Sam paused. "And congratulations. I really am happy for you both."

Sam couldn't read Marcie's face, which was going through the motions of trying to stay upbeat. *She's hurt. And confused. But beyond that* . . . And then Marcie was dragged out of the backyard by a hyper Samus, leaving Sam behind with Harold.

"Well, I guess that's that. Feel better and everything else she said." Harold turned to follow Marcie.

"I really am sorry, Harold," Sam blurted out. "For this, and—"

"What?"

Sam closed her eyes tight, collecting herself.

"After Mike died, I wasn't myself. I don't know how I got through that immediate aftermath, and it didn't get much better from there. But you lost a son *and* a wife—"

"It's not a competition," Harold interjected, but Sam ignored him.

"—and I should've been there for you. I should have been strong enough to have been there for you. But I wasn't. And I'm sorry."

Harold cocked his head, studying Sam. His face softened, and when he spoke, he sounded more understanding than annoyed.

"It was hell for both of us, I'm sure. Still is, more often than not. But we're surviving, as best we can. It doesn't matter how we got here. All that matters is we're here. I don't blame you in the slightest, even if I were to accept your premise that you weren't there for me then. Which I don't."

Harold exhaled. "But I'd be lying if I said I didn't wish you were here for us now." With a rueful shrug, Harold left the backyard to track down Marcie and Samus.

Sam stood alone in her yard. She had been dreading that awkward talk with Harold and Marcie all weekend, but now that it was behind her, Sam still didn't feel any sort of cathartic release. There was no sense of a weight lifting off her. To the contrary, Sam was left with a feeling that she thought was a logical impossibility, given her state of unease over the entire weekend.

She felt worse.

• • • •

Colin was in his basement, firing up his vintage PlayStation, when he heard something on the ground floor above. He recognized those clunking footsteps. *Jeremy*, Colin thought. *Damn it*. Jeremy had a very annoying habit of showing up unannounced, without even a text warning of his arrival. *Probably a remnant of growing up on sitcoms where neighbors comfortably barge in*, Colin noted.

Colin took some solace in the fact that Jeremy hadn't arrived two hours earlier, when Miguel and Sadie were over to go over their plans. Colin could only guess how Jeremy would have responded to learning he had been left out, but he knew, at the very least, that it would have presented a very awkward situation indeed.

Jeremy seemed to know where Colin was; Colin could hear the steps beelining to the door leading to the basement. As he waited for Jeremy to descend the steps, Colin loaded a game and left it on the title screen. Moments later, Jeremy entered the room and glanced at the frozen image on the television.

"Mortal Kombat 3?" he asked without any preamble.

"Yeah. Not for the podcast. I just felt the craving to kick it old school," Colin responded. Jeremy grunted.

"That's the one with the cyborgs, right? I loved this game as a kid." Jeremy picked up the other controller but didn't do anything with it. He just stared blankly, hypnotized by the television, to the point where Colin began to feel somewhat uncomfortable.

With a nod at the tv, Colin asked, "Wanna play?"

Jeremy blinked, emerging from his trance, and nodded. "I call Sub-Zero."

Colin started the game and selected Liu Kang as his own warrior. They played for several minutes, but Jeremy, who was usually atrocious at video games, proved surprisingly adept, managing to closely win two out of three matches.

"Can't believe I remember those combos," Jeremy said, looking pleased as punch. "Seems like you're a little bit rusty."

Colin was annoyed at losing—losing to Jeremy, of all people. *It's possible that Mortal Kombat games are the one thing Jeremy is good at in life*, Colin thought.

"Yeah, well, I hardly ever play with Liu Kang, so you were at a significant advantage to start with." Colin was struck by a thought: *What if he asks to play again? I can't use that excuse twice!* Colin quickly turned off the console and the television to protect himself from that scenario.

"So, you hear anything from Sadie?" Jeremy asked in the stillness that followed, trying to sound nonchalant.

Colin cursed himself. *Dammit, I should have left the game on.* Of course, Jeremy instinctively knew the most annoying question to possibly ask. Colin debated how honest to be in response and realized that he would almost certainly be caught sooner than later for any lie he might have otherwise been inclined to wield.

"She was actually here earlier today," Colin said, trying to sound casual. Jeremy frowned, and Colin added, "With Miguel."

"What were they doing here?" Jeremy's voice was carefully neutral.

Colin again considered lying, and again rejected that strategy.

"Sadie wanted to have a meeting with us before the wedding next weekend."

Jeremy took a deep breath and closed his eyes. Colin waited, but Jeremy didn't stir. Time ticked on, and Jeremy still did not move. Colin, feeling restless, glanced at the television, wondering how Jeremy would react if he started playing a game. *Am I supposed to just sit here while this guy goes comatose?*

After an inordinately long period of time, Jeremy finally spoke without opening his eyes. "She arranged a meeting without me?"

"Yup."

Jeremy's eyes snapped open, filled with barely contained rage. "But I'm the oldest!"

Colin tried not to laugh. *Sadie doesn't care, dude.* But Jeremy looked as if he was on the verge of flying off the rails, and Colin didn't want to push him there.

"For what it's worth, *I* thought it was wrong to exclude you." That was a mild lie, but Colin was confident it would be impossible to disprove. "But Sadie—I think she's still pissed at you."

"For what? I'm the one who should be mad at her!"

"Oh man! You almost hit her!"

"No! I didn't! I was completely in control. She just comes up with excuses to shut me out. You know how she is!"

Colin didn't want to get involved in any drama between Jeremy and Sadie, so he just gave a faint shrug that Jeremy could interpret any way he wanted.

"What did she want, anyway?"

"She really just wanted to stress that we should all plan on flying to Iceland later this week and make sure that we were otherwise all on the same page."

Jeremy shook his head in disbelief at being left out of this planning.

"So, you're going to Iceland." Jeremy sounded skeptical.

"Of course I am. Why wouldn't I?"

Colin had, in fact, been planning on skipping the entire affair. But a significant portion of the conversation earlier in the day had been Sadie tearing into Colin with threats about what she would do to him if he didn't get his ass on that plane, while Miguel sat, uncomfortable, off to the side. Sadie painted quite a bleak image of what Colin's life would look like if he missed his flight, and Colin was fairly certain she could deliver on those promises, if need be.

Jeremy scoffed. "Do you even have a passport?"

Colin rolled his eyes. "Yes, I have a passport."

A few years ago, Colin's girlfriend at the time, a hipster named Amy, had arranged for them to take a trip together to the Dominican Republic. Colin had every intention of going and went through all of the necessary steps to get a passport. As their vacation drew closer and closer, Colin felt increasingly anxious, and he tried everything he could think of to get out of going. Lying about work commitments. Feigning multiple illnesses. Claiming his mother was hospitalized. Amy didn't believe any of it, but Colin ultimately accomplished his goal of staying home when she broke up with him a few hours before their scheduled flight. That notwithstanding, Amy still made a point of getting on the plane. Her Facebook photos, posted the following week, suggested that she managed to have a great time, even in his absence.

Colin's new girlfriend, Sara, had been pressuring him over the past few weeks to go away somewhere. He was considering inviting Sara on the Iceland trip, just to kill two birds with a single stone. *It's not like I'm going to flake on* this *flight.*

He was *nearly* positive he wouldn't.

"Why does Sadie want us to go to this thing, anyway?" Jeremy asked. "I thought she was trying to stop the wedding."

"She said it's important we go to voice our objections in person. She seems to think if we hammer all of this out while we are there, it's unlikely Mom and Harold will follow through with it. Sadie said it would be riskier if we just didn't show at all."

Jeremy considered this explanation.

"Yeah. Maybe. Did Sadie even mention me at this big secret meeting?"

Colin thought it over.

"No. Not that I recall."

Jeremy, once again, struggled to hold his temper.

"Does she even want me to come?" he demanded.

"She didn't say."

"Fine, but what do you *think*?"

"What do I think?" Colin decided to give Jeremy a truthful answer. It seemed the only way to put an end to this uncomfortable conversation. "I don't think she cares one way or another what you do. I get the impression she thinks you can't influence Mom the way the rest of us can, so you're not that useful to her. I think she's written you out of her plans entirely."

Jeremy stared hard at Colin, fuming, before walking away to stomp back up the stairs and out of the house. Colin waited, bracing himself for Jeremy to come storming back in. It was only after he heard Jeremy's car start and peel away that he turned his television back on and restarted his PlayStation.

CHAPTER THIRTEEN

Thursday, October 3, 2019

Jeremy lurked in a pub in the bowels of Penn Station.

It was early afternoon, so the bar was still relatively empty. At least as "empty" as anything in Penn Station ever gets. Granted, there was a collection of people milling about as they waited for a train to take them west to New Jersey, or east to Long Island, or even to another city entirely via Amtrak. But there was plenty of room for Jeremy to find a seat for himself, and another for the large duffle bag he carried at his side.

Polishing off his fourth beer, Jeremy signaled for another. *Am I drunk enough for this?* he wondered. Beer may not be enough, in itself, to fuel his intended course of action. When the bartender brought him his drink, Jeremy also asked for a double shot of Jack Daniels, which he downed immediately before unleashing a choking cough.

Sadie. The name presented itself as a curse in his mind, and Jeremy looked around to make sure he didn't inadvertently say it out loud. No one seemed to be paying him any attention, and Jeremy was mildly comforted that his thoughts hadn't escaped his mouth, as they had a tendency to do.

She turned them all against me, he thought, staring into his beer. *I'm the oldest. I should be the leader, but she manipulated them to the point where they are all conspiring behind my back.*

Jeremy struggled to recall what she had said to him a few weeks earlier. *"Do you really think you're smart enough to kill someone and get away with it?"* Was she goading him into committing murder through reverse psychology? Or was it just a naked insult?

You could go crazy trying to decipher Sadie's mind games, Jeremy thought. "No more!" This time the thought erupted as an exclamation, and a few people in his vicinity shot him a look before retreating back into their own worlds. Jeremy ignored them. He was definitely feeling a bit drunk, but he hoped that would help make his task somewhat easier.

Sadie's not telling me what to do anymore. He placed a hand at his side, feeling for the duffle bag to make sure no one had walked off with it. It was still balanced, somewhat precariously, on the stool at his side.

Jeremy took out his phone to check the time—3:40. It was still unclear when Sam left work on a normal day when there was no scheduled happy hour, but Jeremy figured it couldn't be much before 4:30. He would leave for the subway soon, which would take him downtown to the vicinity of Sam's building in less than twenty minutes. He didn't think he would have to wait too long to track her down.

Sadie thinks she knows me so well, Jeremy thought. *But she has no idea what I'm capable of.*

• • • • •

Sam had struggled to focus at work all week, but that Thursday was particularly difficult. She had originally planned on taking time off to attend Harold and Marcie's wedding in Iceland, but after canceling her flight earlier that week, she withdrew her request for those days off. She didn't see any point in skipping work only to sit home and stew over her decision to skip the wedding. Sam hoped that spending the day in the office would provide some sort of distraction, but, unfortunately, her doubts had no trouble accompanying her on the commute to work.

It was hard not to visualize how her day would have unfolded in an alternate universe where she still planned to go to Iceland. A morning spent packing, if only for a long weekend. An afternoon of trains and a monorail to get her to the airport. An evening flight that would have culminated with the dawn of a new day, twenty-seven hundred miles to the northeast.

Instead, Sam languished in a cubicle, struggling to review a dozen insurance policies relating to a new claim just assigned to her.

Sam entertained the notion of having a last-second change of heart. Before leaving her home that morning, she dug out her passport and packed it carefully away in her purse, acknowledging the possibility of being overtaken by an uncontrollable desire to attend the wedding. But that longing never took hold. Whenever Sam pictured booking a flight to make the wedding, all she envisioned was a sad, damaged girl inserting herself into another family that, by and large, didn't want her there. Her attendance at the wedding would be nothing more than a weak and largely symbolic showing of support for a father-in-law who she ignored when he actually needed her. To be sure, it hurt Sam to sever ties with Harold and Marcie, but that was done and dusted. Changing her mind and going through the effort of reforging those relationships would only lead to that renewed pain at a later date.

As bleak as her week had been, Sam still believed it beat that alternative.

At 4:46, Sam turned off her computer and left without saying goodbye to any of her co-workers. She snuck into an elevator that was thankfully empty and took her directly to the lobby. Sam strode out of the building without looking back, heading straight for the subway that would take her uptown to Grand Central Station, at which point she would take the Metro North home. From there, it was simply a matter of finding a book that could adequately distract her from the flight she had purposely missed.

Sam's role in the wedding was, as far as she was concerned, over. Whether the ceremony went forward or Sadie somehow found a way to stop it, that would all happen without Sam. She had removed herself from the saga of Harold and Marcie. Sam also knew that her part in the story of Marcie's family had finally ended.

It never even crossed her mind that anyone else might think otherwise.

• • • • •

Jeremy followed Sam at a distance as she walked to the subway. His state of inebriation, coupled with the weight of his duffle bag, made the task somewhat difficult, but he managed to keep Sam in his sight. He was a mere twenty feet behind when Sam turned off of busy Water Street onto Pine Street, which wasn't much more than a dark alley flanked by the back entrances to skinny skyscrapers that completely blocked the sun. Up ahead, through the dim lighting, Jeremy spotted a café.

This could work, he thought. Ignoring the handful of nerves that managed to survive his afternoon of drinking, Jeremy accelerated his pace. His long strides closed the distance between him and Sam in a matter of moments. When he was nearly upon her, Sam finally registered his presence and turned—

• • • • •

Sam heard a rustle behind her and spun around to face Jeremy, bearing down on her. His face was unreadable. As her mind raced, Sam glanced about, trying to gauge how much danger she was in. There were a few people further down the street, but no one was particularly close. Jeremy's face looked red, and his eyes looked to be mildly out of focus. *Is he drunk?* Sam was wary, but she couldn't decide whether he posed an actual threat.

Jeremy abruptly stopped, inches from her face. Sam had to arch her neck to look up at him. Jeremy didn't look at her but instead turned his head away, collecting himself. Steeling himself. He was mildly out of breath from the exertion of catching up to her, and Sam was very still, waiting for whatever might come next. Finally, with a deep breath, Jeremy looked down, directly into Sam's eyes, and spoke.

"I owe you an apology."

• • • • •

Jeremy and Sam sat in the café that he had spotted earlier. Sam had selected a table in the middle of the room, surrounded by other patrons. She seemed more at ease being in a crowded space than she had in the alley, which even Jeremy conceded was reasonable on her part.

"So let me get this straight," Sam said, ignoring the latte in front of her. "You stalked me again to apologize for the first time you stalked me?"

Jeremy felt his face flush. "Well, yeah. Basically. I mean, if you put it that way, I kind of sound like an asshole. But sure."

"Alright," Sam said. She finally took a sip of her drink. *What does that mean?* Jeremy thought. *Did she accept my apology?* Jeremy felt uncomfortable in the silence that followed and felt a need to further explain himself.

"It's Sadie," he blurted out. Sam blinked at the non sequitur, but she looked interested in what he had to say. "She has a way of manipulating people. Even me sometimes, I'm embarrassed to say. She knows all the buttons to push to get people to do whatever she wants. I try to fight it when I feel she's trying to operate me like a puppet, but every once in a blue moon, that causes me to do things I don't want to do, just because I'm so focused on avoiding where she's pushing me. Does that make sense?"

After a beat, Sam nodded.

"Sure. I've dealt with Sadie," she said. She took another sip of her latte, looking thoughtful. Jeremy was encouraged by her seeming to understand where he was coming from.

"The last time I ran into you in the city, that was right after Sadie told me not to approach you. Which may have been reverse psychology. Or it may have been reserve-reverse psychology. Anyway, my mind got so twisted about trying to figure out what Sadie wanted—or didn't want—that I was determined to track you down and talk to you for myself. Which I realize was probably creepy, in hindsight. And then I spoke harshly to you afterwards—"

Jeremy trailed off. He again questioned how well his apology was being received. But Sam seemed to soften, if only a bit.

"No harm done," she said. "But maybe, in the future, you should not make ambushing people your primary mode of communication?"

"Fair enough." Jeremy took a sip of his drink, which was bitter and gross. *Is this what coffee tastes like?* He could not recall ever having coffee before, but he felt compelled to get something to drink while he and Sam spoke. *Maybe it needs sugar or something*?

"Looking for you now was a bit of an impulse decision. I'm flying out to Iceland tonight for the wedding." Jeremy looked down at his duffle bag by his feet. "I got my suit in there, ready to go. I'm heading straight to the airport after this."

"You think the wedding will go forward?"

Jeremy barked a bitter laugh. "Who knows? No one tells me anything these days. But if I had to guess, I'd say no. Sadie doesn't want it to happen, and she tends to get whatever she wants."

Sam nodded, seemingly without realizing she was doing so. She looked deep in thought. *She sees Sadie the same way I do!* Jeremy realized. After a lonely and isolating week, Jeremy felt exalted by the discovery that someone else seemed to share his revulsion of Sadie.

"It's a game to her, you see," Jeremy said. Sam tilted her head, intrigued, and Jeremy felt heartened by the unspoken support. "She gets off on just taking the role of a puppeteer, pulling on everyone's strings. She's been that way since I first met her."

"When was that?"

"I was thirteen at the time. In eighth grade. She was in the same grade as me. I suspected her true nature right away, but it became super obvious after her father died and my mom adopted her. She was always going out of her way to get people to bend to her will. She usually fails when she tries it with me because I'm too smart for her."

Sam frowned, looking doubtful. Jeremy pressed on before she could voice any skepticism.

"Now, you've probably noticed that I keep myself pretty fit. I've always been like that. Not necessarily a natural athlete, but a commitment to the gym cures a lot. I wasn't really into team sports in my youth, but I dabbled in all sorts of martial arts as a kid. Karate was my main passion, at first."

"Ok," Sam said, looking confused at this tangent.

"Even though she only enrolled in my class toward the end of middle school, Sadie ended up being one of the most popular girls in high school. Basically, every guy in school wanted to get with her." Jeremy paused before forcing a laugh. "Not me, of course! She was my sister. Of course, she's not a blood relation, so it actually wouldn't be that weird if I—"

Jeremy registered Sam's troubled look and collected his thoughts.

"Anyway, throughout high school, she dated this guy named Jack. Cool guy. Total alpha male. Captain of the football team and the basketball team. He and I were tight."

Jeremy paused, remembering the subtle nods Jack would direct toward him when they passed in the kitchen, before Jack and Sadie made their way up to her bedroom. *Those were nods of respect,* Jeremy thought. *It was a wordless respect. No words were necessary.*

Sam looked confused. "I don't think I understand—"

"There's a point. I'm getting to it." Jeremy took a deep breath. "When I was a junior in high school, I was finally up for the black belt test in my karate class. I was so excited. It was hard to get Mom's attention much back in those days, especially since I was the oldest. Most of her focus was on Miguel, the youngest. Or Colin, the neediest. Or Sadie, the adopted daughter. Basically, everyone but me." Jeremy forced a laugh, but Sam didn't join. Instead, she looked mildly sympathetic toward him, for the first time.

"Anyway," Jeremy continued, "I'm finally on the calendar to get my belt test. I mentioned the test in passing to my mom, and, to my surprise, she tells me that she can't wait to see it! And she added that she is so proud of me, and knows I'll do great."

Those were her exact words, Jeremy recalled. *"I'm so proud of you. I know you'll do great!"*

"I'm not going to lie: I was excited," Jeremy continued. "I wasn't in theatre. I didn't play football. I didn't have many chances as a kid to publicly show off for my mother. So was I pumped that she was coming to my test? Sure. I was."

Sam remained still, hanging on Jeremy's every word.

"The day of my test finally came. Mom and I were going to drive to my class together, and I was in the kitchen waiting as she was collecting her stuff, when Sadie burst in the back door, bawling. Mom rushed over to her and gave her a big hug. I could barely make out Sadie through the tears, but she sobbed something about breaking up with Jack. She was devastated. So maybe you can guess what happened?"

"I think I can," Sam said. She briefly closed her eyes, looking resigned to what was coming.

"Mom apologized to me and said she had to stay home and console Sadie. She knew I'd make her proud, and she explained that she didn't have to worry about me because I was so strong, but Sadie was vulnerable and needed her. And that was that. I drove myself to the class, while Mom stayed home and handed Sadie tissues, for all I know."

"Did you pass your test?" Sam asked. Jeremy blinked.

"I don't remember, to be honest with you," Jeremy lied. *I was very distracted that night*, he thought. *It was Sadie's fault.*

"But here's the messed up part," Jeremy said, leaning in closer to Sam. "I came home that night, and Mom rushed to me to apologize again. 'It's no big deal,' I told her before heading upstairs to take a shower before bed. Once I finally laid down, I was unable to sleep. I just laid there for a while, thinking, and then the door to my bedroom creaked open. I could just make out Sadie's silhouette in the doorway. 'Sorry I pulled Mom away from your karate thing,' she said. 'But I must admit, it is somewhat comforting to know she's willing to sacrifice your happiness for mine.' And then she left."

Sam stared, horrified. Jeremy felt the threat of tears coming, and he tightened his throat to hold them at bay. He took a few deep breaths to collect himself, and only when he was confident that he could continue in a normal voice did he do so.

"I never saw Sadie upset about the breakup after that day. In fact, at school it was Jack who looked devastated. He was, apparently, completely blindsided by Sadie throwing him away. And I think it was all for me. She threw away a three-year relationship just to deprive me of an hour of happiness with my mother. That's who she is."

Sam's lips tightened. Jeremy couldn't tell whether she believed him.

"Why would she do that?" she finally asked.

"Why? I told you. It's a sport to her. That's it."

"Hmmmmm." Sam looked deep in thought. "And now you're off to Iceland for the wedding?"

Jeremy nodded.

"But you said you don't think Sadie would let the wedding happen. That's what confuses me. She told me she was independently wealthy and didn't care about anything she may lose if your mom marries Harold. Why is she so intent on stopping the wedding?"

Jeremy scoffed. "Sadie does *ok* I suppose. Enough to afford a pretty nice apartment at least. I don't consider her wealthy, though. And she is *definitely* not so rich that she doesn't want more."

"And you?"

Jeremy thought it over and let out a deep exhale. "To be honest, I don't know what I want anymore. And my opinions are becoming increasingly irrelevant, so I don't see the point in trying to figure that out. Once this wedding is over, one way or another, I'll be glad to get a break from my siblings."

Jeremy took out his phone and checked the time, prompting Sam to do the same.

"What time is your flight?" she asked slowly.

"I think it's 7:00. Or 7:05. Something like that. Why?"

Sam's eyes widened.

"It's 5:30 now. You're flying out of JFK?"

"I am." Jeremy paused. "Do you think I'll have trouble getting there at this time of night?"

"Are you asking if I think you will hit traffic at 5:30 p.m. on a Thursday in New York City?" Sam asked. Jeremy sensed that the question was mostly rhetorical, and it was with some anxiety that he nodded in response. Sam winced and gave Jeremy a look he had seen too often in his life.

A look that said he had done something stupid.

"I think you might," Sam said, not unkindly.

Jeremy, feeling panicked, quickly stood up and fumbled in picking up his duffle bag.

"I'm sure the plane will wait if I'm just a little late, right?" he asked. Sam looked dumbfounded.

"Have—have you ever flown before?" she asked.

"Yes. Twice. Or four times, since there were two round trips." *My two honeymoons*, Jeremy thought. *Although the exes had handled the planning for those trips.* Jeremy tried to process the ramifications of missing his flight, but his mind was still a bit sluggish from his earlier drinking. "I should probably go," he said, looking down at Sam, who remained in her seat.

Sam nodded, and it seemed to Jeremy like she thought that was very obvious. "Good luck," she said, although it wasn't clear whether she was referring to him making his flight or his life in general. Jeremy, starting to sweat, responded with a tight nod before fleeing the establishment. Outside, he frantically looked for the nearest busy street, where he could hail a cab.

Ideally one with a particularly aggressive driver.

CHAPTER FOURTEEN

Thursday-Friday, October 3-4, 2019

Miguel sat at the airport bar, feeling slightly tipsy and significantly sorry for himself, when Jeremy ran up, panting and sweaty.

"I made it?" Jeremy said, struggling to get his breathing under control.

"You're good," Miguel said. "They announced a while ago that our flight's delayed, for some reason. We may not take off until close to eight now." Jeremy let out a deep exhale and rubbed at his eyes.

"I wish I'd known that," Jeremy said, sounding equal parts pained and relieved. "I was freaking out while stuck in some miserable traffic. Then it took me forever to get through security. I was a wreck the entire time."

"You could have looked up the flight status on your phone," Miguel pointed out. "And that information is on monitors throughout the airport. And—"

"Yeah, maybe," Jeremy said, cutting him off. "But still."

Miguel was about to respond when he felt a hand squeeze his shoulder from behind.

"Hanging in there?" a woman's voice asked.

"Oh, I'm lovely." Miguel answered without looking back. "Just fucking lovely." Miguel felt a gentle reassuring pat before sensing the woman leave as Jeremy looked on, bewildered.

"Who was that?" Jeremy asked after a moment, staring over Miguel's shoulder. Miguel didn't need to follow his gaze to tell where his attention was directed.

"That's Sara. With an *a*."

Jeremy continued to stare at Sara as she walked away from them. "She's got an *a*, alright."

"No, I meant her name ends in *a.* She made a point when I met her of stressing that her name doesn't have an *h.* Of course, Sarah with an *h* still has an *a.* Two of them, actually. So I'm not sure why I called her Sara with an *a.* Stupid of me." Miguel knew he was rambling, but felt powerless to stop it. *I may be drunker than I realized.*

"Jesus, Miguel. I get it. How do you know her?"

"She's Colin's girlfriend. She's coming with him to the wedding. I met her earlier while we were waiting for you. She's really nice." Miguel tried not to resent Sara's presence. He couldn't blame Colin for bringing his girlfriend along. *I wish I could've done the same with Kevin*, he thought.

Jeremy continued to stare over Miguel's shoulder, so, with great effort, Miguel worked up the energy to turn his head to follow Jeremy's hungry look. Jeremy was focused on Sara, her dark hair tied back in a ponytail, as she handed Colin a bottle of water and took a seat next to him near their scheduled departure gate.

"Colin has a girlfriend?" Jeremy asked. "And it's *her*?"

"Yeah, I just said that." Miguel really wanted to get back to drinking alone and sulking.

"She's probably some bimbo, thinking Colin can be her sugar daddy."

"I don't think so. She told me she's a physician's assistant."

"A physician's assistant? That's practically a doctor!" Jeremy stared hard at Miguel, looking horrified. "That's a good job!"

"Yup." Miguel shrugged. "She seems bright. And cool. Yay for Colin."

Miguel was on the verge of turning back to the bar when he noticed Colin and Sara rise together and start walking toward them.

"So," Colin said, chuckling to himself once he arrived moments later. "Looks like Jeremy decided to show up for this flight after all." Jeremy ignored him and turned to Sara.

"You're dating *this* guy?" he demanded. "Don't you know what a loser he is?"

Sara laughed and rubbed Colin's back.

"You must be Jeremy!" she said. "Colin warned me about you!" she added in a teasing tone. But Jeremy remained serious and committed to his cause.

"He just sits at home all day and plays video games! I think this is the first time he's actually left Nassau County."

"I know how committed Colin is to his podcast. It's amazing, don't you think? You can really tell how much effort he puts into it." Sara radiated pride. Jeremy sputtered, searching for additional ammo to support his attack.

"And he eats really unhealthy!" Jeremy finally blurted out in desperation. Sara and Colin both laughed.

"Oh, Jeremy," Sara said with a chuckle. "Colin and I just shared a salad this afternoon for lunch!"

"Yeah, Jeremy," Colin added. "Who are you to talk about eating healthy when the only thing in your fridge is a case of Chicken Nibblers?" Sara's musical laugh only further infuriated Jeremy.

"Yeah, well, those are packed with protein, so you're really just exposing your own ignorance at this point." Jeremy crossed his arms, confident he was winning the debate.

This is so childish, Miguel thought, tuning out of their conversation to resume focusing on his drink. And his self-pity. He felt particularly indisposed to entertain Jeremy's boorishness just then. *It's probably a significant factor in Kevin dumping my ass*, he thought. Granted, Kevin hadn't mentioned Jeremy by name. *"I'm not really in the right place for a serious relationship right now"* was all he had offered as an explanation for the breakup. Miguel struggled to recall what he could have done to signal that he was looking for something serious, and he came up empty. As far as he could tell, he and Kevin were on the same wavelength throughout their time together.

The only potential misstep Miguel could identify was introducing Kevin to his family—specifically, Jeremy and his mother—so quickly. It frustrated Miguel that those introductions were not truly his doing. Jeremy had simply shown up, unannounced, at his home, when he briefly met Kevin. *Seems unfair to punish me for that*, Miguel thought as he polished off another bourbon. Likewise, Miguel hadn't planned for Kevin to meet his mother—they just happened to be in the same general area at the same time. It would have been weird *not* to introduce Kevin to his mother under those circumstances. Still, in hindsight, Miguel wished that his mother had been slightly less clingy upon meeting Kevin, as a prospective boyfriend.

If my family was going to chase him away, it's better that they did it now than a year down the line, Miguel thought, although he couldn't quite convince himself. It made perfect sense from a logical perspective, but as Miguel finished up his drink, it felt like a complete lie.

Miguel fought the urge to be angry with his brother or his mother for any role they may have inadvertently played in him becoming single again. Jeremy and his mother—and his family as a whole—were what they were, and if someone had a problem with that . . . well, that was a dealbreaker as far as Miguel was concerned.

Still, Miguel figured he had earned a few days of self-pity, at the very least.

Miguel noticed that Jeremy, Colin, and Sara had finally settled down. Jeremy seemed to have given up debating Sara on Colin's worth as a boyfriend, although he still looked perturbed by her presence.

"Where's Sadie?" Jeremy asked, looking around.

"She's taking a different plane." Miguel spoke without looking up from his glass. The bartender came over and gave him another generous pour, and Miguel offered a polite nod of thanks. "She has to come in on a later flight because of some work thing she has going on."

Jeremy grunted.

"Wouldn't shock me if Princess booked a private flight to Iceland," Jeremy muttered. Jeremy did a double take upon finally noticing that Miguel, slouched over his drink with his head down, was miserable. "What's with him?"

Sara stepped forward to rub Miguel's back consolingly.

"Miguel is having a bad day," she explained. "His boyfriend broke up with him earlier today."

"I'm not sure if he was my boyfriend," Miguel muttered. Jeremy frowned.

"Was that the guy I met?" Jeremy asked. Miguel gave a slight nod. "Well, you're probably better off. He seemed like a tool." With that pronouncement, Jeremy turned away, signaling his loss of interest in the topic.

Just then, the ticketing agent at their departure gate made an announcement, causing the four of them to look up. They couldn't make out the specifics of what was said, but it must have been a boarding call because, as the agent spoke, everyone in the vicinity started to mill about and, eventually, got into a line in front of the gate.

"Flight time!" Sara announced happily. She grabbed Colin by the arm and pulled him toward the forming line. Colin, who had been successfully hiding his flight anxiety up until that point, looked ill at the prospect of soon being airborne.

"Let's go, Chief," Jeremy said. Miguel, with a stiff nod, settled his tab with the bartender as he threw back the rest of his bourbon before standing up, only to immediately feel woozy. *Damn it*, he thought. *Been sitting a while. Definitely had too much.* Miguel figured it would all be worth it if he passed out on the plane, only to magically wake up at their destination in Iceland. *It will feel like teleportation*, Miguel thought hopefully, cashing in the last remnants of his optimism.

After a brief pit stop at the men's room, Jeremy and Miguel joined Colin and Sara in the line to board. A few minutes later, Miguel found himself wobbling down the narrow aisle of the plane, holding onto various seats to steady himself as he made his way deeper into the belly of the aircraft. Upon locating his window seat, Miguel realized that he was situated in a row behind his brothers and Sara, which suited him just fine. Miguel had just settled into his seat and closed his eyes, hoping for sleep, when he felt a banging at his knees. Jeremy, directly in front of him, had reclined his own seat immediately upon plopping into it.

"Seriously, Jeremy?" Miguel asked wearily into Jeremy's headrest. "We're not even in the air yet."

"I'm a lot taller than you, buddy," Jeremy said over his shoulder. "Sorry, but I need the space."

Miguel sighed and tried to settle back in, but he couldn't find a position that was comfortable. The plane slowly filled, with an elderly Icelandic couple settling in the two seats to Miguel's left. Shortly thereafter—and after a flight attendant instructed Jeremy to put his seat back into the upright position—they were airborne into the night sky. Miguel tried to meditate, like his mother tried to teach him years ago, but he couldn't manage to calm himself. The flight attendants quickly dimmed the interior lights to accommodate the majority of the passengers who were drifting off to sleep. Others donned headphones and found movies or shows to watch. Not in the mood to watch anything in particular, Miguel instead loaded an interactive map of the flight and stared at it, trying to shut off his brain. He had been anticipating a route that took them northeast toward Iceland, and he was surprised when the flight headed due north into Canada. He tried to match his view out the window with what he saw on the map, but it was too dark and cloudy to make out anything on the ground.

Miguel could see through the cracks between the seats that Sara had already fallen asleep. Colin and Jeremy seemed to be watching some action movie together, but at one point Jeremy paused the film to speak to Colin. Miguel leaned forward slightly to listen.

"How you hanging in there?" Jeremy asked. "Your issues with flying kicking in?"

"I'm good," Colin said, forcing a chuckle. "I never really saw how traveling was worth the effort involved, but now that we're up in the air, I'm good."

"It's funny how we can work ourselves up to be afraid of things that aren't such a big deal once we just do them," Jeremy said before pausing to reflect on the profundity of his observation. When Colin went to unpause his video monitor, Jeremy added, "You think this wedding will happen?"

Colin lowered his hand. "I think if it wasn't going to go forward, that would have happened before we all went to stupid Iceland," he said, sounding surly. Jeremy gave a skeptical grunt.

"Maybe," he said. "I wouldn't bet against Sadie though. And besides, if it goes forward, you'll probably have to look into getting a job. A real job. If Harold gets his mitts on Mom's money, as he likely will given what she did with her last few husbands, he's certainly not going to let her continue to baby you the way she does. And even if the wedding doesn't happen . . . Mom is in good shape. She could be around another thirty years or so, easy. You may have to wait a while to see your full share of the money."

Colin gave a slight shrug. He didn't seem overly concerned.

"I'm not too worried about it, to be honest," Colin said. "Things always seem to work out for me, one way or another. I have no reason to think this won't be the same."

"Yeah, you're the embodiment of 'it's better to be lucky than good' alright." Jeremy sounded irritated at the thought.

"Damn right." Colin put his headphones back on and unpaused his movie and, after a moment, Jeremy did the same.

My brothers, Miguel thought. It didn't invoke pride or shame—it was simply a fact. Miguel suspected that, over the course of his life, there would be plenty of people, like Kevin, who would enter his orbit and distort him with their gravitational pull, only to abruptly vanish with little warning. Colin, Jeremy, and Sadie, as flawed as they were, would be constants. And Miguel knew it was preferable to have imperfect constants in his life than be a lonely island unto himself.

Shortly after Colin and Jeremy resumed their movie, Miguel finally managed to attain something resembling sleep.

Miguel awoke a few short hours later, his ears popping with the descent of the plane. He cracked open his window shade and winced as the rays of the rising sun invaded the plane's cabin. Miguel muttered a curse and quickly lowered the shade again.

Seconds later, Jeremy threw open his own window shade, and Miguel found himself assaulted, yet again, by the sun. All of the passengers seemed to collectively wake up at the same time and struggled as a group to shake out the cobwebs before they landed. Miguel felt a stiffness in his neck, and he tried in vain to crack it to remove some of that tension.

The plane landed smoothly at Keflavik International Airport. Miguel checked the time on the monitor in front of him—5:28 a.m., local time. After some quick mental calculations, he translated the time to 1:28 a.m. in New York. *Damn it*, he thought. *I'm not hitting my target of eight hours of sleep today.* He didn't feel hungover, but Miguel thought there was a decent chance that was simply because he was still a little drunk.

Jeremy stood the instant the plane pulled up to the gate and the seatbelt sign was turned off. He hovered awkwardly over Colin, even though they were in row twenty, prompting Colin to sporadically throw dirty looks up at Jeremy. Jeremy exhaled loudly from his contorted position, looking agitated that the passengers were unable to disembark instantaneously. Miguel was content to wait in his seat until the aisle was clear. He glanced out his window, but the airport terminal wasn't particularly remarkable. Jeremy noticed Miguel and looked out the window himself.

"So much for the vaunted beauty of Iceland," he said, staring at a belt loader. The couple next to Miguel gave Jeremy a brief look before politely averting their eyes.

The four of them soon departed the plane and clustered together in the main concourse to get their bearings. A mural on the wall displayed several examples of Iceland's wildlife. Jeremy stared at it before pointing at a bird.

"That's a puffin," he noted.

"No shit," Colin said. "It's labeled."

"It's a beautiful bird, Jeremy," Sara said, sounding a touch patronizing to Miguel's ears.

"Whatever," Jeremy mumbled. "Let's find the car rental place."

They wandered through the surprisingly large airport, each of them too tired to force any conversation. As they approached the exit to the building, Miguel spotted a collection of car rental agencies. Colin tapped Sara and gestured, and she nodded before heading off toward one of them.

"Sara is really good with paperwork," Colin explained. A few minutes later, Sara returned, triumphantly waving a set of car keys.

"We've got a car!" Sara sang happily. Jeremy snatched the keys once Sara was in arm's reach.

"Alright, I'm driving," he said. He looked around, daring someone to challenge him, and he seemed surprised when no one did.

"Better you than me," Miguel muttered. He didn't feel like he was in a position to drive responsibly.

They went outside and located their car, which barely fit the four of them and their luggage. Miguel sat in the passenger seat, with Colin and Sara in the back.

"You're my navigator," Jeremy said to Miguel, shoving a GPS at him before adjusting the car's mirrors. Miguel slouched in his seat and tried to make sense of the device he had been handed.

"Alright, let's go!" Jeremy shifted the car into drive and pulled out of the lot.

A few minutes later, Miguel looked up from the GPS and blinked.

"What are you doing, Jeremy?" he asked.

"Yeah, what are you doing?" Colin asked from the backseat, arching his neck to look out the front windshield.

"What do you mean?" Jeremy asked.

"Why are you driving on the left side of the road?" Miguel said. Jeremy gave a condescending chuckle.

"Did you forget we are in Europe now? Believe it or not, Miguel, not all of the world is like New York."

Miguel peered off at another airport road in the distance.

"But all of those other cars seem to be driving on the right," Miguel said.

Jeremy was on the verge of responding when a car up ahead turned onto their road, heading directly toward them. Miguel braced himself for impact, but Jeremy managed to swerve off to the right at the last second, narrowly avoiding an accident.

"I was just messing with all of you," Jeremy said, trying to play it cool. But Miguel noticed how tightly he was gripping the steering wheel.

They exited the airport and headed east toward Reykjavik. It did not take long for the road to lead them into a rocky terrain, which felt akin to driving on the moon. Off to the right, they could see a giant plume of steam in the distance.

"That's Blue Lagoon," Sara said from the backseat. "It's a nature bath, heated by geothermal activity." Miguel glanced over his shoulder and observed Sara leafing through a tourist guide for Iceland.

"Sure is," Jeremy replied carelessly, as if that was old news to him.

After about twenty minutes, isolated buildings and other signs of life started to reappear on the sides of the road. It didn't take long for the scenery to evolve into a suburban setting, and as Jeremy drove—following Miguel's directions—that suburbia transformed into a small European city. Jeremy maneuvered slowly through the tight streets of Reykjavik, trying to locate the hotel where they would meet up with their mother and Harold.

And, Miguel assumed, Sadie would probably also show up at some point.

Finally, the hotel was in their sights. Jeremy found a space to park on the side of the road, and they all exited, pausing to take in the city.

"Reykjavik, huh?" Jeremy said, and Miguel looked about. Colorful buildings lined streets that flowed chaotically, a far cry from the rectangular grid patterns of New York. The streets inevitably curled out of view after a block or two, severely limiting Miguel's ability to take in much of the city from his vantage point. The layout gave Miguel the feeling of being caught in a giant maze. A fair-haired man, bundled in a winter coat, walked past them and nodded politely.

"Góðan daginn," the man said with a reserved smile before averting his eyes. Jeremy blinked and wordlessly stared at the man as he ambled away from them.

"What was that gibberish?" Jeremy asked once the man was out of earshot. "Was that Icelandic?" No one deemed it necessary to answer.

"Can we head in?" Miguel finally asked. He had left the realm of drunk and was firmly ensconced in hangover town. All he wanted was to lie down—his head felt like it weighed fifty pounds. There would be time enough to wander the city later.

They carried their bags into the small boutique hotel and checked in. Their mother and Harold had made the reservations for them, and Miguel was relieved to see he had his own room—he'd been mildly afraid he would be asked to share one with Jeremy. After getting their keys, the group wandered deeper into the hotel and Sara pressed a button to call an elevator to take them up to their respective rooms. The elevator doors opened seconds later, and Miguel started when his mother and Harold spilled out. His mother's eyes went wide upon stumbling into the group of them.

"My boys!" Marcie cried. She grabbed each of them in an aggressive hug while Harold enthusiastically shook the hand of anyone not ensnared by Marcie. Once hugs and handshakes were distributed, Marcie paused to look at Sara.

"You must be Colin's girlfriend!" she exclaimed.

"Yes, I'm Sara," she said.

"Sara! We are so happy to have you here with us!" Marcie wrapped her arms around Sara as well.

"It's very nice to meet you," Sara said after Marcie relinquished her hold.

"Welcome to Iceland!" Harold said. "It's very nice here. Reminds me a bit of Boston."

"Oh, Harold," Marcie said, swatting at him playfully. "It's nothing like Boston. But it is lovely here, there is no doubt about that. We were just about to head off for a whale watching tour. Would any of you like to come?"

No one immediately responded, and Marcie registered the lack of enthusiasm.

"Forgive me!" she said. "You all must be so exhausted from your flight. Please, rest up. But not for too long! We would like to treat you to a celebratory dinner before the big day tomorrow!"

Marcie gave each of them another long hug before heading off with Harold at her side. Miguel felt like a zombie, and tiredness seemed to be catching up to Jeremy, Colin, and Sara, too. They all trudged into the elevator with Miguel, who hardly registered their presence. Four flights up, Miguel exited and found his room. It was small—there was barely enough room for a bed—but a bed was all that Miguel cared about right then. He found the strength to kick off his shoes and remove his coat before collapsing onto the mattress.

The arrival in Iceland felt ominous to Miguel, like a calm before a storm. He attributed that to Sadie's absence and the assumption that she had something up her sleeve to disrupt the weekend. But Miguel was too tired to worry about Sadie and her plans for long; sleep overtook him almost immediately. His last thought before losing consciousness was that whatever Sadie was scheming, he hoped it had nothing to do with him.

CHAPTER FIFTEEN

Friday, October 4, 2019

Sam's misery had not abated.

She sat in her cubicle, struggling to focus. No matter how hard she tried to concentrate on an item on her to-do list, her thoughts always drifted back to what could be transpiring in Iceland at that moment. She found herself constantly recalculating the time and trying to picture what was happening on that small Arctic island while she sat at her desk. *It's 10:30 here, so that would make it 2:30 there. Everyone would be settling in, perhaps napping after the red-eye flight. Would Sadie have managed to blow up the wedding yet?*

It was maddening.

Sam hoped that her suffering and guilt were nearing an end. By next week, she would no longer be tempted to visualize this alternate reality where she was on the ground in Iceland, looking after Harold and Marcie. She knew the rest of the day would be taxing, and the weekend probably worse, but by Monday, everything would be settled.

One way or another.

Her phone rang. She was tempted, as was so often the case, to let it go to voicemail, but she ultimately decided to welcome the distraction.

"Sam Daly," she said, answering the phone.

"Hey Sam, it's Bob," a voice on the other end said, sounding overly familiar. *"Bob" means nothing to me*, Sam thought, but she continued to listen. "Look, I wanted to give you a call about that mediation from yesterday afternoon," Bob continued. It sounded as if he was calling from his car.

Ah. Sam remembered that there was a court-ordered mediation yesterday on one of her cases that was venued in California. She'd completely forgotten about it. The mediation related to a small slip-and-fall case, not worth more than ten thousand dollars, and certainly not worth the cost of trying to defend it in any protracted litigation. She had given her attorney—whose name she now recalled was Bob—settlement authority of up to twenty-five thousand dollars to get rid of it, which she figured would be more than sufficient given the nominal damages at issue.

"Right," Sam said. "What did we end up settling for?"

"Well, that's the thing," Bob said. "We didn't."

Sam frowned. It was not the response she was expecting.

"The plaintiff, who was there at the mediation himself, *hates* your insured. With a passion. They apparently have some sort of history going back to high school. I guess their relationship didn't get any better after that accident in the parking lot. Anyway, the plaintiff refused to accept *anything*. He insists on taking this worthless case to trial. His own attorney was screaming at him to accept twelve thousand, but he wouldn't. He just kept saying he wanted to turn the screws. The mediator was beside himself. I tried to explain that since there was insurance, he wasn't hurting anyone except you and I, but he wouldn't hear it."

"Huh."

"*Huh* is right," Bob said. "Anyway, I'm about to go into a tunnel. I'll check in next week to discuss a strategy going forward. Maybe we just take a default and let them prove their damages in court? I want to give it more thought, but I'll get back to you."

"Alright, sounds good." Sam was relieved she wasn't being asked to do anything right then and there.

"Yeah, it's a tough one," Bob said. "It doesn't happen often, but sometimes I guess it's just not about the money." He hung up.

Sam's thoughts returned to Iceland the second she put down her phone. She struggled to imagine what Sadie was planning. *They had once organized a collective walkout, perhaps something similar is in the cards?* She hoped whatever Sadie had up her sleeve, Marcie was smart enough not to be manipulated by it.

Although Sam liked to think there was a chance the wedding would go off without a hitch, she didn't view that as a realistic outcome. Sadie had gone through considerable efforts to get rid of Sam, and Sadie didn't seem like the kind of person who would go through that work for nothing. As for whether Marcie and Harold would proceed with the wedding, irrespective of whatever Sadie did, Sam was dubious. Marcie had been inclined to call off the entire affair after the slightest bit of resistance from Colin. Had Sam not intervened, the wedding would have been canceled weeks ago.

And Sadie was considerably more formidable than Colin.

Perhaps Miguel will intervene on his mother's behalf. Hell, even Jeremy showed signs of weakening. Maybe Marcie and Harold aren't as alone as I fear. Still, she couldn't escape the nagging feeling that they needed her.

The entire conflict remained somewhat confusing to Sam. Marcie was rich, and the kids wanted the money. That much made sense. But Harold had told her there was a prenup explicitly providing that Marcie's money would remain solely hers. Even without that prenup, Marcie's children should realize that the marriage would not result in any loss of wealth to their mother. Granted, when Marcie inevitably passed away, if she was survived by Harold, there was a chance the money could be left to him. But it was Marcie's money—she could do whatever she wanted with it through a will, regardless of whether or not she was married. Sam couldn't fully understand why Marcie's children were so opposed to the wedding.

Sometimes I guess it's just not about the money.

Sam froze in her seat as Bob's parting words bubbled up from her subconscious. The money seemed to be such an obvious motive that she had been blind to any other possible reasons behind the objections to the wedding. Marcie's four children were each so different from one another; of course it made sense that they each had a different agenda—a different reason they would oppose their mother remarrying, yet again. Sam thought about Sadie bragging, in her passive-aggressive fashion, that she was independently wealthy and that she was not overly concerned with her mother's wealth. Jeremy had downplayed Sadie's humble-bragging about her own wealth, but Sam realized that there was something driving Sadie other than just dollars. *What is motivating her to do this?* Sam felt the answer to that critical question lurking somewhere in her mind, but she couldn't manage to lasso it.

And even if she did figure it out, she was of no use to Marcie and Harold in New York. Granted, she may have been useless to them in Iceland as well, but—

I could try.

The thought came from nowhere, and Sam winced at its treasonous nature. *Try what?* she wondered. She reminded herself that the entire matter was really none of her business. Whatever was going on only concerned another family, and a small tangential remnant of Sam's old family. The outcome was, as it should be, outside of Sam's control. Why, if the situation were reversed . . .

Marcie would try to help me.

Sam again cursed the weakening of her resolve, but she knew she had stumbled upon a truth.

It wasn't even a hypothetical question. Marcie had set out to guide Sam through her grief before they had even met. Sam, in her own weakness, had initially been repulsed by what seemed to be pity, but, in that moment of clarity, she recognized that Marcie's overture was nothing less than unfiltered compassion. It wasn't a reason for her to stay away from Marcie.

It was a reason to jump to her aid.

Sam shut down her computer and stood. Rising on her toes to peer over the maze of cubicles, she spotted Nick in his small glass-walled office, reading something on his computer. Sam strode to his door and quickly knocked, surprising him.

"Nick, I need to ask you for a favor," Sam said. Nick cocked his head, listening.

"I know it's not even lunchtime, but I have to leave for the day." The words came out of Sam in a rush. "Something came up, so I have to go. I know I haven't been the best employee lately. And you've been incredibly patient with me while I've been working through some personal stuff. I appreciate all of that. I appreciate it so much. And I promise to work more on getting my act together. But for now, I really have to go take care of something."

Nick frowned, looking somewhat hurt.

"Sam," he said. "If you say you have to go, then you have to go. Take care of whatever it is you need to take care of. Capeesh?"

Sam let out a deep breath that she hadn't realized she had been holding. She already felt lighter at her decision, and she was relieved that her job wouldn't be an impediment.

"Thank you, Nick! I won't forget this."

Sam turned to leave, but stopped when Nick, in a hesitating voice, asked, "I don't mean to pry, but will you be back on Monday?"

Sam turned back. She could feel an onset of determination rushing through her veins, and she made no effort to hide it from her grin.

"Of course," she said. "I just have some business to take care of in Iceland."

• • • • •

Miguel was in bed in a semi-asleep daze when his room's telephone rang. Rolling onto his side, Miguel fumbled to pick it up before holding it to his ear.

"Hey, Chief." It was Jeremy. "Family meeting down at the bar in fifteen minutes. Going over the plans for tonight and the wedding tomorrow. Make sure you shower. You really smelled ripe coming off that plane." Jeremy hung up before Miguel could respond.

Miguel tried to sniff his armpits, but the results were inconclusive. He realized, though, that Jeremy was probably right. Miguel figured, as a general rule of thumb, that if the last time you showered was on another continent, you're probably due.

Miguel almost felt human again as he continued to wake up. There was some slight dehydration, to be sure, but Miguel thought he was otherwise ok. He went into the small bathroom in his room and stripped out of his filthy plane clothes. After a minute of finagling with the strange faucets, Miguel hopped into the shower and, as he cleaned himself, drank some of the shower water, which carried a faint taste of sulfur. That water probably wasn't meant to be consumed, but Miguel hoped a bit wouldn't kill him.

Five minutes later, Miguel emerged from the shower stall. Once he finished shaving and dressed, he felt like a brand-new man. The angst he felt the night before about Kevin was already starting to fade. Miguel savored the feeling of being tucked away in a corner of the world beyond the reach of the stresses he had left behind in New York. Miguel had arranged to fly back Sunday afternoon, but he was already regretting not planning for a longer stay.

Miguel took the elevator to the ground level and found a small bar area off of the main lobby. Aside from the bar itself, which could accommodate four stools, there were only five small tables scattered around the room. Jeremy sat alone at the bar, brooding, across from a bored-looking bartender staring into space. All of the tables were empty except for the one occupied by the rest of Miguel's family. Harold appeared to be making small talk with Sara while Marcie was enthusiastically discussing something with an impatient-looking Colin. There was still no sign of Sadie.

Marcie looked up at Miguel by the entrance and waved him over.

"Miguel!" she said. "We are so glad to see you!"

"Nice of you to join us," Harold added sarcastically. He grinned to show that he was just kidding around.

"Where's Sadie?" Miguel asked, looking around the room.

"Who knows?" Jeremy said from the bar, turning to the group. "She's been radio-silent all day."

Miguel noticed that Jeremy's clothes were wrinkled to an absurd degree.

"Are you ok, Jeremy?" he asked. "Your clothes—"

"That's what he gets for stuffing all of his dress clothes in a duffle bag," Colin said, sounding amused. "That's why he looks like he spent the night sleeping on a park bench."

Jeremy grunted.

"Yeah, well the wrinkles will work themselves out when I move around a bit more," he muttered.

"Or, you know, you can just iron them?" Colin looked downright tickled at Jeremy's sloppy appearance.

"I think Jeremy looks wonderful," Marcie said. "You all do. And I'm sure Sadie will be here any time now. We've made dinner reservations for tonight at 7:30, at this wonderful seafood restaurant Harold found. It was hard finding a place that did not serve whale or puffin—I certainly could not handle that—but Harold located a venue that seems perfect!"

Marcie leaned over to pat Harold on the cheek affectionately. Harold seemed embarrassed by the display and gently tried to separate himself from Marcie. Sara and Colin laughed at Harold's discomfort, and Miguel found himself enjoying the dynamics of this new iteration of his family. But that hint of something approaching joy was soon interrupted by a new presence in the room.

Sadie had arrived.

She looked distressed. While she normally took pride in maintaining a carefully crafted look where not a single hair was ever out of place, she now looked as if she had spent the entire day wandering the damp, windy streets of Reykjavik. Her makeup was streaked across her face, and her red-lined eyes looked as if she had been crying for some time.

Without hesitation, Marcie rose and strode across the room to hold Sadie, who didn't resist the embrace. Marcie didn't speak—she simply rubbed Sadie's back while making nonsensical calming noises. Miguel was transfixed by this scene and stole a glance at his brothers to see how they were processing it. Colin also seemed stunned, but Jeremy, for reasons unclear to Miguel, scowled with a cynical arched eyebrow. Miguel took a seat at the bar next to Jeremy and immediately turned around to watch the show.

"I'm sorry," Sadie finally said.

"Whatever for, dear?" Marcie asked, stepping back to look into Sadie's eyes. Sadie paused, seemingly on the verge of tears, and collected herself before speaking.

"Something has been bothering me for some time," Sadie said. She spoke directly to Marcie but projected her voice to allow everyone else to hear. "I hoped this feeling would pass, but it didn't. In fact, it grew. It grew to the point where I was on the verge of a panic attack on the plane last night."

Marcie nodded, sympathetic, and gestured for Sadie to continue.

"I did what I usually do when I'm feeling confused about something. I asked myself: *What would Mom suggest?* And the answer was obvious: meditation and reflection. I needed to tap into a higher consciousness."

Marcie bobbed her head in approval.

"Clever girl," Jeremy muttered, loud enough for Miguel to hear. "She's speaking Mom's language."

"And did your higher self provide you with any guidance?" Marcie asked.

"Not at first," Sadie said quickly, her eyes growing wide. "An answer felt like it was on the verge of my consciousness, but it was hard to hear over the din of the airplane or the airport. I rented a car and found this path to hike outside of the city. Nothing crazy, just a little walk over a couple of hills that led to a geothermal pool. It was quiet there, and I was surrounded by nature in all directions. I felt at peace, and once again I tried to meditate. And this time my higher consciousness was able to reach me and provide an answer to the question I was afraid to articulate."

"And what was the answer you received?" Marcie asked in a soft voice. Sadie paused, looking ashamed. Gathering herself, she blurted it out like she was ripping off a Band-Aid.

"I don't want you to get married again."

Only a handful of people in the room were shocked. Marcie was taken aback and thoughtful while Harold sputtered with indignation. Sara stared wide-eyed, unprepared for this drama. But Miguel, Colin, and Jeremy merely exchanged looks with one another, with small shrugs that communicated: *Well, here we go.*

"It's not that I don't like you, Harold," Sadie added, reaching toward him. "I do. You've made my mom very happy, and that means the world to me. But I was the last child to join this family. I admit, I felt something like an outsider, becoming a part of this family at the age of thirteen. There is nothing any of you could have done to make me feel more welcome, but it was still a struggle to shake the feeling that I didn't belong. That I was an interloper." Sadie had been speaking to the room at large, but she turned her attention back to Marcie. "I was obviously aware that you had married three times before my father. And after my father died of a heart attack just a few years into your marriage to him, I assumed you would get married again, as that seemed to be the pattern. But as time went on, you didn't. You kept my father's name and remained Marcie Porter for over two decades. I know it sounds silly, but that felt like a reaffirmation of my place in your family. As if you were content with where you had landed. And I was a big part of that place, and that helped me feel accepted."

Sadie once again turned to address the entirety of the room.

"These are feelings that have always been in me, but I didn't appreciate them for a long time. Something felt off when I learned you intended to remarry, and it took me a while to pinpoint the source of my angst. I now realize that the sense of being an outsider is resurfacing, with this newest wedding coming up, and I feel like that confused thirteen-year-old girl all over again. I can't handle it. If the two of you are insistent on getting married, well, you should, of course, do what you have to do. But I'm afraid I'm not in a position to support this marriage or bless your wedding. Doing so would dishonor the memory of my father and discredit my place in this family." Sadie lowered her head upon finishing, as if waiting for her penance. Or judgment. Marcie frowned, deep in thought. Harold started to speak but was immediately shushed by Marcie.

"Thank you for telling me that, Sadie," Marcie said. She spoke slowly, still internalizing Sadie's pronouncement. "I appreciate you sharing your feelings with us. You must know that you are a key part of this family, and nothing will ever change that. And yet, I have to respect your greater truth." Marcie looked troubled. "But I have also consulted my higher self over the course of these past months, and this wedding—this marriage—is something my heart truly wants. If I were to honor your wish, I would be betraying my own self."

"Marcie, this is ridiculous," Harold said. "If Sadie doesn't want to be a part of the wedding, she doesn't have to—" Marcie cut him off with a raised finger.

"I would like to hear what my other children think," she said.

Colin looked uncomfortable and turned to Sara. "Hey babe, would you mind giving us some privacy here? It looks like we are having an impromptu family meeting." Sara seemed disappointed by the prospect of missing out, but she nodded her head in understanding.

"Of course. I'll be up in the room." She gave Colin a peck on the cheek and left.

"Look," Colin said once Sara was gone and the door was fully shut behind her. "I told you some time ago that I didn't want to see this wedding go forward. And all I got for that was a cryptic note saying, in essence, *tough shit*. So, I think you know where I stand."

Marcie winced as if she had been physically struck. Harold's eyes darted about—he seemed to realize he was losing control of the situation, but he didn't know what to do about it. Miguel felt ill—he was starting to see where this was heading.

"And you, Jeremy?" Marcie asked.

"What are you doing, Marcie?" Harold asked before Jeremy could respond.

"I want to know what my children think, Harold," Marcie said, calm but forceful. "I can't go through with a wedding that all of my children oppose. So please: Jeremy?"

Miguel glanced to his right to see Jeremy looking down, assessing his options. Jeremy glanced at Sadie and his lips twitched—he seemed to realize he had a rare opportunity to undermine her completely. It didn't take Sadie long to recognize the leverage that had fallen in Jeremy's lap, and she walked slowly and deliberately across the room to him before leaning over to whisper directly into his ear.

"Are you really going to risk throwing away millions of dollars just to annoy me?" she asked, barely loud enough for Miguel to also hear. Jeremy stared straight ahead without responding.

"Or, to put it another way," she added, leaning in even closer to the point where her lips nearly brushed Jeremy's ear. "You have an opportunity here to get back in my good graces. I suggest you seize it."

Sadie walked away, leaving everyone else in the room confused about what had just transpired. Jeremy looked after her, and Miguel could tell from the slight slumping of his shoulders that Sadie had, once again, managed to bend Jeremy to her will.

"I'm not in favor of the wedding, either," Jeremy finally muttered. Harold shook his head, disgusted, and Marcie slowly nodded before looking at Miguel. He found it difficult to meet her wide, pleading eyes.

"Miguel?" she asked. She was struggling to keep her voice neutral, but Miguel could hear the underlying timidity, and it threatened to break him.

Damn it, Miguel thought. He looked about for help, but it wasn't forthcoming. Everyone was frozen as they stared at him. Harold's look seemed to beg for a lifeline. Sadie and Colin looked on, seemingly impassive, but Miguel could detect the urgency in those stares. Jeremy seemed curious, as if wondering whether Miguel would have the strength to do what he could not.

And Marcie simply looked expectant, awaiting an answer.

"Miguel?" she repeated. "If Harold and I got married tomorrow, would we have your blessing at the very least?"

Miguel looked around once again, at his mother and his siblings. He hated the position he found himself in, but he knew neutrality was no longer an option. Five sets of eyes focused on him as he ran some quick calculations in his head before answering his mother's question.

"No."

CHAPTER SIXTEEN

Saturday, October 5, 2019

Although her red-eye flight touched down just around sunrise, it took Sam a fair amount of time to traverse Keflavik Airport. This delay was caused by several factors.

First, upon leaving work the prior day, Sam learned that there was a single flight to Iceland that afternoon with available seating, but the only way for her to catch it was to head straight to the airport directly from her office in downtown Manhattan. There was no time to go home for anything. Sam boarded the plane with nothing more than the clothes on her back and the bag she carried to work, which necessitated overpaying for a winter coat upon arriving at the airport in Iceland.

By the time she was settled on that front, a long line had already formed at the car rental agency. It took her over an hour to get to the desk, where she happily accepted a compact car in a hideous shade of green and a GPS to help her navigate a foreign country she never contemplated visiting up until a few weeks earlier.

Sam was exhausted once those logistics were settled, but she drove toward Reykjavik with a sense of urgency. She had no idea what she was heading into. The wedding could be proceeding as planned, despite Sadie's best efforts to derail it. It could have already been called off, for whatever reason. In any event, it was hard to imagine a scenario that would justify Sam rushing to the hotel. Still, her burning need to know where things stood pushed her to exceed the various speed postings she spotted, confusingly marked in kilometers per hour.

When Sam finally found a place to park near the hotel in Reykjavik, she paused to collect herself. She knew the wedding party was staying there, but she had no inclination of what her course of action should be. *It's hard to plan when you don't know what you're jumping into.* She resolved to find Harold and Marcie to get the lay of the land, and from there . . .

From there it would all have to be improvised.

The hotel was tall but narrow, with a small reception area on the main level. The front desk was vacant, and Sam hesitated to smack the bell resting on it. *What would I even say to the check-in person? If I asked for Marcie's room information, would they even give it to me?* Sam was uncertain.

Sam spotted a door with a glass panel to her right. After looking around to see if anyone was watching her, Sam casually walked to the door and glanced through the window, looking for any sign of a hotel employee. Although she could see a waitress in the distance clearing off a table filled with dirty breakfast plates, Sam disregarded her almost immediately. Her attention was drawn to the other occupants of the room.

Harold and Marcie sat together at a small table, eating in silence. At another nearby table, Jeremy sat with Miguel, Colin, and a woman who Sam didn't recognize. That woman was talking in an excited fashion, but the three men at the table seemed to be paying her little mind. They each seemed lost within their own heads, absently sipping a coffee or juice every now and then. The other tables in the room were empty, aside from some soiled plates, cups, and cutlery. It seemed as if the members of Marcie and Harold's wedding party were the only ones in the small hotel taking advantage of the complimentary breakfast at that time.

Sam scanned the rest of the room—no sign of Sadie. *Is that a good thing, or a bad thing?* Sam wondered. *Well, only one way to find out.*

She pushed the door open and entered. Marcie looked up and her face instantaneously brightened. Harold, following her gaze, spotted Sam and shook his head with a small rueful grin. The other table soon also picked up on Sam's arrival. Colin scowled and whispered something to the woman next to him. Jeremy stared blankly, as if trying to decide how he should feel about Sam showing up. Miguel, oddly enough, flushed upon seeing her and averted his eyes when they briefly connected with Sam's. Sam again surveyed the room, looking for Sadie, but it was—with the exception of hotel staff filtering in and out to clean the breakfast plates—otherwise empty.

Sam braced herself for impact when Marcie leapt out of her seat and headed toward her.

"I knew you would come," she whispered as she ensnared Sam in a tight hug. "I knew it."

"It's true," Harold said, walking up to them. "She wouldn't even let me cancel your room reservation." He paused, before adding in a slightly chiding tone, "Although we paid for a room last night for no reason, with your late arrival and all."

"Oh, hush," Marcie said as she let go of the embrace. While she studied Sam, Marcie's smile slipped. With a glance back at her three sons, Marcie gently guided Sam to a far end of the room, with Harold following.

"I'm so glad you came," Marcie said in a lowered voice. "But I'm afraid you may have wasted your trip. We have decided not to get married." Harold scowled.

"It's ridiculous, Marcie. And I certainly was not part of that decision." But Marcie shook her head.

"No, Harold. It has to be this way." Turning back to Sam, she added, "Iceland is truly magical though. I hope you have some time to enjoy it."

Sam felt her stomach drop. *Am I too late?* she wondered.

"What happened?" she asked. Harold merely shook his head, too disgusted to respond. Marcie placed a calming hand on his arm before answering Sam's question.

"Last night, after Sadie raised some concerns of hers, we all had a discussion about whether or not we should proceed with this wedding. I made it quite clear that I would not go through with it if all of my children opposed it. And we had an open and frank conversation, and it turns out that none of them are willing to give this marriage their blessing."

"None of them?" Sam looked back at Miguel, who caught her glance and once again looked away, ashamed. Sam turned back to Marcie and Harold.

"That's—" Sam paused. "I'm sorry that happened. And I'm sorry I wasn't here to support you last night. I know if I had a few minutes to speak with Miguel, I could turn him around. I could probably even do the same with Jeremy—" Sam trailed off as Marcie shook her head.

"No, Sam," Marcie said in a gentle tone. "After last night, I spent a lot of time in my room praying for guidance and meditating to open myself up for a response from my higher self, and I came to the realization that I could not get married again unless all four of my children were at my side. I told my children this morning that I would not go through with the wedding without all of their blessings. It was my hope that it may have prompted a change of heart, but their position was unchanged. So here we are."

"You've got to live your own life, Marcie," Harold said in a pleading tone. It was clear that this was a mere continuation of an argument they had been having over the course of the past day.

"Harold, I love you, and I have no intention of leaving you," Marcie said, ever patient. "And as much as I was looking forward to memorializing our love through a wedding ceremony, I am not willing to do that without the support of all four of my children."

Harold threw his hands up in response, frustrated, and wandered back to his table.

"I feel for him," Marcie said, watching him depart. "This isn't easy for him to understand. I wish it didn't turn out this way, but—" Marcie shrugged. "Everything happens for a reason, I suppose." She did not sound particularly convinced.

Sam didn't know what to say. *I'm too late*, she realized. *The damage has already been done.* She didn't know what she could have done had she been there a night earlier, but guilt gnawed at her regardless. Marcie sensed Sam's discomfort and reached over to gently rub her arm.

"Please, do not worry about us," Marcie said. "We will be fine. And we are all here, together, for at least another day. We should try to make the best of it. You must be exhausted from your flight. Why don't you go up to your room and rest for a few hours? We will have a wonderful time, regardless of this hiccup."

Sam nodded dumbly. Exhaustion swept in to replace adrenaline as the realization that she had failed took hold. Sam turned and trudged back toward where she had entered—she had no desire to greet any of Marcie's children. But as she neared the door, a tall, lithe figure entered, nearly bumping into Sam.

Sadie. Sam felt dying embers inside her flicker with renewed life.

"Oh, Sam," Sadie said, blinking in surprise. "I had no idea you were here. Did you just get in?" When Sam didn't answer, Sadie continued. "I never had a chance to apologize for the last time we saw each other. I must've sounded so insensitive! It's bothered me so much since then, knowing that I may have played a part in you leaving early from the silent retreat."

Sam continued to stare blankly at Sadie, who was unfazed.

"Anyway, you must be exhausted. I know how tired I was yesterday after that red eye! I'll leave you to go rest, and hopefully we'll get a chance to catch up once you're feeling better."

Sadie beamed at Sam and walked toward an open seat at the table with her brothers. It didn't bother Sam at all that Sadie thought she had won. Sam did not feel any sense of competition and was indifferent to any internal gloating Sadie was conducting just then. Sadie was the only participant in whatever game she was playing, and Sam was not inclined to partake in that twisted contest.

Sam slowly trudged toward the reception area.

And slowed to a stop.

I cannot give up. The thought was powerful enough to pause Sam in her tracks.

Not because of Sadie, or any of her brothers. She had no desire to fight against anyone. But she wanted to fight *for* Harold and Marcie, who were asking for so little—just a simple ceremony to celebrate their love—yet even that was eluding them. Marcie had, without invitation, stepped in as the mother that had been missing to Sam for so long. And Harold—

Sam lacked the ability in the past few years to support Harold when he truly needed someone, but at that moment, she felt reserves of strength that had been unattainable to her for some time. She was strong enough, Sam realized.

Strong enough to try, at least.

"If you don't mind," Sam called out to the room. Everyone stopped what they were doing and looked up at Sam by the door. She waited for all of their attention before continuing. "I'd like to have a word with the children. Alone."

Sadie smirked at the subtle insult and shifted in her seat, looking forward to whatever was coming. Harold and Marcie whispered to one another before standing in tandem. Miguel and Jeremy exchanged a glance, both of them looking somewhat apprehensive.

"We will be up in our room," Marcie murmured to Sam as she walked past. "Room 32."

"What are you planning?" Harold asked in a less subtle voice. Sam shrugged.

"I'm not sure," Sam said, truthfully. Harold looked confused.

"Good luck with that, then," he said, before exiting with Marcie.

The woman next to Colin tentatively stood up, signaling for Sam's attention.

"Ummmm, should I leave, too?" the woman asked.

"Well," Sam said. "I'm not quite sure who you are."

"Oh, I'm Colin's girlfriend. My name is Sara." Sam frowned, thoughtful, and the silence seemed to make Sara uncomfortable. "It's spelled without an *h*," Sara added with a nervous titter.

"Nice to meet you, Sara. I'm Sam. Also spelled without an *h*."

Sam and Sara smiled at each other well past the point of awkwardness. Sam won the staring contest when Sara broke their eye contact.

"I'll head up to our room, too," Sara said.

"Thank you," Sam said. "I appreciate that."

Sara exited, leaving Sam alone in the room with the four half-siblings. In the eerie calm that permeated the area once the door had closed behind Sara, Marcie's children, as if driven by some deep-seated instinct, took to spreading out around the otherwise empty room. Jeremy stood up to take a seat at the bar, while Miguel shuffled to a window. Colin slinked off to another table on the side of the room, leaving Sadie alone at the table where they had been sitting together. No matter where Sam looked, someone was in her blind spot.

It was ominous. Sam realized she was badly outnumbered, but even worse, she had allowed herself to be flanked before even starting a conversation. Even though Sam didn't believe the conversation would become heated to the point of getting physical, she couldn't shake the feeling that she was surrounded.

• • • • •

Colin watched from the side of the room where he had resettled. From there, he could clearly see the faces of his siblings, as well as Sam's, looking a bit panicked, like she was on the verge of trying to improvise a speech at a big conference. It was hard for Colin not to laugh as he watched Sam looking wildly around the room, trying to address all four of them at once.

"I understand that you have all convinced your mother not to get married later today," Sam said, clearly stalling for time as she collected her thoughts. Across the room, Sadie crossed her arms, demonstrating a lack of regard for such preliminaries. Colin thought Sadie looked like someone suffering through an opening act while impatient to see the headliner.

Colin, by contrast, found himself savoring Sam's desperation. He still resented her for undoing his work in convincing his mother to forgo the wedding weeks earlier, and he enjoyed watching her struggle to find some magical combination of words that would convince all of them to change their minds. *I'm certainly not changing* my *position*, Colin thought. He was relieved Sara had been dismissed from the room. She didn't fully understand why the wedding wasn't proceeding, and Colin was happy to let her believe that Sadie was the sole cause of it. Colin had been apprehensive about what Sam might say in Sara's presence about his own role, and he had considered fleeing the room altogether once Sam made it clear that she wasn't going to let the issue die a natural death. But with Sara gone, Colin didn't see any harm in antagonizing Sam a bit.

"I really don't see how any of this is your business," Colin said with a sneer. Sadie arched an eyebrow, impressed by his moxie.

"I'm friends with your mother, and she's obviously upset about it," Sam replied. "That makes it my business."

Colin snorted, unconvinced. The others remained silent.

Sam paused.

She has no idea what she's doing, Colin realized with glee. *She's just humiliating herself.* But Colin didn't have any sympathy for her.

It served her right for getting in the way of his legacy.

• • • • •

Sam surveyed the room, trying to formulate a plan. *I can't just convince one of them to change their mind*, she reminded herself. *I have to somehow run the table.* She glanced about, wondering where to start. *Where is the weak link?*

Miguel, trying to hide by the window, remained a mystery to her. Sam had no idea what would have prompted him not to support his mother, and, as such, she had no idea how he should be approached. Jeremy, at the bar, seemed focused on how Sadie was reacting to these events. Sam had a vague idea for how she could bring him to her side, but she knew it would first require a showing of strength on her part. And as for Sadie, it would take some time to wrestle open the jar to that lid. Which left—

Sam turned to face Colin head on.

She was sure Colin, with his love of video games, would be offended at being perceived as a level one boss, but it made sense. Sam knew he was driven entirely by greed, and money was the basest of motivations. She thought that would be straightforward enough to navigate.

"Your girlfriend seems very nice," Sam said in a pleasant tone. Colin squirmed—he was not comfortable having Sam's attention focused on him.

"Thanks," he said, defensive and suspicious as to where this was heading.

"What does she make of you convincing your mom not to go forward with the wedding?"

It was subtle, but Sam noticed Colin's face flush. *He lied to Sara*, she thought. *Maybe he blamed his siblings for the betrayal?* It really didn't matter—it was enough to know that it was a point of embarrassment, if not shame, for Colin.

"Don't worry about her," was all Colin said in response.

I won't, Sam thought. *I just wanted to plant that seed in that spoiled skull of yours.*

"I assume," Sam continued, "that your primary goal in preventing the wedding from going forward was a fear of what would happen to your mother's money once she married. Do I have that right?"

Colin tightened his jaw, determined not to respond.

"But maybe you don't think of it as your mother's money," Sam added. "Your father earned it, after all. So I can almost see why you would feel some sense of entitlement to it. But what doesn't make sense to me is why this wedding matters to you at all. Are you worried your mother will share her wealth with Harold once they are married? If that was a risk, why would they go through the effort of having a prenup in place making it clear that their individual assets would remain separately owned after the wedding?"

Colin blinked and glanced at Sadie, who ignored him. *Maybe they didn't know about the prenup after all*, Sam wondered. Either way, the revelation did not cause Colin, or any of the others, to withdraw their objections to the wedding.

"That means that when they get married, the money will unquestionably stay with your mother." Sam shrugged. "How are you possibly any better off now with the wedding not proceeding?"

Colin bit a lip, fighting the urge to say anything. In her periphery, Sam noticed Sadie place her elbows onto the table before resting her chin in her palms. A dramatic gesture conveying she was intrigued, but not at all concerned. *I'll deal with you later*, Sam thought before refocusing on Colin.

"Maybe," Sam said, thinking out loud, "you're worried about what happens when your mother dies?" Sam gave a slight disgusted shake of her head. "It's always a sign of a great son when he is more concerned about the financial ramifications of his mother dying than, you know, the dying itself, but again, how could this wedding change anything? Whether you like it or not, it's legally your mother's money, and it will stay her money if she marries Harold. She can leave her estate to whomever she wants. If she wants it to go to Harold, it will. If she wants it to go to you, it will. How does—"

Sam trailed off. She could tell from the brief involuntary glance Colin threw at Sadie that she had somehow drifted off the path. Sam racked her brain and recalled something Marcie once told her: *"I don't like to think about money."*

And that piece, at least, finally clicked for Sam.

"Ah. Your mother doesn't have a will." Sam knew from Colin's reaction that she had hit the mark. *What does that mean?* Sam thought, trying to put it all together on the fly. *When Marcie passes, may it be a long time from now, she will die without a will.* Sam remembered from somewhere that dying without a will was called intestacy, but she didn't know the full ramifications beyond that. *I should have pestered Nick a bit more when I was talking to him about prenups*, Sam thought. Still, Sam figured that it stood to reason that if Marcie was married and died without a will, then a good amount of her estate, whatever the percentage might be, would pass to Harold by default.

"You're afraid that even with a prenup, most of your mother's money will go to Harold if they are married and she dies before him," Sam said aloud. Sam hated to think about Marcie and Harold's eventual deaths, and she resented Colin and his siblings for forcing her to do so.

Colin continued to stay tight-lipped. *Good*, Sam thought. *I have plenty more to say anyway.* Sam noted that Colin looked tenser than he had a few minutes earlier, which she thought was at least some confirmation she was on the right track.

And she knew what she had to do.

"Assuming I'm right about this," Sam said, "which I think I am, you're operating under the belief that if your mother does not marry, her wealth will pass to you—at least in part—when she inevitably passes away, whether it be six months or thirty years from now, because she no longer intends to get married. But you're missing something."

Colin stared at her, trying to maintain his refusal to speak. Sam patiently waited, and Colin's curiosity soon got the better of him.

"What's that?" he asked harshly.

"I think you know that I've become pretty good friends with your mother. And she listens to me when I give her advice." Sam paused to allow Colin to recall how she successfully convinced Marcie to proceed with the wedding despite Colin's attempted manipulation a few weeks earlier. "And I know your mother isn't interested in material things. But there's a lot of good she can do with that money. Maybe even set up her own charity. She told me she doesn't like to think about her finances, but I'm sure once I start showing her all of the good in the world she can do with it, she will become addicted to applying it to the right places and get it in the hands of people who really need it. Because, like I said, your mother listens to me."

Colin processed this with a small frown. As he mulled that over, his tongue absently moistened his lips.

"It sounds like you may have an alternative proposition in mind?" he said. He glanced at Sadie, but she didn't seem overly concerned with his display of weakening. *Why should she be?* Sam thought. *She knows she can veto this entire thing herself if she has to*. Sam pushed Sadie out of her head once again—she wasn't ready for her yet.

"This is what I propose," Sam said. "We've established that the money will stay with your mother whether or not the wedding happens, and it should be clear that she has no intent to share it with Harold in any event. I convince your mother to execute a will naming the four of you as her sole beneficiaries, and you withdraw any objection you have to the wedding. It's a better situation than you're in now."

Colin thought this over.

"What makes you so confident that my mother would even agree to this?" he asked.

Sam rolled her eyes, exasperated.

"Because instead of running around trying to manipulate her, I actually take the time to talk and listen to her. You should try that when this is all over with. I think you'd actually get a lot out of it."

Colin ignored the slight. His greed had him zeroed in on the ramifications of Sam's proposal. He was quickly assessing his options, and Sam could see the resistance leave him upon realizing that the arrangement presented by Sam was his best-case scenario.

"I suppose I might agree to go along with the wedding if my mother agreed to a will along the lines of what you laid out," he finally said.

Sadie arched an eyebrow, looking more amused than annoyed by Colin's concession. Jeremy and Miguel exchanged a surprised look, but they also didn't voice any withdrawal of their objection to the wedding. Sam was disappointed, but not surprised, that she still had more work ahead of her. Sadie and Jeremy sat expectantly, waiting to see where Sam's next move took her. By contrast, Miguel stared into space with his face scrunched. *Calculating*, Sam thought. *Miguel looks like he is recalculating something.* But his motivations remained a mystery to her.

That's another problem for later, Sam noted, dismissing Miguel from her thoughts. She could only work with what she understood.

Fortunately, Jeremy was quite easy for Sam to decipher.

What drove Jeremy could be reduced to a single name: Sadie. His interest in Sadie seemed to run the gamut between outright lust and a fervent desire to put her in her place. Sam couldn't help him with the former. But the latter . . .

Sam walked toward Jeremy, who gave her a wary look as she approached. She needed to speak with him privately, but she was afraid of losing the rest of the room out of boredom if she took too long. Sam suspected it was only a sense of perverse curiosity that was keeping Sadie rooted to her seat, but once she left, any small chance Sam had of salvaging the wedding dwindled down to zero. She only had time to whisper a few sentences to Jeremy.

Leaning close to Jeremy's ear, Sam breathed, "I don't want to announce this to the room, but our talk the other day is what prompted me to change my mind and come out here."

Jeremy twitched, but Sam sensed he was grateful about not being thrown under the bus by her a second time.

"Listen: I'm about to take down Sadie," Sam added softly. "I can do it, but not alone. I'll need your help when the time comes."

Sam suspected that Jeremy was instinctively drawn to follow strength. When he was growing up, Sadie's dominance was often the gravitational pull that directed him, however much Jeremy might resent it. But Sam knew what Jeremy wanted above all else was to see Sadie humbled and, better yet, to be a part of her humbling. Sam held out hope that her successful negotiations with Colin would be enough to convince Jeremy that she was a formidable force herself and prompt him to jump on her bandwagon against Sadie.

Jeremy hesitated, torn between his fear of incurring Sadie's wrath and his need to see her humiliated. Sam tensed, wondering how much longer she had before Sadie or Miguel got fed up with the entire affair and left. But then Jeremy looked Sam straight in the eyes and gave the smallest of nods, which was all Sam needed.

She allowed herself the briefest of smiles before turning back to Sadie and Miguel.

• • • • •

Sadie was delighted.

She took a fierce pride in driving Sam away from Iceland for the wedding, but part of her regretted that doing so deprived her the opportunity to go head-to-head with Sam. Sam's absence had allowed Sadie to accomplish her goal of having the wedding called off, but that victory felt anticlimactic.

Sam's unexpected arrival presented itself as the best of both worlds.

It gave Sadie the opportunity to spar with a rival without any real stakes at hand. Her mother had made it clear that she wouldn't proceed with the wedding without all of her children on board. Sadie knew she held all of the cards, and she had nothing to lose. It didn't matter that Sam had weakened Colin. It also didn't matter if she somehow got Jeremy and Miguel to withdraw their objections. The end result would not change. And it would be a joy to see Sam waste her efforts and look the fool in the process.

Sadie was unconcerned when Sam approached Jeremy to conduct a sidebar. She could not fathom what Sam was telling him, although she knew it was possible Sam could just be bullying him into making the same concession that Colin had agreed to earlier. After a few moments, though, Sam stepped away without Jeremy having said a word. Sam looked satisfied even though Jeremy didn't voice any change in his position. It was somewhat perplexing, but Sadie ultimately deemed it immaterial.

Sam positioned herself to face Sadie and Miguel. She looked back and forth between them, as if conflicted on how to proceed. Sam gave Miguel a hard look, her brow furrowed. *She's confused by him*, Sadie realized. Miguel was an open book once you got to know him, as Sadie did, but Sam was at a disadvantage in that regard. Sam tore her eyes away from Miguel with a grimace and aimed them squarely at Sadie.

And Sadie smiled—

• • • • •

—a wolfish grin that Sam interpreted as an invitation to get to it. Sam wasn't particularly interested in the fight, but circumstances had made Sadie an unavoidable roadblock. She didn't know if this was a battle she could win, but she was resigned to do her best. And as for the only workable strategy she had, well . . .

This is going to suck, Sam thought. But she didn't see any other viable path. Sam took a deep breath to steel herself.

And then she began.

"Hello, Sadie."

A curt nod. "Sam."

"It's nice to see you again."

"Is it?"

"Well, I thought we were connecting at that retreat."

"I thought so, too. Until you bolted in the middle of the night, at least."

Don't allow yourself to go down that road, Sam cautioned herself. *Stay on point.*

"It's been difficult for me since Mike died," Sam said in an apologetic tone. "Sometimes, emotions just hit me out of nowhere. That was one of those nights. I'm sorry if I led you to believe you did something wrong."

Sadie pursed her lips, thoughtful. *She had been hoping I would start lobbing paranoid accusations at her*, she realized. Sam was thankful she opted to take the high road in that exchange.

"I have to admit," Sam added, "that I was a bit confused when I heard you had come out against the wedding. You seemed so supportive that weekend, and I know your mother dotes on you. And you explained to me how you're independently well-off, so I couldn't imagine there being any significant financial concerns on your end."

Sam recalled how Jeremy had described Sadie to her: *Not so rich that she doesn't want more.*

"And in any event," Sam continued, "as I was just discussing with Colin, I think we can all reach an agreement that protects any monetary interests you may have. With all that in mind, do you mind telling me your reason for opposing the wedding?"

Sadie nodded graciously, as if Sam's request was eminently reasonable. Sam had suspected that Sadie would not remain hushed, as Colin largely did. Doing so would be tantamount to a concession that she was no match for Sam. Sam knew that Sadie would never do anything to ever suggest such a weakness on her part.

"As I explained to my family last night," Sadie said, stressing the word *family*, "it was very difficult for me as a child when my father remarried after my biological mother passed. It was even harder when my father died, and I was adopted. I felt like an interloper to the family, but our mother did not remarry again, and things finally settled down for me. It was only then did I feel like I truly belonged. But now, I have found that our mother remarrying, yet again, has been a triggering experience, although it took some time to self-diagnose in that regard. Only last night did I find the strength to give voice to my struggles, and Mom and Harold were incredibly understanding."

Sam nodded her head slowly, as if considering this explanation. The quick glance exchanged between Jeremy and Miguel confirmed for her that Sadie was entirely full of crap.

"I can understand that," Sam said. "But, truth be told, I'm still somewhat surprised. You seem like such a strong, well-adjusted woman. It's hard for me to imagine you being bothered by anything, let alone something like your mother remarrying over two decades after your father passed away."

Sadie's mouth tightened. Sam knew she didn't like finding herself in a position where she had to concede any weakness.

"Sometimes it is necessary to put on a brave face to show the world," was all Sadie said in response.

Sam paused. It had been a long shot, hoping Sadie's revulsion to admitting any imperfections would cause her to back off, but it had not yielded anything Sam could use.

Sam saw no choice but to play dirty.

"You were only a teenager when your father died, right?" Sam asked. Sadie didn't respond, and Sam opted to treat that as a *yes*. "I can't imagine what that was like. You lost both of your biological parents in a matter of years and found yourself under the care of a woman who you didn't really know all that well, who had three children of her own. That must've been incredibly difficult."

"Thank you for your concern, but you needn't trouble yourself with revisiting the hurdles I faced as a child," Sadie said.

"Please!" Sam said. Their tones were growing increasingly hostile, yet they continued to go through the motions of having a polite conversation. "We spent so much time at the retreat discussing me, we never had a chance to touch upon you. Or your issues. Fairly narcissistic of me, I admit. But since you're feeling so triggered, helping you, to the extent I am able, is the least I can do for you now."

Sadie frowned, and Sam noticed Jeremy stifling a laugh behind her. Miguel continued to look thoughtful.

"If *I* were in your shoes and was adopted like that?" Sam rubbed her chin, deep in thought. "I think I might feel inferior to the siblings with a biological connection to my mother. I'm sure *inferior* is the wrong word, but I'd probably wonder whether I was loved as much as they were. At least subconsciously. Don't get me wrong—I know that wasn't actually the case for you. But I think it would be normal to feel lesser, at some level, under those circumstances. And maybe that's something I would want to test, if only to confirm my suspicions."

Miguel stared, slack-jawed. Colin was also leaning forward, actively listening. Jeremy nodded his head slowly, and Sam suspected that she might have tapped into something that was real. Sadie adopted a face that was completely impassive, but Sam could tell she was being extra careful about betraying anything she was feeling.

"But how to test it?" Sam asked. "I suppose the only way would be to pit myself against my competitors. Force my mother to choose between me and her biological children. That would certainly tell the tale. Granted, doing that would probably involve some manipulation—putting my mother in a position where she had to choose between me and her other children. I'd feel bad about it, but I could see how it would be worth it to get some peace of mind."

"Shut up," Sadie muttered. Her three brothers looked at her, shock written over their faces. They were clearly not used to seeing her even remotely lose control. "Don't act like you understand me," Sadie added.

"I don't fully understand you," Sam admitted. She tried to reinsert compassion into her tone—she took no joy in rattling Sadie—before continuing. "But I would like to. Your mother obviously adores you, and if you don't appreciate that, I'd like to help you there. Because as I stand here, all I see is a woman arbitrarily withholding her blessing for her mother's wedding, solely to get one more piece of evidence that her mother loves her above all else. Proof that your mother values you even over her own happiness. Please tell me if I'm off base."

Sadie didn't respond. She eyed the exit, as if wondering if she could leave without sacrificing any dignity. Whatever she was thinking, she remained rooted to her seat.

"Or maybe it's about the power?" Sam added. "There is power in manipulation, I'll grant you that. The power to have others dance as you work the puppet strings. I've seen you wield that ability already with your brothers, getting them to turn against their own mother. The way you convinced them all to storm out after her engagement announcement, while you stayed behind like a dutiful daughter? Even now, I can't quite figure how you convinced them to do that."

Colin, Miguel, and Jeremy each shifted in their seats, uncomfortable. They had been so focused on conspiring against their mother that they had been blind to the fact that Sadie was manipulating them as well.

"But maybe I'm wrong," Sam conceded. "It's just difficult to get my head around why you would want to cause this needless pain to a woman who seems to radiate love toward the entire world, all while asking for nothing in return. I don't think that kind of spitefulness is who you are."

Sam didn't necessarily believe the last part, but she tried not to dwell on it. Instead, she flicked her eyes to Jeremy, hoping to catch his attention. He jolted at the eye contact and sat up straight, ready to play his part.

Sadie was shaken, but she was doing her best to hide it. Sam had spoken for a while without interruption, and Sadie knew she had to respond to the litany of allegations. Sadie opened her mouth to speak, but the words caught in her throat. Sam waited patiently for Sadie to collect herself, and Sadie seemed to resent even that small drop of pity. With great effort, Sadie calmed her breathing and stood, armed with her sweetest smile.

"I enjoy these little mind games you are trying to play with me, Sam," she said. "But I don't—"

"Enough."

Sadie blanched at the interruption and turned to face the declarant. Jeremy, also standing, met Sadie's glare and held the eye contact. It was hard for Sam to imagine Jeremy facing off against Sadie for long without eventually backing down, and she didn't know what would happen if he were to lose his nerve right then. As Jeremy and Sadie squared off, Sam strategically repositioned herself behind Sadie to ensure that she would also be in Jeremy's line of sight. She wanted to remind Jeremy that he had an ally, at least for this particular dispute.

An ally, Sam hoped, who had demonstrated to Jeremy that she was stronger than Sadie.

"Sam is right," Jeremy said, without taking his eyes off Sadie. He sounded almost confident—nothing like the broken man who had begged Sam's forgiveness two days earlier. "If Mom agrees to sign a will, and there's a prenup making it clear everything stays Mom's, we get everything we want. Withholding our consent for the wedding at this point would be cruelty with no purpose. I, for one, want no part of that. So, if Sam can deliver on that promise, I would withdraw my objection to the wedding as well."

Sadie's nostrils flared, and her stare at Jeremy promised payback at a later time. If Jeremy was intimidated, he wasn't showing it. Instead, he looked thrilled at his part in knocking Sadie back onto her heels.

Sam stole a look at Miguel. He looked thoughtful once again, like the numbers in the math problem he was mentally processing had changed and warranted a recalculation. Miguel seemed resigned upon arriving at whatever answer he computed, and he looked pained as he walked toward them.

"For what it's worth, I agree with Jeremy," he said, stopping in front of a vacant chair. He stared at his feet as he shuffled them absently. "Mom asks for nothing from us. If she really wants to get married, we shouldn't stand in the way." He plopped into the chair, as if his proclamation had sapped him of all his energy.

Sam was more confused than ever. *What the hell changed for him?* Sam wondered. *He must've realized before now that they were being unkind to their mother.* Sam vowed to corner him later to get an answer.

But Sam still had one holdout to deal with.

"Congratulations," Sadie said. "You've managed to charm my brothers. But the fact remains, I stand by my—"

"Don't you see you've won?" Sam interrupted in a soft voice, and Sadie froze. "You've won," Sam repeated. "If you wanted to prove that your mother was willing to give up her own happiness for you, and that of your brothers, you've done it. She plans on flying home a single woman. You have nothing left to prove. Can't you just give your mother this bit of happiness?"

Jeremy and Miguel nodded their agreement. Even Colin looked like he was inclined to agree with Sam. Sadie seemed to sense that the room had turned against her and was weighing her options. Sadie could choose to be the lone objector, thereby alienating herself from her mother and siblings.

Or she could back down.

"Fine." Sadie spat the word. "I don't see why she's so hung up about this symbolic ceremony, but fine. I'll go along with it, since it's apparently so important to all of you." She looked darkly around the room at her brothers, still digesting their betrayal. Her brothers, for their part, looked stunned at witnessing the breaking of Sadie. Sam figured it may have been a first for all of them.

The room was tense, and Sam figured that if she hung around, it would only give someone a chance to change their mind. Common sense told her to get out of there while the tide was in her favor.

"Lovely!" Sam said brightly, as if their agreement hadn't involved a fair amount of duress. "Let me go clamp down the other half of this arrangement."

She hustled out of the bar area before anyone could object. She couldn't imagine what Sadie might be saying to her brothers in her absence. *At least her rage should be diluted between the three of them*, she thought.

After a short elevator ride, Sam located Marcie and Harold's room on the third floor. She knocked and entered at Marcie's muffled invitation. Marcie and Harold sat in two chairs, looking like they had been in the midst of a serious conversation. As Sam walked in, Marcie looked up at her with hopeful eyes.

"Did you accomplish anything?" Marcie asked, breathless. Sam nodded.

"Yes," she said. "We have a deal." Sam sat on the foot of the bed, facing Marcie and Harold. "Well, maybe."

"Maybe?"

How do I put this? Sam knew it would only hurt Marcie if she repeated her entire conversation with Sadie and the others. She would avoid what she could, but some parts had to be addressed.

"I think it's fair to say that your children's objections were primarily based upon financial considerations," Sam said. Harold and Marcie exchanged a shocked look.

"I find that hard to believe," Marcie said. "All of them are doing quite well and are not wanting for anything." But Sam thought her tone was aspirational, and she did not sound like she necessarily believed that to be true.

Sam shrugged.

"Be that as it may, it was a sticking point for them. They are concerned about what will happen to your money if you get married today. And also, if you are married, what will happen to your estate if you were to die before Harold without a will." Sam paused to let Marcie and Harold process this information before continuing. "I understand you already have a prenup, but if you were to also execute a will in your children's favor, they said they would withdraw any objections they have to the wedding."

Even though Sam was only the messenger, she felt dirty for communicating such a proposal. Harold looked angry but held off on sharing his thoughts to give Marcie a chance to speak. Marcie looked down at her feet, hiding her face from the rest of them.

"They indicated as much to you?" Marcie asked in a small voice. Sam waited for Marcie to look up before nodding in response.

Marcie looked into Harold's eyes. They seemed to be communicating telepathically, with Harold looking increasingly agitated. Finally, he turned away with a defeated sigh, gesturing to Marcie to do whatever she wanted.

"I think we can come to terms," was all Marcie said. Sam held out for more of an explanation, but none was forthcoming. *Oh well,* she thought. *I've done all I can at this point.*

"Ok," she said. "I'll take you to them."

Sam led Marcie and Harold out of their room to the elevator, which they took back to the main floor of the hotel. Marcie's children remained alone by the bar, each sitting alone with their own thoughts. Although Sam had envisioned harsh words erupting between the siblings once she left, it seemed like they had simply languished in an icy silence. The arrival of Marcie and Harold caused each of them to stand, looking uncertain as to what would come next.

"Sam told me that you'd each agree to bless our wedding if I were to execute a will having my estate distributed among all of you." Marcie said it without emotion; she was simply summarizing established facts. Her children each mumbled their assent before looking away. Marcie rubbed her chin, thinking.

"I can do you one better," Marcie said, prompting her children to look back at her, curious. "You seem to know that Harold and I have a prenuptial agreement that explicitly states that we each keep whatever we are bringing into the marriage as our individual property. When we get back home, I will immediately have my attorney draft a will providing that everything I have will be split equally among the four of you when I pass. And not only that, I will swear to you, right here and now, that I will not spend another dime of my money from now until the day I die. I will live entirely off of Harold. You will not have to worry about me depleting my estate, as it stands today, if that was a concern any of you have."

Harold blinked. "Marcie, are you sure—"

"I'm quite sure, Harold." Marcie turned back to her children. "If I were to do all of this, would you bless our wedding?"

The four siblings wordlessly considered this, looking for a loophole. *It is a better deal than what I had worked out with them,* Sam realized. *They are each guaranteed to get a fourth of Marcie's substantial estate.* Marcie's children seemed to reach a similar conclusion after exchanging looks with one another. Colin was the first to speak up.

"If that's the case," he said, sounding tentative, "can't you just give us the money now?"

Marcie didn't answer, but, instead, merely looked at him impassively. She wore an expression that suggested there were limits to the extent she was willing to let herself be extorted by her children. Colin, uncomfortable, picked up on the implied message.

"Ah, never mind," Colin muttered, rubbing at the back of his head. "Yes, that would be acceptable to me." The other three nodded their agreement, with Miguel in particular looking embarrassed about the entire affair.

"Excellent!" Marcie was trying to put on a bright face, but Sam could tell she was disappointed in her children's haggling. She turned to Harold.

"Do you think you could get back in touch with the officiant?" Marcie asked. "I wonder if he's still available, after you told him we were canceling?"

Harold blinked, confused.

"What do you mean I told him we were canceling? You said you'd call him!"

"No, Harold," she said in a calm tone. "You told me last night that you would call him first thing in the morning and—"

Marcie stopped and laughed as she realized that the issue was no longer relevant.

"It doesn't matter," Marcie continued. "It looks like the universe did not want us to cancel after all!"

CHAPTER SEVENTEEN

Saturday, October 5, 2019

Once the negotiations were wrapped up and the dust had settled, there wasn't much left to say in the hotel bar.

Which left a vacuum of awkwardness.

Sam couldn't imagine how the day would proceed after that drama. Marcie seemed inclined to let bygones be bygones, but everyone else looked like they were struggling to release their emotional baggage. Harold was visibly put out, and he refused to look at any of Marcie's children. Miguel appeared humiliated by his role in the affair and could not manage to meet anyone's eyes. Sadie sat, looking somewhat sulky, as she reflected upon the events that had brought her to this point. Colin and Jeremy, apparently realizing that it would be odd to be overly celebratory about a wedding they had objected to only an hour earlier, milled about the room, giving unwarranted attention to any and all insignificant bits of paraphernalia decorating the walls.

Marcie, reading the atmosphere, leaned over to whisper to Sam.

"I think we can all do with a bit of a break from each other, no?" Before Sam could answer, Marcie announced to the room, "If you don't mind, Harold, Sam, and I are going to excuse ourselves. Sam rushed out here without any luggage, you see, so we will have to take her shopping to get ready for the wedding. And don't worry—I will make sure Harold pays for everything. I did not forget my promise already!"

Without waiting for a response, Marcie took Sam by the elbow and firmly led her out of the room with Harold trudging along behind. Harold started to speak in the lobby, but Marcie shushed him with a look and led them all upstairs, back to her room.

"What was that about, Marcie?" Harold demanded once the door closed. Sam wasn't sure what he was referencing.

"Not now, Harold," Marcie said. "We'll talk about it later."

Marcie turned to Sam.

"I figured it would be a good idea for the three of us to make ourselves scarce for a few hours. There have been lots of emotions flowing back and forth in the past day that I am sure we are all still processing. Some time for everyone to reset is just what the doctor ordered, I imagine." Marcie beamed as she added, "Not that it won't be fun to take you out shopping!"

"With my money," Harold grumbled. Sam noted, though, that he didn't sound particularly upset about it. He seemed more confused than anything.

"With your money," Marcie said with a smile. "Of course. Well, shall we?"

They exited the building without running into any of the others. Marcie and Harold, having spent the week at that hotel, were generally familiar with the area and led Sam through the meandering streets to an avenue lined with restaurants and boutique shops. Sam noticed a sign that identified the street as Laugavegur.

"What do you need?" Marcie asked. "A dress, I'm sure. Maybe a few outfits to change into? And I think we can do better than that coat—it will be very cold at the wedding ceremony later. Oh! You'll definitely need some boots. And a winter hat. And gloves and a scarf."

"You're being very generous with my money," Harold said. But again, Sam noted he did not sound annoyed about it—there was an ironic tilt to his words that she didn't comprehend. *Perhaps he's just more benevolent than I've given him credit for?* she thought.

"Ah!" Marcie cried, stopping abruptly in front of a small boutique. She got close to the glass to peer at an elegant dress imprinted with squirrels in various poses. "This is you, Sam!"

Sam wasn't quite sure how to respond to that.

They went inside and Harold immediately wandered off to examine the price tags on assorted items of clothing. Sam stayed at Marcie's side as she glided around the small shop, stopping here and there to pick up bits of clothing for Sam. Sam didn't feel comfortable voicing any objections to what Marcie was selecting for her, given that she was being treated to the shopping spree.

"Thank you for all of this," Sam finally said, as Marcie handed off a bundle of clothing to the shop owner to put aside for Sam to try on. "And I'm sorry I was so late in getting here, and arriving empty handed." But Marcie waved her off.

"Are you kidding? We cannot thank *you* enough. My heart has been overjoyed at the thought of this wedding, and it bothered me more than I was willing to admit when my children came out against it. But you turned them around. We will forever be in your debt."

Sam, not knowing what to say, gave a small nod. And then a question came to her.

"Do you think the wedding itself will be—" Sam paused, looking for the right word.

"Uncomfortable?" Marcie ventured.

"Sure. *Uncomfortable*. Given that your kids will be there, and they were against the wedding a few hours ago." Sam definitely felt unsettled at the thought of later trying to celebrate with Marcie's children under the circumstances. Marcie thought it over, before shaking her head.

"My first husband, Barry, was so stoic. So many times, I saw him calmly navigate situations that would have caused anyone else to pull their hair out of their head. And he taught me that drama, or awkwardness, needs fuel to survive. And without that fuel, it will just flicker out of existence. If my children are uncomfortable about changing their minds with regards to the wedding? Well, I'll simply ignore it and not allow that reality to take hold. You will see. It will all be wonderful."

Sam nodded, although she remained skeptical. "It's funny that Jeremy's father was so calm. Considering that Jeremy is—"

"A bit hot-headed?" Marcie inserted with a laugh. "Oh, yes. Sometimes, blood ties mean nothing, and we are all so different. It is quite extraordinary. It certainly makes things interesting. I often think Barry had more of an impact on me than he did Jeremy. I tried to adopt his sense of calm, even if Jeremy went in a different direction." Marcie paused, contemplative. "You and I discussed this before, but I often reflect upon how each of my prior husbands played a part in who I am today. If you knew them, you would certainly recognize their imprints. And I'm sure the same will be the case for Harold."

"Have you figured out yet how Harold has changed you?" Sam asked, curious.

"He taught me the value of laughter," Marcie replied without hesitation. "The joy in laughing at myself, or at the little quirks life throws at us. He has done wonders for my sense of humor!" Harold came bumbling over from across the shop.

"Are you talking about me?" he demanded. A twitch at the corner of his mouth suggested he was joking, and that it was mere coincidence that he hit a bullseye.

"Of course!" Sam said. "Marcie was just telling me about how you've rubbed off on her."

"Absolutely!" Harold said. "Where do you think she gets her patience from?"

Marcie threw her head back and laughed loudly.

"Do you see what I mean?" she said. "Such a wonderful sense of humor!"

Sam shrugged. "Once in a while, I suppose." Harold frowned, and Sam grinned at his consternation.

"Hey!" Harold took out his credit card and waggled it under Sam's chin. "Don't forget who's funding this Pretty Woman excursion of yours!" But he seemed pleased by the gentle ribbing from Sam.

"Of course, you're right. I apologize." Sam gave a slight curtsy. "You're hilarious, Harold. A real gift to the world of comedy."

"Damn right."

After Marcie had picked out nearly a dozen dresses for Sam—far more than she could envision wearing in the next year or two—they left the shop and continued down the street. Marcie handed the clothes to Harold and instructed him to bring them back to the hotel.

"We just need a few more things," she told him. "We'll be back soon, and then we'll get ready to go to the ceremony."

"I can't believe you're making me do all of this manual labor on my wedding day," Harold grumbled. Marcie patted him on the cheek.

"I have no doubt a big, strong man such as yourself won't have any issue with carrying a couple of dresses for a few blocks!"

Harold threw a pained look at Sam. "You see how she treats me? Completely exploiting the fact that she has me wrapped around her little finger!" He shook his head and trudged back in the direction of the hotel with the dresses. Marcie looked tickled as she watched Harold struggle down the street with Sam's new wardrobe.

"The thing about Harold is he loves to complain," she said. "I think I am doing him a kindness by giving him things to whine about."

Sam laughed. "That's one way of looking at it, I suppose. I doubt he'd agree, though."

"Of course not! Harold doesn't see the fun in being agreeable." But Marcie said it with affection, and the dynamic between Marcie and Harold—polar opposites by just about any conceivable metric—started to make some sense to Sam. *She loves the banter and the mild friction. He does, too.* Sam supposed that could be enough to sustain a relationship, if there was genuine love underneath it all.

Which there seemed to be.

"This is so much fun!" Marcie said once Harold was out of sight. "I've never been that into shopping back home, but it is such a wonderful excuse to explore this city, isn't it? Let's just get you some winter gear for the ceremony. It will be a cold one!"

They found a store that seemed to have everything Sam would need to avoid freezing to death. It didn't take long for Sam and Marcie to find a coat, boots, thermal socks, gloves, and a wool hat. Sam donned the items before leaving, which seemed like a better option than trying to carry it all, and they walked slowly back to the hotel.

"One day, you will have to tell me how you convinced my children to withdraw their objections to the wedding," Marcie said. "It saddens me that money was the main issue, but surely there was more to it than that?"

Sam hesitated before answering. "I got to know all four of them fairly well over the past few months. It gave me a pretty good idea of what they each needed to hear." Sam frowned. "Although, to be honest with you, I'm still a bit unclear on what I did to change Miguel's mind. Or why he was against the wedding in the first place. He seems like such a sweet, caring guy."

Marcie bobbed her head in agreement.

"Ah, but he is! And now that I think about it, I'm sure that was his issue."

"Huh?"

"Here is the thing about Miguel: his father, Ramon, bless his heart, passed away when Miguel was only two years old. I'm sure Miguel has no memory of him whatsoever, aside from whatever remembrances he manufactured for himself by looking at old photos. And even though Colin and Jeremy were also very young when their fathers died, I think Miguel feels that absence of a father much stronger than they do. Had Ramon lived, he would have introduced Miguel to an entire world—a different culture—that I failed to ingrain in him no matter how hard I tried. I did what I could to keep that world alive for Miguel, but all I could offer was a weak sampling of what I thought Ramon would have delivered to him. There is a part of Miguel that I fear is missing, and he very much feels that absence."

Sam frowned. "I don't understand."

"What I am saying is that Miguel, more than any of my other children, understands the power of family. What it can give. And what you lose when it is gone." Marcie sighed. "I don't want to put words in Miguel's mouth. But you should speak with him about what he did and why. I think he may surprise you."

The hotel was quiet when they arrived back. Marcie stopped Sam before she returned to her room.

"The ceremony is at 5:00, but we should try to leave here an hour early. We'll all meet down here around 4:00—we've already arranged for cars to take us there. And promise me you'll dress warm!"

Marcie grabbed Sam for a tight hug, which Sam returned. She knew Marcie would take her time, so she committed herself to staying in the moment and appreciating the showing of love for what it was. As she and Marcie held each other, it occurred to Sam that her time with Marcie had made it much easier for her to surrender her cynicism, when she put her mind to it.

Once Marcie let go, Sam went to the desk to check in while Marcie scurried away to the elevator to go back to her room. After finding someone to help her, an employee informed Sam that someone had already checked in on her behalf, but she was given an additional key. Sam took the key and went upstairs, and upon entering her room, she spotted her new dresses, strewn unceremoniously on the bed. *You couldn't take ten seconds to hang them up, Harold?* Sam thought.

After showering, Sam surveyed the mass of clothes she had accumulated in the past few hours. She knew the ceremony would be outdoors, although she was fuzzy on the details. It was hard to see how she could wear any of the dresses Marcie had selected without suffering from hypothermia. In the end, Sam opted for basic pants with a green blazer, although she planned to be too bundled up for anyone to actually get a good look at her outfit. She knew the plan was to come back to the city after the ceremony for a dinner, and she figured she'd have time then to run back to her room for a quick wardrobe change.

Sam headed downstairs a few minutes before 4:00. She dreaded running into Marcie's children and having to deal with any lingering drama, but the lobby was empty. There was still no one to be found once 4:00 came, and Sam settled into a chair opposite the elevator to wait.

Almost immediately after Sam sat down, the elevator doors opened to reveal Miguel, sporting a woolen sailor's hat and a dark navy winter coat. Miguel flinched upon seeing Sam, and, in a panic, pushed the button to reclose the doors.

"Seriously, dude?" Sam asked from her seat. Miguel, realizing what he'd just done, sheepishly emerged. Sam stood up to face him.

"How's it going, Sam?" he asked, looking uncomfortable.

"It's been a busy few days, but I'm getting by."

"Yeah, my first day here was rough, too."

They both smiled tightly at each other—merely something to do in the absence of conversation.

"Listen, about before," Miguel finally said. "I'm sorry you had to go through all that. And for what it's worth, I'm really happy with how things worked out."

"Are you?"

"Yes, of course."

"Well, why wouldn't you be? You're getting your money, after all."

For the first time, Miguel looked Sam directly in the eyes.

"Do you think I objected to the wedding for the money?" He sounded offended.

Sam shrugged. "I don't know why you did it, although your mother acted like she has an inkling. If it wasn't the money, then why?"

"It doesn't matter now. Just leave it be."

"For what it's worth, it *does* matter to me. I like you, Miguel, and I want to continue to like you. It really is important for me to understand."

Miguel shoved his hands into his pockets and started to walk away. Sam thought he was leaving, but he soon pivoted back to face her.

"Sadie. Jeremy. Colin." Miguel aggressively ticked off each of his siblings' names on his fingers as he recited them. "If I didn't stand with them in opposing the wedding, they would never forget it. My relationship with them would effectively be over."

"Ok," Sam said, holding back her thoughts for the moment.

"Even though I wasn't proud of what I did in standing with my siblings, and I knew it would hurt my mother, I had no doubt that *she* would ultimately forgive me. And I'd still be in my siblings' good graces. Do you see? It was the only option I had to keep this family together. We're barely holding it together as is." Miguel looked hard at Sam, as if willing her to believe him. Sam didn't doubt Miguel's sincerity, but she still took issue with his explanation.

"It sounds to me like you were punishing your mother for being kinder than your brothers and sister," Sam said. Miguel winced—she had hit a nerve.

"I know that's how it sounds. And I can't tell you how much it killed me to do that to her, or how thankful I am that you were able to sort it all out and keep our family intact. Once you convinced Jeremy to challenge Sadie, I felt unburdened. It was no longer a question of turning against all of my siblings. I just had to pick a side. And I finally had the freedom to do what I considered to be the right thing."

"Did you ever consider that if your siblings are forcing you to turn on your own mother, then maybe those aren't relationships worth saving?"

"Maybe," Miguel said right away. He looked like he had already asked himself that exact question on multiple occasions. "They are far from perfect. But they're all I have."

Sam shook her head. It didn't make sense to her. Maybe it never would. But at least she had some clue as to what was going through Miguel's head that morning.

"Are you mad at me?" Miguel asked.

"Yes. No. I don't know." Sam started to walk away and stopped to turn back. Miguel looked chagrined, and Sam felt compelled to add, "But if I am mad, I know it won't last that long." Miguel let out a small breath and, with a grin, tipped an imaginary cap at her.

Colin and Sara arrived next, bundled up to deal with the nearly arctic weather. Sara greeted Sam with warmth, and Colin even threw her a respectful head nod. They were soon joined by Jeremy, dressed in a dark suit that was wrinkled beyond belief.

"Oh man!" Colin exclaimed. "Still couldn't find that iron, huh?"

"Well, at least I'm wearing a suit, bro. You are *significantly* underdressed."

"Jeremy!" Sara said in a mothering tone. "You're going to freeze to death. Where's your coat? You know the ceremony is outside, right?" A flicker of doubt passed Jeremy's face.

"Yes," he said. "Of course."

Sadie was the next to arrive, managing to look slender and beautiful even in bulky winter gear. She didn't greet anyone upon arriving in the lobby. Instead, she made a great showing of playing with her phone, as if she was involved in some time-sensitive transaction.

Finally, Marcie and Harold arrived.

"Let's go, let's go!" Harold called out, clapping his hands. "We're late!" He didn't acknowledge that he was the last to arrive.

Marcie, wearing a thick coat that extended to her calves, ignored Harold's commands and took her time going around the lobby to give everyone a long hug. Harold waited for a beat, impatient, before darting outside. He came back almost immediately.

"The cars are here," he said. "We have to go."

The group left the hotel. Colin and Sara hopped into the back seat of one of the two cars waiting for them, and Jeremy, hugging himself for warmth in the cold Icelandic air, clambered in after them. Sadie, after taking a second to weigh her options, got into the front seat of the same car.

Miguel sidled up next to Sam. "Hope you're no longer fuming at me. Because I think we're stuck in the same car for the next hour." Sam looked at Marcie, bouncing with excitement, and felt inspired to let go of any lingering resentment she may have had.

"No fuming here," she told Miguel. "Let's go get these two married."

Miguel hopped into the front seat of the remaining car, and Sam took a window seat in the back, with Marcie sitting between her and Harold.

"I feel bad that you're stuck in the middle on the way to your own wedding," Sam told Marcie after they had been driving for a few minutes.

"Don't be silly," Marcie responded. "What better spot to be than in the middle of three of my favorite people? I am the meat in a sandwich of love!"

"Oh God, save me from this eternal optimism!" Harold groaned, winking at Sam. "If you keep this up, I'm calling off the wedding myself!" Marcie laughed and took a hold of Harold's hand.

It didn't take long to put the city behind them as they journeyed north. Soon, they were surrounded by green countryside, sprinkled with stout Iceland horses with long, thick hair—a testament to evolution's ability to adapt to nearly any climate.

"It's so beautiful," Sam breathed, staring out her window. "I had no idea it was this beautiful." She turned back to the others. "It breaks my heart that I have to leave tomorrow. I'd love to just spend two weeks or so here, wandering about. Disconnected from emails, phone calls, all of those daily stressors. It would be amazing."

"You should do it then," Harold said, making it sound like it would be the easiest thing in the world. "Come back here when you have more time." Marcie nodded in agreement.

"Maybe I will." Any time that Sam had taken off from work in the past two years was mostly spent at home, reading on the couch. *Perhaps I deserve a little trip at this point*, she thought.

After an hour of driving, the two cars pulled into a small lot that was mostly empty. As she exited the backseat, Sam heard water running in the distance, but all she could see were trees in the midst of shedding orange and red leaves. Harold hopped out next and, after looking around the lot for a spell, found a running car where a man sat alone. Marcie followed along, and Sam assumed they were greeting their wedding officiant. After they chatted with the man for a few moments, the officiant got out and walked toward a path. Harold and Marcie gestured for the rest of the family to follow along.

As Sam walked, the sound of running water intensified until she turned into a small clearing, at which point she stopped, awestruck. Sam sensed those around her also stopping in their tracks to stare at what was before them.

A cobalt blue river ran directly below, walled off by a lava field facing the group. Glacial waters ran off the wall in scattered chutes, cascading into the river and causing the otherwise calm waters to come alive in fits of white. These waterfalls stretched into the distance and seemed to continue even after the river curved out of their line of sight.

Sam was breathless. *How are there not a thousand people here, right now, to see this?* Outside of their little group, she only spotted a couple of tourists snapping photos of the wall of waterfalls.

Sam looked about and saw that she was not the only one stunned into reverence. Jeremy, clearly freezing, stopped hugging himself and stepped close to the ledge, craning his neck to try to get a better view. Colin, after a moment of processing, took out his phone to take a picture of Sara posing in front of the falls. Even Sadie looked impressed, with her hand holding her phone dropping to her side, momentarily forgotten, as she took it all in.

"These are the Hraunfossar waterfalls!" the wedding officiant declared. He sounded proud, as if he had designed the spectacle himself. "And that river below us is Hvitá. A wonderful place to celebrate this union of love. Come!"

He arranged Marcie and Harold in front of him, facing each other, as he stood with his back to the Hvitá. Jeremy, Colin, and Miguel stood at Harold's side, and Sadie glided to Marcie's left. Not knowing what she was expected to do, Sam took a position next to Sadie, who ignored her.

Sam couldn't hear much of the short ceremony over the rushing water. It was like watching a silent movie, only with the turbulence of the falls serving as the soundtrack. Which was fitting, Sam realized, because she was witnessing a story that didn't require language. From her vantage point, Sam could see Harold's face, radiating love without a hint of his usual trademark grumpiness. Marcie also turned around often to throw a warm smile to Sam or Sadie, and Sam realized that it was the first time in her life she had truly witnessed unadulterated joy.

You did this, Sam. She tried to release the immodest thought, but it proved impossible to shake. It was simply too fulfilling to have played a part in bringing about such happiness. Sam was too selfish to relinquish the pride she felt in helping to make it happen, but, given what she had gone through over the past few years, she felt no need to apologize for it.

After a few minutes, Harold kissed his bride, and Sam and Marcie's children all cheered them on. Miguel looked overjoyed, but even the others seemed to have gotten caught up in the magic of the moment and applauded with enthusiasm. After the kiss, Harold said something Sam couldn't decipher, but she could tell from his face and the others' reactions that it was some sort of inappropriate joke. Marcie, with good humor, rolled her eyes and turned back to Sadie to embrace her. She then came to Sam and ensnared her in a hug, which Sam was happy to return.

"Do you feel them?" Marcie asked, speaking directly into Sam's ear.

"Who?"

"The fairies. They are very elusive, so you won't see them, but if you pay careful attention to your other senses, you will feel them. They are here. And they are happy for us. Do you feel them?"

Sam closed her eyes, holding her cynicism at bay. She stretched her senses beyond the power of Marcie's hug, and beyond the tumult of the waters below. She pushed the tendrils of her consciousness into the rocky cliffs that surrounded them, and deep into the earth. She allowed the essence of her being to radiate from her body, spreading beyond the sparse clouds above and permeating the brisk air that purified her lungs with every breath. And only once Sam reached out as far as she could in all directions did she whisper her truthful response.

"Yes, Marcie. I can feel them."

CHAPTER EIGHTEEN

Tuesday, December 17, 2019

Two months after the wedding, Sam returned to Iceland alone.

After spending a few days exploring Reykjavik, she rented a car and drove to the northern end of the island, where she settled in at a small hotel sitting on Lake Mývatn—a largely undeveloped region of Iceland punctuated by clouds of steam emanating from natural hot springs, volcanic craters, lava fields, and other assorted natural anomalies generated by the scraping of the North American and Eurasian tectonic plates far below the surface. Sam mostly spent her days reading in front of an enormous window at the hotel that looked out upon the lake itself, tranquil in Iceland's early winter. In the evenings, she made a short drive to the Lake Mývatn Nature Baths, where she would soak in the dimly lit geothermal pools and enjoy the privacy afforded by the steam, which made it all but impossible to see the other occupants of the baths. The freezing temperatures constantly froze her wet hair, and she delighted in repeatedly submerging herself in the warm waters just to defrost her exposed head.

Sam honored her intention of avoiding the phone and emails while she was away. She couldn't shake the feeling that she was on a different path than the one she had been on months earlier, and Sam instinctively realized that what she needed above all else was some time to reflect and meditate—she was not at all tempted by the hotel's wi-fi. She took solace in being so far removed from the rest of the world, in a restorative state of solitude, and she soon felt something changing in her that was not quite healing, but perhaps a precursor to healing. Like removing clutter from a countertop before wiping it down. Even if only an incremental step, Sam felt like she was moving in the right direction.

Sam felt refreshed when she finally flew back to New York. Despite being awake for nearly nine hours, it was just after noon when the plane finally touched down at JFK. It was with a heavy heart that she turned on her phone after landing. Sam didn't regret holding the world at arm's length for a few weeks, but she knew there would be a backlog on her phone left for her to reckon with.

As the plane taxied to a gate, Sam was surprised to see she had received multiple voicemails from Miguel while she was away, the first of which was delivered only a few days after she departed for her trip. Sam listened to them in chronological order, and her heart thumped more and more aggressively with each message. "No," she found herself muttering after finishing each voicemail, staring out the window to hide her face from her fellow passengers. By the time she reached the last, Sam was struggling to hold herself together.

"No," she whispered, yet again.

As if that would fix anything.

• • • • •

Sam couldn't bring herself to return Miguel's calls or to even call anyone else. Like a zombie, Sam navigated her way home from the airport, struggling to process the messages Miguel had left for her. Upon arriving at her house, Sam quickly dropped off her luggage and went straight to her car. She drove, aimlessly at first, and only about halfway into the drive did she realize where her subconscious was taking her.

A little over an hour later, Sam parked on the street in a residential area. A light dusting of snow painted the landscape white, and even though it was only late afternoon, the sun was already well into its descent. Sam walked toward a small stone bridge, taking care not to slip in the coating of snow on the asphalt.

As she neared her destination, Sam was surprised, but not shocked, to see the old man halfway across the bridge, standing a lonely vigil as he watched the creek flow toward the setting sun. He didn't register Sam's approach—his attention was focused westward on the rolling waters below.

The waters that had carried the ashes of his wife to the Hudson River.

Which would take her to the Atlantic Ocean.

And from there, to the rest of the world.

Sam froze, before abandoning care to run through the snowy street.

"I didn't know," Sam tried to call out as she moved, but the words caught in her throat. She coughed before crying out again. "I didn't know!"

Harold turned, startled, as Sam staggered toward him, arms outstretched.

"I didn't know!" she cried yet again once she was nearly on top of him. Harold shushed her before taking her in his arms. He held her as Sam sobbed against his shoulder.

"I know. I know," he told her as he patted her awkwardly on the back. "It's ok. It's ok."

Sam wept into Harold's jacket for some time, but he didn't try to rush her. Once Sam felt collected enough to speak, she gently pushed herself away and faced him.

"I only just heard," she said. "I was away and—"

"I know," Harold said. "Believe me, I know. I wanted to reach out to you. You sent me your hotel information before you left, so I could have tracked you down. But Marcie was adamant that I not ruin your trip because of her. 'Don't you dare ruin that girl's vacation,' she told me repeatedly." He let out a small humorless laugh. "Her last words were practically 'Let Sam enjoy her time away.'"

Sam shook her head.

"It was just a vacation. I wish I knew. I would've flown back. Maybe I could have at least said goodbye."

Harold shrugged, defeated. "I don't know. Maybe I should have reached out to you, regardless of what Marcie said. It's hard not to honor the requests of your dying wife, though. But I guess I might've done the wrong thing. Feel free to be mad at me, if you want. Just please don't feel guilty at all. That's the last thing Marcie would have wanted."

At the invocation of Marcie's name, Sam turned her head and looked at the creek below.

"She showed me this spot a few months ago," she said. "She told me that she wanted this to be her final resting spot." Harold nodded.

"Toward the end, she showed me this spot on a map and gave me some very detailed instructions. I wasn't even sure if what she was asking me to do was legal, so I came here in the dead of night over this past weekend to deposit her ashes. I haven't been arrested yet, so I suppose I got away with it."

A car drove slowly past them on the narrow bridge, taking care to give them as much room as possible. It was the first car Sam had seen since arriving. It wasn't difficult to imagine how quiet this area would have been in the middle of the night.

"I've gotten in the habit of driving up here since then," Harold continued. "I still hear Marcie wherever I go, telling me what to do, or not do, but it's always a bit easier to make out her voice from this spot."

"What is she telling you?"

"Oh, you know, the usual." Harold raised the pitch of his voice in a rough approximation of Marcie: "*Be strong for the rest of the family. Don't use my death as an excuse to stop living. Don't make toast while taking a bath.*" Harold let out a small laugh—he could never go too long without making a joke, no matter the circumstances. After a beat he grew serious once again. "Mostly just telling me she's glad she had a chance, however brief, to be my wife." Harold looked away, and Sam saw him bring a hand up to his face to wipe away a tear. After a beat, he turned back to Sam.

"That all sounds like her," Sam said in a soft voice. With a small twitch of her lips, she added, "And you really shouldn't need Marcie to remind you not to use the toaster in the bathtub."

Harold chuckled. He seemed to appreciate the moment of levity, however small.

It occurred to Sam that she was having a conversation with Harold on a bridge, buffeted by December winds, without once having the need to repeat herself. She frowned and peered at the side of Harold's head.

"Did you get a hearing aid?" she asked. Harold grimaced, and his hand flew up to cover his right ear.

"Can you see it?" he asked, looking embarrassed. Sam shook her head.

"No, it's just—you're talking at a normal volume, and you can hear me."

"Well, yes. I did get a hearing aid. Marcie convinced me to do that about a month ago." He paused. "I think her exact words were 'You have so much wisdom to share with the world. It would be a shame if you could not hear when it was needed.'" Harold shook his head. "It's amazing how much she changed me in such a short time. I think she's still changing me somehow, even though she's gone."

"What happened?" Sam asked, and Harold blinked in confusion. "I got a couple of voicemails from Miguel about Marcie being sick and all, but he didn't go into details."

"Ah." Harold collected himself, and Sam sensed he was bracing to tell her a story that brought him pain. "Well, the short version is that I started seeing Marcie this past spring, and we hit it off right away. We were just having fun, enjoying each other's company. Certainly no plans to rush to a marriage. And then in August, Marcie told me that she had been diagnosed with MDS."

"MDS?"

"Myelodysplastic syndrome," Harold recited. It was clear he had heard the technical term enough over the course of the past half-year to repeat it phonetically. "It's a cancer that impacts the blood-forming cells in bone marrow, or something like that. I never really fully understood it, as much as I tried. But it's serious." As Sam processed this, she felt an irrational and misplaced anger toward Marcie begin to form, and she struggled to suppress it.

"She hid it. There wasn't a hint she was sick," she said. She looked Harold square in the eyes and felt tears forming once more. "There wasn't a single hint, Harold!" But Harold was unfazed.

"She was remarkable at covering it up, but she had her share of days where she felt dizzy or weak. I'm sure she was even concealing a fair amount of her symptoms from me, just so I wouldn't worry about her."

"But why hide it?"

Harold grimaced. "She told someone else, other than me, right after she was diagnosed, and it—it didn't go well. From that point on, she resolved to keep it to herself for as long as she could."

"Then that's what killed her? This MDS?"

"Ultimately, yes. It's not necessarily fatal in and of itself, although there was always a risk it would evolve into something that was. Given Marcie's age, that risk was not insubstantial. That's why Marcie and I had a very frank conversation." Harold paused, looking again at the creek and working up the nerve to recite the next part of his story. "She told me about her diagnosis, and what it possibly meant for her life expectancy. And she told me she would understand if I didn't want to be with her under those circumstances. She gave me an out, but I didn't accept it. And once I made it clear that I wasn't going anywhere, she told me how relieved that made her. She said she loved me, and she told me that although she didn't know how much time she had left on this earth, she would die a happy woman if she was married to me." Harold squirmed, uncomfortable with even repeating that sentiment. He added, a touch defensively, "I thought she was nuts for saying it, but she did. And she seemed to mean it, so we made plans to get married. And that's around the time I 'broke into' your home."

"You didn't break in," Sam muttered. She had nearly forgotten about the manner in which Harold reentered her life over the summer.

"We both wanted to get married fairly quickly. We never discussed what a worst-case scenario would look like, but I think we each realized that time would not necessarily be on our side. Still, it would be pointless to rush a wedding that wasn't special to Marcie, so we had to take a bit of time. I didn't even understand what a 'special' wedding would be like to Marcie. But you helped her find it that weekend when the two of you came up here together." He looked earnest and grateful, and Sam was tempted to give him another hug. But Harold quickly became uncomfortable with the tender moment and continued.

"And then actually getting to the wedding itself proved a bit trickier than either of us envisioned. And you helped us clear those hurdles as well. So, thank you again. From both of us."

"It was my pleasure."

"We got married, enjoyed our honeymoon in Iceland, and then we came home. And a few weeks later, we learned that Marcie's condition had evolved to AML. That is 'acute myeloid leukemia.'" Again, Harold recited the technical term, making it clear that it had been drilled into his head over the past month. "That would have been a week or so before you left for Iceland. And from there, things got bad, quick." Harold's shoulders sank. He looked depleted from reliving this narrative.

"And then it was over," Harold concluded with a small defeated shrug. Sam shook her head, struggling to process this.

"I spoke with her right before I left," Sam said. "She sounded—"

"Fine? I know. I'm amazed by the reserves of strength that woman had. She spent so much time at the end writing letters, giving me instructions, yelling at me anytime I suggested trying to contact you in Iceland. She was a marvel."

"Jesus." Sam placed her hands on the cold stone wall of the bridge and looked down at the creek. Harold joined her in looking out over the water.

"Sometimes I think back to that choice she gave me early on. About getting clear, early in our relationship, to avoid all of this. And the thing is, I can say with one hundred percent certainty that if I had a chance to do it all over again, I would not have done anything differently."

Sam said nothing, and Harold seemed to interpret her non-response as doubt.

"It's true," he insisted. "Even now, in the midst of all this, I don't regret it."

"I believe you," Sam said. "I've just struggled historically with holding a clear view of the positives when I'm wallowing in grief."

"I know what you mean, but . . ." Harold trailed off, gathering his thoughts. "I was only twenty-five years old when I married Carol. A few years later, Mike was born, and Carol and I both adored him. I thought I was in love with Carol back then. Maybe I was. But we were kids, and we were still growing. By the time I was in my forties, I was a completely different person than who I was two decades earlier. Same for Carol. And we didn't necessarily grow in the same direction. We got along well enough, but, over time, it felt like we were more acquaintances with a common interest—that being Mike—than soulmates. It was never bad enough that we seriously entertained any notion of splitting up. But after Carol and Mike died on that Mother's Day, I realized that she and I had largely been going through the motions with our marriage. Which I don't mean as a knock on her, by any means. She was a wonderful person, and Mike couldn't have had a better mother. I just mean, for me personally, there was something missing in that relationship that I didn't even comprehend until I met Marcie."

Harold stole a glance at Sam, as if checking to see if she was displaying any visible signs of disapproval with what he was saying. Sam gave him a reassuring nod to continue, and he did.

"With Marcie, I felt joy. Not just passing puppy love, but something deeper. I didn't know how long it would last, but I knew I couldn't voluntarily give it up."

Harold shivered. The sun was barely visible through the barren deciduous trees ahead of them, and the winds were picking up. He blew on his ungloved hands for warmth before stuffing them into his coat pockets.

"I guess all I'm saying," Harold continued, "is that even a short period of authentic love is worth all of the pain that I'm feeling now."

He paused, reflecting on that truth. Sam was silent as she processed it herself. She attempted to imagine the love Harold was describing. Sam replayed the last few months in her head, trying to make sense of that history by seeing it from Harold's perspective. She was so invested in reassessing the saga of Harold and Marcie that she was caught completely off guard when Harold looked directly at her and spoke again.

"I imagine it was the same for you and Mike."

The words hit her like a physical blow. Sam felt a sharp pain in her chest as the import of the non sequitur fully registered. She felt blindsided by the reference to her own doomed marriage and unprepared to deflect it using any of the tricks she had developed over the past two years. With a jolt, Sam turned to face Harold, but she could only hopelessly look at him, as language had escaped her.

Perhaps it was the result of Sam being exhausted from her unnaturally long day, which started four time zones to the east. Maybe it was just a matter of her emotional barriers having already been stripped bare by the shock of Marcie's passing, leaving Sam's heart defenseless and unprotected. Whatever the reason, Sam felt the levees she had erected over the course of two years become overpowered by the flood of memories, leaving her powerless against the ensuing torrent. Sam felt herself being dragged against her will into something she had managed to avoid since Mike disappeared from her life.

Sam found herself remembering.

Bracing for the onslaught of pain, Sam closed her eyes tightly.

• • • • •

When she opened them, she was at a crowded bar, her coat strategically placed onto the stool next to her to keep it vacant. Granted, several men had already tried to claim the seat for themselves, the coat notwithstanding, but after some polite but firm exchanges, Sam managed to avoid relinquishing that valuable territory.

Sam felt a gentle tap at her shoulder and braced herself to send another man away, when the tapper asked, "Excuse me, are you Sam?"

Sam turned and looked at the man in front of her. Even seated, she could tell that she was significantly shorter than he was. The man was tall and skinny, but not quite lanky, and clad in a winter overcoat covering gray khakis and a blue collared shirt. Sam surmised, from the settled wrinkles in his clothes, that he had come straight from work and was still wearing what he had put on that morning. His brown eyes displayed mild nervousness, which he was trying to cover up with an over-enthusiastic grin.

"You must be Mike," Sam said, extending a hand. Mike shook it, taking care not to hold on for too long.

"I am." They smiled uncomfortably at one another. *Uh oh, ten seconds in and we already have an awkward moment*, Sam thought. She took her coat from the stool and hung it over the back of her own before gesturing to the empty seat.

"Please. Sit."

Mike looked absurdly grateful at having a small task to do while he gathered his thoughts, and he took his time in hanging up his own coat on the back of his stool. As he settled into his seat, the bartender dropped two beers in front of Sam.

"Don't mind me, I like to double-fist when I'm nervous," she said. Mike looked mildly horrified, and Sam laughed. "I'm just kidding. I saw you a while ago through the front window, and I ordered you a beer. I figured it wouldn't take you too long to find me in here. You look just like your profile picture, so you were easy to identify." She pushed a bottle in his direction. "No pressure to drink it if it's not your beverage of choice."

Mike looked relieved as he picked up his beer.

"Thank you. Cheers." They clinked bottles, and Mike surveyed the establishment.

"This is a nice bar," he remarked. "I don't really come out in this area of Brooklyn that often, but this is a cool place."

"I've only been here a few times, but I like it," Sam said, looking around. It was probably as nice as a bar could get without losing the label of *dive bar*. "Thanks for coming out here, by the way. The last date I was going to go on, the guy wanted me to come out to his town in Jersey."

Mike blinked.

"You said 'going to go on.' Did you end up not going?"

"Well, yes. I caught a 'cold' at the last minute and had to cancel." Sam put down her beer to emphasize her finger quotes. "Anyway, I appreciate you coming all the way out here from Long Island."

Mike waved her off. "It's literally the least I could do. But I feel a debt of gratitude to that guy from Jersey for setting the bar so low for me."

Sam laughed and felt a touch more at ease.

"If the commute was less than two hours, I would've gone," Sam said. "I like first dates."

She paused, waiting for the follow up question. After a beat, Mike took the bait.

"You *like* first dates?"

"Sure." Sam took a sip of her beer. "They're either good, or they end up being a good story. Win-win in my book." Mike grinned.

"Well, if I feel our date start to go south, I'm going to be as boring as possible. I won't let you get a good story out of me."

Sam pretended to pout. "That's immature."

"And I'm an accountant on the verge of tax season," Mike said. "My boring gets *real* boring." Sam thought that over.

"Now I'm oddly intrigued. I wonder if it's possible to get so boring that it crosses back over into interesting?"

While Mike chewed on that query, Sam stood up.

"Bolting already?" he asked. He was joking, but Sam thought he sounded at least a little nervous.

"Just heading to the ladies' room," Sam said. "I had about six beers before you got here, you see, and—" Sam laughed at Mike's confusion. "I kid. I should warn you: I have a tendency to turn into a wise-ass when I'm nervous. I'm not normally this insufferable."

"It's fine," Mike said. "I'm just glad you aren't leaving. And you're not insufferable. And if you're nervous, I can't tell."

"Not bolting. See?" Sam nodded at her coat, which she left on the back of her seat. "I left you collateral."

As Sam walked away, the strap of her purse caught onto her stool. Mike stared, wide-eyed, as she stumbled—

—and caught herself on the stone wall of the bridge. She felt the uneven masonry under her hands and tried to make sense of that flashback. It was not a two-dimensional memory, like watching an old movie. It was a fully immersive experience, with Sam reliving moments beyond the imperfect reach of language. The smell of the stale popcorn in the bar. The sound of a dozen conversations happening in the background at once, merging into a vague white noise. A full realization of sensory inputs that could otherwise only be described in the vaguest of terms. *What is happening to me?* She struggled to push herself up off of the short wall. In her periphery, she could sense Harold reaching out toward her as she propped herself up on the side of the bridge. Sam turned—

—and walked back into her small bedroom, which barely fit a queen-sized bed.

In her absence, Mike had redressed himself in a plain gray t-shirt and a pair of boxer shorts and was lying comfortably above the covers, waiting for

Sam's return from the bathroom. Sam lay on the bed next to him and nestled under his arm.

"You get shy afterwards, huh?" she said, plucking at his clothes.

"Well, maybe. But mostly it's just that your apartment is freezing."

Sam felt goosebumps forming on her exposed skin and knew he was right. She burrowed under her thick comforter, and Mike soon followed her lead.

"When the radiator comes on, you'll be sweating, I promise. The temperature in here jumps back and forth between forty-five and ninety-five. I've learned to adapt on the fly."

"Ah." Mike stared up at the ceiling. Sam knew, after only dating him for a month, that he was working up the nerve to ask her something he deemed important.

"So, are we, like, a couple now?" Mike finally asked. Sam thought he was trying very hard to avoid coming off as shy and, as a result, ended up sounding overly casual.

"Wow, you also get clingy afterwards, huh?" Sam said with a grin, and Mike laughed. It had taken him a while to fully understand her dry sense of humor, but he had gotten used to it over the course of the past several weeks.

"No, it's not that," Mike said, his eyes twinkling. "I was really just concerned about STDs—" He was cut off by Sam elbowing him in the side.

"Idiot," she said, but she found herself laughing hard. *He's learning to give it as well as he takes it*, Sam thought with a bizarre sense of pride.

"But seriously," Sam said once the laughter died down. "Are you asking me if I'm your girlfriend?"

"Yeah. I guess I am."

Sam pretended to give the matter deep thought before answering.

"Sure. Consider us 'going steady.'"

Mike's hand found Sam's under the covers, and he gave it a gentle squeeze, which Sam returned. A stillness descended upon the room as Mike and Sam each contemplated the upgrade in their relationship. *This is nice*, Sam decided. *This feels right.* Feeling content, she closed her eyes—

—and opened them again. Her vision was obstructed by tears, but she could make out a blurry version of Harold looking at her, worry written across his face. Sam tried to explain what was happening to her, but she was still unable to speak. *I am drowning in my memories.* Sam wiped at her eyes with a hand, dislodging two tears. Sam managed to follow those droplets as they plummeted to the asphalt, and through the tumult in her head, she imagined she could hear the sound of impact. *Plunk, plunk*—

—and Sam looked impassively out the window as the rain assaulted the grounds outside. *Plunk, plunk, plunk.*

A flurry of activity stirred behind her. Wedding attendants rapidly carried chairs up to the second floor, setting up an impromptu venue for an indoor ceremony. Mike paced about while fidgeting with his phone, trying to get the most up-to-date information on the unexpected squall. Their officiant—a balding man in his mid-fifties—kept glancing at his watch, constantly recalculating how long he would have for the service in light of the delay. Everyone who had been summoned for the pre-ceremony wedding photos, which was really just the wedding party and immediate family members, shuffled about uselessly.

"You know, rain on your wedding day is a sign of good luck!" Mike's mom said to Sam in a cheery voice. Harold laughed nearby.

"Come on, Carol," he said. "You know that's just something they say to keep brides from losing their minds when it rains."

"That's not helpful, Dad," Mike remarked without looking up from his phone. He strode to Sam's side and spoke softly to her. "We're already ten minutes behind because of this rain. We'll just have to squeeze everyone into that room upstairs and get through the ceremony. It's no big deal."

"It's fine," Sam said. "Truly. You seem more worked up about it than I am."

"It would have been beautiful out there," Mike said, gesturing out the window. It was almost completely dark beyond the window, but Sam knew Mike was pointing toward the water. "It would have been nice to get married right on the Long Island Sound." He sighed. "Ah, well."

The wedding coordinator approached Mike and Sam. He wore a broad smile, as if trying to convey that everything was still going according to plan.

"We are all set up now, and the guests are being led into the indoor chapel upstairs. We can start in a few minutes."

"Great," Sam said, forcing a smile of her own. The coordinator gestured for Sam and Mike to follow him. After walking away from the window, Sam and Mike stopped and wordlessly exchanged a confused look. Something had changed, and it took Sam a moment to place it. And then she realized:

It had stopped raining.

Sam and Mike rushed to the window. A few drops of water continued to fall from the roof, but otherwise the rain had stopped completely. Whatever dark clouds had been obscuring the sun also continued to drift eastward, and the sky slowly brightened like someone was turning a dimmer switch.

"The rain stopped," Mike said to the coordinator. The coordinator went through the motions of looking out the window with an air of mild curiosity.

"How about that?" the coordinator replied as he gazed outside. He turned back to Mike. "But since we have everyone set up upstairs—"

"We should get married outside," Mike interrupted. The coordinator tightened his lips, trying to hide his annoyance.

"All of the chairs outside are wet," the coordinator pointed out. "It will take time to wipe them all down. And then we have to relocate about one hundred and fifty people outside—"

"Hey, a rainbow!" Harold said as he peered out the window.

Sam and Mike looked outside again, and, indeed, there was a rainbow forming over the water that had been meant to serve as the backdrop to Sam and Mike's wedding ceremony. Mike wheeled back to the coordinator.

"I'll run out there myself and wipe down the chairs," he said in a rush. "But given the option of having a half-hour ceremony under a rainbow or a forty-five-minute ceremony in a windowless closet, we are going with the outside option."

Mike then realized that he had been speaking for both of them and glanced at Sam to see if she agreed. She gave a slight nod of encouragement, trying not to laugh at him. *My Groomzilla*, she thought, feeling tickled.

The coordinator gave a tight nod that was only a touch sulky.

"I'll try to find some towels for the chairs outside," he said before walking away.

Thirteen minutes later, the wedding guests were resituated outside, and Mike and Sam watched them through a window.

"I really caused a lot of extra work, didn't I?" Mike asked. He was breathless from the exertion of wiping down dozens of wet chairs.

"I didn't know you had it in you," Sam said, impressed, and Mike shrugged.

"I just want today to be perfect for you," Mike replied. He looked guilty. "I'll beef up everyone's tips later for my being such a pain in the ass. Anyway, I should probably get out there, and let you do your fancy walk down the aisle. You're a stunning bride, so try not to be self-conscious when everyone is staring at you." Mike kissed her gently on the head, careful not to disturb her hair or makeup.

"I'll see you out there," Sam said. "Get a good look at the rainbow now. You can't be too distracted by it while the ceremony is ongoing." Mike nodded with a smile before growing serious.

"Thank you for marrying me."

"It's my pleasure. And right back at you."

Sam watched Mike walk away and saw him emerge outside a few seconds later to take his position in front of the officiant, who was situated near the water's edge. In her reflection in the window, Sam noticed that despite Mike's best efforts, her hair had been slightly disturbed by his farewell kiss. She raised her hands to her head—

—and pressed her fingers to her temples, squeezing hard, as if she could take a physical hold of the uncontrollable thoughts hammering throughout her skull. She could sense the trajectory of her remembrances and dreaded where they were heading. Still, she was powerless to resist. It felt like being dragged by an undertow out to sea: all she could do was wait for it to be over and try not to suffocate in the interim. Harold stared at her, concerned, and Sam couldn't imagine what she looked like to him just then.

Harold moved as if to grab her, before stopping. From his frozen position, arms outstretched, he asked, "Are you—"

—"Ok." Mike sounded pleased as he surveyed the house from the sidewalk.

"Ok, what?" Sam asked.

"Just that we got the closing over with. And after two hours of sitting around signing documents, the fun finally starts." He flourished a set of newly acquired keys.

"By 'fun,' are you referring to the cleaning or the moving?" Sam asked.

"Both! It's our house! I'm excited to get dirty making it our home."

They moved up the walkway to the front porch, each of them taking in their new dwelling. It was an old colonial, constructed in the 1930s, with a small porch area leading to a red front door. The rest of the house was white, with the exception of dark gray shutters surrounding all of the front windows. There were only three bedrooms, which would prevent it from feeling too big for the two of them, but it would still be spacious enough to give them options to deal with whatever life threw at them down the road.

"It's funny," Sam said as they strolled down the path. "It's the biggest purchase I've ever made, but I only saw it for a few minutes before we put the offer in and a few minutes at yesterday's inspection. I don't think I could sketch out a map of the inside if I had to."

"It's a nice house," Mike said. "I remember that much."

"Can we afford it?"

"Yes. Of course." Mike paused and frowned. "I think so."

"You're not sure? You're the accountant—I trust you for this stuff!"

"We'll be ok." Another pause. "I think."

They made their way up the porch steps, and Mike inserted the key into the front door. After he was unable to turn it, Mike muttered a curse and took to wiggling it.

"You make much more than I do," Sam said as Mike tried to finagle the door open, "so it's up to you to make these mortgage payments. I'm totally screwed if you run out on me. Or get hit by a bus."

Mike grinned while he continued to manipulate the key. Sam knew he always viewed the dark humor they shared together as some sort of secret they kept from the rest of the world.

"If I run out on you, you'll clean up in the divorce and have no trouble paying the bills," Mike said. "And if I get hit by a bus, you can use the life insurance proceeds to pay off the mortgage. But I'm not going anywhere. In any sense of the word."

Mike finally managed to work the key and opened the door with a flourish.

"After you! Unless you'd prefer that I carry you over the threshold."

Sam gave him a wry look before purposefully stepping forward—

—and then found herself once again holding herself up by the stone wall of the bridge. She felt something on her back, and it took her a second to realize it was a comforting hand from Harold. He was saying something, but the words didn't register. With her hands clenched, Sam lowered her head to the top of the wall; her skull suddenly felt too heavy to hold. A fresh cascade of tears was coming; she felt them stirring deep within. She gasped for breath, trying to calm herself down, but the gravitational forces that had conquered her head seemed to spread to the rest of her body, and she lowered herself to the ground, hugging her knees to form the shape of a ball. Harold spoke again and she looked up—

—and noticed that Mike was walking in front of her wearing khakis and a dress shirt that had just come back from the dry cleaner. She lowered the book she'd been reading and stared at him, confused. *Why is he dressed up? Should* I *be dressed up?* Mike noticed Sam looking at him and stopped.

"What's wrong?" he asked.

"You're all dressed up," Sam noted. "Are we going somewhere?"

"I've been in this outfit for the last hour and a half, and you only just noticed?" he asked, sounding amazed. Sam shrugged.

"This book is really good. I guess I lost myself for a bit."

He bent to look at the cover and grunted. "Well, let me know if they ever make a movie out of it." Mike was not a reader himself.

"Do I need to get fancy for anything?" Sam asked. She was dreading being pulled away from her book, which she was a mere fifty pages from finishing.

"No, you're good. You're all set to stay in your sweatpants and read. I'm taking Mom out for a Mother's Day dinner, remember?"

"Ah, right." Sam had forgotten. She briefly cherished the notion of an empty house in which to finish reading, but she quickly suppressed that selfish thought. "Are you going down to her?" Mike nodded.

"I made reservations for this place on Long Island, maybe half an hour from her house. Dad is whining that he's not invited. His FOMO is legendary. He keeps saying he's going to starve tonight without Mom around to cook him dinner." Mike shrugged. "I'll bring him a couple of donuts to hold him over—that should make him happy."

"You're such a good son." Sam said. She stole a peek back at the page she had been reading. Mike noticed and took the hint, leaving her to read.

Twenty minutes later, Mike resurfaced in the living room.

"Alright, I'm heading out," he said, before adding with a lascivious wink, "Don't wait up."

"Dude. That's your mom you're talking about."

Mike looked moderately ashamed.

"Too far? Ok, I take that back. In all seriousness, I should be home around ten or so. Try not to have too much fun without me."

"I'll try," Sam said. As she dove back into her novel, Mike swept by the couch and kissed her on top of the head before heading to the door.

Sam waved goodbye without looking up from her book.

CHAPTER NINETEEN

Tuesday, December 17, 2019

Sam hugged herself on the ground in the middle of the bridge. The dam had broken, and no power on earth could have stemmed the tears that poured out of her. Sam sobbed, trying to catch her breath as emotions she had held at arm's length over the course of the past two years overtook her completely, reducing her to a blob of anguish, writhing on the snowy ground.

Harold wordlessly stood at her side to protect her from any traffic that came across the bridge as Sam continued to fall apart. But all was still, save the blowing of the wind and Sam's outpouring of grief.

Sam didn't know how long it took, but the tears eventually stopped, leaving her depleted and gasping for breath. Harold watched her carefully as she regained control before fishing in his pocket for a tissue. It was rumpled, but it looked clean, so Sam took it gratefully and wiped at her face before blowing her nose.

"I've had a few of those myself," Harold said calmly, looking down at Sam. He extended a hand to help her get back up, which Sam took. "You have to let that out of you every now and then."

Once she was back on her feet, Sam took another wrinkled tissue from Harold and tried to clean up her face as best as she could manage.

"It's hard for me to imagine you breaking down like that," Sam said in a choked voice that was slowly recovering. "You're always joking around, no matter the situation."

"Men don't have the luxury of crying out in public," Harold explained. "We have to do it behind closed doors."

"That's not actually true," Sam said, but she knew Harold believed it. "But anyway, you're right. My time with Mike was worth everything that came afterward. As much as it hurts. You raised a good son."

Harold, with a sad smile, nodded in agreement before turning away. He took one long look at the creek before blowing it a kiss with a flourish of his hand.

"I'll be back tomorrow, Marcie," he said to the gentle waters below. Turning to Sam, he asked, "Can you come with me to my car? I have a couple of things for you."

Sam decided not to pester him with questions and simply fell in beside Harold as he walked off the bridge, heading to the side opposite from where Sam had parked. Although her multiple fits of crying had left her feeling empty inside, she also felt lighter—like she had released a weight that she hadn't even realized she'd been carrying.

"How are Marcie's kids doing with it all?" Sam asked as they walked down a quiet residential street.

"It's hard to tell with them," Harold admitted. "Miguel seems heartbroken, but the rest of them kind of hold their cards close to their chests, if you know what I mean. I'm sure they are all grieving, in their own ways."

Sam still had leftover resentment for the hoops they had made Marcie jump through to get married, and she couldn't help blurting out with some bitterness, "At least they got Marcie to execute that will for them. I suppose they 'won' in that respect."

Harold stopped walking and blinked, as if he had only just remembered something. Sam stopped and gave him a quizzical look.

"Oh, right," Harold said. "Well, about that . . ."

• • • • •

Sadie was the first to arrive, and the receptionist directed her to an empty conference room. The attorney's office was small and unglamorous, and the conference room looked like it couldn't fit more than a half-dozen people.

Exactly the kind of lawyer I would have expected Mom to hire, she thought. She took a seat at the foot of the table in the room and waited.

She hadn't felt right since Iceland, and the passing of her mother only further complicated her internal turmoil. It was taking Sadie time to process her mother's death, and she was somewhat surprised—and a bit concerned—by her lack of a significant emotional response to that event. Which is not to say that Sadie allowed any semblance of indifference to manifest at the service for her mother—she was the model of a grieving daughter. But Sadie had always loved her mother, albeit in her own way, and she suspected that her true feelings would hit her at some point.

Or so she hoped.

But most of Sadie's disquiet stemmed from what transpired in Iceland. *You locked up your share of the inheritance*, Sadie repeatedly reminded herself. *And Mom got to have her quirky wedding, and a few weeks of a happy marriage. You won.* And yet, no matter how many times Sadie reminded herself of this, she remained unconvinced.

Sadie knew from experience that had she truly "won," she wouldn't have needed to repeatedly remind herself of the victory.

Part of the reason she felt so unfulfilled was regret over how she had conducted herself in Iceland. Sadie was not prone to missteps, and with the gift of hindsight, she could clearly see where she had erred over the course of the day leading up to the wedding. *I shouldn't have engaged with Sam*, she thought. By staying to listen to Sam at all—and even worse, in front of her brothers—Sadie had allowed Sam to create that narrative about her manipulating her family because of some deep-seated insecurity. *It was an absurd theory*, Sadie reminded herself. *But my brothers were stupid enough to buy into it.* And that, Sadie realized, is what ultimately emboldened them enough to stand up to her.

Even though she had attained all of her intended goals with regard to her mother's estate, Sadie realized, as she sat alone in the conference room, what she had lost in the process: her brothers' respect. She hadn't communicated with her family much since Iceland aside from a few polite words to each other at the service, but, looking back at all of their interactions since the wedding, she now saw that her brothers were no longer treating her as the leader of their group. They had once looked to her to make decisions on behalf of them all, but Sadie recognized that they now only looked at her with something akin to pity.

Sadie grimaced at the self-diagnosis, but she was not overly concerned. *Now that I've identified the issue, I can get to work on correcting it.* Sadie's lips twitched as she realized it may even be a blessing. She had been looking for a challenge since the whole affair with Marcie and Harold had concluded—working on reestablishing herself to her half-brothers just might be the stimulation that she had been missing over the past few months.

Jeremy was the next to arrive. He nodded politely at Sadie and then took a chair at the opposite end of the table from her. Sadie pursed her lips, deep in thought. *A few months ago, he would have salivated at the opportunity to sit next to me*. Sadie had always been repulsed by his infatuation, but she was even more appalled by the fact that his longing for her appeared to have dissipated over the past few months. Jeremy's apathy toward her only further confirmed her suspicions regarding the diminution of her role as the leader of the family.

Once he settled in, Jeremy took to playing on his phone, largely ignoring Sadie. Sadie stared at him, trying to determine if the snub was intentional, but he didn't register her look. Finally, she felt compelled to break the ice.

"How are you holding up?" she asked, prompting Jeremy to lower his phone to his lap.

"It's been rough," he said, sounding as if he meant it. "I miss her. And to be completely honest with you, I feel somewhat relieved with how everything worked out. I'd feel awful if we convinced her not to go through with the wedding. At least she got a few weeks of happiness before the end, right?" He shrugged. "And you?"

"I'm getting by," Sadie said. When Jeremy realized that she wasn't going to say more, he gave a half-hearted nod and resumed fiddling with his phone.

He wasn't ignoring me on purpose, Sadie concluded. *He's simply not interested in me.* That was not a problem for her, in and of itself, but it was a symptom of the larger issue Sadie had identified.

Miguel and Colin then entered together. Sadie had wondered whether Colin would come, but she supposed that for him the day was close enough to Christmas to warrant a venture outside of his home. Colin, with a half-hearted wave at the room, took a seat between Sadie and Jeremy, but Miguel took his time in greeting everyone, including giving Sadie a sad hug.

"This is hard, right?" Miguel asked the room. His rough voice suggested that he was struggling not to cry.

"This should be painless," Jeremy said, misunderstanding Miguel. He checked the time. "We're all here. Is this guy really going to make us wait long?" No one answered the rhetorical question. Jeremy sighed loudly and spun about in his chair like a child before stopping abruptly.

"Hey, Colin," he said. "How are things with you and Sara?"

"Things are proceeding *quite* well, actually," Colin said with a chuckle. "She just moved in."

"Congratulations!" Miguel said, patting Colin on the back.

"What?" Jeremy looked shocked. "Won't that make it harder for you to hide the fact that you don't do anything but play video games all day long?"

"I don't have to hide anything from her," Colin said, sounding cocky. "She loves me for who I am." Jeremy shook his head in disbelief.

"You weren't kidding when you said things just work out for you. Even the timing of all of this." Jeremy gestured around the conference room. "You won't have to get a job once you get your share of the estate."

"As you know, I consider my podcast to be—"

"Yeah, yeah, yeah," Jeremy interrupted. "I've heard it all before."

The door to the conference room opened, and a middle-aged man with a ponytail entered. He smiled at them all warmly, although Sadie thought it was a bit forced, and sat, holding a small file. *Of course Mom would hire a hippy attorney*, Sadie thought.

"Hello, everyone," the man said. "My name is Tim Russo. I am truly sorry for your loss—your mother was a very kind and gentle soul. As you probably know, I was your mother's attorney. And as you are also undoubtedly aware, she executed a new will—or her first will, I should say—several months ago, and she named me as the executor. She also mentioned to me at that time that she had come to some sort of agreement with all of you regarding the disposition of her estate, and she asked me to have a reading of her will shortly after her death to assure you that she lived up to her end of the bargain. I have to tell you: aside from the movies, it's very rare to have an actual will reading. This will be the first of my career. But your mother asked for it, and you all showed up, so . . ." Tim shrugged. He fished a document out of the file and gave it a quick read before putting it down again.

"Look, the disposition of your mother's estate is very straightforward. You are each getting a quarter of it, which I understand is what your mother told you she would do. I'll get you each a copy of the will before you leave for your records. Your mother also has some personal artifacts of no significant economic value but that may be of sentimental value to you. You are welcome to those, and if you are not able to work out how to divvy them up among yourselves, I will be happy to get involved. But hopefully it will not come to that."

Sadie noticed Colin nodding his head, pleased. He had pushed for so long to get a bigger share than the rest of them, but Sadie assumed he was content with where things ended up.

"If I may," Colin began. He waited for a polite nod from Tim before continuing. "We are all glad that our mother did what she said she was going to do with her will, but are you able to give us an idea of the size of her estate? I think we'd all be interested in hearing what we are actually getting."

Colin looked around, looking for the others to jump in and voice their agreement, but he was met with silence. Tim nodded at Colin to show his request was reasonable before flipping through the file. Moments later, he settled on a page with handwritten notes. He scrutinized the page carefully before looking back at Colin.

"In reviewing your mother's estate, it appears that she has a checking account with a current balance of $18,547.22."

Colin nodded, impatient for Tim to continue.

But he didn't.

Sadie suddenly felt ill. *Oh shit,* she thought, trying to maintain an impassive face. *Oh shit, oh shit*. Her brothers were slower on the uptake.

"Ok, what else?" Colin finally asked, sounding annoyed. Tim shook his head. He was trying to look impartial, but Sadie thought she detected a hint of satisfaction on the attorney's face.

"Aside from the sentimental items that I mentioned, which have no significant monetary value, that is the entirety of your mother's estate. Each of your shares of that account will be $4,636.80. Give or take a penny."

Colin's mouth moved wordlessly. Jeremy looked confused as well, and soon all of the brothers were looking to Sadie for an explanation. Sadie maintained a stoic face, but her mind was reeling. *How did I screw this up so badly?* she wondered.

"What about her house?" Jeremy finally asked. Sadie's face blanched and the struggle to remain calm intensified. *It was transferred to Harold over the summer*, she thought. *I thought nothing of it at the time, it being such a small piece of the estate. Oh God, it was right in front of me, but I ignored it. She got rid of it.*

She got rid of it all.

"I was authorized by your mother before her passing to share that she divested herself of most of her assets, including the home, this past August. It is also my understanding that your mother agreed not to touch any of her remaining assets after entering into her agreement with all of you concerning her estate, and I can confirm that the amount in her bank account has not changed since that time."

"What happened to it all?" Colin asked. He looked wildly between Sadie and Tim, hoping one of them would answer. Sadie knew the answer, but she didn't speak. Her attention was focused on not vomiting on the conference room table.

"Your mother came to me in August for my assistance in transferring all of her assets, with the exception of the funds in the bank account I mentioned, to her fiancé. I am not aware of the circumstances that led to her doing so."

His eyes flickered toward Sadie, and Sadie immediately realized two things. The first was that Tim very much knew what had prompted their mother to get rid of her estate. The second thing Sadie realized was the reason her mother rid herself of that estate.

And it was me, Sadie thought.

"This makes no sense," Colin said, starting to sound belligerent. "How can all of the money be with Harold? They got married, for Christ's sake! Wouldn't that make it—"

"They had a prenup," Sadie muttered. Tim Russo's lips twitched—he was clearly enjoying their collective discomfort. "We thought it would ensure that Harold had no claim to any of those funds, but it will do the opposite. It makes it crystal clear the money is not Mother's."

Sadie abruptly stood up. She wanted to bolt out of the room, but an overriding need to maintain a sense of composure helped her resist the impulse. But before she could walk away, Tim gestured for her to reseat herself.

"Please," Tim said. "There is something else." Sadie reluctantly sat back down.

Tim removed four envelopes from his folder, each with a different name written on it. He briefly shuffled through them before passing the envelopes around the table. Sadie's name was written on the envelope she received in handwriting that she recognized as her mother's.

"Your mother asked me to deliver these to you as well. Again, I'm terribly sorry for your loss." With an ironic twitch of his lips, he added, "I know how much you all cared about your mother." With that, Tim gathered his papers and left the conference room. Sadie noticed Tim looking self-satisfied as he left, but she was too preoccupied to care.

The half-siblings each looked at each other before opening their respective envelopes. Colin stupidly held his upside down after opening it and shook it, as if expecting a wad of cash to fall out. But each envelope only contained a single piece of notepaper. With some trepidation, Sadie removed hers and read.

She skimmed it quickly, and her hands were shaking by the time she finished. Taking a deep breath, she tried to calm herself before reading it again.

My dearest Sadie,

I have been thinking much on the things I want to tell you while I still can. It is unfair of me to put all of this in a note, depriving you of the chance to respond, and I must beg your forgiveness for that. In fact, I feel like there is much for which I owe you an apology. There are many ways in which I am afraid I have failed you as a mother, but I promise you, none of those failures stemmed from a lack of love.

I confess that I was disappointed by the entire affair relating to my estate. It took me a long time to completely let go of the anger I felt following our conversation in August, and I admit that some resentment reasserted itself in Iceland after that business involving you and your brothers. As I write this, I can assure you that any bitterness I felt is long gone—life is simply too short to hold on to such negative energy. Still, I suspect that I allowed that negativity to cloud my judgment prior to the wedding, and I am not proud of the way in which I handled things.

Although I took care to never lie to you or your brothers, I feared that being completely forthcoming would have alienated us completely. It was so important to me that you be at my side when I married Harold, and when I had an opportunity to secure your blessing, I felt compelled to take it, even if doing so required me to walk a path that fell short of complete honesty. Had I been stronger, I would have been entirely truthful with you all and accepted whatever consequences there may have been. But I was weak and selfish, so I must beg your forgiveness for hiding certain things from you all regarding my finances. Such matters were never important to me, but they apparently mean a great deal to you and your brothers, and I should have had greater respect for your feelings in that regard.

I used to wish that you and I could have a relationship where we were more comfortable being open with one another. Over time, I've learned to stop wishing for things I did not have and to cherish all that I did have. Our relationship is unique and beautiful, and I would not change it for anything. But there is one point I want to make clear, as I know I would never be able to rest if there was any confusion on your part as respects this issue:

You entered my life when you were already a young woman, and I know that must have been confusing for you. It was not lost on me how you seemed to compete for my attention with your brothers, even though you were always in my thoughts. Looking back on my life, and yours, it is possible that you may have devoted so much energy to establishing that I loved you like *a daughter that you became blinded to a greater truth:*

I love you as *my daughter.*

I hope when I am gone, and you have had time to reflect on our time together, you can forgive me for my shortcomings and appreciate the love I have for you, which never wavered, and will never waver. And although this may be presumptuous of me to say, should you ever reach a point where you harbor your own regrets about our interactions, please know this:

I forgive you.

All of my love,

Mom

Sadie carefully folded the note and placed it back into the envelope. She glanced around at her brothers, who were each studying their own messages. Sadie couldn't get a read on the nature of those notes; none of her brothers' faces gave anything away. After Miguel finished reading his, he calmly rose and walked to the window to look outside. Sadie could make out a faint reflection of his visage in the glass and frowned when she noticed Miguel smiling quietly to himself. *What the hell does he find so funny about all of this?*

Sadie stood up, and Colin and Jeremy were startled out of their respective reveries.

"What does this all mean, Sadie?" Colin asked, sounding like he was on the verge of panicking. "Can we do anything about this? Can we sue Harold or something?"

"I think you may have to get a job after all, bro," Jeremy said. "Do you even have a resume?"

"Shut up, Jeremy," Colin said without taking his eyes off of Sadie. "Sadie, what do we do? We're going to do something, right?"

Sadie stared at him for some time before walking out of the room, her note in hand. Her brothers looked at her in confusion as she left, but no one tried to stop her. Tim, the hippy attorney, saw Sadie exit from down the hall and called out to her.

"We will get you a copy of the will, if you want one." Sadie ignored him and left the building altogether. She walked slowly through the parking lot to her car. Once there, she flicked the note from her mother onto the passenger seat and turned the key in the ignition, but after the car came to life, she didn't shift the gear out of "park." Instead, she stared into space with her hands on the wheel, unable to move as she listened to the hum of the car idling.

And then she let it all out.

It didn't take long for Sadie's scream to fog up the entirety of the windshield.

• • • • •

"Here's the deal," Harold told Sam as they walked. "After Marcie got her initial diagnosis, she told me all about it. She also wanted to tell her children, and she started with Sadie. I think she spoke with her right around the time I was telling you about the engagement. Marcie's conversation with Sadie, it . . . didn't go well."

"What do you mean?"

Harold rolled his eyes. "Marcie opened herself up completely to Sadie, telling her all of her fears and what the diagnosis might mean. Sadie listened to it all and then proceeded to tell Marcie that it was more important than ever that she get a will."

"No!"

"Yup." Harold looked uncomfortable. "Marcie was hurt by the response. She tried to put a positive spin on it. 'Oh, Harold, she's just in shock, I'm sure.' But it troubled her greatly. I think Sadie's response was why she didn't tell any of her other kids. It would have hurt her too badly if any of them reacted in a similar way. But shortly after that, Marcie told me she wanted to be rid of all of her money. Everything, even the deed to her house. She viewed it all as a curse, and she didn't want it. We talked about donating it all to a charity, but she was scared of how her children would respond to that. She wanted time to think about it, 'to pray to her higher self.' But she was certain she wanted to be rid of it. It was like it was burning her, just being in her name. Finally, because she was so adamant, she convinced me to take it all away from her. Transferring that wealth proved to be a major pain in the ass, and I still haven't figured out how much we screwed ourselves tax-wise by rushing it like that. But Marcie didn't want anything to do with that money, even after we were married. Her attorney advised her to get a prenup to avoid any possibility of it being considered hers down the road. It's usually the spouse with all of the money that insists on the prenup, but here, it was the woman who made herself destitute and wanted to ensure she remained that way." Harold chuckled to himself. "Marcie was nothing if not outside of the box." Sam stopped walking, jaw agape, which prompted Harold to pause as well.

"So, you are a multi-millionaire?" she asked in disbelief.

"For now, yes." Harold and Sam resumed walking. "But I have no intention of keeping any of it. Like I told you before, I wasn't marrying Marcie for her money."

"What are you going to do with it all?"

"I've been thinking about what Marcie would have wanted. I'm leaning toward giving half to charity and splitting the rest between Marcie's kids. She was never opposed to them getting it, and she certainly wouldn't have wanted her money to cause any ill feelings."

"That sounds like a reasonable plan," Sam said. "But they won't be happy only getting half."

Harold snorted.

"They'll be a hell of a lot happier than if they get zero!"

"Touché." After they walked a bit further, Sam asked, "Do you actually think it will make them happy?"

"Probably not," Harold admitted. "Not by itself, anyway. But I don't think it's my job to deliver that particular lesson to them. That's one of those things they need to figure out for themselves." Harold gave Sam a sidelong glance, as if he just had a thought.

"Unless you want some of the money?" Harold asked, a twinkle in his eye. "I'm happy to make you a millionaire if you like?"

Sam thought it over, but she wasn't particularly tempted.

"No, but thank you."

"Yeah, I figured you'd say that. Anyway, I may need your help in finding charities that Marcie would have been into. You seem to understand that side of her much better than I ever did."

Up ahead, Sam saw Harold's car parked on the side of the road. She thought she spotted movement in the back seat, and as they got closer, she was able to identify it.

"You brought Samus?" she asked. The dog, much larger than when Sam had last seen her, was wildly bouncing around upon seeing Harold. "Why did you leave her in the car?"

"She's too wild!" Harold said. "She'd never let me just have a moment of peace while she was out here. It's ok—it's not that cold out and I cracked the windows for her. And I took her for a walk when we first got here."

Harold opened the passenger door to reach into the car and, after giving Samus a quick reassuring pat, grabbed a small package from the seat. He handed it to Sam, who noticed it was addressed to her.

"Never got around to taking it to the post office," Harold explained with a sheepish shrug. "It's from Marcie. I want to walk Samus for a bit, so feel free to look at it now, if you're so inclined."

Harold opened the back door and Samus immediately tried to bolt. As he struggled to hold the dog with one hand, Harold managed to affix a leash to Samus's collar with the other. Samus happily bounded out of the car, practically dragging Harold down the street.

Sam watched them depart and then turned her attention to the package. She ripped open the paper wrapping to reveal a small book with a blank cover. Sam flipped through the book, which was filled with notations in an elegant handwriting. Tucked in the pages as a makeshift bookmark was a single piece of notepaper. The handwriting looked much the same as that in the book itself, albeit not as elegant. Sam surmised that Marcie must have written the note in a significantly weakened state.

Bracing herself, Sam read the note.

Sam,

First and foremost, I hope you had a wonderful return to Iceland. It is a magical place, and I am so glad you were able to guide me into visiting it so I could appreciate its beauty with my own eyes.

I have no doubt that I will see you again, in this world or another, but for now, let me just say that I am so happy we had a chance to become friends. The light you brought to my life these last few months was a fringe benefit of marrying Harold that I never could have imagined. You have so much strength and compassion, and the world is a better place for your being in it.

I had previously mentioned to you that after my first husband passed, I took to journaling to try to quiet all of those thoughts that were rattling around my head. I found it very therapeutic to put my ideas to paper, and they helped me define what I was going through and cope with emotions that were too large to stay inside me for long. Given the similar experiences you and I have gone through, I thought the book may be of some interest to you. If I have managed to accumulate any wisdom during this life of mine, it would please me greatly to share it with you (and you can add it to your own undeniable reserves of wisdom).

Thank you for all you have done for us. You are loved for it, and for everything else that you are.

XOXOXO,

Marcie

Sam stood alone on the side of the road, reflecting upon Marcie's goodbye to her. There was solace in hearing Marcie's voice again, even if only in writing. Sam hefted the journal, filled with Marcie's ruminations over the course of decades. *I have no shortage of Marcie's voice right now*, she thought, but it was a source of comfort rather than obligation.

A minute later, Harold reemerged from a bend in the road, half running as he tried to keep up with Samus.

"Samus!" he shouted. "Samus!" Samus, gleefully prancing down the street, stopped abruptly to smell a bush along the side of the road, and Harold nearly toppled over her. Harold glared at Samus as he returned to Sam.

"I guess I have Colin and Marcie to thank for training this dog so well," he muttered. "Although I suppose Marcie had a decent excuse. Anyway, I gave you one of the things Marcie wanted you to have, so here is the other." He extended the leash to Sam, who laughed.

"You want me to take your untrained dog?" she asked.

"No. Marcie wants you to take our untrained dog."

Sam looked hard at Samus, who stared back with large, trusting eyes. *You poor girl*, Sam thought. *You have yet to get settled in anywhere, huh?*

"Won't you miss her?" Sam asked.

"Sure. She's a good puppy, even if she's constantly climbing up on the table to steal my dinner. But I'm sure I'll still have plenty of opportunities to see her. Besides, you could use a good guard dog to help you deal with all of those creepy old men breaking into your house to play with your undergarments."

Sam tried to hold back a laugh and ended up snorting in the process.

"How untrained is she? Does she know 'sit'?" Sam asked. Samus lowered her haunches to the asphalt, wagging her tail.

"See?" Harold said. "She knows 'sit.' Samus the wonder pup! Here." He gently took Sam's wrist and transferred the leash into her hand. Samus looked from Harold to Sam as if she could sense the change in ownership that was happening. Staring at Sam with eyes begging for another walk, Samus stood up to stretch and let out a gentle whine.

"She's much calmer with you," Harold noted, glaring at Samus. "Probably because you're so tiny."

"Dogs feed off energy," Sam said. "I radiate tranquility. And you—"

"Do not," Harold finished for her. "I get it. Come, she wants to walk. Let's see if you can do better than me."

They wandered down the street. Samus stopped to sniff on too many occasions to make it a comfortable walk, but she always continued onward after some gentle prodding from Sam.

"What do you see happening from here?" Sam asked. "Do you think you'll maintain a relationship with Marcie's kids going forward?"

"I don't know," Harold admitted. "That's largely up to them. I'm open to it." Harold's face brightened as he remembered something. "I'm actually playing golf with Miguel this weekend. Well, an indoor driving range, at least. I played with him a few months ago. He's atrocious—it's unbelievable. I think he may actually be left-handed and just never realized it. Anyway, you should come. It would be fun to teach you to golf."

Samus stopped again to sniff at a piece of litter on the ground, but Sam didn't rush her.

"I don't know," Sam finally said.

"Come on. What's the problem?"

"It's just—I don't know. Is it weird for me to hang out with my deceased husband's father and my deceased husband's father's deceased wife's son? Because, honestly, it feels a little weird to me."

Harold scrunched up his face, gathering his thoughts, as Samus continued to smell the same piece of debris.

"Let me tell you something," Harold said at last. He bent over to pick up the litter Samus had been smelling, and Samus finally continued to walk. "Early on, when Marcie and I decided to get married, I told her that I'd love to have a relationship with her children, but I was concerned about not being a blood relative. And Marcie told me, 'Blood ties are great if you need a kidney or something, but otherwise, "family" means whatever the hell you want it to mean.'" He paused, thoughtful. "Granted, she didn't put it *quite* as eloquently as that."

Sam laughed, despite herself, and Harold looked delighted.

"See? You do get some of my bad jokes sometimes!"

"I always get them," Sam told him. "And once in a while, they aren't bad."

As if on cue, Sam and Harold turned to go back to Harold's car. Samus took one longing look down the road before turning around to join them. *She's a good girl*, Sam thought. *She wants to be good.*

"Alright, I'll golf with you," she said, and Harold beamed.

"Awesome. Maybe we can all grab lunch and a beer afterwards?"

"That'd be fun," Sam said. "Do you think I'll be better at golf than Miguel?"

Harold snorted. "You couldn't possibly be worse. You will be amazed, I'm telling you. I've never seen someone so uncoordinated with a golf club. But he had a blast last time anyway."

"I'm looking forward to it," Sam said. She was only somewhat surprised to realize she meant it. Harold leaned into his car to turn on his ignition once they got back before standing up to face Sam.

"I'm sorry you had to find out this way," Harold said over the sound of the car engine warming up.

"And I'm sorry for your loss," Sam said. "I don't know if I ever got around to saying that before."

"Our loss," Harold gently corrected her. "It's funny: I miss her, of course, but the one thing that makes this almost bearable is that I know, with certainty, that the last thing she would want is for me—or you, for that matter—to sequester ourselves in grief. I feel obligated to keep living to honor her." Harold paused and looked contemplative, like he only just realized the exact nature of the obligation Marcie had left for him. "Anyway, I'll give you a call during the week to set up this golf thing."

Harold gave Sam a quick hug and bent down to pet Samus before ducking back into his car and driving off. The sun had nearly set, and Sam's own car was a few blocks away, on the other side of the bridge.

Sam walked back to Marcie's resting place with Samus at her side. As she crossed over the small bridge spanning the creek, she reflected on Harold's parting words. *An obligation to keep living.* Sam wondered whether Mike had likewise imparted such an obligation upon her. If he had, she wasn't sure she had satisfied it. But she was young. And there was still time.

Not many goals can be reached with a single step, but there is power in embarking on the proper path. A comfort that lies in simply making a choice that takes you in the right direction.

Sam glanced down at Samus, panting slightly from all of the walking, and realized that, at some point over the course of the past few months, she had made such a choice. She wasn't where she wanted to be—not yet—but for the first time in years, she felt herself being drawn closer to that indescribable destination rather than drifting aimlessly away from the target. It took Sam a moment to identify the nature of the choice she had made, but as she and Samus walked across the bridge through the winter twilight, the answer came to her.

She had chosen life.

EPILOGUE

samisreadingbooks Greetings, Bookstagram! It feels like it's been forever since I put up a book review, but there's a reason for that. And the reason is that it's been forever since I've managed to actually read a book. A published book, at least. But more on that in a bit.

My lack of reviews notwithstanding, I wanted to check in and give you all something of an update (and maybe a bit of an explanation as to my absence here over the past few months).

In short, I've been through a fair amount lately. I've gotten a new puppy, although she's practically bigger than me at this point, who goes by the name of Samus (and no, she's not named after me). I often describe Samus to others with the expression "she means well," which is really a testament to the fact that she doesn't always "do" well. Her training is a work in progress and has eaten up most of my free time, but she's making huge strides. I've already spent enough time with Samus to know she has a tremendous heart, and she loves me as much as I love her.

On a sadder note, I also recently lost a friend named Marcie, and I've been processing her loss for the past several weeks. Marcie came into my life much too late and left much too early, but I can't begin to describe the imprint she left on me in the brief time we had together. Mourning her passing has also, somewhat surprisingly, helped me deal with some other emotional stuff that I've been actively trying to avoid for a long time. To put it another way: I used to dive into books to avoid spending too much time in my own head, but, I'm pleased to report, the inside of my head is no longer as scary as it once was. I used to run from memories that should have been joyful out of a fear for where they might take me, but it's getting somewhat easier to embrace those positive remembrances and accept that they will ultimately overpower the bad. For the first time in years, it feels like I'm at least in a place where I can begin to heal (even if that healing, like Samus's training, is a work in progress).

And aside from the puppy and my self-healing, I've also taken up golf. I am not yet good, but I am not atrocious (and the two guys I play with swear I am still getting better), so I've already surpassed my meager goals. So, as you can see, there hasn't been a great deal of free time for me to lounge around with a book.

There is, however, a notable exception to the book slump I find myself in. Marcie and I, as it turns out, carried a lot of the same baggage (primarily relating to loss), and she told me some time ago that she kept a journal to help her process her trials and tribulations. She left that journal to me upon her passing, and I have spent a significant amount of time exploring it since then. It has been enlightening and cathartic to read about her perspectives, particularly since we had so much in common with our respective histories.

The book in the picture above is Marcie's journal, and the backdrop is Sawkill Creek, which was Marcie's final resting place. I have no intention, of course, to "review" this particular book. In fact, at first, I thought it would be a betrayal to share any portion of Marcie's journal with the world at large. But after reading and reflecting upon her writings, I realized that Marcie had so much to share, and it would be selfish of me to keep it all to myself. I cannot shake the feeling that Marcie entrusted me with the power to let her continue to touch the world, and I am determined to help her do that.

With that in mind, the following is an excerpt from Marcie's journal that I wanted to share. I have no doubt I'll feel inspired down the road to post other snippets, but for now I will leave you with this passage, which has resonated with me since I first read it a few weeks ago:

My first husband passed away when I was only twenty-nine years old. Several years later, I remarried, only to become a widow again after a few years. This cycle continued into my early forties. At that point, I was a completely different person than the girl who married for the first time sixteen years earlier. I had been reshaped by my life experiences, of course, but also by the relationships that made me stronger, even through the pain of loss that consistently drove me to my knees to beg a higher power for answers.

Those answers were not always attainable but, over time, I found that I had been gifted a question. At first, I thought this was a problem in search of a solution, but I soon began to appreciate the rhetorical nature of the inquiry. As I grew older, the question slowly evolved into a mantra, one that I found myself chanting into the dark on those lonely nights where sleep was elusive and unattainable. On such occasions, I managed to suffuse myself with a sense of calm and peace and a feeling of oneness with the universe, simply by proposing the following:

How can we consider anyone truly "gone" when they continue to touch the world through those of us who knew and loved them?

ABOUT THE AUTHOR

When he is not writing, Daniel Maunz works as in-house counsel for a major insurance company. He currently lives in the Hudson Valley region of New York with his wife Lynne, their son Patrick, and their two cats: Admiral Meowy McWhiskers and Captain Cutie (or "Admiral" and "Captain" for short). His debut novel, *Questions of Perspective*, was published by Black Rose Writing in May 2020. *Hyphenated Relations* is his second novel.

NOTE FROM THE AUTHOR

Word-of-mouth is crucial for any author to succeed. If you enjoyed *Hyphenated Relations*, please leave a review online—anywhere you are able. Even if it's just a sentence or two. It would make all the difference and would be very much appreciated.

Thanks!
Daniel Maunz

CPSIA information can be obtained
at www.ICGtesting.com
Printed in the USA
LVHW091050220223
740093LV00005B/26

9 781685 131890